Alice, or The Wild Girl

Alice, or The Wild Girl

Michael Robert Liska

Copyright © 2025 by Michael Robert Liska

All rights reserved. No part of this book may be reproduced in any manner without the express written consent of the publisher, except in the case of brief excerpts in critical reviews or articles. All inquiries should be addressed to Heresy Press, 307 West 36th Street, 11th Floor, New York, NY 10018.

Heresy Press books may be purchased in bulk at special discounts for sales promotion, corporate gifts, fund-raising, or educational purposes. Special editions can also be created to specifications. For details, contact the Special Sales Department, Heresy Press, 307 West 36th Street, 11th Floor, New York, NY 10018 or info@skyhorsepublishing.com.

Skyhorse Publishing® is a registered trademark of Skyhorse Publishing, Inc.®, a Delaware corporation.

Visit our website at skyhorsepublishing.com.

HERESY PRESS LLC
P.O. Box 425201
Cambridge, MA 02142
heresy-press.com

10 9 8 7 6 5 4 3 2 1

Library of Congress Cataloging-in-Publication Data is available on file.

Cover design by Dana Sellers
Print ISBN: 978-1-949846-72-0
Ebook ISBN: 978-1-949846-73-7

Printed in the United States of America

From earliest boyhood, my heart went out in admiring love towards those great navigators whose discoveries have caused their names to be inscribed on the scroll of the world's immortals. . . . In the world's early days, the command of God to man was to subdue the earth, to conquer it, and to civilize and fit it for the habitation of the human race. Nor did God's command apply to this portion or that only, or merely to lands where nature smiles in loveliness; nor yet to the forest primeval, the cloud-capped hills, the far-stretching plains, or the regions of eternal ice and snow; but to the whole earth *in its completeness. This should be man's mission.*

– Charles Erskine, cabin boy of the USS *Vincennes*

CONTENTS

The First Part *Islands*

1.	The Wreck	3
2.	Deaf and Dumb	13
3.	Mr. Rand's Proposal	23
4.	The Wild Girl	33
5.	An Island	39
6.	Mr. Rand's Complaint	48
7.	Alice	57
8.	Another Island	61
9.	A Charitable Offer	74
10.	The Piglet	79
11.	. . .	82
12.	Low Islands	87
13.	Called Home	94
14.	Another Island	100
15.	Southern Latitudes	118
16.	. . .	125
17.	Apocalypse	131
18.	Portsmouth, January 1857	134

The Second Part *Portraits*

1.	Correspondence	165
2.	The Tour	175
3.	. . .	193
4.	. . .	201
5.	The Impresario	207
6.	A Warm Reception	213
7.	. . .	219
8.	The Ship	230
9.	The Wild Girl of San Francisco	235
10.	. . .	244
11.	High Society	246
12.	. . .	253
13.	Sketches	267
14.	. . .	280
15.	An Uninvited Guest	291
16.	Pistols	303
17.	. . .	310
18.	Another Duel	323
19.	Awakening	329
20.	. . .	332

The Last Part *Ghosts*

. . .	339

The First Part
Islands
1856–1857

1.

THE WRECK

Lieutenant Henry Aaron Bird first saw the child as he was slumped on the shore, coughing and sputtering. Wet sand was caked on his face and uniform. Breakers crashed at his feet and disappeared into foam. One of his boatmen had dragged him from the waves, then ran off to help the others without offering so much as a salute; Bird's first thought was to admonish the sailor for this oversight, but he found that he couldn't because he was retching up seawater and trembling like a newborn lamb.

Lieutenant Grady stood waist-deep in the ocean, flailing his arms to direct the survivors in salvaging what they could from the foundered boat. Their empty water casks rolled along the tops of the swells, as if trying to decide whether to land themselves or float farther out to sea. Bird put the blame for their wreck squarely on Grady's shoulders—Grady had been the one to direct the landing, as Bird sat in the prow of the longboat, considering possible names for the island. He'd only accompanied the watering party because of the possibility, however remote, that it remained uncharted. Nothing was marked at this location, and he would maintain that American charts were the best that could be had in the world. The chance to put his name on something, even such an insignificant rock as this, was too much to pass up at this late point in his career. His thinking at the time, safe in his cabin aboard the *Fredonia*, was that if he would name it after himself, it was only fitting that he be the first to put his foot upon it. An involuntary shudder passed through him as he considered that this was an ambition he'd nearly died for. He imagined what his epitaph might have been, if he'd indeed perished on that day: Lieutenant Henry Aaron Bird: He Sailed All Around the World for Years and Years and Still Accomplished Nothing.

He was brooding in this manner, on the subject of his own inevitable disappearance from the world, when he caught sight of her. She was little more than a dusky smudge among the confusion of ferns that marked the forest's edge. He squinted through a salt haze to confirm what he saw: a small face; a child of indeterminate gender, or perhaps some type of pygmied native, peering from the tree line. He pushed himself to his feet and staggered up the shore. His hat had been lost, and the sun beat down on his bare crown and the few wisps of hair that remained there, stirred into salty tangles. He'd managed to retain both of his boots, a small mercy. Whoever it was, he hoped the little fellow would accept one of his coat buttons to guide him to fresh water, which would save them from traipsing across the island for hours. But as he halloed and waved his arms, the face abruptly disappeared.

There was no sign of the childlike figure once he'd entered the dimness of the forest, no track he could find. Thorns scratched at his hands and face as he pushed into the interior. There was some satisfaction to the activity, to the life of the chase and the feel of his own breath rattling with moisture—he often told himself that he was not one of those prim officers who feared to muddy their coats, unfortunately so common these days. His boots sank into the soft loam. At his approach, a parakeet ruffled and lit from its branch, sweeping away in little arcs just above the brush.

It was only now that he began to consider the curiosity of the figure's appearance—from the ship, they'd found no evidence of any native habitation. The shore where they'd been attempting to land was the only accessible portion of the coast. The outer shore of the island's curve was rocky and high, and the Polynesians almost never built their villages in the highlands. They clustered themselves always at the beaches or lagoons, as if they were magnetically drawn to the sea. Bird didn't encounter so much as a game trail as he continued to climb toward the island's high western shore, and he began to wonder if the child might have been nothing more than a hallucination brought on by his ingestion of seawater.

At some point, he realized he was lost. There was no landmark he could recognize, only featureless vegetation and a thick canopy that blotted out the sun, slicing and diffusing the light that filtered down to him. He paused to listen for the sound of the breakers to guide him, but the forest was impressively silent. No breeze or noise from the sea penetrated this far inland. Not even insects marred the absolute stillness. The scene reminded him of that moment which must have just followed the Creation, all of the world unpeopled and quivering with expectation.

Three quarters of an hour later, he emerged somewhat north of where they'd wrecked, drenched in sweat, his flesh mapped by long red welts, in a foul mood. The *Fredonia* was visible, two miles out past the reefs, still sitting quietly at anchor, unaware that her commander had been stranded. He wondered with pre-emptive annoyance how long it would take Lieutenant Rand to send a rescue party.

As he undertook the long walk back along the shore, small crabs circled around him on the sand and waved their futile claws at his approach.

A disorderly scene awaited him upon his reunion with his men. Deprived of his oversight for even a short while, their discipline had fallen to shambles. They were idle and many had removed their clothing to dry on a stretch of sunlit rocks. The marines sat smoking (how any of their tobacco remained dry was a mystery) and the middies were engaged, like rambunctious children, in a nude wrestling competition in the surf.

"Can you explain this, Mr. Grady?"

"Sixteen casks have survived, along with the arms, though the powder is ruined. We have only one spade remaining."

Grady was a ponderously dull man in his middle forties, with a doughy face and an altogether undistinguished character. Bird thought it a great injustice that the man wore the same number of epaulets as he. He waited for Grady to note his displeasure.

The second lieutenant flustered. "They were only letting off steam. Sir."

Bird called for Mr. Hooper. There were two Hoopers on his staff, young brothers from Connecticut. The midshipman was still pulling on his trousers as he arrived. "Which one are you again?" Bird inquired.

"Samuel, sir."

"Take the marines inland, to dig for water. Cask only that which has a fresh taste. I will not have it brackish."

"There is only one spade, sir," Grady reminded him.

"I suggest then that you take turns," Bird added.

Grady was tasked with surveying the island, though much of the necessary equipment had been lost in the wreck. To ensure the success of this mission, Bird also assigned Messrs. Dowd, Minnie, and Elliot to accompany him. Minnie at least was competent. Bird had thought at first to lead the surveying party himself, but after the day's misadventures he found he'd lost the spirit. Instead, he elected to remain at the beach, where he might sit on a rock to rest his knee and direct the remaining members of the boat crew in the gathering of wood for a signal fire.

As he watched them scouring the edge of the forest for downed wood, of which there was little, Bird allowed himself to relax and return to his earlier, more encouraging line of thinking. He considered *Bird's Land*. Simple but evocative. Perhaps too evocative, though? He wondered if that name might not inadvertently provoke the image of an island with an abundance of sea birds? Once, when he'd been a young middie himself on the Wilkes Expedition, he'd visited an island that was nothing more than a rock dusted with some dry shrubbery, every inch of it blanketed by nesting boobies. It had been the foulest-smelling place he'd ever encountered, littered with an admixture of feather, droppings, and the scattered carcasses of birds rotting in the sun. He wrinkled his face, to think of his name being permanently affixed to such an image.

∼

Dowd returned later in the afternoon to report that his party had found something of interest. "A settlement," he explained, out of breath from his trek up the beach.

"Natives? Or French?"

"It is difficult to tell, sir."

Bird frowned dismissively. "And how, Mr. Dowd, do you find it difficult to distinguish a Kanaka from a Frenchman?"

"They are all dead, sir."

Bird looked out toward the *Fredonia* and found no approaching boat. Though their signal fire burned on the shore, the palm wood and dried grass were quickly consumed, and the wind scattered the smoke. He turned to the boat crew, loath to leave them without supervision but finding no alternative, and said, "You are to remain here, to await Mr. Hooper and watch for any sign from the ship. And keep that damned fire burning."

The island was crescent-shaped, about three miles from one tip to the other and a mile across at its widest. The supposed settlement was located near the southern tip, where the cliffs of the western shore dwindled to meet the sandy beach that stretched along the inner curve. The site appeared at first to be nothing more than a stony meadow overgrown with dune grass. There was some dried lumber and copper sheeting, which seemed to have been prized from a ship's hull, scattered over a large area. Bird considered that it might all be nothing more than flotsam. But then Dowd showed him evidence of several shoddily constructed shelters—the only timbers left standing were three leaning posts that appeared to have marked the corners of a house. These were not native constructions. At some point, there had been white men here, perhaps the survivors of a wreck. It was impossible for him to determine how long the settlement had been deserted— the islands of the Pacific, he'd seen, had a stubborn way of renewing themselves. Native dwellings, left unoccupied for only a few years, he'd seen so thoroughly reclaimed by the forest that one could hardly tell there had been a house there at all.

Mr. Dowd presented him with the entire inventory of items located among the wreckage: a carpenter's hammer, a few ragged strips of cloth, two leather belts, a case knife. The leather coverlet of a Bible with only a few faded pages remaining.

"Where is Mr. Grady?"

"He is overseeing the excavation, sir."

Grady was in a nearby clearing, out of sight of the main settlement. Broken fragments of ship's spars had been planted in the ground at regular intervals, a few feet apart, none higher than a man's waist. They stood at odd angles, resembling two rows of drunken soldiers trying to stand at attention. One was engulfed in jungle creepers that seemed to pull it toward the earth. Grady was covered in sweat and endeavored to holler encouraging statements to the seamen, who grunted and swatted at the ground uselessly with hatchets and stones.

"Exactly what are these men digging for, Mr. Grady?"

"I believe these are graves, sir."

"I have gathered that, Mr. Grady."

Grady continued to survey the work and shouted, "Look to Jim, see how he puts his back into it!" To one of the sailors he added, "Fine work, Jim," with a nod of approval. The sailor briefly glared at Bird and Grady from his widening hole before resuming his futile pecking at the stony ground.

"You have not answered my question, Mr. Grady."

"My apologies, sir. I thought you had gathered that as well."

"Your thinking is beyond me, Mr. Grady."

"We are digging them up, sir."

"And what might we learn from some moldering bones, I wonder?"

Grady wiped his brow and said, "I thought we might discover pertinent clues, sir."

"Clues," Bird repeated dryly. It was baffling to him that such a man could rise so far in the service of his country. "Well. Put an end to it at once, Mr. Grady. We will not be robbing any Christian graves today."

Disappointed, Grady went to the task of dispatching the sailors as Bird wandered among the spars. There were no markings on the graves that could tell him anything about the men who'd met their fates on this lonely rock.

"Walk with me, Mr. Grady. I am feeling pensive."

Together they made their way back to the shore. Bird paused on a promontory buffeted by the wind. "Mr. Grady. I would like to present a line of thinking that I have been developing. I ask you, what do you see to the east?"

Grady squinted at the horizon and took entirely too long in answering. "The sea, sir."

"Very good. And now I ask you, what direction do you expect storms would blow in from?"

"The east, sir."

"So I assume that even you can now apprehend my point." It was clear from the man's dim expression that he did not, so Bird explained: "These are our *clues*, Mr. Grady. It is an exceedingly poor place for a settlement, exposed as it is to the sea and the weather. I would not be surprised if it was reduced to this state by the first winter's storms. I would say that they were inexperienced and ill-prepared."

He tried to detect any note of admiration for his powers of deduction on Grady's face, but the second lieutenant only said, "Shall I have the men fill in the holes, sir?"

"No," Bird said. "Leave them as they are. Organize the men into parties to search the island. I believe there is a survivor."

After sundown, the entire company was gathered on the shore. They were near-silent, the only sound the crackle of grasses being thrown onto the dwindling fire. Sparks circled upwards to be consumed by a clouded sky. The officers sat upon the filled water casks while the others stood or sat in the sand, awaiting the arrival of the boat the *Fredonia* had finally dispatched shortly before dusk. The lantern that marked its prow bobbed over the dark sea, a distant prick in the night.

Though the search parties had spent the remainder of the day crisscrossing the island's length and breadth, they'd found no sign of the child. Mr. Minnie's party had located a scrawny herd of goats in the highlands, no doubt also survivors of the wreck or their descendants. At the time, Bird had made a comment about the remarkable wisdom and tenacity of nature—impressed as he was by the fact that the goats had lived and thrived while the foolhardy men had perished—which was not fully appreciated. Minnie's party had shot all of the goats, and now hunks of their flesh roasted slowly over the fire on a spit.

Bird was arranged just outside of the firelight, his leg elevated on another cask to reduce its swelling. A chill wind had risen, which made him wish to be closer to the warmth, but he would not be seen being overly familiar with the crew. His thoughts remained fixed on the mysterious child he'd seen: Why was he now so sure it had been a child? Perhaps it had been a small-featured woman. Or a tiny man, a dwarf or pygmy or such? No, Bird thought—leave it at a woman, a more attractive fantasy to explore: a poor delicate soul cast upon this shore and struggling to survive, praying for her rescue . . . but why then would she flee from him?

Just then, at the edge of his vision, he caught a furtive glint of motion from farther down the beach. He let his eyes settle on the darkness there and found a small, hunched silhouette, crouched in the shadow of some rocks by the water's edge.

He looked away, as if he'd seen nothing. After a few bated moments, he rose and slowly made his way toward the fire.

"Mr. Grady," he said without alarm. Grady was staring at the roasting goat with naked anticipation.

"Sir?"

"I believe that we have our quarry."

Three middies were quietly dispatched to trek up the shore in the opposite direction—Bird's design was to have them backtrack through the forest in order to emerge behind the figure, thus cutting off any possibility of escape.

He waited, resisting the temptation to look, lest he scare her off. When they came upon her, there was a barely visible scuffle. Bird heard their distant cries as they gave pursuit. Mr. Minnie was the one who finally dragged her into the fire's light, an almost unrecognizably feral creature who dug her heels into the sand to resist him.

"What is it?" someone asked.

"It is a girl," came the reply.

It was indeed a girl, browned by the sun though Bird still adjudged her to most likely be of European stock. She was so much less than he'd imagined that he found himself pining now for the pygmy, or at least the dwarf, which would have somehow been less freakish. She was completely naked, her ribs and spine plainly visible, her face sunken from malnourishment. Her lips were curled in a snarl and she made a frightened, unintelligible hissing noise, but she was powerless against Minnie. Blonde hair, bleached nearly white, hung in thick dirty clumps over the burnt edges of her scalp. Her breasts were slight buds, barely rising from her chest. He guessed her to be no more than ten years old.

Finding no escape as they formed a circle around her, she crouched anxiously by the fire, her gaze locked upon the ground. She would not respond to any greeting, not in English or French, Dutch or Portuguese.

"For God's sake, someone give me a coat," Bird snapped.

He did not have much experience with the treatment of children—he'd never known a mother and his father had spoken to him only briefly, and of practical matters, the spacing of seed and the diseases of livestock, of jobs done poorly and how to correct them. So he spoke to her as he might have tried to soothe a skittish horse, clucking his tongue and saying *There now* . . . as he extended a hand to offer its emptiness.

She shrank from his approach, backing toward the fire until she could retreat no farther. He slowly moved to drape Dowd's offered coat over her shoulders, and she flinched at the touch of the fabric.

"There," he soothed her. "Isn't that much better?" Her eyes moved frantically over the sand.

"I am the commander of a ship." She sniffled as the wind turned to send smoke at her, but made no sign that she'd heard him. "We are of the United States Navy," he said. "You need not worry. You are safe now."

"My God, what has happened to her?" Mr. Grady asked.

None attempted a reply.

She was offered a portion of the goat when it was served, but only sniffed at it and dropped it into the sand. Bird could not believe that she wasn't hungry. How long had she been stranded there? Perhaps years, from the look of her. And another question: How had she survived while the others had perished?

A seaman named Fernandes thought to see if she was a Christian and dangled his golden cross on a string before her. This drew her attention; whether due to the symbol's meaning or only because it was a bright, shining object, Bird could not tell. She snatched it quickly from the sailor's grasp and held it tightly clasped in her fist, and afterwards could not be coaxed to release it.

2.

DEAF AND DUMB

Lieutenant Rand had arranged a hero's welcome for their returning commander. The entire crew was lined along the starboard, with lamps lit up and down the length of the ship, and the band greeted Bird with a meager version of *Hail, Columbia* as he climbed onto the deck. There was little true musical talent on board—they had only four instrumentalists and two drummers—and the climate ensured that their instruments were never in quite the same tune. The crew did not offer much to admire, either. Much of their original complement had deserted in Honolulu, vanished into the raucous music halls of that city, and the other portion had returned, Dr. Mallory confirmed, with every manner of venereal disease known to the medical sciences. Bird had filled out his crew list in Sydney by taking on whatever could be had; men with no country, who shipped out only when they ran out of funds for whoring and drink. To avoid further losses, he'd kept them confined to the ship for more than a year, a period of time in which none of them had had contact with a woman of any variety. Currently, they appeared confused and irritated, half of them roused from their sleep for the occasion, as the boatswain and his mates patrolled the rows blowing their whistles into men's faces.

Bird had judiciously ordered that the girl, still dressed only in an officer's coat, wait in the boat with Mr. Grady until he could bring her aboard with as little fuss as possible.

Rand greeted him with a salute, in one of the crisp uniforms that he steamed and pressed with a hot iron in the galley. Twenty-four years old and already a first lieutenant. A small bitterness Bird carried: It had taken him thirty years in the service to rise so far, due to his lack of influential relations such as the young man possessed. Still, Rand was a fine officer and possessed an enthusiasm for scheduling the watches that rivaled Bird's own.

"Is there not enough work, Mr. Rand? Have we time now for celebration?"

"Sir?"

"Put out these lights at once. Unless you have some idea of where we might replenish our oil. It is a terrible waste."

"I only wished for the crew to pay their respects, sir."

"And that is a fine ambition. But next time, please do it with more sense."

"Yes, sir. Will that be all?"

"No," Bird said. "There is one other thing. Have the storeroom just aft of the steerage arranged as a private cabin. We are to have a guest aboard."

In Bird's dayroom, Mr. Dowd and one of the Hoopers attempted to get the girl into a long sailor's shirt of white duck cloth that might serve as a dress. Bird had expected no trouble from her—she'd been entirely docile in the boat, leaning sleepily against the gunwale with a blank stare—but as soon as the two middies put their hands on her, she returned to all of her previous wildness. She scratched at Hooper, who'd been given the unenviable task of trying to hold her still, drawing lines of blood on his forearm with her broken nails. She wriggled free of the shirt before Dowd had it fully over her head and resumed her sibilant hissing, which Bird now observed was not unlike that which one might make to clear a cat from the dining table. She kneed Dowd in the stomach and twisted from Hooper's grasp to flee across the small cabin. Dowd gave clumsy pursuit, but she was surprisingly agile and managed to avoid recapture by scrambling over the furniture. Less usefully, Mr. Hooper stood frozen with a look of panic on his face.

In the chaos, she jostled the Lieutenant's writing desk, toppling his inkpot. The thick, black India ink seeped along the edge of the table and dripped to the floor.

"Damn it, can you not handle a girl?"

"Sorry, sir," Dowd muttered.

Finally, they cornered her. She crouched in terror, her breath whistling through her teeth. Something about the scene moved Bird to pity. "Oh, leave her be," he said. Dowd and Hooper backed away from her and she seemed to settle in her corner, watching them without taking her eyes fully from the floor. When her fear had quieted, Bird addressed her: "I will have you know that you are a guest here and you will not be harmed. But you must understand that this is a Navy ship, and you will not be permitted to run about naked like an animal."

There was still no sign that she understood any of his words. Dowd and Hooper stood uncomfortably to the side, unsure of whether to watch her for any further sign of trouble or to avert their eyes from her nakedness. His boy Victor came in with a requested bowl of pork and biscuits, and stood gaping at her body.

"You will give the girl some privacy while she eats," Bird scolded him, but it was no use. The boy was unable to look away, until Bird added, "You are dismissed," and sent him scurrying from the room. The pork and biscuits, placed on the floor in front of her, remained untouched.

Dr. Mallory ducked through the portal and touched his hat to acknowledge Bird. He studied the girl indifferently as he put down his bag.

"We found her on the island. She does not speak," Bird explained. He searched for the proper medical terminology. "She suffers possibly from some . . . *delirium*."

Mallory rummaged in his bag and brought out a brown glass bottle. "Hold her," he instructed the middies as he filled a dropper. With both Hooper and Dowd holding her still the surgeon was able to prize her mouth open just long enough to accept the medicine. As he tried to remove the dropper she snapped at him with her teeth, briefly getting ahold of the webbing between his thumb and forefinger. Mallory gave out a little cry as he pulled his hand from her, and regarded the slight wound she'd made with horror and disgust. Within a few moments, her struggles began to ease, and she sagged like a discarded puppet in Hooper's lap.

"Put her in the armchair," Mallory suggested.

"Is that necessary?" Bird asked, unenthusiastic about the idea of this filthy creature being placed in his favorite chair.

"Unless you wish for me to examine her on the floor."

She was neither asleep nor awake, her eyes hanging open enough to watch them with a dull interest as they deposited her on the armchair.

"Should we dress her now, sir?" Dowd looked to Bird for an answer.

"Don't bother," Mallory said.

Bird sent the middies from the cabin as Mallory began his examination. The surgeon probed her ribs, ran a careful finger around the inside of her mouth to check for sores. He bent to press an ear against her sternum, which stood out sharply beneath her skin. Under the influence of the laudanum she was still and had relaxed her features—for the first time Bird felt he could truly see her face. Blue eyes and a small nose that showed damage from the sun. She was about four and a half feet tall, small-shouldered, her forearms and calves so thin a large-handed man could get his grip completely around them. He imagined her under different circumstances—in a proper dress, with a neat braid down her back—and judged her to be, if not beautiful, at least on the cusp of pretty.

"There is no fever," Mallory declared. "No sign of scurvy."

"What prevents her speech?"

Mallory stooped and snapped his fingers right near her ear. She made no reaction. He stood and clapped his hands once, sharply, before her face. Still nothing.

"Most probably deaf and dumb."

Bird frowned. "How old?" he asked.

"Difficult to say. I see adult bone development. She might be mature."

"But so small," the Lieutenant mused.

Mallory said, "Malnutrition can work all manner of mischief on human development. Delay the growth, the sexual maturation. I would guess she was stranded for some time."

He retrieved again the brown bottle and put a few more drops on her tongue.

"She will sleep now."

Bird poured two whiskies at the sideboard and offered one to Mallory, which the surgeon accepted without comment, and they stood regarding her slumped form. A line of spittle ran from her mouth.

"She is some manner of idiot," Mallory stated flatly. "Probably would have been best served if you'd left her where you found her." The surgeon grinned mirthlessly at the Lieutenant, showing off his dentures—he'd fashioned them himself, from animal teeth affixed to a leather fitting. They rotted quickly and needed to be replaced often, but for chewing Mallory insisted there was no substitute for natural dentation. He'd offered to make a bridge for Bird, who was missing four in a row on his bottom left, but Bird had declined. He couldn't square himself to the idea of chewing his food with teeth that had once been in a doe's mouth.

"Is it possible, though, that she might be cured? Perhaps she is not a true idiot." Bird strove to sound *scientific*, conscious as he was of his lack of education. He was thinking about cases he'd read of, those of children who had been raised in the wild, outside of human society, who'd run on all fours and howled at the moon, deprived of speech and all custom. There had been a famous French case, where a doctor had partially cured just such a wild boy. He'd been made to wear suits and recite his name, things like that. "Perhaps, because of her long isolation . . ." Bird ventured, "I mean . . . might it be the case that she has simply *regressed*? To some kind of animalistic state?"

Mallory frowned as if he tasted something sour in his whiskey.

"Like that French boy," Bird added. "Have you heard of him? The one they found suckling a she-wolf?"

"You mean the German boy?"

"No, I think he was French. There may have been a German one as well."

"Pure nonsense."

With a thumb, Mallory pulled the flesh below the girl's eye to reveal the red crescent beneath, and tilted his head to look through the lower part of his spectacles. Her pupil wandered lazily, and her mouth hung slightly open to reveal two rows of small, uneven teeth.

"How can you be so certain?"

"Even if there have been such cases," Mallory said, "it is a very rare phenomenon. And idiocy, I would say, is much more common. Hence, my diagnosis."

He should have known better than to attempt to engage the surgeon in this kind of speculative thinking—the man was about as interested in science as a clam. He knew Mallory to spend most of his time sequestered in the sick bay, composing verses of poetry and eating through the ship's store of opium to ease the pain of a bullet he claimed was lodged in his shinbone.

"You are dismissed, Dr. Mallory."

After the surgeon had left, Bird took up the discarded sailor's shirt and gently guided her into it. Once she was dressed, he returned to his sideboard to fetch his last remaining orange, which he offered to her. The girl regarded it with a wrinkle of confusion, then reached out to slowly remove it from his hands. She brought it to her lips and dug her teeth into the outer rind.

"No," Bird corrected her. She paused in her chewing guiltily, like any child that had been caught at some mischief. He reached over to take it back. Her fingers went loose and she relinquished it, still not meeting his eyes. He took up a knife and began to pare away the rind and let the peelings drop to the cabin floor, then returned the peeled orange to her and watched as she ate it slowly but greedily, licking the juice from her palms as it tried to escape. The surgeon was a fool, Bird thought. She was no idiot.

"Well," he said to her, "we know your stomach and your ears work well enough."

∼

The *Fredonia* sailed on through the night toward the Marquesas Islands, untroubled by the additional passenger. After the girl drifted off and was carried to her quarters by Mr. Dowd, Bird remained awake in his cabin. The room was austerely furnished, containing only a table and chairs, his now ink-stained writing desk, a shelf of books he occasionally pawed without enthusiasm, and his liquor cabinet above the sideboard, which saw quite a bit more use. He'd been exhausted by the day's excitement but knew he would not be able to find sleep. He poured himself another whiskey and sat smoking his pipe until the bowl became so hot that he was forced to hold it by the stem. The windows were dark but he could hear the sound of water rushing against the hull.

Being given command of the *Fredonia* had been the crowning achievement of Bird's life, the fulfillment of almost all of his youthful ambition. When he'd first left home to enlist, at fifteen, his head had been full of tales of travel and adventure, the voyages of Drake and Cook. He'd thought to take his place among the world's great explorers. He was an old man now—at fifty-five, the same age that his father had been when he collapsed in his fowl pen from a bad heart—and he was sometimes possessed by the disturbing notion that his life was nearly over, and he'd spent all of his years waiting for it to begin. Before this, he'd been stuck for years on a packet that delivered mail up and down the sleepy California coast. The command of an important diplomatic mission to the South

Pacific was just the sort of post he'd long dreamed of gaining, but they'd been at sea for three years already and the voyage had thus far presented him only with a series of disappointments. He hadn't been promoted to captain before taking command, as he'd expected to be, which put him in the awkward position of wearing the same amount of epaulets as many on his staff, a discrepancy that rankled him and, he felt, needlessly undercut his authority. The South Pacific was not as he'd expected to find it, either. It had been two decades since the Wilkes Expedition, and in that time the region had been overrun by European missionaries and American whalers. Even in the most remote locations, he found drunken white sailors living in huts on the beaches, eager to trade or translate or begging for passage to some other island. It had occurred to Bird more than once that he'd been born a few decades too late for his ambition; it seemed there was nothing left in the world that remained waiting to be discovered. At every sleepy outpost of civilization, he was forced to endure an endless, dreary procession of society dinners. He dined with the captains of the whalers and merchantmen to inquire into the state of their commerce. He dined with missionaries and local governors. Once, while taking a gourd of steamed breadfruit from a tray carried by a smiling Tongan house servant, he had thought to himself: *I am dining my way across the Pacific.*

Their voyage had been prompted by an incident, on the 14th of May, 1852, during which a party of the Nantucket whaler *Genovese* had encountered violence from the inhabitants of Uonukuhahake, among the Friendly Isles. The cause or origin of the conflict remained obscure, but in the end the landing party had been largely stoned to death. Upon learning that white men had been slain by savages, the public had demanded that something be done, regardless of fault, though by all accounts a thorough retribution had already been taken by the remaining crew of the *Genovese*. Bird had confirmed this. Nothing in the reports which had been appended to his orders had prepared him for the devastation he found there. He had at first been unable to locate the village at the coordinates indicated. When communicating with a local fisherman who spoke some English, the man had seemed confused by Bird's inquiries concerning the whereabouts of the village. *Village no more*, he'd said, waving toward a distant and forested shore. *Tapu now.* Bird found little evidence there that such a village had ever existed. A large patch of charred ground and a blank-faced stone monument were all that remained. Young coconut palms and island grasses had already reclaimed the area. Pressing farther inland, Bird's party had discovered the remaining inhabitants, mostly women and children and old men, still residing in the forest nearby. Whether they lacked the means to rebuild their village or the desire, Bird could not ascertain. They retreated at the approach of Bird's party, like quiet, frightened spirits. There had been nothing for the Navy to accomplish there.

Privately, and only when he was drunk, Bird would grant himself permission to wonder if their mission ever truly had any purpose at all, or if it might have just been a bit of politicking, meant to quiet angry constituents. When he was *very* drunk, he wondered if the type of man who would be chosen to lead such a mission was a fool.

The ship required little of him. Rand and Grady had the crew well in hand, though he suspected this was mostly the doing of Mr. Rand. He had a competent sailing master in Mr. Whitlocke, who could perform all of the more monotonous tasks of navigation. Most days they sailed on flat, calm seas. Rain fell on the ship for a few minutes every day, a clockwork downpour like a bucket overturned in the sky that drenched the boards. Rain or shine, the heat was inescapable. His handkerchiefs were all stained yellow from the sweat he mopped from his brow when forced out of his cabin and into the sun. The nights at sea were even worse—each a long, dark crossing that seemed impossible to traverse without the assistance of alcohol.

But now, something had finally *happened*. He'd discovered perhaps the last rock in the Pacific that still required a name, and rescued an actual castaway, something he'd only read about in adventure novels as a boy. He imagined that when word of these events spread, there might even be some form of public outcry when it became known that a man of his experience had not been granted a captaincy sooner, and then the whole stinking corrupt mess of Washington would be uncovered.

His first order of business, he considered, would be to record the day's events in the ship's log. He didn't wish to entrust such a momentous record, one which might well someday be the subject of much scrutiny, to his clerk. And besides, the man was so adept at hiding himself on the ship that Bird rarely knew his whereabouts. Bird righted the spilled inkpot and regarded the mess. He tried to sop up the ink with a rag but found he only smeared it, and so instead he just laid some sheets of paper over the spill, both on the desk and the floor, to prevent him from tracking it around the cabin.

∼

Apart from a brief mention in the passenger list of the clipper Lady Fortune *preserved at Boston Harbor (which notes that Thomas Kelly and his wife boarded "w/child"), the logbook of the* Fredonia *provides the first surviving documentation establishing her existence—any birth certificate or earlier record being lost. In this rare instance, it is authored and signed personally by Bird, rather than his clerk:*

> *"Put in at a small island, believed to be uninhabited, to refresh water. Boat foundered on an unseen reef, owing to faulty observations on the part of Mr. Grady, thus stranding us for part of the day until a rescue could be accomplished. At the urging of my crew, and finding no land on record for this location, we did nickname the place "Bird's Land." There we encountered the remains of a camp and a single living survivor of what is assumed to have been a wreck. She is a girl of perhaps ten years, of American or European origin, who has been left in a speechless and pitiable state. I have thus adjudged it our duty to assist and provide every courtesy of our Nation to such a desperate soul, and take sole responsibility for her presence aboard this frigate the USS* Fredonia. *17 Feb 1856."*

3.

Mr. Rand's Proposal

Rand found himself standing in a desolate valley, looking toward the crown of a great, bare hill. On all sides the landscape was featureless, not even a shrub marked it. He felt only a mild curiosity about his location, or how he'd gotten there. More importantly, his uniform was in poor order, and he fussed over it for some time, smoothing wrinkles, testing the strength of buttons, straightening his epaulet. It seemed to him that even in his present circumstance, his appearance was of the most vital importance.

Just then he was startled by a sudden great sound from the heavens that nearly shook him from his feet: the blast of a horn so loud and deep it made him quake with fear. It filled the sky and passed over him like a wind, stirring the dust all around him.

The shock of the sound was slowly replaced with a growing panic, as he realized that it had been the great trumpet blast of the angel Gabriel. Rand had been taken unawares, surprised at the Last Judgment in an act of vanity, and now there was no time left to repent. He looked up to the crown of the hill. He could hear fifes and drums in the distance. An army was approaching. He turned in bewildered circles, looking for anyplace that he might hide himself, any rock or tree that might conceal him. There was nothing, and nothing to do but await their arrival. Then he saw the first of them crest the hill. They were marching proudly, holding colorful standards. He could hear them singing joyous music. It was the army of the Saved, risen from their graves and given new bodies to live in the Paradise to come. And he knew with a deep, sinking certainty that he would not be deemed fit to walk among their number.

He woke to a small cabin that was heavy with the lingering smell of Grady's flatulence. He couldn't see the top bunk from where he lay, but knew that Grady must be absent. Even in sleep, the man shuffled and breathed heavily, like a swine. Grady didn't have *all night in*, as he did, but the privilege of sleeping through the night was only a small comfort for Rand, as he was woken every four hours by the second lieutenant clumsily bumping him in the tight space as he either removed or donned his boots. And when Rand did sleep, it was always the same disheartening dream.

The bell had not yet rung to announce the morning watch—he could tell by the unhurried voices that drifted from the wardroom. These few quiet moments upon waking were all he would have to himself until after dusk. It was during these times that he allowed himself to dwell on happy memories of home. His two hound dogs, Jake and King, who would bound toward the door whenever he entered the house. His comfortable old room overlooking the ships in Providence harbor. The sound of his mother playing the piano in the parlor.

Rand hadn't wished to be a naval officer. He didn't know what he wished for—but not this. It was not the sea that he minded, nor sailing. It had always given him pleasure as a boy, to sail with his father and brothers in the harbor. He admired the curvature of ships, and was enamored of sleek vessels cutting through the water, their neat rigging snapping in the wind; he even admired the sight of Navy men in their flashing uniforms. It was everything else about Navy life, though, which he found unpleasant: the cramped quarters, the heavy smell of unwashed men, the joyless routine, the tiring vigilance that was required of him to keep the entire company from sliding into a moral chaos. The South Pacific, to him, may as well have been the surface of the moon—there was nothing in it he could recognize, nothing familiar. To think that the Lord had seen fit to create such a place, populated by brown-skinned heathen, hideously tattooed from head to foot, their breadfruit and cocoanuts provided to them like manna, isolated on their scattered islands to exist without any labor save for their constant fornication. For what purpose in the Lord's plan did such a place exist? It was not for him to know.

As much as he hated this life, Rand's family had produced only Navy men back to the Revolution, and who was he to break from that tradition? What other grand purpose could he find for himself? Because he had not been able to answer that question, he'd gone to the academy and then to sea in accordance with his father's wishes. And he comforted himself with the notion that wherever he was, he could strive to be a good Christian, a beacon of charity, and to help uplift his fellow man.

He'd taken pains to decorate the cabin, to make it as cheerful as possible. The ship's carpenter had built him a wall shelf where he could display the souvenirs he'd acquired on the cruise: masks and decorations of the Polynesians, woven of dyed cocoanut husk or carved in sandalwood. A *bêche-de-mer*, which had an appearance he could compare to nothing but a dried turd. He'd acquired it to demonstrate to his brothers the ridiculous superstitions of the Celestials, who believed that the consumption of these disgusting sea-turds would increase their male potency. On the floor was a rug purchased in Honolulu, woven from the native tappa. His mother had advised him that it was important to keep mementos of home in sight as well, to maintain his spirits, and to this end he'd brought with him an ivory hairbrush that belonged to her, though he hardly needed it for his own neatly-cropped hair, and a small hassock she'd embroidered with a cross of lace, which he now used to kneel for his morning prayer.

In his prayers that morning—along with an already long list which included his family, his fellow officers, the crew whose lives were so bereft of uplifting influence, the heathen of the islands, and the French missionaries, who after all were trying their best to do the Lord's work despite the misfortune of being born as papists—he included the poor girl who had been brought onto the ship the night before. A shipwrecked child, he was told. He'd hardly seen her. She'd only been a small form in an overlarge coat, and he struggled to recall her features so that the Lord might know where to direct His grace.

When he'd finished, he laced his boots, braced himself for the day to come, and entered the wardroom. Mr. Fledge was reading a very old French newspaper, crumpled at the edges from its long voyage. He looked up to Rand and nodded. They had agreed, all of them, to keep the wardroom informal. Mr. Piper was contemplating a soft-boiled egg he had yet to crack, and Dr. Mallory was speaking to no one in particular.

"I don't know what the Pelican expects to do with her . . ." He used their private nickname for the commander.

Mr. Piper responded as he tapped the egg with a spoon. "She's a wild one. I heard tell she bit one of the reefers and he still bears her tooth marks."

"I'll show you tooth marks," Mallory complained, presenting his lightly injured hand as if it were a broken wing. "And let us hope it doesn't fester. Who knows what diseases she might carry?"

Rand took up a china cup from a peg on the wall, poured himself half a cup of coffee from the pot on the table. "What else is known of her?"

Mallory shrugged. "She was wrecked."

"For how long?"

"There is no way to tell. She does not speak."

Their conversation was interrupted by the Pelican's boy, Victor. He was flushed and anxious, as if he had run there chased by devils. Rand had never seen the boy look otherwise.

"Begging your pardon, sirs."

"Oh, what is it?" Fledge said without looking up.

"Lieutenant Bird requests all the officers of the wardroom at his quarters following the muster."

Rand was surprised—it had been months since the Pelican had addressed all of the officers at once. Their commander was a private man who preferred to remain shut up in his cabin, drinking himself into a stupor. He normally only communicated via cryptic, scrawled notes to the line officers. Rand had received one the day before which read, in Bird's customary tight scrawl:

TODAY THE PEOPLE WILL HAVE FRESH PICKLES WITH THEIR MEAT

They had not had any pickles, fresh or of any other variety, for several months, a fact of which Bird was obviously unaware. And what was a "fresh" pickle, anyway? Weren't pickles, by their very nature, a preserved foodstuff? Such were the ambiguities of dealing with the lieutenant commander. Rand had considered the necessity of entering into a written dialogue with his superior about the state of the ship's pantries, but opted instead to ignore the directive entirely, confident that Bird would never notice.

Mr. Fledge said, "I suppose we're finally to be introduced to our guest."

Rand finished his coffee in two sips and began to make his way up to the spar deck. Before the steerage, he paused at the door of the converted storeroom where the girl was being quartered. Newly installed on its outer surface was a simple iron bar latch, securing the door. He felt an indignant ripple run through him—for what purpose was she being confined? Surely a small, speechless girl could pose no threat to the ship. He listened at the door but heard no sound from within. Before he could contemplate any further action, the bell rang, calling them for the muster, and every man on the ship sprang into motion at once.

Sailors on the berth deck parted for him like the sea as they pulled on stockings and rolled up their hammocks. He climbed to the gun deck and his attention was drawn to the starboard, where Mr. King shrieked at a seaman who seemed to be attempting to eject himself, rear-end first, through one of the cannon ports.

"On your feet or I'll put you the rest of the way out!" King screamed, swatting the man with a length of rope.

"Mr. King, I would like to ask you what this man's offense is, which requires his deportation?"

King snapped to attention and touched his hat. The middie was younger than Rand only by a few years, and was eager to make good on his threat. "Got hold of a laggard, sir."

The sailor had a greenish pallor. It was one of the sheet anchor men, an old salt with a long white beard, whom he assumed to be a victim of the spoiled water casks which had necessitated the previous day's adventures. His thesis was confirmed as Rand heard a sickening noise erupt from the man's hindquarters. The old sailor moaned pitifully.

Rand addressed the sailor. "You are ill, seaman?"

The old man mustered a weak, grateful nod. "Yes, sir, thank you so much for noticing."

"Have this fellow sent to the infirmary," he said, and then added privately, "and keep in mind, Mr. King, that throwing seamen overboard is not on the punishment list."

Rand climbed up from below and took his place on the quarterdeck with the other officers, the entire ship's company assembled before them for the morning muster: three hundred men standing in absolute silence as the chaplain delivered a morning prayer from the area of the mainmast, barely audible at this distance. It was a fine, clear day, the ship moving at a good clip and no land in sight. Sailcloth rolled under the breeze. He breathed in the fresh air, thankful to be out from below. It always amazed him, to regard the company all at once and be struck by the miracle of their continued existence, all of these souls crowded onto a four-hundred-foot bark, eating, sleeping, living their entire lives in the presence of one another, a little city of men surrounded by nothing but blue and more blue as far as the eye could see. Every soul on board must know by now of the girl, he thought. All of them wondering the same as he: Who was she?

Trying to hide his curiosity, he searched the quarterdeck for her as best he could without drawing notice. Around him he saw Fledge, Grady, Piper, the sailing master Mr. Whitlocke. The middies gathered around Mr. Harvey, their professor, like schoolchildren. Dr. Mallory appeared to be a creature out of place in the sun, holding a slim book above his eyes to block the glare. At the end of the line, he found the Pelican standing smugly, his hands clasped behind him. But the girl was not among them.

He was almost the last to arrive at Bird's dayroom, due to several issues on the deck that hadn't really required his attention. There was a shuffling of chairs at the long table to make room for him. A respectful nod from Mr. Harvey, his tiny spectacles perched on his nose. Next to him sat Mr. Thomas, whom Rand could smell even at this distance to be already drunk at eight in the morning. The windows were brightly lit by the sun, illuminating some lingering smoke though none smoked that he could see. The sailing master, Mr. Whitlocke, an old Puritan with his face squarely bordered by a neat beard, scratched slowly and methodically at a wiry gray tuft of hair that protruded from one of his ears. Piper and Grady colluded off to one side, a slight guffaw escaping from Grady that he quickly stifled when he noticed Bird waiting for their attention.

In moments like this, Rand could not help but to compare Bird unfavorably to the image of his father, who was a natural leader of men: broad-chested, with a booming voice and a full, snowy head of hair. Bird, on the other hand, was tall and thin, nearly bald and sun-spotted on his pate, his skin hanging loosely from his neck. Rand thought he resembled nothing so much as a weary office clerk or an accountant who'd happened to accidentally don an officer's uniform.

Finally, Dr. Mallory entered. He nodded and smiled at the assembly, as if he gave them permission to begin. The purser, Mr. Fledge, had brought along another pot of coffee, retrieved from the galley, and offered to fill everyone's cup.

"If you don't mind, sir, as we've just finished our breakfast."

"As you will." Bird allowed them to settle. "Thank you for joining me this morning. As I'm sure you're all aware by now, we have a guest on the ship. A girl. We assume her to be the survivor of a wreck. She has not spoken and her condition is poor."

"What is wrong with her?" Mr. Thomas asked.

"She is malnourished and . . . Dr. Mallory, would it be fair to say she suffers from some form of delirium?"

Mallory shrugged. "I've given my full opinion on the matter. The girl is an idiot."

Bird frowned at the surgeon and continued, "Nevertheless, she will remain on the ship until such a time as we can offer her to the proper authorities. And I will expect your full cooperation in this matter." He searched their faces for any sign of dissent. "Because she has not been able to tell us her name," Bird continued, "I have decided that, for the time being, we will refer to her as *Lucy*. I urge you to use this when referring to her, in the hope that the possession of a name might begin to warm her again to the ways of civilization. Do you all find this to be acceptable?"

He was met with a stony silence.

"*Lucy*," Mr. Fledge finally repeated, as if trying it out. "And when will we meet this Lucy?"

"A more difficult question," Bird mused. "It has been necessary to confine her to quarters, for the present. She is to be permitted no visitors. I will personally oversee her care, so as to avoid any disruption to your present duties."

Rand had not intended to speak. It was a bad habit he'd possessed since childhood, that of speaking his mind. His father had counseled him that the way to get ahead in the service was to avoid making waves, but he often found words in his mouth like unwanted guests. His mother used to tell him that at these times, he was being moved by the Spirit.

"By what authority do you keep her as a prisoner?" He felt the discomfort in the room at once. Whitlocke, who detested all conflict, began to slowly chew his own lip.

"Mr. Rand, I do not apprehend your meaning."

"She is not under naval jurisdiction. She is a civilian. You can do as you like to Navy men, but you do not have the right to keep her locked away."

"It does seem inhospitable," Mr. Fledge offered helpfully.

"If you saw the girl, you'd understand," Mallory said. "There is no other option."

Lieutenant Bird rapped his knuckles on the table to restore order. "I am the commander of this ship, and I have judged it to be in the best interests of the mission to keep her apart."

Rand answered, "Surely there is no danger to permitting her above decks, to take the air? I would be glad to chaperone her."

"This is a ship in the service of the United States Navy, Mr. Rand, and we are not in the custom of operating a nursery. I assume you already have enough duties to fill your time. And I suppose you have not considered the moral life of the crew. There is a reason, after all, why women are not permitted on our ships. Even at your tender age, I am sure you understand something of these matters?"

Rand bristled at the insult, but took a moment to steady his voice so it wouldn't betray him. "Allow me to make another proposal, then."

Bird nodded without enthusiasm, his lips drawn thin.

"You must appreciate that a woman is a more delicate creature than a man, not designed by the Creator to face such terrors as she must have endured . . ."

Mr. Thomas interrupted to state his agreement—he stifled a belch and then cited the fact that when he was at home, he'd often witnessed his wife weeping for no discernible reason.

Rand ignored him and continued, "Consider that this young woman . . ."

"*Lucy*," Bird corrected him.

"Fine. Consider that *Lucy* has been bereft of any company for some time now, we cannot even guess how long. And has not pleasant society proven to be almost the equivalent, for the female of the species, of meat and bread?"

"This is not a courtroom, Mr. Rand, and we are not a jury to be flattered. What do you propose?"

"I would like to extend an invitation for her to dine with us tonight, in the wardroom. Surely there is no reason you will object to that? We'll show her some hospitality, won't we boys?" He scanned the room, looking for support among his fellow officers, but found little save for a paltry *Hear, hear* from Mr. Fledge.

Bird sighed. "Mr. Rand, I simply don't think that would be a very good idea."

4.

THE WILD GIRL

Despite the Lieutenant's best efforts, the adoption of *Lucy* as the girl's name refused to take hold. As word of her spread, the sailors began to weave fanciful theories about her. Some claimed to know her true identity. They had seen her years before, in some far-off port. Her name was *Elizabeth*, they said, or *Ann*, or *Ruby*. She was a harlot, or the daughter of a sea captain; she was even claimed, in one of the more far-fetched stories, to be the bastard child of Danish royalty.

"They say she does not speak," Victor explained, "because her tongue has been cut from her mouth." The boy served as Bird's eyes and ears among the crew.

"And why would anyone do something like that, I wonder?"

"To keep her from sayin' her true name," Victor answered quickly. "Or else she would get the crown. From her cousin."

"I see it has all been worked out down to the pin."

The old sheet-anchor men, the boy reported, unanimously declared her to be bad luck, and claimed that she would bring misfortune to the ship. Bird paid it no mind—these were men who considered it an ill omen if the cook dropped an onion to the floor.

"And what is your opinion of all of this?" Bird asked him in a serious tone. "Do you believe what they say?"

Victor's character was unmarked by anything extraordinary. Bird thought he would be lucky enough to become some form of ship's tradesman, if his career advanced that far. He had none of the ambition Bird had possessed at his age. As a matter of fact, Bird had noticed, early in the voyage, an alarming amount of hair on Victor's upper lip and on the backs of his hands, a sign that he might have misrepresented his age to continue a comfortable life as a ship's boy, rather than taking on the more rigorous work of a grown man. Still, boy or young man, he had a knack for going unnoticed.

Victor was disinclined to offer his own thoughts, if he had any. He knew what Bird wished him to say. "No sir. My thinking is they are just making up tales."

"Good boy," Bird said. Then he asked, "Do any say she is a wild girl?"

"No, none say that, sir."

~

For her first days on the ship, the girl was affected by a terrible seasickness, during which she could not stand, even to relieve herself, and lay in a puddle of her own waste. She continued to refuse all food, and vomited only thin streams of bile or made painful, dry retching sounds that produced no issue at all.

Bird did not cease in his efforts to reacquaint her with the necessity of clothing. Each time she was discovered in the nude, he sent Dowd and King into the close space of her cabin—only the span of a man's arms across, with a bunk affixed to the wall occupying half of it—to pin her to the ground and force her back into the same soiled shirt.

Looking in on her was Bird's first order of business each morning, after his first coffee, his first pipe, and his first whiskey, always enjoyed in that order. She would squint her eyes against the light and look up at him without recognition. When it seemed the worst of her sickness had passed, he decided that she would have a bath. Perhaps warm water and cleanliness would awaken something in her. At the very least, he thought, it would be a comfort. He summoned Mallory to liberate her of her filthy hair. Despite her weakened state, the surgeon would not touch her without first liberally dosing her with laudanum. She swayed without objection as he sheared mudded clumps of the stuff from her scalp with a razorblade, leaving her with a short and uneven stubble, so blonde as to be almost clear and revealing the scabby pink of her scalp. Dealing with her womanhood properly and with respect was Bird's most vexing concern. It seemed more proper to him if Mallory would also be the one to wash her, but the surgeon refused. "First you use me as a barber, and now you wish for a governess. You have no use for a surgeon here." With that, he stormed off to the sick bay to stew on his humiliation, and would not exit for any reason for the rest of the day.

The girl's bath required a complex orchestration of bodies; Messrs. Dowd and King positioned themselves around a zinc tub, filled by Victor squeezing around them as he ran back and forth to the galley for pails of hot water. Through all of the proceedings she seemed to sleep, and only woke briefly when they lifted her up by her armpits. She looked pleasantly astonished, to be suspended in the air.

She let out a gasp and pulled her legs up as her feet touched the water. She clung to Mr. King's neck like an orang-utan until they pried her loose and pushed her into the tub. She gave a single kick that soaked Mr. King's shirt, and then drooped lazily in the water. Her breath was shallow and quick and her skin flushed from the tub's warmth. Dowd and King scrubbed her with rags tied to the ends of short poles, a plan Bird had devised to preserve what he could of her honor.

His shirtsleeves rolled up to the elbows, King reached into the water to bring up a foot. The sole was hard calloused and gray. Her toenails were jagged and broken stubs, one gouged and half-missing. She made no reaction to the washing of her feet, but when they arrived at her chest she made a queer noise, like *huh . . . huh*. She was, Bird guessed, laughing.

As they pulled her out of the tub, Bird reviewed her and said, "Now, you are almost presentable."

King propped her up as Dowd fumbled with the sleeves of the dress the steward had fashioned for her, one that could be fastened between her legs so as to be more difficult to remove. Scrubbed to a rosy pink and drowsy from the heat and steam and laudanum, she fell almost instantly into a deep and peaceful sleep in King's arms, and he gingerly placed her on the bunk and covered her up.

When Bird returned to her the next morning, thinking to hand deliver her breakfast and see if he could coax her toward speech, he found her once again nude and sleeping on the floor, in a nest of freshly-soiled blankets.

She was dressed and brought up to his cabin for a few hours each afternoon, so that she might move about in more spacious quarters and enjoy the light that seeped in through the thickly-paned windows. During this time, he was content to simply observe her, and allow her to acclimate herself slowly to his company. After the menacing figures of Dowd and King were banished, she would quickly forget about Bird's presence and begin to explore her surroundings. He sat in his armchair, moving only to lift his pipe or his glass to his mouth. She moved in a low crouch around the edges of the room, as if afraid to stand fully upright. She touched the spines of his books one by one, an activity whose purpose he could not divine.

Whenever she turned to regard him, he would smile and call something out like, "HELLO LUCY! HOW ARE YOU TODAY?"

He began to present her with small objects that he thought might interest her: his golden wedding ring which he'd never lost the habit of wearing, a shaving brush, one of the small hand mirrors that so fascinated the Polynesians. She would not take them directly from his hand, but only when he left them for her on the floor and had fully returned to his armchair. She did not long regard the mirror, but an empty tin that had contained peppermints, and which still bore their scent, occupied her for some time. He held before her a photographic card he had purchased in Sydney, commemorating the opening of an opera house. All of the investors stood in three rows on its front steps, dressed in dark coats and tall hats. He studied her face, to see if her eyes focused on the picture or hinted at any recognition of the image it held. She stared past it, past him, her eyes twitching in their sockets. He turned to the windows, where she was directed, and caught the last flicker of a sea bird's passage.

He noted in his private journal: *She shows no understanding of a photograph or even a mirror, as would be expected of any girl her age. When not directly threatened, she seems to have no concern for her situation. She is partial to certain sounds from without, such as the ship's bell, to others such as speech she seems entirely deaf. Her attention is much like that of a dog's, wandering unfocused from one object to the next, each a source of momentary fascination which is then entirely forgotten.*

He had once known a ship's dog named Royal, on the schooner *Maryann*; he recalled he'd earned the dog's loyalty not by boxing its ears, as the other sailors did, but by giving it crumbs from his meals, and endeavored now to apply the same principle to the girl. At first, she'd eaten only fruit, of which there was precious little remaining on the ship, but through patient experimentation he discovered that she would also eat cheese, and hardtack as long as it was first soaked in tea or wine to soften it. He could not interest her in stewed pork, but she would drink the broth, lapping at the rim of the hot bowl and tilting it with her hands until half of its quantity spilled onto the floor. She would not sit in a chair or eat from the table, no matter what prize he offered her. When several bream were pulled aboard one day, the Lieutenant sent a request to the cook that his be prepared in a sauce of butter and capers, and that another be sent up whole and raw on a plate. This, he placed across from him at the table with a knife and fork arranged optimistically beside it. Though she had no interest in meat, he wondered if, during her period of isolation, she might have survived by eating the carcasses of fish that had washed ashore?

When she saw the fish she approached the table quickly and reached for it—she was starting, he thought, to feel quite at home—but Bird slid the plate away.

"First, you must sit properly," he told her.

She leaned over the table, unable to take her eyes from the fish. She did not even seem aware of Bird's presence, or Dowd and King hovering behind her.

"Sit," he repeated, motioning toward the chair. "Mr. King, if you would show Lucy how we sit at a table . . ."

King took hold of her from behind and pressed her into the chair. She tried to twist out from beneath him but he held her fast.

"There now," Bird said. "Now, we can eat our supper like ladies and gentlemen." He slid the plate back across the table. Once the fish was within her reach she seemed to forget all else, and dug into its silver skin with her fingers.

"You may let her go," Bird said, and nodded at Mr. King. He did, and stepped back. She remained in the chair, once again leaning crookedly over the table to bring herself closer to her meal. After a few moments Bird tucked his handkerchief into his shirt front, picked up his fork and knife, and proceeded to dine with her, thoughtfully chewing small morsels and pulling the bones from his teeth as she shredded the bloody fish with her fingers, stuffing it into her mouth skin, bone, and all.

5.

An Island

At dawn on March the 11th, a cry came down from the foretop—land had been sighted. Bird looked to Mr. Whitlocke for an explanation, but Whitlocke only scowled and said it could not possibly be one of the Marquesas group.

Bird squinted into the distance but saw nothing. His eyesight had diminished and he refused to wear spectacles, considering any accommodation to his advancing age to be a kind of failure. It came to Bird as less of a surprise than it probably should have that their sailing master had no clue where they were. The South Pacific was like a handful of sand scattered across an impossibly large table, so littered with small islands and reefs as to be impossible to chart with any precision, and a hellish task to navigate. All that mattered was: they were somewhere. An island. The morning sky purpled and then became bright as Whitlocke tacked the ship into the wind under half-sail. Finally, Bird could see it. A thin gray line, no more than a smudge on the vast intersection of sea and sky.

As they approached, it was discovered that the island was high and dry, with little vegetation upon its imposing cliffs. Bird called for a course around the leeward side to search for a suitable harbor. As the ship rounded a protruding cape, there came into view a small village nestled in a deep valley, surprisingly lush with breadfruit trees.

"Perhaps we might ask *them* where we are," Bird joked to a gaggle of middies within earshot. He indicated the small brown figures already launching their canoes from the shore. The middies shuffled and stared at their feet. An observation Bird had often made: younger men, in or out of the service, rarely possessed a well-developed sense of humor. Take Lieutenant Rand, for example, who had control of the deck. There he stood at the mainmast, fervently shouting commands, looking so regrettably *earnest*. As if the approaching canoes constituted a war party and he was preparing to repel boarders. Dozens of the craft approached over the gentle swells of the harbor. Bird adjudged their intentions to be peaceful: the approaching canoes were loaded with fruit and other items, no doubt for trade, and the men sang as they rowed.

There was no greeting from below as the natives reached the ship, no request to come aboard. They paddled up to the sides and then clambered onto the deck, using the gun ports to gain purchase. Before any of the officers could react, the ship was crowded with the islanders. They were tall, some six feet or more, and they towered over the sailors. Most were tattooed over much of their bodies, which even Bird was forced to admit made them appear warlike, though they quelled this impression by immediately presenting their trade goods to anyone who would give them a moment's attention. They offered nothing substantial: woven mats and little ornaments made from palm leaves. Bird wondered why they hadn't boarded with any of the fruit he'd seen. One man had a collection of smooth stones which he seemed to indicate were of incredible use and value, though he had little English and could not explain any further. In return for these trinkets and souvenirs, they unanimously requested tobacco, which they pronounced as *bacca*. Some admired their distorted reflections on the polished tops of the capstans, or squatted on their hams to regard the sailors with curious, limpid brown eyes.

"Permit them to board," Bird sarcastically called down to Mr. Rand, who was flummoxed.

Their chief was a man near Bird's age, with a scruff of sparse white beard on his chin. He greeted Bird and the officers on the quarterdeck, accompanied by his own group of advisors, a grave-faced line of native men dressed in mismatched articles of Western clothing. The chief himself wore a worn British officer's coat; his name was announced as Kahauolupea.

The ship's translator was a New Zealand Maori known as John Black—not for the color of his skin, which was a gentle cocoa-brown, but for the dark tattooed bands that encircled his arms and legs and extended even over his face. He'd shipped with them in Sydney and had been of incalculable use. Now the sailor took up a long and halting conversation with Kahauolupea. Their languages were not a match, but similar enough. "He say he friend to British," the New Zealander finally relayed. As if corroborating this, Kahauolupea reached within a coat pocket and produced a dog-eared and worn photograph of Queen Victoria. He offered it for Bird to admire. So as not to insult him, Bird regarded it with mock admiration for a moment before returning it.

"Very good!" he confirmed. Turning to John Black, he said, "Inform him that we are a vessel of the United States of America."

Another round of conversation came back with the answer:

"He friend to all white mans."

Kahauolupea possessed a monopoly among his people, Bird was made to understand, over the dispensation of the most desirable commodity the islanders had to offer: a flotilla of cocoanuts had been moored to the side of the ship, each tied to the next by strips of their husk so they were made into a great raft. Bird was determined to have them all. It was so unbearably hot, and their water so tepid and stale, that he'd developed a habit of drinking as many as twelve per day when they were available, their milk mixed with gin and lemon juice, an astoundingly refreshing cocktail recipe he'd learned from a British beachcomber in Tahiti. "Mr. Grady," Bird called over his shoulder, "bring up the hatchets."

Along with their supply of cheap hunting hatchets, crates of other goods were brought up to impress the chief. They had a smaller reserve of polished hand mirrors, which Bird had found to be useful for those times when a hard bargain needed to be sealed. There were also barrels and barrels of iron nails, which were distributed liberally as gifts wherever they anchored, in order to build good feelings with the locals. Across the Pacific they were a treasured commodity, as the Polynesians used them to make fishhooks.

Kahauolupea inspected the hatchets without emotion and spoke rapidly with a member of his retinue. He handed the hatchet he was holding back to Mr. Fledge, and walked away somewhat abruptly, in what Bird assumed was some form of dramatic negotiation tactic. He strode to the bulwark and looked back at the island. Then he spoke angrily into the air without turning, as if he was addressing it.

"He say he want you trade gun and powder," John Black relayed. Then the translator consulted quietly with a lesser chief, a slight old man leaning on a staff. "There is war," he finally explained, after listening to the old man speak softly for a while with worried eyes. The lesser chief made gestures with his hands in an attempt to communicate to Bird how terrible their enemies were, and the extent of the degradations his people had suffered. Throughout all of this, Kahauolupea remained apart, apparently so distraught at this topic of conversation that he could do nothing but moan and grasp at his hair.

"Tell him I can offer a small amount of tobacco," he said to John Black. He hated resorting to that, but he doubted the hand mirrors would impress the man. Bird had powder to spare, but he would not help them to slaughter one another.

After it had been firmly communicated to Kahauolupea that no weapons or powder would be offered, there was a heated conversation among the retinue, too rapid for Black to glean much of its meaning. Bird observed how they all clustered around their chief, jockeying for the position nearest to him, searching his face for any sign of joy or displeasure that might inform their own bearing. Just as naval officers had their epaulets and medals, the chiefs were adorned with the evidence of their contacts with Europeans and Americans: they wore rosaries and had ornamental broaches pinned to their sashes. One possessed a watch fob with nothing attached to it, which he let dangle from the buttonhole of what appeared to be a lady's velvet jacket.

Bird could feel the cocoanuts slipping from his grasp, until, born solely of his desperation, he said to John Black, "Tell him that there is a way, I think, that we might help him with his war . . ."

John Black listened as Bird described his proposition, and then relayed it to the chief, which took some time. The eventual reply sounded stern and dismissive to Bird's ear. But then Black explained: "He say it good trade, but you give hatchet and tobacco too."

With the trading concluded, Bird declared a half-holiday and a festive atmosphere took hold. Sailors skylarked freely with the Polynesians, racing them up and down the masts; a table and chairs were brought up so that Bird and the officers could dine with Kahauolupea and his own lieutenants on the quarterdeck. Even Dr. Mallory had risen from below, a rare sight, to barter medicinal gin for the right to extract a few teeth from the natives. He'd noted in their travels that the Polynesians knew no tooth rot, and intended to fashion himself a superior set of dentures.

Chaplain Parker had assembled a queue who wished to be baptized and given Christian names. Rand watched the process with some distaste. He'd learned that the peoples of the Pacific were hungry for the Word, but he doubted their sincerity. *In their limited understanding,* he'd written in a letter to his mother, *I believe they only seek to benefit from the worship of more powerful gods. They see all the splendor of a sailing ship and think that our deity must be mightier (if only they knew the truth of that!) and will bless them with all of the same riches. They have no true desire to receive the Spirit, but only to profit from its receipt . . .* The letter had been entrusted to a passing whaler months earlier, and he wondered now if it had ever reached her, and what his mother would think if she could see the eager heathen lined up along the bulwark. Chaplain Parker sprinkled water on their foreheads and dubbed them Frances, Christopher, Daniel, William . . . when his store of names was exhausted he returned to the beginning of the list and gave them all out again.

Rand had control of the deck, but Bird had instructed him not to police the crew too rigorously as they taught dice games to the islanders in little obscuring clusters. He also ordered the remnants of a whiskey barrel watered down and distributed to the men, who normally only received a single tot per day to keep the worst drunks among them from trembling.

Rand was able to check his growing disapproval only until Bird allowed the tribe's women to board. They swam up to the sides of the ship like mermaids, with flowers in their hair—they were forbidden to set foot in the canoes, due to some heathen superstition—and climbed the sides of the ship as readily as the men. They were all entirely unclothed. Their arrival caused the crew to throw their hats into the air with glee. The women began to cavort shamelessly with the sailors. To his horror, Rand saw two pairs of legs, one brown and one white, the white with its duck trousers pulled down to the ankles, poking out from underneath one of the boats, right beneath *Old Glory* on the mainmast as it flapped in the wind.

"This is inappropriate," he stammered to Bird, who was busy demonstrating the basic function of a sextant to an obviously disinterested or uncomprehending Kahauolupea.

"Really, Mr. Rand. I can't imagine you're as ignorant of such matters as you pretend to be. You'll no doubt have a command of your own someday, and I urge you to remember this bit of wisdom: a good commander knows when to be vigilant, and when to avert his gaze."

Unwilling to bear witness any longer, Rand gave control of the deck to Mr. Piper and retreated below. He sat alone in the wardroom and listened to the commotion above as the Pelican set his absurd plan into motion: stomping feet, the rumble of the cannons being pulled back on their steel rails, the cries of the gun captains. He braced himself for the noise but still it shook him. A volley of cannon fire on the deck above. They were firing the starboard cannons harmlessly out to sea. Rand was so badly startled by the noise that he inadvertently gripped the sides of the wardroom table. All the hanging cups quivered on their pegs and the plates and saucers rattled in the cupboard. After a second volley was fired, he wadded some scraps of cloth and stuffed them in his ears.

Bird's plan was to create as great and noisy a spectacle as the ship could accomplish, with their cannons and Congreve war rockets, in an attempt to demonstrate the power of the United States. This would hopefully frighten the tribe's enemies across the island by convincing them that Kahauolupea possessed mighty allies. A harmless and empty threat, Bird had explained, but still, it violated the very purpose of their mission. They were meant only to tour the region and show the flag, to establish respect for the American whalers who relied on these islands to resupply. But now they were tampering in local politics. And all because the Pelican desired cocoanut milk to mix into his cocktails.

Each volley was followed by a brief period of silence. Slowly the wardroom began to fill with smoke. With the noise of it in his ears and the acrid stench of burnt powder in his nostrils, Rand considered that he might as well be on a ship bound for Hell, though he did not even believe in such a place. Chaplain Parker might preach of such un-Biblical nonsense, but he would have none of it. The Scriptures were clear on the matter: The dead would wait in their graves until the Lord's return, and then would be judged accordingly, either to be granted new life or cast forever into darkness.

His thoughts went to the girl, shut up in her cabin, and with no explanation of the terrible noise. He imagined her cowering in fear, with none to comfort her. As another volley rattled the cups and saucers, rattled the table, rattled his teeth, he rose and moved into the passageway that connected the wardroom with the steerage, wading through the thick smoke. When he reached her cabin he rapped twice on the door, loudly.

"Hello? Young lady? Are you within? Are you well?"

There was no response. The cannons fired again. In the brief lull between volleys, he thought he heard a terrified whimper from behind the door.

"May I enter?"

He heard a slight shuffle inside the cabin, but nothing else. The Pelican could be damned, he thought. He wouldn't sit idly by while a child was made to suffer. He looked toward the steerage to confirm that he would not be witnessed, then lifted the latch to open the door.

He recoiled at first from the smell—the girl was being kept in rank and filthy conditions, penned like an animal in a space no larger than a horse's stall. The floor was a tangle of bedding and the scent of urine prevailed. The only source of light was a lamp hanging in the corridor without, and he considered that for weeks now she'd spent most of each day caged in this foul darkness.

But where was she? His eyes searched the small space twice and then he saw her tightly curled beneath the bunk. Her knees were drawn to her chest and her face lost in shadow. As he approached, he realized with dismay that she was unclothed. He should turn away, he thought, but the thought was distant and he made no move to do so.

"I'm sorry . . ." he said without reason. "My name is Lieutenant Evan Rand." He realized he still had wads of cloth in his ears, and quickly pocketed them to make himself appear less ridiculous.

The cannons were directly above her cabin, and the next volley was deafening. The girl let out another pitiful noise and kicked her bare feet at the floor, trying to scramble farther into the tight space.

"They're firing the cannons," he said when the noise had subsided.

His words did nothing to ease her. What did one do, he thought, to comfort a girl? Rand had been brought up with only brothers. He continued to approach the bunk and lowered himself until he could place a reassuring hand on her knee. As the next volley was released, he felt her entire body tense.

"Can you say a prayer with me?" he asked her gently. "Do you know the Lord's Prayer?"

She made no answer, but her breath briefly paused and then resumed, somewhat slower—he took this to be some small indication that she understood him. If she was indeed a Christian, of any variety, he was sure the words would be known to her, their sound and cadence, a familiar comfort to remind her of the Lord's presence even in places such as this.

"Our Father who art in Heaven . . ." He spoke the words of the prayer in a steady, low chant, not bothering to compete with the cannon fire. He provided his voice to her like a line thrown out, for her to cling to. In case she was deaf, as they said she was, he directed the words toward her face, hidden beneath the bunk, so that she might feel them on his breath.

"For thine is the power and the glory and the kingdom, forever and ever," he finished. Just a moment before, a volley had fired, but now there was blessed silence rolling across the ship. Rand waited a few moments, but no further sound came. "Perhaps the Lord has heard our prayer, and given to us this blessing," he whispered to her.

He could feel the girl ease. She shifted forward to regard him in the light, and he could see her face. Small and delicate features. An intelligence in her eyes, their color a muted blue-gray.

"Can you tell me your name?" he asked her.

He heard sounds from ahead in the steerage—men were descending. Suddenly he became embarrassed by the terrible impropriety of it, sitting here in the dark with an unclothed girl. He stood to leave and straightened his coat.

"I will come to see you again," he whispered. "Just as soon as I am able."

As he turned to exit the cabin, he heard a small sound coming from her. It was her voice, so coarse from disuse that it was only a tiny, thin croak. She spoke only one word, but he heard in it both an offering of gratitude and a desperate plea.

"*Alice*," was all that she said.

6.

Mr. Rand's Complaint

Bird sat in his armchair to watch as she played on the broad Persian carpet that covered the floor of his dayroom. He'd provided her with a handful of chestnuts and she seemed to take great pleasure in placing them in small, orderly arrangements, sometimes moving them slowly along the lines of the carpet's pattern as if they were little toy horses.

"Are those your dolls?" he asked her.

She froze at the sound of his voice, her hand suspended a few inches above the floor. She waited for him to speak again, without raising her eyes, and when he did not she resumed her quiet labors.

It had occurred to him that her rescue would be met with more enthusiasm by the press if he could present to them, by voyage's end, with a proper young girl who had a harrowing story to tell, and perhaps a grateful family to return to, rather than a damaged and senseless creature of no account. And there had been many small but encouraging signs. She'd begun to relent in her determination to remain naked; he did not know if it was her displeasure at being forcefully handled or something else, but she seemed more inclined to remain in her clothing even through the long hours she was left alone in her cabin. No amount of coaxing, however, could persuade her to wear a pair of shoes—when they were placed on her feet she would fall to the floor as if she was crippled or in pain. Flesh began to fill in the valleys of her sunken cheeks as Bird plied her with johnnycakes and breadfruit sprinkled with sugar, plum duff with molasses, and any other manner of treat he could produce. She knew the use of a spoon, though it was clear she still preferred her habit of lowering herself to sip directly from the bowl. When he provided her with the duff, he'd noted with amusement that she took the time to carefully remove the raisins from it, plucking them out with her fingers each time one came to the surface and tossing them to the floorboards.

He found that laudanum served as a reward even more effectively than food. He'd secured a vial from Mallory, overriding the surgeon's objection that it was wasted on her, and provided her with a drop or two on the tongue whenever she demonstrated some simple task, such as turning the page of a book or sitting straight in a chair. Too much, he quickly discovered, sent her into an almost lifeless torpor. A small amount, though, seemed to relieve her moodiness and irritability and had the added benefit of sharpening her concentration. Under its influence, she showed more of a willingness to tolerate his company, and to participate in the little games and experiments he devised.

Bird wondered if he was growing sentimental in his old age. She eased a loneliness in him that he hadn't even realized he felt. Of the three hundred and fifteen souls aboard the ship, he spoke with perhaps a dozen, and only as his duty required. He'd always kept what he felt to be a necessary distance between himself and his line officers, so there would be no hint of favoritism. He often consulted with Mr. Whitlocke concerning the ship's course, but the sailing master was of that old Puritan type who would not mar their discourse with a single unnecessary syllable. Before the girl had come aboard, his most frequent companion had been Victor, though the boy had never tugged at the strings of his affections like this. Something about her stirred in him the long-dormant paternal feelings which he thought the years had rid him of. He'd been a husband once, and a father, but briefly. He'd married a woman named Margaret he'd met at an officers' dance. She had been unmarried in her late twenties, and he found her to be adequate—not offensive in her looks and, most importantly, willing to live the life of a sailor's wife. He'd been a bachelor of almost forty. He left her with child after their first month together. Fourteen months later, in Orange Bay, he'd been informed in a letter that both mother and child had perished in the birthing. His father-in-law had been thoughtful enough to make a photographic portrait of them together for him, deceased mother and child arranged by a photographer on a chaise longue. Margaret's eyes had been mercifully closed. The child—a daughter, he discovered—was swaddled in her lap, her eyes half open and empty as they stared at the portrait machine. He took the photograph to sea with him, but then burned it. These women, he thought, he did not even know who they were. After that, he hadn't felt inclined to start a family again.

There were times when he began to suspect that the girl harbored tender feelings for him as well; he thought he could sense this in the fact that she was more guarded when others, like Dowd or King, were in the room. When she was alone with him, she took on an easiness, moving about more freely, even sometimes making little inarticulate sounds to herself or to her chestnuts that was like whispering.

One day, he witnessed her attention fall on the silver service bell that was resting on the table, the one he used to summon Victor. She was sitting on the floor next to the table, her legs tucked beneath her. To encourage her curiosity, he picked up the bell by its handle and gave it a shake. It gave off a bright, brash tinkling.

"Let us see what arrives," he said mischievously.

Victor had been instructed to remain within earshot at all times. Still, it took several more insistent shakes before he appeared.

"Yes sir?"

"Ah, it is our friend Victor."

Victor's face wrinkled with confusion, unsure if he was being spoken to.

"Say hello to Lucy, Victor."

The girl looked over briefly at his entrance, but then returned her attention to the polished bell.

"Aye, sir," was all the boy replied.

"That will be all, Victor. You may go."

"Is that all you're needing, sir?" On his face Bird read a kind of intelligence, or lack thereof, which was entirely different from the girl's. He was able to speak, follow rules, accomplish simple tasks, but really there was nothing inside of him. It was the caliber of boys these days, Bird thought sadly. It had been going down for some time. The girl, however . . . no matter how wild she might be, he saw something in her eyes that looked unmistakably like cunning.

Bird raised his eyebrows. "*Go,*" he said to the boy. "*Out . . .*"

"Aye, sir."

"Wait just outside," he explained quietly.

The boy closed the cabin door behind him. Bird waited until his footsteps ceased and looked to the girl, her eyes once again fixed on the bell.

"Come sit with me," he said. "Come up here, and have a look at it."

She slunk up from the floor and half-sat, half-leaned upon a seat across from him, her hands gripping the edge of the table. He pushed the bell across to her. "Go ahead," he told her. "Play it as you will."

She cautiously pulled the bell toward her, sliding it over the table, then picked it up in both of her hands. Her shoulders were hunched inwards, her elbows almost touching each other as she looked to him for permission.

He repeated himself, to assure her. "Go ahead and ring it, if it please you." With his hand, he mimed a shaking motion.

She shook it once, with both of her palms still wrapped around the sides. It made a muted clank. Apprehensively, she twisted in the seat to look toward the door. *She could recall*, he thought. She understood that the bell would summon the boy. Unfortunately, the dull sound had not been enough to stir Victor.

"Victor!" he called out. "Did you not hear the bell?"

The boy re-entered.

The girl's face twisted into a smile. It was like a dog with all of its teeth bared, grotesque and almost pained, but also the first thing like joy he'd seen in her. She was delighted, he thought, simply to discover her own agency.

"Ah! He has arrived!" Bird clapped with satisfaction. The girl shook the bell again and began to moan, he assumed with pleasure.

"Do you have anything to say to Victor?" he asked her.

"Sir?"

"I am not speaking to you."

"Aye, sir."

She had nothing to say, of course, but when he sent Victor away once more, she was quick to shake the bell again, this time with more success. Her pleasure at seeing him rush back in was undiminished.

"I think that she likes you," Bird said to the boy. He instructed the boy to pour him a drink, and then sat back to watch, with great amusement, as they sent Victor scurrying in and out of the room for hours.

～

Bird always knew when something was troubling Mr. Rand, because when he was troubled the first lieutenant huffed and puffed like a woman, waiting to be asked about the source of his displeasure. Several times Bird had discovered Rand hovering expectantly before his cabin door, as if he'd just been about to knock. Bird had asked him to stop this, because it gave him dyspepsia to think that at any time Mr. Rand might be standing there just on the other side of the door, silently wringing his hands.

Rand finally mustered the courage to approach one afternoon on the quarterdeck, looking sheepish and especially well-groomed, his eyes downcast as if still rehearsing what he wished to say. Bird studied the sky. The ship proudly cut the water under full sail, with nothing in sight but vast stretches of cumulus clouds. The men were tarring down the masts, scurrying on the yards like insects with their pails and brushes. The smell of it always put Bird in mind of a campfire.

"I wonder, sir, if I might speak frankly . . ."

"I expect it has something to do with the upcoming Easter holiday, does it not? Honestly, Mr. Rand, I expected you days ago."

"Sir, I . . ."

"Know that I am prepared to allow another half-holiday. I believe, as I know you do, that the moral life of this ship could use some uplifting. You will organize the Biblical readings, of course, as I do not claim to have any talent at that. I will say a few words to the people, as a sermon. Don't you think that's a fine idea? I feel they have not seen enough of me lately, and I might use the moment to inspire them."

"Yes, sir."

"In addition, I would ask you to arrange for some kind of musical performance. Perhaps a singing group from among the officers. And if any wishes to organize it, I will permit a theatrical. If we're going to have a holiday, I think we should go the whole hog, don't you?"

"Of course, sir. I will make the arrangements."

"Very well. That will be all for now, Mr. Rand, but let us not drop this baton of comradery, in the months to come, now that we have taken it up."

He drew on his pipe and returned his attention to the sky, searching for any detail he might have missed. When Rand made no motion to leave, he said, without turning, "You are once again at your hovering, Mr. Rand."

"I would like to make a complaint, sir."

"Well, speak up. Don't buzz in my ear. I find it intolerable."

"It is the girl, sir. I do not believe her treatment to be Christian."

Now Bird turned to face him. "And what do you know of her *treatment*, as you call it?"

"She is kept in poor conditions. Her cabin is filthy, and you keep her locked in there like an animal."

"Lucy's conditions are those of her own creation. I send my boy in to clean it and she fouls it again as soon as he leaves. And she is brought up to my quarters every day for the light and the air. I can assure you she is comfortable."

"I still do not see the necessity of her confinement."

They were both momentarily distracted by a shout from Mr. King—Bird gathered that a sailor being lowered on a rope to tar the stays had been dropped several feet. His tar-bucket had slipped from his grasp and fallen to the deck.

Bird pursed his lips. "So, you cannot see the . . . *necessity* . . ." he pronounced the word as if it were a dead rat, tail held in his fingers, "of one of my decisions. I do not see why this should be something of my concern. Not only that, but allow me to remind you that we have already discussed this matter at length. I feel as if we are repeating ourselves, Mr. Rand."

"With all respect, sir, I think that if you would only have more compassion . . ."

"Mr. Rand, this girl has been stranded alone on an island for God knows how long, and you suggest that I lack compassion because she has been provided a dry, secure cabin, with plenty to eat and passage, if not to her home, at least to a more civilized place, even after I have quite probably saved her life? The girl's situation at present has been vastly improved from what it was previously, you would have to agree."

"Yes, I admit, her situation has been improved. But only for her *body*. I ask that you consider her *spirit*. If you would allow it, I would pray with her. Perhaps prayer would provide her a comfort that food and a bed cannot."

Bird considered the request, turning his attention back to the sea. Then he said, "I do not think it wise for the girl to have visitors at this time."

"Why not? What harm could it possibly cause?"

Bird paused, taking the time to form a judicious reply. "I do not think we are that far from one another in our thinking, Mr. Rand. Some, like the good doctor Mallory, have given her up for a lost cause, but not us! We believe she can be saved! I too wish to give her more liberty, but you forget that she was brought onto this ship as a naked and wild thing, barely sensible, I would add. And before she is granted more liberty, she first must be brought under control. This is still a Navy ship, after all, and I am still the commander. Before anything else is accomplished, she must be taught to respect my command. How would we accomplish this if we show her two faces? If I serve as the cruel ogre who confines her, and you become her gallant savior, coming with soothing words and the comfort of prayer? No, I fear it would only confuse her, and further delay the granting of her liberty that we both desire. I will not permit it at this moment. But I am prepared to make a concession. I will say that Lucy has made remarkable progress from the state we found her in, and I fully expect her to continue. If this is the case, which I hope but do not guarantee, I see no reason why we cannot look forward to permitting her to attend the spiritual portion of our Easter program. So you see, once a friendly tone has been established, there is often a give and take of this nature. You have expressed a desire, and not an unreasonable one, given your vantage on the situation, and I have offered you a partial answer. I hope that will satisfy you."

"That does not satisfy me."

"Then I encourage you to revisit the matter with me following the Easter holiday. At such time, perhaps my feeling will have changed. You are dismissed, Mr. Rand."

Rand stood for a moment, as if considering another comment, and then decided against it and turned to take his leave. Then he turned sharply back to the Lieutenant.

"She can speak, you know."

"Excuse me?"

"She has spoken to me. She told me her name and it is Alice."

Bird attempted to hide his displeasure. "Wonderful news. As I have said, she makes great progress. At what point, may I ask, Mr. Rand, have you had the opportunity to converse with her?"

"While the heathen were aboard. I entered the girl's cabin to determine her safety. I feared that one of the savages you allowed onto the ship might have found his way belowdecks."

"This was in direct violation of my order."

"I believe the circumstance was exceptional."

"In what way, Mr. Rand, was the circumstance exceptional?"

"If the ship was on fire, and you were not there to amend your order, would you have us run past her door and leave her to burn?"

"I do not apprehend your point, Mr. Rand, as the ship was not on fire."

"It is of the same order. The ship was full of savages and I thought the girl to be in immediate danger. I had heard a sound."

"What type of sound was that?"

"A shuffling, sir."

"A shuffling!"

"Yes, coming from the girl's cabin. So I entered."

"And did you find her to be in any danger, Mr. Rand?"

"No, sir."

"And, having secured her against the villainous heathen who were not in fact present, did you then tarry?"

"I did not," Rand said.

"So you are telling me that, just as you entered her cabin, this girl, Lucy or Alice or whoever she is, who has not spoken a word to anyone, leapt up and spoke her name to you?"

"That is what happened."

Bird let a long trail of pipesmoke leave the corner of his mouth and did not speak until it was exhausted. "I find that implausible," he said.

"Perhaps if you would just show more compassion, as I have urged, she would speak to you as well."

"I thank you for that advice concerning my personal failings, Mr. Rand. We should all strive for self-improvement, I have always said."

Bird's eyes remained hard on Rand's back as he huffed off to his duties. Again, like a woman. Beyond him, a new bucket of tar swayed on a rope as it was being lofted toward the sky.

7.

ALICE

Bird chewed on these revelations for several hours, drinking whiskey alone in his cabin. He had the unmistakable feeling he was being made a fool of—though he was not quite sure how or whom to blame—and was determined to do something about it. At some time during the night he roused himself and made his way to the deck below. A sentry, one of Lieutenant Thomas's marines, stopped to salute him and asked if he was in need of assistance.

"Do I look like I need assistance?" Bird slurred, finding the wall for support.

"I just thought . . . it's not your habit to go walking at night, sir."

"Can a man no longer walk on his own ship?" Bird asked him. "You can assist me by getting out of my damned way."

He fumbled with the latch on the girl's cabin door. She looked up sharply as the door opened, as if she'd been startled out of some activity, though what she'd been doing was unclear.

"I would like a word with you," Bird said. He realized how ridiculous he sounded. How ridiculous he looked, standing in a doorway to address a girl. *This is what women do to men*, he thought with some disgust, directed both at himself and toward femininity in general. Even a nothing of a girl such as this has the ability to stir up these petty jealousies.

"I am sorry to say, your friend Mr. Rand has betrayed you. He has informed me that you are in fact able to speak. Is this true?"

There was no change on her face, no sign. She appeared as terrified and innocent as a hare at night, revealed in a woodsman's lamp.

"I will not play games with you. Speak or do not speak, it is your choice. But it is my duty to tell you what will happen to you, in either case. We will soon arrive in a place where there are French authorities. Because of your refusal to speak, I am not currently aware if you are French, or British. Or if you are a citizen of the United States. If you wish to be left off with the French, to fend for yourself, it is within your grasp. You must simply remain in your ungrateful silence, and soon you will be rid of this ship forever. But if you wish to remain here, you must say so. I must at least know your name and your country."

His words caused no change in her. Let her chew on them, he thought. He would not stand there waiting upon a child.

"That is all I have to say. Good night, Alice."

At the sound of her name she flinched once, like a fly had troubled her eyelid. Then he closed the door and left her again in darkness.

He did not visit her for several days, nor was she permitted to his dayroom for activity. Twice daily, Victor went down to bring her a meal and empty her waste pail. During this time, Bird busied himself with various duties he'd been neglecting. He made a tour of the entire ship and sent several corrective notes to the attention of Mr. Rand. Things he would like repaired, polished, replaced, removed, or left just as they were. He attempted to sit down and begin work on his Easter sermon but he could not find the words, and several times wound up in a drunken state, unable to accomplish anything further that day save for a nap, without a mark made upon the page. He found spiders in the officers' pantry and, purely for the satisfaction of it, he removed a boot and spent some time knocking them from their webs.

When he could find nothing else to occupy himself, he perched on the quarterdeck like an old crow and watched the men climbing in the rigging and crawling over the deck. It was an appealing scene, something like an ant hill, when seen at a distance: an apparent chaos, but actually a great and magnificent order, each man with his prescribed duties, moving along familiar lines.

"The people appear to be quite well rested!" he commented to Mr. Grady.

"Which ones, sir?"

"The crew!" Bird repeated, raising his voice in case it had been obscured by the wind.

Mr. Grady brought himself closer. "What about them, sir?"

"I was only commenting that the crew seem to be in high spirits."

Grady squinted toward the fore. "I suppose so, sir."

"To what do you attribute that?"

"I assume it is their faith in God and country, sir."

Bird studied him but could not tell if the man meant it as a joke.

Before they arrived at Nukahiva, Bird had the girl brought up to him by Mr. King. She stood before him, blinking, and Bird could find no indication of whether or not she'd understood she was being punished. He dismissed Mr. King and stood examining her for some time. She had on her arm a bit of dried blood.

"Come here," he said.

She took a few halting steps toward him in his armchair.

"What country were you born in?" he asked her.

She made no response. He waited.

"Should I leave you with the French?"

"No," she said. The word was hardly more than a puff of air. But it was an intelligible sound, in English.

"Ah. I see you have learned some better manners."

She just shifted uncomfortably on her feet.

"You may tell me just by nodding your head. Are you American?"

She nodded only once, an incline of her head so slight Bird might not have even noticed it.

"Why do you refuse to speak, if you are able?"

". . ."

"Are you afraid?"

". . ."

"Are you in distress?" he asked her.

"No," she said.

"Well, this is an improvement."

He tamped tobacco into his pipe with his thumb, watching her from the corner of his eye. "Would you like anything to eat?"

"Yes," she said.

"What would you like?"

". . ."

Her actions spoke loudly enough. Her gaze was fixed on the laudanum bottle, resting on the side table.

"You require medicine?" he asked her.

She gave another barely perceptible nod. As he took it up and filled the dropper, she leaned forward and opened her mouth to receive it. He gave her two drops and then he lit his pipe and blew a fat cloud of smoke. They both spent a quiet moment watching as it uncurled in the air between them.

"Is there anything else you would like to tell me?" he asked.

"No," she said quietly.

8.

Another Island

Twin promontories guided the *Fredonia* into Anaho Bay. They were known as Cape Jack and Jane. Or some called them Cape Adam and Eve. The sea rolled gently into the bay; the clear waters took on the faintest blue reflection. Three sharks that had been following them for many days, Bird noticed, turned their fins away and vanished beneath the waves as the ship drifted into shallow water.

A French corvette rested in the harbor, alongside a battered whaler flying the colors of the United States. A vast sprawl of Marquesan dwellings rose gently away from the shore, intermixed with the whitewashed domiciles of the French. Farther on he could see the walls of the fort and the foothills of Mount Ua-huna. Orange trees, breadfruit trees, large stands of island chestnut. Ua-huna's summit scraped the clouds. Bird sometimes wished he had the means to have a painter follow him around the world, to capture majestic scenes like this so he might later relive them.

A fisherman stopped paddling his dugout to observe their approach. The boatswain blew his whistle and they dropped anchor. Ten minutes later, a boat approached, carrying a French officer. Mr. Rand ordered the band to strike up *La Parisienne*.

The French lieutenant was given a brief tour of the deck by Mr. Rand. His name was Lévesque and he spoke English well; he was trim in most regards, save for the fact that he badly required a shave. He offered an invitation for Bird and his officers to dine at the fort that afternoon, where more formal introductions would be made. "And if you have any whiskey or rum . . ." Lévesque suggested. Bird assured Lévesque they would attend and promised to check the status of their liquor stores.

After the Frenchman's departure, Bird ordered Mr. Piper to accompany him over to the whaler, so that he could greet the captain, as was customary. Piper, a small-statured and oft-overlooked man, was pleased to have been selected, and made a great show of calling the crew's strokes as they bobbed across the harbor.

They were permitted to board by a mate, and climbed to a deck that was near-empty and filthy in places with dried blood. "Are you in need of mops?" Bird suggested. The mate stared as if he didn't understand the question.

He left Mr. Piper to socialize with this miscreant and went below to find Captain Snow in his cabin, in a drunken and disagreeable state. He was a squat man in his late middle years, with flushed skin that made him look as if he'd been singed. His stateroom was drab and permeated throughout with the smell of boiled onions. Like his mate, he didn't seem to register any of Bird's questions about the state of his business. He complained of back pains and of the French, and made Bird several offers of rum, which Bird refused only because there was a thin coating of whale oil spread over all of the room's accoutrements; the man's glasses were all marked with smudged fingerprints. Snow barely seemed to notice when Bird stood to leave; staring off at nothing in particular, the last thing Bird heard him mutter was, "Have that bastard bring me my eggs."

∽

With a few hours of liberty at his disposal, Rand went ashore. He shared the boat with several of the middies: Mr. Elliot, Mr. Letcher, Mr. Dowd, Mr. King, and both Hoopers. The twin brothers were rowdy with drink and chattered indiscreetly about the native women—they hadn't dared partake in the revel aboard the ship, but on shore it was another matter. Rand made a displeased noise and gave them a look, and after this they rowed to the island in a newly uncomfortable silence.

Nukahiva was what passed in this part of the world for a bustling metropolis. Everywhere there were Americans of the lowest sort, no doubt the crew of the whaler. He could smell alcohol as if it was in the atmosphere of the place. The entire village seemed drunk. A motley assemblage crashed from a thicket: a bare-chested Polynesian woman laughing shrilly, sandwiched between two sailors, all leaning on each other and swaying like buoys, somehow miraculously not falling over as they wove an erratic course among the huts. Only the church house was empty, save for a pale Jesuit under a wide-brimmed hat who was carrying a bucket of water to some pigs. A child with the mark of smallpox on his face was curled in the shadow of a doorway, and followed Rand impassively with his gaze.

He moved at a brisk pace, keeping his eyes downcast. The thoroughfare was lined with men and women who'd spread wares on woven mats, carvings of driftwood and coral and bone. They offered him fruit, strips of roast pork, elaborate jewelry made from shells. He stopped at one such trader, an old man who offered small, carved animals. Rand saw among them several fish and several pigs, something that resembled a sheep or a goat or a dog. The carvings were similar, rounded shapes with lightly-carved features to distinguish them. He squatted by the man's blanket. The vendor smiled at him as he picked one up and found it to be surprisingly light. It was a bird; he could tell by the impression of a wing. It was hollow and had several open holes along its back, another at the tip of its beak. It was a kind of flute, he guessed. He raised it to his lips and blew. It produced a thin note.

Rand offered a Dutch coin but the vendor refused. He wanted tobacco.

"I have none and do not recommend it. But what you do with the coin is your own business."

After a few more attempts at refusal, the man took the coin.

Rand still had hours before he was due back at the ship. Seeking out an easy path among the stones and boulders, he climbed up into the foothills, loosely holding onto the carved bird in his pocket.

On a small promontory overlooking the sea, he sat down on a stone and gathered himself. The sun cast a perfect warmth over his skin. The noise of the surf was a distant susurrus; he could more prominently hear the wind rustling the branches of the acacias. It was at moments like this, faced only with the beauty the Lord had provided to man and none of the wickedness he'd created for himself, that Rand felt he could see everything clearly. For a long time, he now realized, he'd been angry at his father: for sending him away to this God-forsaken place, for not preparing him at all for what he would encounter on a Navy ship. His father had spent a dignified and uneventful career on the Mediterranean Station, mostly residing at port in Spain or Italy. Rand could not remember him ever mentioning anything like what he'd seen on the *Fredonia*. Their commander and most of the other officers were unrepentant drunks, soused and stumbling through their duties. It was a wonder the ship hadn't foundered. The crew engaged in constant swearing, fighting, self-abuse, he even suspected sodomy. On one occasion, he'd come upon two sailors on the orlop deck, hidden behind some bolts of sailcloth. Both had their pants down around their ankles and one was bent over a barrelhead. The rest of the officers on the *Fredonia* turned a blind eye to all of this. Whenever he brought the subject to anyone else's attention, they would simply speak around the issue, or ignore it completely and change the topic. It was as if they believed that if only they refused to put it into words, it did not exist.

For three years, Rand had tried his best. He'd set up various services to help uplift the crew, such as organizing a small lending library of books and a weekly group devoted to scriptural study. The books were gradually all stolen or lost and the study group poorly attended, only by a few drunks who wished to pray away their desire for drink. Rand often felt as if all his efforts to counter the tide of immorality were for nothing; he might as well have been fighting against the sea itself.

He recalled something his mother was fond of saying: that it was always best to *tend one's own garden patch*. Her meaning was that all one could really do in the world was to manage one's own affairs well, and try to find some small corner where one could do good. Rand could not alleviate all the sinfulness of the world, he understood this now. But in the girl, Alice, he saw a small place where he might be of use, a small amount of good he could achieve. She would be his garden patch.

A tiny kingfisher with his long, pointed beak hopped from one branch to another, settled, and regarded Lieutenant Rand quizzically. It looked very much like the carved flute he'd purchased, something he took to be an auspicious sign, one of those small moments of grace wherein the Lord reveals Himself. The bird only remained for a few moments and then started off into the forest without making a sound.

∽

For their visit to the French fort, Bird chose Messrs. Grady, Piper, Fledge, Harvey, and Dr. Mallory to accompany him, along with Minnie and Darling, the only two passed midshipmen whom he could rely upon not to embarrass him.

On the boat that pulled them ashore, Bird noticed that Grady was missing two buttons on his coat. "Really, Mr. Grady," he scolded the man, "we don't want to give the impression that American officers are slovenly." Grady mumbled the excuse that he thought the buttons had been stolen by the natives who'd come aboard, as if that explained why he'd let a week go by without replacing them. When Bird pressed him on this point, Grady claimed he was also out of thread.

Lévesque met them on the beach to provide an unenthusiastic tour of local landmarks. He pointed out a trading post with nearly empty shelves, a small church of whitewashed stone, a wooden house surrounded by a neat picket fence that they were told belonged to an Australian trader named Walker, someone Bird took to be a notable figure. The village was crowded with white figures, who must have existed now in direct proportion with the native inhabitants. The French fort sat on higher ground, overlooking the thickly-settled valley. Within the fort's low walls there were orderly rows of bunkhouses and small bungalows for the officers.

In the center of it all, there was a wide house with every window open to the breeze. Captain Hugo Chardin came out to the veranda to greet them. He looked to Bird like a typical Frenchman: he carried a paunch and his hair was plastered to his skull with some kind of glistening substance. Bird had brought along a single bottle of Madeira to present him as a gift, which Chardin graciously accepted as he called for a corkscrew and two glasses. He filled them both, handed one to Bird, and made a toast.

"To the Americans." He raised the glass and Bird noticed Lévesque eyeing it like a wolf. "I apologize that I can only offer your men tea," Chardin said in crisp English. "We have not had a ship from Papeete for some time. Do you have any spirits to trade?"

"Unfortunately, we do not," Bird informed him. "And tea will be acceptable."

He silently clenched his teeth in preparation for the evening. There was nothing in the world more irritating, he believed, than a sober Frenchman. Save, perhaps, for a dozen of them.

They had a billiards table and an upright piano; Chardin informed them that it had unfortunately become out of tune due to the heat, and no one had been able to locate their tuning fork. They sat at a long table and Polynesian women served them tinned mutton and an array of breadfruit dishes, all of which, to Bird's taste, were mealy and bland.

The French side of the table was occupied by a dozen officers who'd arrived in twos and threes. In a mix of French and English, they discussed news of the islands and some limited home politics, though both French and American knew to fastidiously avoid the subject of Napolean III, which would no doubt divide even the French. Bird's attention wandered. He nodded occasionally. As they ate, he noticed a curious phenomenon: every so often, a native would enter and wait silently beside a door in the next room, visible through a wide arch. Each time this happened, one of the French officers would rise from the table, walk over, and unlock the door with a key that hung on a string from his belt. The native would then enter and the door would be locked behind him, and the officer would return to the table without comment. While all of the officers prattled on, stuffing their faces with olives and bread, Bird counted six Marquesans enter, all men, and none ever came out.

"What in the devil are they doing?" he leaned over to ask Chardin.

"They are prisoners," Chardin explained. He told Bird of the difficulty he had in policing the natives—there were so many who had run afoul of the laws, he did not have the space to keep them all permanently confined. "And where could they flee to?" he added. Instead of jailing them, Chardin had arranged for most to pay fines or do service. Even those who represented the worst criminal class were only required to report to the fort by nightfall, so that they might sleep there under lock and key. They spent their days hunting goats in the hills nearby, or working the kitchen garden for a salary of six *sous* per month. Bird had to admit that the arrangement seemed very civilized.

The meal finished, and the room filled with pipe and cigar smoke. A game of billiards was agreed to between Mr. Piper and one of his French counterparts. Some small wagers were made.

Chardin took Bird aside on a couch, to discuss "official matters." The Frenchman seemed weary and beleaguered. Bird was sympathetic to the man's plight. Nukahiva lay at the farthest extent of France's ambition; nearly a thousand miles of roughly charted waters lying between it and the rest of the squadron at Tahiti. He served the whims of a mad emperor: Within a decade of escaping from prison disguised as a pauper, Bonaparte's nephew had managed first to be elected president and then had declared himself emperor and trampled the remains of the Republic into dust. Who knew why he even wanted these insignificant archipelagoes? Perhaps for use as penal colonies once he'd completely filled Algeria? Chardin's position was not unlike Bird's own: the celebrated Admiral Dupetit Thouars had long since staked the wide borders of France's claim and returned to Paris to be feted and honored, while minor officers like Chardin were the ones left to watch the outskirts, abandoned for years at a time to rot away in the tropics playing cards, endlessly drilling their troops under the overbearing sun to maintain the tattered remnants of their discipline. He and this French captain were similar, Bird thought, in that they represented the noble, unrecognized men who did the real day-to-day work of maintaining empires.

Chardin warned Bird that there was smallpox running on the island. Half of the native population had died. He suggested that Bird keep his crew confined to the ship if they wished to avoid its spread.

Chardin became confidential and said, "If there is something you can do for us . . ."

"Certainly. What is your difficulty?"

"It is these whalemen," he complained. "They are *swine*. They spread their disease . . . *tout les maladies*. They claim they have no liquor to trade but look . . ." He waved an arm in the direction of the village, visible through the open windows. "They give it away to the people. You must understand . . . give these people liquor and they become uncontrollable. They begin to steal and run wild."

"What would you like me to do? Perhaps you could put a law in place that prevents them from coming ashore?"

Chardin shook his head. "*Merde*, make them go away. They have been here for a month. It is too long."

Bird promised he would do what he could. His word seemed to reassure the Frenchman, who rested a hand on Bird's thigh as if they were old friends.

It was Mr. Grady who first mentioned the girl, and afterwards the French wished to speak of nothing else. In Grady's telling of her rescue, she seemed even more wild than she actually had been. Mr. Minnie spoke up to claim that she'd run on all fours, trying to escape him on the beach, something Bird doubted had actually occurred—he'd never known the girl to walk any other way than upright, with a slight stoop when she was frightened. Dr. Mallory allowed the French to inspect his hand where he'd been bitten, though there was hardly even a mark left.

"Her name is Alice," Bird intoned from his chair, taking his time to light his pipe afterwards, to allow their attention to settle on him. He imagined that this was news even to his own officers. "Though I do not claim any great education, like some of my staff," he said, nodding at Mr. Harvey, "I must admit to an interest in natural history, and I have studied the girl thoroughly . . ."

He had just begun to explain his theories about her wildness when Dr. Mallory interrupted him. The doctor had taken a pinch or two of cocaine and ranted wildly, "The man cannot abide the simple fact that the girl is an idiot. *Id-i-ote*," he said with an exaggerated accent. "Do you see? Even the French understand the word. But not our commander. No, to him, she must be a *wolf-girl* or some such nonsense. Really, it is beyond my understanding . . ."

Bird tried to quietly maintain his dignity under this insubordinate assault. Chardin displayed solidarity with his fellow senior officer by ignoring Mallory completely.

"Is it possible that she is French?" he asked Bird.

"We know very little, as she is hesitant to speak. But she has indicated that she is an American."

"But you must let us view her! I would be most curious to meet this *enfant sauvage*. It is so rare that something happens."

"I do not think this would be possible. You see, the girl is of a delicate temperament."

Chardin affected a chiding mock formality. "Ah, but *Henri*, you know that as the governor of these islands, it is my right to inspect your ship. If I am to pay a visit, I would rather it be under pleasant circumstances, no?"

Bird wondered if he was bluffing. He cringed at the thought of entertaining the French aboard the *Fredonia*, though it looked like he would not be able to avoid it without giving offense. Once they were aboard, it would also be unconscionably rude for him not to offer them liquor from his private store, which he'd carefully rationed to last him through the voyage. In an attempt to get ahead of the problem, he suggested they repair to the *Fredonia* that very evening for a nightcap. At least then he would have the lateness of the hour as an excuse to send them back to their fort before they'd decimated his liquor cabinet.

There was little for Rand to occupy himself with while the Pelican was ashore. Anaho Bay was quiet. A few terns were circling and plunging into the calm waters of the bay, searching for a meal. Oh, he thought, to live a life so simple as those birds! With no choice but up or down, rest or flight. No duty save to fill their bellies. On the anchored whaler he could see a few figures moving slowly along the deck, a man smoking a corncob pipe and staring back at him in a way that made Rand deeply uncomfortable.

He waited until Bird's party had disappeared into the distant fort and gave command of the deck to Mr. Stewart, adjudging him to be the most capable of the middies who remained. Then he made his way below, still fingering the trinket in his coat pocket, feeling its smooth grain and the tiny holes that marked its surface. He waited until the wardroom was clear so none would see him entering the girl's cabin. He did not think that Bird truly had the authority to forbid him to visit her—she was a civilian, and his position thankfully insulated him, to some extent, from the whims of his commander—but still, Bird had made his desires clear and Rand saw no reason to trample them outright. He would be forced to suffer the Pelican for at least another six months, perhaps a year, and Bird could still, if he so wished, make the voyage even more unpleasant for him than it already was.

This time, he did not bother to knock. As he undid the latch and entered, she looked up sharply from a scattering of chestnuts on the floor. He searched her face for any sign of accusation or anger at his having betrayed her secret, but only found a simple joy at his arrival, an open-mouthed smile that revealed her small and perfectly white teeth.

"I've brought you something," he said to her. He took the trinket from his pocket. She reached for it, but he said "Wait, look . . ." and brought it to his lips. The sound that emerged was a high and thin whistling, like the wind over the top of a reed. "You can make the little bird sing its song," he explained.

He offered it to her. She took the bird from him and held it against her chest with both hands, like she was trying to push it inside of herself.

"You must blow on it," he said to her. He pursed his lips, took a breath, and expelled it slowly.

Alice wrinkled her face in concentration and brought the bird to her mouth, but she did not blow. "Like this," Rand said. He came close to her and blew on her forehead, stirring her short hair with his breath. When he gave it back to her, she brought it to her lips and made a sound with her voice, a brief *uhhh*. It looked as if she was trying to speak to it. Then she dropped the bird to the floor in frustration.

"Here, I will play it for you," he said, taking it up. He sat on the bunk and blew the few different notes it could produce, arranging them at last into a simple melody that walked up and down its short scale. He tried to hand it back to her but she caught his hands and pushed them away.

She whispered, "Make it sing."

He took it up again and blew, and she reached out to gently brush the bird's beak with her fingers as he did, as if she wished to catch the notes as they escaped.

~

There were fires in the village after dusk, a multitude of winking lights. Rand was again on the deck, regarding them and the flickering shadows they created. He heard an occasional whooping in the distance; be it from Marquesans or American seamen, he could not tell.

Two boats pulled from the shore. Rand watched them until they resolved from the darkness. One contained the *Fredonia*'s returning officers, the other, a dozen or more French, an impressive feather-plume in their captain's hat.

"Mr. Stewart," he called out. "Ready the band."

Following several rounds of saluting and the firing of rifles, Chardin toured the deck and complimented Bird on its orderliness.

"I am fortunate that my first lieutenant, young Mr. Rand here, is as competent as he is fastidious," Bird said, as an introduction. He instructed Mr. King to fetch Alice to his cabin, and turned back to Rand. "You may join us, if you wish. Captain Chardin wishes to view the girl."

Bird's dayroom was scarcely large enough to accommodate the audience. There was not even room enough to sit. Bottles of brandy were uncorked. Mr. Thomas, who'd become completely drunk that afternoon by himself in the wardroom, in bitterness that he'd not been invited ashore, wandered in proffering a bottle of applejack that he'd carried all the way from his home state of Maryland, loudly touting its medicinal benefits. Lévesque, quickly red-faced, offered to pour brandy for Rand, but Rand declined. Once, when he was at university, Rand had penned an essay on temperance for his school's journal. His thesis: that liquor made men lose their manners, their reason, and their souls, in that order.

By the time Alice was brought in, the French officers seemed more like a rough tavern audience than a gathering of gentlemen. When she saw the assembled officers, all chattering and gaping at her and jostling each other for a better view, she tore free from Mr. King, who let go in surprise. She was caught by Mr. Letcher, who'd been entering behind, and was pulled into the room by both men.

"And here is Alice," Bird announced. To her, he said, "Young Alice, please join us for a moment. There are some French gentlemen here who wish to make your acquaintance."

She sunk into a crouch and stared at her feet as they all ogled her strangeness. Dr. Mallory made the display of shouting into her ear to prove her deafness and seemed pleased by the result.

"It is remarkable," Chardin said. "She was entirely alone?"

"There was evidence that others were wrecked along with her, but we found only their graves. How long she was on her own, we don't know. I suspect for some time."

"It is a miracle of God she has survived."

"She is very fortunate we came upon her," Bird remarked. "As I have said, the island was off the trades, and she made no attempt to signal any passing ship. She did not even seem to desire her own rescue."

Captain Chardin took her chin in his hand and lifted it so he could see her features. Her eyes moved wildly in their orbits. Then she pulled her head from his grasp and swatted an arm at the Frenchman, knocking his brandy glass from his other hand and spilling its contents onto the carpet. His own officers roared with amusement.

"Please forgive her," Bird apologized. "I have mentioned her temperament."

Rand could not watch it any longer. He said, "I believe we should allow young Alice to retire for the evening. Sir."

At the sound of his voice, Alice looked up and found his eyes in the crowd. She ran to his side, pressed herself against him with her face hidden against his coat.

"Ah," Bird said. "There is nothing in the world that can diminish the attraction a girl has to a dashing young officer in his uniform, isn't that right, Hugo?" Bird dropped his tone into something more serious to add, "But I agree with Mr. Rand entirely, perhaps this would be a good opportunity for all of us to retire, before the hour grows any later . . ."

9.

A Charitable Offer

The Australian trader, Walker, was in possession of a daguerreotype machine, and Chardin enthusiastically arranged for him to capture the girl's image. The French wished for a document of the wonder they'd seen: the girl who'd survived alone on a Pacific island, living like an animal, who had run on all fours, who'd lashed out like a cornered stoat to scratch their commander.

The camera and its operator were brought aboard the *Fredonia*, accompanied by the French captain. The camera was less than impressive—Bird had expected more than a largish, black wooden box with a lens affixed to one side. The Australian's crown was bare, but tufts of bushy white hair like raw cotton clung to the sides. The man jabbered as he set up the equipment and staged his scene. Bird found him to be one of those interesting and eclectic sorts of men who found their way to all of the world's remote corners. Walker claimed to have traveled extensively and had lived for some time in China. In addition to maintaining several economic ventures on Nukahiva, including a fledgling mail service, he had learned the native language and endeavored to make a full translation of the Bible for the island's inhabitants, a fact which for some unfathomable reason had made him into an enemy of the Jesuits. Walker declared that Bird's dayroom, with its wide bank of windows, possessed sufficient light, and the girl was given a healthy dose of laudanum to keep her still. She would need to sit for some minutes, Bird was told, for the camera to capture her form. She tottered on a stiff-backed wooden chair.

"Where would you like me to stand?" Bird asked him. "I thought perhaps behind her, and to the left."

"Stand?" Walker asked.

"Yes, for the portrait." Before their arrival, Bird had polished up his coat, straightened out his single epaulet, and gotten his hair into manageable form with an oiled comb. He'd not before had the opportunity to have his photograph taken, and was excited by the prospect.

Walker looked to Captain Chardin. "Did you want the Lieutenant in the impression?"

Chardin's tone was delicate. "Ah. You understand, we only thought to photograph the girl."

Bird bristled. "Surely you would wish for your portrait to include the one who has discovered her? For the historical value?"

Chardin turned to the Australian. "Can we create two of the impressions?" he asked. "One with the Lieutenant, and one without?"

"But I have only prepared one plate."

Chardin was defeated, and motioned to the Lieutenant that he could take up a place behind her.

Despite the laudanum, over the course of the quarter hour they were required to remain in the same position so the image could take hold, Alice continued to sway gently in her seat. The finished plate, which Lieutenant Bird went ashore to view the following day, was a failure: her form was so blurred that Bird couldn't even tell she was a female. She looked like a smudge of dark and light somehow sitting in a chair. Behind this inky blob, in sharp contrast, stood Bird, standing so still that you could make out every strand on his epaulet and every stray hair on his head, both now the same luminous gray. He was staring at the camera with an intensity that he'd thought at the time would appear dignified, but which now resembled something like a demented bewilderment.

"The image," Bird said to Walker. "It is spoiled."

"Yes, it was unfortunate. You can keep it," he said, leaving Bird in possession of this unbecoming portrait of himself, standing watch over some shapeless thing.

∼

It would be one of two photographs known to be taken of her, both of which would survive into the twentieth century in a privately-held collection of memorabilia related to her brief career. The other portrait would be professionally done in a studio in San Francisco, by Mr. George Robinson Fardon, and would become the sole evidence we have of what she actually looked like.

In what came to be known as the Nukahiva Photo, her form was in fact so blurred that one historian would dispute that it was even her, though this theory was later disproved by the discovery of Captain Chardin's correspondence from this era, tucked away in an attic, which confirmed Alice's presence. It remains the only photographic portrait of Lieutenant Henry Aaron Bird that was ever taken.

∼

The *Fredonia* remained at anchor in Anaho Bay for two weeks as the crew worked on refitting the ship. Uneager to revisit the fetid onion cloud that hung in Captain Snow's quarters, Bird delayed meeting with the man, as he'd promised Chardin he would, for as long as possible. Then two of Snow's men were arrested for the murder of a native. They had gotten into some sort of disagreement concerning the Marquesan man's wife and had beaten him to death with a chain.

On the whaler *Sea Witch*, a magnificent transformation had occurred that Bird could not account for. Everything was spotless from stem to stern, the crew readying everything to sail. Even Snow's cabin had been tidied and aired out. Snow looked puffier, with his hair sharply parted in the middle. He apologized for his previous drunkenness. He'd been four years crisscrossing the Japan Grounds and claimed that he only drank—for one month straight—after the conclusion of a successful voyage. "We took in a few big ones," he smiled. "Normally I am a Bible man," he said, patting the leatherbound book upon his table gently, like a sleeping pet.

Of his arrested men, he said, "Let the French hang them for all I care. Though I can't see to killing two white men for one Kanaka. That doesn't sit square with me."

Thankfully, Bird's promise to rid Chardin of the whalers was easily kept, as Captain Snow planned to sail on the morrow. He volunteered to take the *Fredonia*'s mail, as the *Sea Witch* would make the States long in advance of them.

"And what of this wild girl?" Snow asked.

There was not a soul on the island, it seemed, who had not heard of her. Bird thought it remarkable how quickly word spread. The islanders had even given her a name: *kakahutamahina*, which was translated to him, quite unflatteringly, as *biting girl*.

"What of her?" Bird asked.

"Where are her people?"

"She has not spoken of them."

"Well, wherever they are, I expect she'd be pleased to have her feet on land again."

"I expect that is true."

Snow considered Bird and then said, with a tone of admission, "I have heard of this girl and I have prayed for her, and the good Lord has given me my instruction to help her in any way I can. My ship is at her disposal, and I can have her in the States in twelve weeks. And when we arrive, I can take her into my home until we do find her people. I have six daughters of my own, so I do not think the missus will even notice another for a spell."

Bird felt a grave misgiving. Had the man really changed so quickly from the besotted drunk he'd met earlier to this charitable Christian? The Bible on his table now seemed like a prop, a decoration in a scene carefully designed to win him over. But what could he possibly want with the girl? Before seeing the reaction of the French, he hadn't considered how great the public's curiosity might be. A disgusting image entered his mind: Alice being displayed at some traveling show, a besotted Captain Snow collecting pennies into his grimy hand to allow the curious to gawp at her. A bit of profit added to his voyage.

He looked at Snow's hands, folded before him on the table, and saw he wore no wedding band.

"I thank you for the offer. You are a good and charitable man. But she will remain with the *Fredonia*. She has been through much and I see no need to disrupt her further, now that she has just grown accustomed to life on our ship. And besides, I do admit she has become something of a good-luck charm for my crew."

Snow nodded solemnly.

"May God bless and keep you both," he offered.

10.

The Piglet

Forty swine were purchased from the French before the *Fredonia* departed from Nukahiva, along with one piglet, selected by Bird for a special purpose. Two days out from the island, Bird stood at the edge of the makeshift pen that had been constructed on the gun deck, watching them squeal and jostle one another. He'd always found the perambulations of livestock to be soothing, ever since he was a boy. The solemn chewing of a milk cow, the casual flick of a horse's tail; these things never failed to put him into a contemplative trance. Whenever he emerged from this state, he'd feel rejuvenated, as if he'd just been awakened from a deep sleep.

He called over the nearest middie. The man's hair was mussed and his coat was buttoned crookedly so he looked as if he'd slept in a haystack.

"Which are you?" Bird asked. "Your name, Midshipman."

"Elliot, sir."

Bird stared long and hard at him. "Have I seen you before?" he asked.

Elliot was confounded by the question. "I have been here since the beginning," he answered.

Without acknowledging this, Bird returned his attention to the pigs. "Do you see that piglet there?"

"Yes, sir."

"Have it brought to my cabin."

Elliot hesitated. "Alive, sir?"

"Yes, Mr. Elliot. Alive and fully intact."

In his dayroom, the piglet nosed at the legs of his chairs and his writing table, searching out every nook and depression with its snout. It was a fine, handsome piglet, its body covered with downy white fur, with curious eyes and a delicately curled little tail. He had Alice brought up as well, and she squatted on her hams to watch its movements with an alert attention. The piglet took no notice of her as it continued its investigation of the furniture. Bird's hope was that the animal might stimulate her maternal feelings, as a civilizing influence: Did not all women fawn and coo over the young, even from their earliest years? As the pig ambled within her reach, she reached out to grab it by one of its ears. It jerked itself free and fled across the room. She did not pursue it. Bird stood to try to corral it with one of his feet as it ran along the wall. It neatly jumped over his foot and disappeared beneath the sideboard.

"Wait, look here," he said to her. He reached into a pocket to retrieve a handful of dried corn. Gently, he tossed a few kernels onto the boards.

The piglet did not appear for some time, and then cautiously began to sniff its way out. It nosed the nearest few kernels and then appeared to inhale them.

"Would you like to feed him?"

He offered her some of the corn, which she closed in her fist and seemed reluctant to surrender. He placed a reassuring hand on her back, and felt her heartbeat through her warm skin. It felt rapid and slight, like a canary fluttering in its cage.

She squeezed her fist tightly, then made a small, ecstatic noise as she cast the entire handful at the animal, scattering the kernels across the floor, bouncing them off the boards and the cabinet doors like a sudden deluge of hailstones. The piglet flinched away, but then realized the nature of this bonanza and began to suck up everything in sight.

"Isn't he fine?"

She crawled along the floor toward the pig, kernels of corn sticking to her hands and knees. He knew that she was listening. He'd come to believe that she in fact heard and understood everything that was said to her.

"I have decided that you may keep him as a little pet, if you like. But there is one condition. Tomorrow is Easter Sunday," he said. "You will be permitted to come onto the deck to view our church service and our singing group. You will carry yourself properly at this time, do you understand? If you carry yourself well, I will allow you to keep the piglet."

The piglet had slowed considerably after its buffet, and now moseyed after the last traces of corn it had missed. Alice followed behind it in a lazy circle, still on her hands and knees. She reached over to scoop it up and brought it into her lap. The piglet squirmed to escape her grasp but settled when it found itself to be powerless.

"*Cat*," she whispered. She looked at him.

"Swine," he corrected her. "But what shall we name it?"

He didn't expect her to answer, but then without warning she whispered something that sounded like *Marcy*.

He raised an eyebrow. "Marcy?" He didn't know if he'd heard her correctly. She did not repeat herself. He suggested the name of Royal as more appropriate—the piglet was a male, after all—but Alice had drifted away. It was an effect sometimes, of her medicine. She held the pig in her lap and both she and it lapsed into a kind of silent reverie, each one staring off at nothing, their breathing slow and rhythmic, almost but not quite in unison.

11.

. . .

Alice sat in the darkness of the cabin, waiting for the door to open. On the island she had not been waiting for anything. She'd walked where she pleased, over sandy shore and through the forest, wandering like an aimless ghost among the trees. She listened to the whistling of birds and spent her days sitting on the shore to regard the unending entertainment of waves that crashed and receded. The cabin possessed few such entertainments. She had felt along every inch of it, mapped every joint in the boards with her fingers. Her days on the island had been divided by the sun and moon, by the brief rains that visited her, by a thousand small features of wind and tide and cloud. Now she was surrounded at all times by the same heavy darkness, the shuffling of boots above and below, incomprehensible voices, the blowing of whistles, and the scratching of rats. She had tried to count the ship's bell to mark the passage of time, but it did no good. It rang once, and then some while later it rang twice, and then later still it would ring three times . . . it counted up to eight rings and then began its meaningless pattern all over again.

She searched in her blankets for a small thing she desired, a momentary distraction. Her hands at first found other things she'd saved: a chestnut with a point on its tip, a chipped coin, a coat button . . . and then she had it: a small, empty tin. She felt the raised impression on the lid, recalling the image she had seen there before. It showed a woman in a long gown, standing on a shore, holding a lamp aloft—she could feel the shape of the woman's body, the curving line of her golden hair. She traced her finger along the woman's contours; her awareness traveled down her arm, through her fingers, until it seemed to leave her completely, and then for a brief merciful time she forgot herself and became that woman, holding her lamp to shine light upon the waters.

The sound of footsteps in the corridor called her back. The piglet, which had been quietly sleeping next to her, at once rose and began to pace. She heard the bolt being lifted from its catch on the other side of the door, which opened to reveal the disappointing figure of the boy. He entered her cabin without a word, carrying a plate in one hand and a small stub of candle in the other, melted into the mouth of a bottle. A whisk was tucked beneath his arm. He placed the plate and candle on the floor and used the whisk to tidy the floor. The piglet cautiously sniffed its way toward the plate and began to lap at the food with little sucking noises. The boy took no notice. He was gazing at her.

"Girl . . ." he whispered. "Girl, you girl . . ."

She remained still; it felt as if she could not move when his eyes were upon her. She waited for him to withdraw his gaze. Finally he did, but only to peer into the corridor and softly pull the door closed.

"I wish to tell you something," he said in a soft whisper. He crouched before her and took her hand into his own. "Can you hear me? I wish to tell you I have grown sweet on you."

His hand was hot and his smell like soured vinegar. She gave him no answer.

He stood over her for a long while, breathing heavily and saying nothing else. Then he began to fish in his trousers.

"It is only fair that I show you mine," he said, "because I have seen your titties."

He came out with his prick in his hand. It was a hairless and blind and pink thing, like a worm or a baby mouse. She thought it looked funny; she had never seen a prick before, and now that she had she wondered at how small and harmless it was. Just a little mouse that hid in a man's pants. He put it away almost at once, then crouched and put a hand on her shoulder to say, "There. Now we are even." He tried to look into her eyes but she evaded him. "Do you fancy me?" he asked her.

The sound of more footsteps from without caused him to take up his whisk and his candle. A small bubble of anticipation in her chest, swelling with each footfall. But the door opened again to reveal only the old man, Bird, who stooped to peer within the cabin. Another disappointment. He never entered, only stood stooped like this, his head bent under the door's low frame so that he looked like some monstrous old stork, smelling of tobacco and bootblack and whiskey.

"Victor?"

"Just finished, sir."

"Very good, boy. Remember that tidiness of one's environment leads to tidiness of the mind."

Bird moved aside to allow the boy to pass into the corridor with his burdens. Then he removed a vial from his pocket and she rose to receive it. The taste of the medicine was bitter on her tongue, but it helped for her sickness, she knew this to be true. When she had it, she felt as if some inner tide had receded, to reveal all of the shells and precious things that had been covered by the waves.

The old man said that it was Easter Sunday, and she tried to recall what these words meant. She could conjure only an image of a roast goose. She could remember the shape of the goose, and that its crisped form had terrified her, because she'd been able to recognize it as a thing that had once flown and honked and she realized that it would never honk again. The edges of its wings had been charred to black. She asked him, "Where have the feathers gone?"

Bird had been saying something, and he paused.

"What was that?"

"The feathers of the goose . . ." she said quietly.

Bird tsked. "This is exactly the kind of behavior I am talking about. You will stop this at once."

She searched inside herself for a response, but found nothing. At one time, she had been full of words—she could dimly recall as a child when she would babble to her father or mother about the things she had seen, or ask them endless questions about the world. But that had been so long ago. She had not spoken in so long a time that she had lost the habit of it, and words felt useless and unnecessary. She could not find the right ones, and even when she did they would dissipate in the air and lose their meanings as soon as they were spoken.

"Ah," Bird said, stooping to pick up the plate that the piglet had emptied. "I see you have finished your breakfast."

Soon after, Bird took his leave and two other men came to guide her through the corridors of the ship. She floated between them; the action of her feet seemed impossibly distant. She thought she was being taken to Bird's bright cabin, but then she was led to the foot of another ladder. One of the men picked her up and she hung on to his neck as they ascended, up again and through a hatch that was flooded with light.

The naked sunlight that she hadn't known . . . for how long? . . . now blinded her. A fresh breeze blew over her skin and she could smell tar warming in the sun. She looked down to see that her feet were no longer on the boards. She was being carried along by the men, each with a hand under her armpit. She felt a chair rise up beneath her. All around her, the quiet commotion of men in blue coats arranging themselves in chairs around her.

As her eyes became accustomed to the light she looked up to see again the blue of the sea, the blue of the sky. She was looking out over the entire length of the ship and all along it she could see men, more men than she had ever seen before in one place, all of them crowded upon the deck or hanging in the rigging, lined up on the yards and tops like crows perched on branches, their legs dangling beneath them. Young and old, fair and dark-skinned . . . it was a delegation in which all of the forms that men took in the world seemed to be represented. She saw Lieutenant Bird near the mast. Above him the sails flapped as he spoke more words . . . he was always speaking . . . but even though he shouted the words through a trumpet they were lost to the wind. It did not matter. None of the assembled sailors were watching him. Every pair of eyes across the entire deck was directed at her. This seemed fitting; for her husband William had promised her that one day she would be a queen and men would come to worship her, and that when she died she would be carried to Heaven by a flight of angels. And she was given another thought that caused her to flicker with joy: that all of these men had been gathered there for her. That they ate and moved and breathed upon this ship only to be her witness. And surrounding them all, the familiar endlessness of the sea.

And that is the true meaning of Hospitality, Bird declared through his trumpet. The officers seated around her seemed to stumble into a polite applause that quickly tapered back to nothing.

And then men were rising around her, shifting positions. From her chair, she was the still form that they seemed to revolve around. A figure approached her, bathed in bright sunlight. It resolved into the form of Mr. Rand, with his uniform neatly buttoned, his hair wet against his scalp as if he'd just doused and smoothed it with a hand. Her joy bloomed and filled her up—here at last was the one she'd been waiting for.

"Alice," he said as he smiled, the sound of her own name still so unfamiliar to her. He bent to whisper a message only for her ears: "Do you know that today is the day that the Lord has risen?"

And she did, she truly did. But there were no words she could find which could possibly express this.

12.

Low Islands

For weeks they sailed among the Puamotu group—the archipelago was a vast and crowded stretch of low coral atolls, barely visible until you were right upon them, nearly all ring-shaped around a central lagoon. The ship's progress was slow and cautious; they could hardly show any sail for fear of crashing into a reef. Whitlocke spent long stretches of time standing on a stool at the fore to peer over the bulwark, studying the water for any change in its color. From his perch on the quarterdeck, island after island drifted into Bird's view and out of it, approaching and retreating, identical and endless, as he sipped his gin concoction from the carved-out husk of a cocoanut.

The islands of this group appeared forlorn and uninhabited at their approach, but this was not the case. The natives built their villages exclusively on the inner lagoons, where the waters were peaceful and the fishing easier. They were a superstitious folk, and considered the outer shores of their islands to be haunted places. The *Fredonia* anchored at every island they found which possessed a sizable population and showered the natives with gifts meant to demonstrate the generosity and goodwill of the United States. Bird remarked in his journal that the peoples of the Puamotu group were slightly shorter than their Marquesan neighbors, and more prone to petty thievery. On one occasion, a man had snuck up the side of the *Fredonia*; he'd grabbed hold of an iron hoop and then threw himself back overboard. He was quickly apprehended—he attempted to make his escape by swimming, and was easily overtaken by a boat—and then was returned to the ship, where Bird had him soundly whipped on the foredeck so that his fellows on shore could witness. Dr. Mallory's collected native tooth specimens had also gone missing, which caused him to raise a terrible fuss. Though Bird thought they'd also probably been filched by the thieving natives, the surgeon insisted on having all of the crew's belongings turned out, which only uncovered a single yellowed molar, possessed by a sailor, which the man claimed had belonged to his mother and brought him good luck.

Bird could not understand the lives of these Polynesians. They were almost entirely idle; with weather that never changed, there was no need to store for any long winter, and they had no thought save for the present day and the satisfaction of their few rudimentary desires. Food was plentiful, breadfruit and cocoanuts in such ample supply they need only pick them up from the ground. If they wished to eat fish, they went and caught one. The sea was an endless bounty. If they wished to fornicate, they did so, freely and without shame or, as far as Bird could tell, any sense of animosity, competition, or jealousy among their sexual hierarchies. They harbored no ambitions of greatness, nothing *drove* them, not the pursuit of wealth or fame or achievement. They didn't even record their history. They lived and died on their islands without making any mark on the world at all. It made him shudder, to think of living such a meaningless, dull existence.

∽

Bird began to permit Alice to walk abovedecks for one hour each afternoon, when the weather was clear. To prevent her from leaving the quarterdeck, where she would be safe among the officers, he affixed a rope tether to her waist and gently tugged her back whenever it looked as if she might wander beyond the aft mast. Sometimes she followed her piglet on a rawhide leash, and the three of them—Bird, Alice, and the piglet—would drift from one side of the ship to the other like a chain of blind men, led by the whims of the pig.

She enjoyed watching the sailors at their work and especially seemed to enjoy gazing out at the sea. The middies greeted her with mock gentility, bowing and doffing their hats. Mr. Minnie tried to make a game of hiding coins around the deck, but could not long interest her in the search. Those few that she found, she flung over the bulwark into the waves. Mr. Whitlocke ignored her completely—though the man had fathered eleven children, he saw them as a frivolity, better given over entirely to the care of women. The first and only time the girl dared to approach him as he stood at the wheel, the sailing master had only turned to scowl slightly, like a man who'd just noticed his wallpaper peeling.

Even from afar, the common sailors gaped at her like a bunch of schooling guppies, slack-jawed and slow to work. Whenever this occurred, Bird would instruct Mr. Rand to better engage their attention with drills in the rigging; some days he had them running up and down the masts, furling and unfurling the sails, until well after dusk.

Her speech continued to return to her—not all at once, but in small, spontaneous bursts. She would sometimes be of a mood to grant his questions short replies, words and phrases, or else only a nodding of her head. He learned to be patient, as any attempt to force her would cause her to revert to her stubborn silence, sometimes for days, and he was content to record whatever tiny bits of information she let slip. They were like puzzle pieces that he could not yet assemble into a complete picture, but slowly he began to see the shape of it.

Bird brought her up onto the deck one night to show her the constellations. It was exceptionally clear, and dark, and above the ship Bird could see the grand whirl of the Milky Way. He asked for the lamps on deck to be extinguished and once the ship had been darkened he directed her gaze upwards into that brilliant cacophony of stars. Did she know of Orion or the Northern Cross? He named them for her and pointed, as he remembered his older brother doing for him, but she refused to look at the sky.

"Are you thinking of something?"

She shifted.

"Will you tell me what you are thinking of, or shall I try to guess it?"

"William," she said plainly.

His mind immediately returned to the tiny, makeshift graveyard on her island. The spars cast at odd angles.

"I would like to know more about William," he said

He could sense her slipping from his grasp, retreating into memory.

"Who is William?" he repeated.

She looked up with a confusion in her eyes. "He is my husband," she said, as if surprised that he would ask such a thing, as if it was the plainest fact in the world.

"You are married?"

She nodded.

He wondered if this could possibly be true. Or if it might not be some childish fantasy. She was, in his opinion, a bit young to be wed, but it would not have surprised him. His own stepmother had only been fourteen when she entered into the house, closer in age to her stepchildren than her husband; his father, already in his forties then, had almost bartered for her with a neighbor. But even if Alice had been married, when could such a wedding have possibly occurred? When he'd asked her how long she'd been alone on the island, she'd only given the answer *For a very long time* . . . He considered what Mallory had said about the extent of her malnutrition: perhaps she was older than he believed.

"Your husband is William?"

"He is dead."

Bird paused to reflect on this. He could hear light swells sloshing against the ship, unseen.

"Was he with you?" Bird asked gently. "On the island?"

He thought that she nodded. He tried one further tactic.

"After your ship wrecked?"

"No," she said. "The ship did burn."

He knew from the way her voice trailed off that he would get no more from her. The light of the slim moon caught her eyes, and for a brief instant it looked to him as if whatever memory she'd visited was somehow visible there: a ship, in the distance, burning in the night.

The *Fredonia* lay in the mouth of a lagoon too shallow to permit them entry, with only a single small fishing village on its western shore. Bird called for a boat to be prepared. When Mr. Rand asked after his intent, he said only that he had taken a notion to walk on the island. And he would bring the girl, he added. He thought to reward her for her recent progress with a pleasant afternoon's excursion.

The boat crew bent their backs to propel their craft across the flat surface of the lagoon. Alice, seated in the prow next to Bird, peered over the side to witness the coral formations and flickering schools of fish that passed beneath them.

They beached on the uninhabited eastern shore of the lagoon. As soon as they hit the sand she jumped from the boat and Mr. King, given the task of keeping her close, fumbled over the side to chase after her. His concern was unnecessary: she hopped up the beach a few steps, bent over and ran her fingers through the sand. After another few steps, she turned to search Bird's face. He gave her a nod of approval.

They walked along the shore, Alice hovering around at the edges of their party, happier than he'd seen her on the ship. She collected seashells as they walked, and when her hands were full she began to discard them one by one.

They encountered only a few of the island's inhabitants, a small group of sun-dried fishermen mending their nets beyond the reach of the surf. Bird had nothing to offer them and parlay proved impossible, but still the island men seemed interested in them; they strolled casually along behind the party, conversing in their own language. They were especially interested in the girl—Bird surmised it was not often they saw a white woman. Alice did not even seem to notice them.

Walking in the sand began to tax Bird's knee, so he turned their path inland. The forest was full of small, mottled brown birds that rose from the trees in clouds as they approached. The terrain was flat and much of it formed of sharp coral limestone. After only a few steps into the interior Alice discovered it to be intolerable to her bare feet, and she would proceed no farther. She picked her way carefully onto a patch of loamier ground, ringed by the stone.

"Now you understand why you must wear shoes," he scolded her. "Mr. King, if you will assist her."

Mr. King huffed his large frame over to her and then kneeled to offer her a ride on his back. She seemed to misapprehend his gesture and took a cautious step back.

"He will serve as your elephant," Mr. Minnie encouraged her. "And you shall be an Arabian princess."

"Mr. Minnie," Bird said. "Please. This is not helpful."

She was finally coaxed to climb up onto King's back and she grasped his forehead as he trundled over the landscape. Mosquitos buzzed incessantly around them, which she amusingly tried to fan away from King's head. Bird had not often seen mosquitos before among these islands, no doubt another gift brought from the civilized world. He swatted at a sensation on his neck and then regarded his palm to find a smear of blood and some scattered insect parts that looked as if they could not have possibly once been assembled into an entire creature.

They made slow progress over the island's uneven terrain. As they neared the outer shore, the native men who followed grew silent and trailed farther behind, eventually vanishing altogether.

Their party broke from the trees onto the windswept shore that faced the open ocean. The beach here was of an entirely different character than that which faced the inner lagoon. Here, the vegetation was sparse and hardened by the elements. Craggy shrubs grew among the limestone outcroppings. The surf threw itself at the island's edges, sluicing into narrow fissures of stone. It was so unlike the green and gentle shore of the lagoon that it was difficult to imagine they were on the same island. The wind off of the ocean was strong; it had cleared the mosquitos and its gusts bent the dune grass that grew among the rocks. Witnessing this scene, Bird understood why the natives considered these places haunted.

He chose a knob of stone and instructed Minnie to drape it with a blanket. Then, with a small, inadvertent groan, Bird lowered himself onto it. As he'd aged, things had become heavier, more difficult. He could remember on the Wilkes Expedition, going ashore with the scientifics, how he could traipse across islands all day without tiring. Thinking back on those days, he was struck with a pang of nostalgia, not only for himself at that age, but for the world as it had been. He lamented that time and progress both moved only in one direction.

The sun on his face was strong, and he had a desire to retreat into the shade. But that would mean rising, and so only wiped his brow with his handkerchief and squinted out at the sea.

"A low island has the sea within, and the sea without," he explained to Alice, pointing uselessly where she was already looking.

Mr. King had set her down on the hot stone and she was standing beside him. She flinched as a thunderous breaker pounded against the stone, the dissipating white surf rushing toward them among the cracks.

"In a hurricane, the sea might even o'ersweep the entire island," he explained. "Like the deck of a ship in a storm."

The girl's blankness was difficult to read; she made no outward expression. But the way she stared out at the ocean, wide-eyed, he believed that he could know exactly what she must be feeling. Could any child stand at the edge of such a vast and powerful body of water and not feel awe, and terror, at the thought of how easily it could sweep over the slim fingernail of ground they stood upon, to swallow them up?

13.

CALLED HOME

A man slipped and fell from the rigging one day while Rand was on duty. He heard only a brief, sharp cry, and then the commotion of men rushing up the shrouds.

By the time he arrived, the man was already dead, not twenty feet from the deck, his eyes and tongue bulging out from the force of his drop. He'd become tangled in a line that had snapped his neck. His body twisted gently as one of his former companions sawed at the line with a jackknife.

The deceased sailor was a Portuguese named Fernandes. Rand had most likely seen the man hundreds of times over the course of the voyage, but didn't recall him specifically. He imagined Fernandes waking that morning, eating his breakfast and hearing the chaplain's prayer, entirely unaware that he would soon meet his end. If any sins lay on his soul, he would be forced to carry them until the Judgment.

Rand brought the news to the Lieutenant. He found Bird sitting at his writing table. It looked as if he was reviewing something that he'd written, but there was a chance he was asleep, given the way his head was cocked to the side. The cabin stank of the gin being extruded through the old man's pores. Rand cleared his throat.

"I am here to inform you that Seaman Fernandes has fallen to his death."

Bird was awake, now at least. "Who?"

"Fernandes, sir. A seaman of the foretop."

"Oh. Good man, was he?"

"A solid reputation, I am told."

"Well. Have him sewn up."

All hands were called for the funeral, with only a few sharp-eyed men left in the tops to watch for reefs. The body of Seaman Fernandes was laid on a plank near the mainmast, the outline of his Roman features dimly visible beneath a sailcloth shroud. The crew gathered in a quiet circle, their heads bowed and tongues for once silent. The sheet-anchor men removed their caps. Chaplain Parker read some words from Paul's epistle to the Galatians, which in Rand's opinion bore absolutely no relevance to the occasion. Rand had come to believe that the chaplain opened his Bible at random, and the words he spoke were arbitrary, more meant to fill a span of time than to carry any scriptural meaning. At that morning's prayer service, he'd spent an inordinate amount of time mumbling an anecdote about a parrot or parakeet—he used the words interchangeably—who repeated the bad behavior of others and wound up in Damnation. This, sadly, had been the last spiritual guidance Seaman Fernandes ever received.

Rand's faith did not reside in this incompetent chaplain, or in any sect or church, but only in the Bible itself, and its words that were handed from God to man. Only the scriptures, he thought, were incorruptible. At one time, he'd considered himself a Millerite. When he was a boy, he'd accompanied his mother to see Miller preach in a schoolhouse. It was a snowy day and he'd driven the buggy with a loaded rifle in his lap because his mother was afraid of stags. It was that day that he'd first truly felt the presence of the Holy Spirit, summoned to him somehow through the passion in Miller's voice, the warmth of the stove and good feeling in the room, the proud fact that he'd escorted his mother alone. Miller had presented arguments as to the exact date of the Return, but ultimately he'd been mistaken. Rand had been twelve on the appointed day, known by his followers as the Great Disappointment. His mother had wept in the parlor, and he'd wept too, but only because he'd been affected by her tears. The only thing he'd retained of Miller's teaching was a feeling he could not shake: that the time of the Return was not distant, but close at hand. Sometimes he stood on the quarterdeck in the evening and looked at the darkening sky, imagining that it might crack open at any moment to reveal what lay behind it. It felt as if all of the souls in the world sat poised at the edge of a great precipice they might fall into at any moment.

As Chaplain Parker made the sign of the cross over the shrouded body, Rand felt a dull stab of anxiety for the man's soul. Then the board was tipped over the bulwark and Fernandes' mortal vessel splashed into the ocean and disappeared in an instant, dragged down by the weight of the cannonball that had been sewn in with him.

His belongings were put into the lucky bag to be auctioned off to the rest of the crew. The only item of any value was a small golden cross. A glimmer of hope in Rand: perhaps he would be Saved after all.

Rattled by the death of Seaman Fernandes, Rand nervously drank four cups of coffee with his afternoon meal, too much, and now had a throbbing headache. It wasn't the first time a sailor had died. There had been a few cases of fever, a knife fight, and an old-timer who'd expired in his sleep, but none of them had died so suddenly, right within Rand's sight. He couldn't rid himself of the image of the man hanging there with his eyes bulging. He considered this event to be a warning, an omen—that time was running out for them all, and their souls must be prepared.

That night, he waited until the fourth bell of the middle watch, when the wardroom was darkened and disturbed only by the sawmill noise of Mr. Whitlocke snoring in his cabin. Those seamen who weren't fast asleep would be gathered on the weather deck to smoke. Quietly, he filled a tin cup with water from the wash basin, and took with him only a small candle to light the way.

He'd been visiting her every night, to prepare her for this moment. He hoped she was ready. She knew how to clasp her hands, and he'd intoned the Lord's Prayer for her until she began to mouth the words herself. He thought that he could feel the love of Christ in her eyes, the way she stared at him in the near-dark. He did not know if she'd ever been baptized, and as each day passed his anxiety had grown, to think that her soul might remain in a naked state. What if the ship went down? Or she was swept from the deck in a storm? He couldn't bear to think that something so precious as her immortal soul might be thrown so carelessly into the void.

She was waiting for him in the darkness, her piglet curled asleep against her leg. He drew her onto her knees and they prayed, her head bent forwards so it almost touched his. She echoed the last word of each line: *Heaven . . . name . . . come . . . be done . . . Heaven . . . bread . . .* When they came to *trespasses* she quieted and did not resume. He finished for them both.

"I have something for you," he whispered. He reached into his coat pocket and drew up a loop of string. Hung from it, the small golden cross that had belonged to Seaman Fernandes.

She reached for it at once but he held her hand away and placed the cross on the floor. Then, he drew from another pocket the little bird-flute that she loved to hear him play. He placed it next to the cross.

"You must choose," he said to her. "Please." He had no idea if she could understand the importance of her decision. He trusted the Lord to guide her. She did not hesitate. She reached again for the cross and enclosed it completely in her fist. He felt his heart swell with hope to think that even this poor, lost creature could yearn for the Lord.

"I must ask you some questions now," he said, "and you must answer me truthfully. Will you do that?"

She nodded. He took up the tin cup from where he'd left it, and felt the lukewarm water splash the rim.

"Do you reject the Devil, and his evil works?"

". . ."

"You must say it. Will you cast out the Devil?"

She nodded.

"Do you know that Jesus Christ is the son of the Lord, and that he came to save us?"

"Yes."

"Do you love him?"

"I do."

She allowed him to tilt her head back and he poured the water over her face. As he did, she looked up into the stream and blinked her eyes as it ran over them. It was done. She had been Saved.

Then, before he could stop her, she leaned forward and pressed her mouth against his. He could feel the dry skin of her lips, the scrape of her teeth. Her small breasts flattened against him. He grabbed her shoulders and pushed her away with too much force. She tumbled backwards in the small space and crashed against the bulkhead, a look of shock and incomprehension on her face.

"I'm sorry," he said, though he did not know if he meant for shoving her, or for the kiss, or for something else. These were the only words he could call into his mind.

He took up the candle and quickly left. When the cabin door was safely closed behind him, he paused to collect himself. In his haste to exit, the candle had snuffed itself out. He was breathing heavily and had to replace the latch by feel. He waited until his breath slowed and listened for any sound within the cabin. But then he heard something else. A small noise from the direction of the steerage.

"Hello?" he whispered.

"Well, look at this."

"Who is that?"

"It is I, sir."

"Victor? Do you have a match?"

"I do not."

There was something he did not like in the boy's tone. They were both silent for a moment.

"What are you doing here?"

"I was just listening."

"To what?"

"To you. And the girl. I did hear some things."

"I do not think I like your tone."

"Well, I do not care what you like."

If it hadn't been so dark, he would have grabbed the boy by his ear. Instead, he hissed, "Watch your tongue, boy. Or I will grab your ear and drag you onto the deck and thrash you."

There was no sound. Had the boy left?

Then his voice appeared, from farther away. "I do not think you will do that. Because then I would tell the Pelican a good story."

"What have you heard? You have heard nothing."

"I have heard you and that girl, carrying on in private. But I would not tell if you gave me five dollars."

"Excuse me?"

"You heard me, you molly."

Rand lunged in the dark and managed to get hold of a tuft of the boy's hair. Victor cried out and then Rand felt a sharp blow on his ribs that knocked the wind from him. He let go.

"You will . . . spend the rest of . . . the voyage in irons," Rand stammered as he tried to regain his breath. But he realized he was talking to no one, in an empty corridor. The boy was gone.

14.

Another Island

They were first greeted at Mangareva by a number of goats cavorting on the barren slope of Mount Duff, who bleated at the ship as it made its way into the harbor. Bird was surprised by the lack of vegetation. The entire island looked as if it had been clear-cut, or else maybe nothing had ever grown there. The village of Rikitea was a quiet cluster of white stone houses stretched along the shore of the bay.

A boat approached, containing a Jesuit in his dark habit and a crew of Polynesians all in spotless white. The priest was permitted to board and provided a note to Mr. Grady without comment or introduction. Grady in turn gave it to Bird, who split the seal and saw that the missive was written in French. He called for Mr. Piper, who'd been following behind him, waiting to be called upon.

"It says we will not be permitted to land, sir."

The letter was signed by Pater H. Laval.

"What is the meaning of this?" Bird asked the Jesuit. "Have we offended you somehow?"

"No English," he said.

"You send a man who speaks no English to greet an American ship?"

"No," the priest said, somehow seemingly in agreement.

The Jesuit declined a tour of the deck. After he'd taken his leave, Bird extended his spyglass to study the village. Perhaps there was plague? He could find no sign of it. The village was neat and orderly. He saw pigs in pens and clothed Polynesians working in little garden plots. Everything perfectly orderly, perfectly serene. A brown-frocked priest, nearly identical to the one who had so recently vacated the *Fredonia*, directed a team of native men in the slow labor of building a stone wall. Whatever tactic these Catholics had used to tame the native spirit, he mused, it had worked. In fact, in some ways Rikitea appeared to be the most civilized place he'd encountered in the entire Pacific. In the center of the village stood a magnificent church, so large he could see it over the other rooftops. An ornate stone structure with towers three or four stories tall, whitewashed to the very top. It was a wonder—he had seen nothing so grand as this, not even among the palaces of the kings and queens of other islands. It was rare in the Pacific to even find a structure of two stories. Bird's glass found a dark figure standing at the highest window of one of the church's towers. A man with snowy white hair. It seemed for a moment, though it could not be possible at such a distance, that he looked directly at Bird. Then he turned and retreated within.

Bird declared that they would remain at anchor for the day. If nothing further came from the Jesuits, he would send a messenger ashore requesting permission to land for firewood and water. With the treeless state of the island, he wondered if there was even firewood to be had.

That afternoon, the middies entertained themselves by trying to capture a white tip shark that was lazily circling the ship. They could not get it on the hook, and eventually Mr. Elliot shot it. It disappeared, leaving only a bloom of blood that hung loosely at the surface of the water.

The island contained a further surprise: later in the day, another boat appeared from the north. Uncapping his spyglass again, Bird discovered that this one contained an oddity: a Polynesian man, dressed in a dandyish European fashion. He wore a jacket and pants of green wool, a smart gray hat adorned with what looked like an ostrich feather. A silken cravat was tucked into his shirt. Even more curious, his boat appeared to be crewed by raven-haired women in flowing robes. As they hove closer, though, he realized they were not quite so strange as that; they were men, Chinese coolies.

The well-dressed islander was much friendlier than the Jesuit. He introduced himself as Bill and shook the hand of every man he encountered, both officers and crew. He spoke some English and was quite tall. Even Bird squinted up at his smiling face as he delivered his message: an invitation for the captain to dine with someone named Monsieur Baptiste, the man's employer Bird assumed, who owned a coffee plantation on the northern side of island.

"Why are we not permitted to land here?" Bird asked.

Bill shook his head and waved at the village. "This place is all for priest."

"And when would Mr. Baptiste like to receive me?"

"You come now," Bill said.

Bird's officers had been cool to him as of late and he wished to snub them, so he invited only Mr. Piper to accompany him, with four marines to safeguard their party. Before leaving, he instructed Dowd and King to prepare Alice to go ashore as well—if Baptiste's plantation was half as civilized as what he'd seen in Rikitea, he had no fear for her safety, and she'd been showing so much progress that he hoped to begin to acclimate her to polite society. In order to assure her cooperation in this, he gave her three drops of laudanum when she was brought up, and pocketed the vial in case more was required.

They left in two boats, one carrying the men of the *Fredonia* and the other Bill and his crew. The boats cut across the harbor and then followed the shoreline until even the spire of the grand church was no longer visible. Alice sat alert at his side; she understood, he thought, that she had received a special privilege.

Most of the island seemed as bare and desolate as Mount Duff. Then finally, some greenery was visible on the crest of a hill. As they passed beyond the hill, Bird saw that the rest of the island was blanketed almost uniformly with rows of coffee trees, rising into the highlands. After an hour of rowing, Bill signaled that they should land. They beached in a small inlet where a single-masted sloop was anchored. Several smaller boats were pulled up onto the sand beyond the tide line. Bill led them along a packed earthen road that wound away from the cove, up into the hills. Mr. Piper accompanied Alice, taking her hand and steering her in the correct direction as the marines followed behind. On either side of the lane, at work in the fields, more Chinese were so busily occupied they did not even look up as the group passed.

Bill proudly described the plantation's output as they walked: copra as well as coffee, both of which were grown not only on a thousand cultivated acres on Mangareva but also on several smaller islands nearby. Bird admired the efficiency of the operation; there seemed to be nothing frivolous, nothing spare. All around them, the coolies moved among the trees, filling their gunnysacks with the red berries, loading the full sacks onto mule carts. A team was digging an irrigation canal. Where before there had been nothing but a barren rock, and the useless disorder of nature, here was a brilliant clockwork of men and animals and trees planted in orderly rows. Bird looked forward to meeting the man who had accomplished all of this.

Bird said to Bill, "You speak English very well. May I ask how you learned?"

"Listen to English, speak English. Is not *difficile*." As far as Bird could tell, the man never stopped smiling.

"I admire your spirit. You mean to say, 'It is not *difficult*'."

"What is this?"

"You have used the French. *Difficile*. The word in English is *difficult*."

"French and English," Bill said, "it is the same," and Bird could see no point in arguing with him.

Baptiste's house sat on a cleared hill and was visible long before they arrived. A white fence encircled an ample yard of bare red dirt that contained a garden and a chicken house. It was similar to many of the ranch houses he'd seen across the Pacific, low and wide and open to the elements. Baptiste was seated on the veranda and raised his hat at their approach. He gave an impression, even at a distance, of fragility. He wore a wrinkled white linen suit, and had a single leg propped on a wicker ottoman, covered with a thick blanket despite the warmth.

"Please excuse me, that I do not rise," he said after their introductions were made. "The leg pains me so."

"We have a surgeon on board," Bird offered. "I could have him give his opinion. And perhaps provide you with opium for the pain?"

Baptiste laughed at this. "Opium I have!" he said. "Wherever there are Chinese, there is opium." Even as he said this, his attention was drawn to Alice, who hovered uncertainly behind Mr. Piper.

"Bill has been telling me all about your production." Bird looked to find the Polynesian man but he'd casually slipped off to feed some chickens in the yard. The marines waited by the gate, already looking bored and hot.

Baptiste mopped his brow. "I would deal in pearls as well but these Jesuit swine have control of the pearls. Please sit. Would you like a drink?"

Bird and Piper reclined on the veranda's wicker furniture. Alice had sat down on the porch stairs, fascinated by the chickens in the yard, and Bird did not disturb her. Her attention was immediately drawn to the two Polynesian women of exceptional beauty who emerged from the house, one carrying cut glasses and the other a pitcher of something colorful. They wore calico dresses, and one, obviously the younger, had flowers in her raven-dark hair. She could not have been more than fifteen or sixteen. She placed the glasses on a table and the other woman, who carried herself more seriously, took great care in filling them up almost to their rims. Bird accepted one with a silent nod of gratitude and found that the beverage was a delicious rum punch.

"My wives," Baptiste finally introduced them, with a weak smile. "This one is Anna," he said of the younger. "And this is Kalilea." The older woman had tiny lines gathered at the corners of her eyes.

As Anna passed by her, Alice reached out and touched her dress. Bird was about to scold her, but he saw Anna smile and decided to let them be. Anna had also brought out a bowl of goat's milk for Alice, which she drank eagerly in two long draughts, allowing tiny streams of the milk to run down her chin and onto her chest, soaking the front of her garment.

Baptiste was of course most interested to know why a young girl was traveling with a Navy ship, and Bird told of her rescue. After he'd finished, Baptiste turned his attention directly to her and said, "You are welcome here, *jolie*."

Bird said, "Alice, can you say hello to *Monsieur* Baptiste?"

When she was addressed, Alice looked down at the boards of the porch and remained still.

"I have told you she does not speak much," Bird explained.

Baptiste was a fine and gracious host. Before dinner, he invited Bird and Piper inside to rest and refresh themselves. Bird assumed that Alice would accompany him, but seeing his concern, Baptiste said, "Don't worry. Anna will take care of her." Alice did seem attached to the young Polynesian woman, who walked hand-in-hand with her in the garden as the chickens pecked around their feet.

He allowed Kalilea to show him into the house, to a small room with a sliding wall, partially open to permit the breeze. Within, there was a washstand and a hammock hanging by a wide open window. After splashing water on his face and hands, Bird collapsed into the hammock and fell into a long, hazy nap, during which he thought he heard the sound of Alice stirring the water in the basin with her fingers, though she was not there.

∽

The village of Rikitea was quiet, like a dog sleeping in the sun. Gentle swells rolled across the harbor and crumbled into froth at the shore. The men sat idle in the tops, engaged in contests to see who could spit farthest over the bulwark. Lieutenant Rand brooded on the quarterdeck, his mind scarcely on his duties, when he was approached by four middies: Mr. Minnie, Mr. Dowd, and both of the Hoopers. Minnie spoke for them.

"Permission to take a boat out for oysters, sir."

"Mr. Minnie, you are aware that none are to be permitted ashore."

"We do not aim to land, sir. We will keep to the surf."

"Very well. Proceed."

It was a small and petty rebellion against the Pelican. He considered Bird's displeasure, upon hearing that he'd permitted it, and imagined his own retort: *but you said nothing of the surf* . . .

He was barely aware of the preparations as their boat was lowered onto the waters of the harbor. He was busy chastising himself for having surely, though unwittingly, encouraged the girl's affections. He should have seen it for what it was much earlier: She, alone and afraid, surrounded by strange and unfriendly faces. He, visiting her in the dark of night, in her private quarters. The powerful intimacy of prayer. The suggestive nature of woman.

The sun moved across the afternoon sky. Mr. Fledge brought him a report on several sacks of flour that had become infested with weevils. The man was holding one of the culprits pinched between his thumb and forefinger. The beetle circled its legs in the air helplessly. Rand let the words enter his ears and gave some sign of acknowledgment. He resolved that he would not visit her again. She had been baptized and her soul was secure—any further contact would only put them both in jeopardy. But he could not banish the memory of her, damp with perspiration, pressed against his body in the darkness. Sometimes in his mind, he saw her without her clothes, her arms wide open, yearning for his embrace. Her hair cut short like a boy's, her small body taut and ropey with muscle.

Two gunshots rang out in rapid succession from the shore, snapping Rand from the confusing muddle of his thoughts. He looked to the village and saw a number of identical priests hurrying in one direction. He felt a walnut-sized lump of anxiety in his stomach. There was no sign of the oyster boat.

"What are your orders, sir?" Mr. King asked him.

"What is going on?"

"Shots have been fired."

"I heard them, Mr. King."

The priests all moved out of his sight, and the village once more appeared sleepy and peaceful. Rand gave no orders—he could not think of any to give. Not long after this, a boat was launched from shore, carrying the same priest who'd first greeted them. Rand nodded at King to permit the man, and met him as he stepped onto the deck.

"The commander is not present at the moment. I am First Lieutenant Evan Rand, and you may speak to me as the current authority on this ship."

The priest was sweaty and urgent, and suddenly had a better grasp of English. "Jacob Minnie and Samuel Hooper, these are your men?"

"Yes, why?"

"They have been arrested."

"For what crime?"

"For violating the law," he answered unhelpfully.

Rand's throat closed. His words, rising through it, felt as large as eggs.

"There were four men in their boat. What of the other two?"

The priest's face darkened. *"Monsieur, ils sont mortes."*

Baptiste's dining room was elegantly furnished: a hutch displaying ornate china and crystal stood against one wall, the other a wide open window that overlooked the coffee fields. Bird considered the silverware, the china, the delicately decorated teacups and saucers, all of it no doubt carried here over hundreds of miles, packed in straw like precious eggs. Baptiste was already seated at the table when Bird was roused for dinner, his leg still propped on a chair and covered with a blanket. Alice was brought in by Anna, and Bird was shocked at the girl's transformation. She wore a blue gown of taffeta, her short hair brushed back against her scalp with a purple flower tucked into it. Around her neck, tiny shells strung on a wire.

"*Très très bien*," Baptiste said, mirroring his thoughts. She was no great beauty—her features were average, but the work Anna had done seemed to put her in a proper context to be admired. The dress was overlong and dragged on the floor, causing her to walk slowly, as if she was balancing on a wire, which lent an elegance to her entrance.

She took her seat beside Bird, and Anna retreated to the kitchen to begin serving them. The variety of the meal was incredible: a roast pheasant stuffed with canned pears (*Bill has shot it only this morning*, Baptiste informed them), lamb in aspic, poached fish and eggs, boiled turnips with parsley and butter, beef gravy, also from a tin. A fresh loaf of real bread, not johnnycakes or ship's biscuit, was brought out warm from the oven and broken into hunks by their host. Throughout, the women carried in steaming trays and refilled their plates whether they requested it or not.

Alice ate little, accepting only a single boiled turnip which she tried to crush in her hands. It was too hot at first, and she gasped and silently fluttered her scalded hands above the plate.

"Do you like the pretty dress? And the necklace I have given you?" Baptiste asked her.

Alice looked at him, her hands covered with turnip pulp.

"You may keep them. If you like, I shall have my wives make you another dress if you wish. Would you like to pick the cloth?"

"That is very generous of you," Bird thanked him. "I would like to express our gratitude, for your hospitality."

Baptiste did not respond, but raised his wineglass in a toast that Bird and Piper joined as Alice licked turnip pulp from her fingers.

Their dinner conversation focused on Baptiste's business ventures, and the politics of the island. "Why do you bring in the Chinese?" Bird asked him at one point. "Could you not have the natives perform the labor and save the expense of transporting them?"

Baptiste waved off the idea. "The Chinese make me rich. The Kanaka, you understand, has a dread of hard labor. Did you know that there is a word in their language . . . *akaturuma*, which means to sit down by your work and return home with nothing done?" He made a face that was inscrutable, some combination of disgust and humor that seemed to Bird to be particularly French. "Some of them leave the village to come here, and at least I pay them for their work. The priests make them gather pearls and say that it protects their souls. I feel sad for these people. Do you know how Laval keeps them from fornicating? He locks the women in prison every night, and releases them in the morning. There is a cliff on the side of Mount Duff, *te rerega-o-te-ahine* they call it, which means *the place where women jump off*. They cast themselves into the sea rather than live for another day."

Piper made a noise like *humph*, to remind everyone that he was still there. Their host was breathing heavily, as if exhausted by even the small expenditure of energy that conversation required. "I do not mean to give you a poor impression of our little corner of paradise," he added. "The church cannot touch us here . . ."

Bird had been noticing Mr. Piper growing more unsteady over the course of the afternoon, and now he said, a bit too forcefully, "I see that you have more than one wife . . ."

Bird thought it rude, but Baptiste took it graciously. He said, "It is the custom, here and in many parts of the world. Let us not forget that even Moses and Solomon of old kept several wives."

"I would be happy to find even one," Mr. Piper said. It was clear that the alcohol had gone to his head. He continued, uninvited, "A good woman, someone who will support me. Not one of these fly-by-nights."

"Mr. Piper, have you finished your meal?" Bird asked. "I wonder if you would go outside and make sure the marines are well-occupied."

"The marines, sir?"

"Yes, Mr. Piper."

After Piper had grudgingly departed, Bird nodded an apology to Baptiste, who seemed to understand his embarrassment.

"It is hard to find good men," Baptiste said wistfully. "I am very fortunate, to have Bill. He is a fine man. He can read and write in three languages."

"He seems fine," was all Bird could come up with. The rum punch had been piling up in his stomach as well and after the food his thoughts began to feel sluggish.

Baptiste studied Alice with his drink in his hand. "What will become of her?" he asked Bird. Alice was drawing slow lines on her plate with the fork, though she hadn't touched it while eating.

"We will return her to the States, of course."

"Yes, but who awaits her? Where are her people?"

"Every effort will be made to locate her people."

"And if she does not have any?"

It was a question Bird had considered, but he had no answer. It had lurked in the corners of his mind for all of the time she'd been in his care. He'd considered that, if no relations could be located, she might end up in a workhouse, or worse, a madhouse. All he said was, "I assure you that she will be well cared for."

Baptiste seemed to accept this, and again tried to coax her into conversation. "I see that you are fond of Anna. Would you like to stay here with us?" To Bird, he added, "I would be willing to care for her, and I am sure Anna would like to have another girl in the house so close to her own age."

"A very generous offer, but as I have said, I'm sure that after spending so long abroad, Alice would prefer to return home to the States."

"And is that what you would prefer?" Baptiste asked Alice.

Alice looked up and surprised them both by speaking. "I don't wish to stay here," she said, and Bird felt an unmistakable flicker of pride. Then, confidently, she reached across the table for another turnip.

Baptiste smiled graciously. "But of course, *mademoiselle*."

The meal was cleared by his women, who also took Alice away, and Baptiste bid them to bring out cigars that had come all the way from the Caribbean and good Spanish brandy. Something else Bird admired about Baptiste: no matter how much he drank, the man's demeanor and presentation did not seem to change a jot. He could hold his liquor—it was an attribute that Bird had, in his life, come to equate with soundness of mind and a clean conscience.

"You must stay the night," Baptiste said. "It is far too late to be returning to your ship."

Bird considered the proposition. He couldn't remember the last time he'd spent a night on land, but his growing drunkenness and Baptiste's hospitality made it an attractive offer. Baptiste had just uncorked the brandy and he was about to accept when they were interrupted by Kalilea, followed close behind by an unexpected Mr. King, sweating and out of breath as if he'd run all the way there.

"What's the meaning of this, Mr. King? Why are you here? I do remember giving the order that all hands should remain on the ship."

"Your presence is requested, sir. Something terrible has happened."

Rand was ferried ashore with Mr. Thomas and ten marines. The marines stared dully at the island, at the officers, or fiddled with weapons. Once ashore, a priest led them through the village, toward the towering structure of the church. The inhabitants of Rikitea kept their distance from the procession. They leaned on their tools or peered cautiously out of the windows of their stone houses. Everything whitewashed, the people clothed in white linen. White sheets on clotheslines.

The church in Rikitea was even more ostentatious up close, towering above all else in sight, painted with bright colors and decorated around every window with white and black pearls set into the mortar. On a sign board outside, he saw two billets, one in French and one, he assumed, in the Mangarevan tongue. The French was a list of the village's rules and regulations. He could read only a handful as they passed by: PAS DE BOISSON ALCOOLISÉE OU D'ALCOOL DUR . . . PAS DE DANSE . . . LE SABBAT EST RÉSERVÉ À LA PRIÈRE . . . LE CHANT NE SERA AUTORISÉ QUE DANS L'ÉGLISE . . .

Father Laval met them at the door of a windowless structure that lay in the church's shadow. He was not the stern character Rand had imagined: he was a kindly-looking man, with soft, almost feminine features. He had thick hair, all stark white. The bodies of Hooper and Dowd were laid out on a table in the front room. Hooper's shirt and jacket were dark with blood.

Rand examined the bodies. Dowd had taken a bullet in the temple and the wound was eerily clean, a little hole and nothing more. Examining Hooper's body, he realized he couldn't tell which brother it was.

Rand said, "I ask your leave to bury them in sacred ground. They were both to my knowledge baptized Christians."

"Yes, of course."

"Regarding the men you have placed under arrest, I'll see that they are unharmed and then I'll hear what you have to say."

Laval nodded. "Follow me," he said, and nodded toward an iron door.

They were led through a long hall lined with unassuming wooden doors. As Laval opened the door of one of the cells, Minnie and the other Hooper stood and sheepishly saluted. They had been sitting side by side on a bench. Hooper's face was slack and pale, almost green, nearly identical to that of his brother's corpse. His mouth hung open as if he was going to be sick. Minnie was better able to report on the incident: the two men had dueled with pistols to settle a dispute that had originated weeks before, the details of which were meaningless.

"He said that my brother was pigeon-livered," Samuel Hooper added morosely. His words hung dead in the air. Even he seemed to realize their absurdity.

To Laval, Rand said, "None of your people have been harmed, so I'm sure you'll allow me to take these men into my custody, to be punished according to the laws of their own country."

Laval nodded, as if he'd expected this. "Yes. And of course, you must pay the fines." He donned a pair of spectacles and motioned to a younger priest nearby to provide him with the fee schedule, so he could show Rand all of the costs he'd incurred.

Bird winced when he heard the sum that was paid out to the Jesuits and rubbed a hand on his sun-beaten brow.

"It appears that I cannot leave this ship even for a moment, because you are incapable of handling it. And you have no answer as to why you permitted these men ashore despite my order to the contrary?"

The words that Rand had hoped to spit back at his commander seemed small and petty now that two men were dead. And so he said nothing.

The sun was setting over Mangareva, the reddened sky crisscrossed with low wisps of clouds that looked as if they'd been scattered by a broom. "Very well then, Mr. Rand. I am disappointed in your performance, I'll have you know that. I shall be in my quarters until the funeral."

"What would you have me do with the seconds?"

"Oh. Hooper's brother, and Minnie?"

"Yes."

"Give them a tongue lashing and let them loose. It was, after all, a matter of honor."

Rand and the other officers were permitted ashore for the funeral. The atmosphere in the two longboats that carried them across the harbor was something like that of a picnic outing. In one of the boats, Minnie retold the story of the duel to Piper and Thomas and Chaplain

Parker. Mr. Harvey, leaning over the side, attempted to identify the tropical fish that flitted around beneath them. The Pelican showed only a slight annoyance at having to waste his day, but he was curious to view the village up close. Aside from Rand's, the only other solemn presence belonged to Hooper's brother, who sat on a bench with his hands folded, a look on his face like a man attempting to awaken from some terrible dream.

Two Jesuits led them all back through the village toward the imposing spires of the church. When they arrived at the gravesite the cemetery was already attended by a dozen more dark-frocked priests, most of them young and clean-shaven. Gathered at a farther distance was what seemed to be the entire population of the village. Men, women, the old and the young, children pressed against their mothers' legs. Rand wondered if the priests had coerced them all to attend, or if they'd come only to satisfy their own curiosity.

The Jesuits had cleaned Dowd's and Hooper's bodies and put them into fresh uniforms, delivered from the ship. There was not enough mature wood on the island for caskets and so they were wrapped in sailcloth and carried by four marines the short distance from the church to their places of rest. Parker read a long passage from Deuteronomy that seemed to try the patience of even the Jesuits, and then he led them all in a prayer for the departed men. The Catholics bowed their heads respectfully. After Parker committed the body, Laval stepped forward to provide a brief funeral service in Latin, after which he addressed the gathered Polynesians loudly in their own tongue. His tone was stern and frightening.

"What is he saying?" Mr. Thomas said, bringing disapproving looks from the gathered priests, and from the Pelican.

Laval had obviously heard, because when he'd finished he turned to the officers and furrowed his thick eyebrows: "I am telling to the people that only death will come to those who make use of firearms."

The two men were lowered into the ground and Mr. Thomas raised and lowered his sword to signal the volleys of the seven-gun salute. Rand felt responsible, and he knew so little about either of the men who'd died, despite having sailed with them for years. He fought back tears, both of sorrow and of shame, as he thought about the threads of their lives, all of their boyhood adventures, their longings and designs, all coming to an abrupt end here at the ends of the Earth, where their graves would be trod upon in perpetuity by these Catholic idolaters and the naked brown feet of those natives they tasked with pulling the cemetery weeds.

After the embarrassment of this incident, the *Fredonia* remained at Mangareva only for a few more days, to complete some refittings in the harbor. Before raising sail, Bird took a boat to Baptiste's villa once more, at another invitation brought by Bill, who explained only that his employer would like to make a business proposal.

Curious, Bird went alone, save for his boat crew, whom he bid to wait at the small cove while he trekked up through the coffee fields with Bill. He couldn't fathom what Baptiste wanted—he had a partner in San Francisco who brought him laborers and supplies three times yearly, and Bird assumed it must have something to do with this. He was optimistic about the prospect—naval service, after all, brought more prestige than it did profit, and he'd known many officers who'd used their connections to establish themselves in more lucrative fields. As he walked through the coffee fields, watching the Chinese at their work, he thought he could do much worse than to throw his hat in with a man like Baptiste. Here in the Pacific, at the edge of the world, a man could still be the king of his own small domain.

The Frenchman was in his customary seat on the porch when Bird arrived. Bird realized that he'd never actually seen the man standing. Amazingly, he had before him a fresh bottle of Kentucky bourbon—it was unlabeled, but Bird knew it the moment it touched his lips.

He wasted no time in getting to his business. "The girl," he said. "I would purchase her from you."

Bird was caught off guard with a swallow of whiskey in his mouth, and had difficulty finding a way to get it down.

"Money is no object, I have more than I need. You will see that such an arrangement would be to the benefit of all of the parties. I offer to take her as a wife, and I can give her here a life better than anything that waits for her, this you will know is true. And you will profit very well, Lieutenant."

The thought of someone proposing marriage to Alice was more than he could comprehend. "But . . . *why?*" was all he could say.

Baptiste grew wistful. "Who can explain love? She reminds me of a girl I knew when I was young."

Bird was still fumbling for words. "I have to say . . . I am in amazement at this request. I do not know how you do it in France but in the United States we do not buy and sell white women like horses."

"I will give you forty thousand dollars of United States currency. Will you take a banknote? Or if you like I shall provide it in gold?"

The amount sent Bird into a shocked silence. He considered all that he possessed: a few thousand dollars on deposit at a savings and loan, a small two-room house in Norfolk. Everything he'd accumulated in his long and thankless career at sea. This amount of money would make him, in one swoop, a man of substance.

"You have heard her say herself that she would not remain here."

Baptiste scoffed. "You do the young woman a disservice. I wish for you to present her with my offer."

"Unequivocally, my answer is no. Good day, *Monsieur* Baptiste."

Bird hadn't expected to be returning right away, and after he'd walked alone back to his boat his knee was so shot through with pain it was all he could do to climb over the side and take a seat on the bench as his crew pushed him out into the waves. As they re-entered the harbor of Rikitea, where the *Fredonia* lay anchored, he noticed that the village again seemed curiously empty, as it had on the day of the funeral. Then he heard a sound from the direction of the church, and remembered that it was Sunday.

Father Laval was leading his flock in song, a hymn in French that Bird did not recognize, accompanied by a wheezing pump organ. The congregants did not seem to know the song either, many singing *oohs* and *aahs* in place of the words. It sounded like a room full of school children all speaking at once, without melody or rhythm, a pointless muddle of words spilling out of the church's open windows that followed him as his boat bobbed over the swells.

15.

SOUTHERN LATITUDES

Victor moved onto the foredeck, where he presented himself to Mr. Rand with a salute.

"Commander wishes to speak with you in his quarters, sir."

Rand stared at him incredulously, and found no acknowledgment of what had occurred between them. He hadn't mentioned the incident to Bird, or to anyone, and whether this was from shame at the circumstance or something else he did not know. The more he considered the events of that night, the more they seemed unreal, like a tangled dream.

"Victor, do you recall our meeting the other night in the steerage?"

"Meeting, sir?" The boy's face appeared entirely blank.

"Yes. When we collided, in the dark."

"I don't know your meaning, sir."

Rand searched him for any sign of deception or subterfuge, and found none. If the boy was play-acting, he deserved an ovation.

"Very well. You are dismissed. But we will speak of this again."

"Whatever please you, sir."

Rand made his way below and found Bird seated at his table with a glass of wine in one hand and an unlit pipe in the other. He'd been expecting this, but was surprised it had taken so long. They'd left Mangareva behind almost a week earlier. Rand saluted. Bird did not rise. He squinted at Rand, as if he'd been pulled from some deep, distant rumination.

"Mr. Rand, you have arrived."

"Indeed, sir."

"You have received the message? From my boy?"

Rand nodded. Bird seemed satisfied by this, and took a sip of his drink. "I wish to have a talk with you, Mr. Rand. About a few things. Why don't you sit?"

"I would stand."

"Very well," Bird said. "After giving careful thought to the matter, I have decided not to proceed with formal charges in response to your conduct at Mangareva. We both know how a court martial would turn out. It might put a black mark on your record, but with the influence of your father you could hope to weather that. Far be it from me to prevent the rise of another star into the heavens."

"I urge you to do whatever your duty requires of you. I request no favor."

"Nor will I be issuing formal charges for your repeated acts of insubordination. As I am sure you are aware, you have violated my orders regarding our passenger."

"Has the boy told you this?"

"It has not been difficult to figure you, Mr. Rand."

"I have only prayed with her," he finally said. Was this a lie? His face grew hot.

Bird nodded. "I expect this is true. It changes nothing."

He took a swallow of his wine and regarded Rand anew, as if he'd just entered and no words had passed between them. His lips were stained a rich purple. "Why don't you have a seat? I would like for you to pour yourself a drink. Take a cup." He motioned toward the sideboard.

"I do not imbibe, sir. I am sure you are aware of this by now."

"Oh, just have a damned drink."

"I will not. You cannot require another officer to violate his morals in that way, sir. It is outside of your authority."

"Hell's bells, but you are difficult." Bird said this and then fell into a deep silence.

Rand waited, standing with his hands clasped behind him. After a while he reminded Bird, "I await your command, sir."

"I have been at a loss, I admit, as to what to do with you. I might confine you to your quarters for the short remainder of our voyage, but I do not see what good that would do. You will be on another ship before long and there you most probably will resume this type of disrespect for your superiors." Another silence and a long sip of wine. Bird let out a little silent belch, which he stifled with a fist. Then he continued: "I have decided instead that I will endeavor to make a true man of you, Mr. Rand."

"I do not follow your meaning, sir."

"It has occurred to me, Mr. Rand, that all of our difficulties may stem from the simple fact that you lack experience. You have the fire of youth, with none of the tempering that hard use can bring. You have been in the service of your country for how long?"

"Six years, sir."

"Only six years! And already a lieutenant! It is remarkable, don't you think?"

"I would like to think that the Navy Commission has seen my ability and placed me accordingly."

"Yet, you have never learned the ropes, as we say. Due to the protection afforded by your family and position, I can only require so much from you. But know this: Before your feet touch land again, I will do my best to work you as you have never been worked before. And I wish for you to understand that I do this with no malice whatsoever. I do it to help improve you, young man. For the sake of those seamen who will serve beneath you in the future. For the Navy," he said.

He raised his glass for a toast, but then realized that it was empty, and Rand had none. Still, he attempted to drain the last few drops.

∼

Bottles of champagne were uncorked in the wardroom after Bird gave the order to sail for the Cape. Rand stood off to one side, not partaking, providing a forced smile to those who raised their glasses in his direction. Though he'd long yearned for this day, he could find no joy in the thought of finally returning home. He was too exhausted. The meaning of the Pelican's promise to *make a man of him* had soon become clear. Victor appeared before him several times per day, still seeming entirely ignorant of anything that had occurred between them, to present notes from the Lieutenant requesting that he oversee the accomplishment of endless lists of tasks: cataloging and sorting the hold, holystoning the deck, drilling the crew in the rigging until they seethed and glared at him with murder in their eyes.

In addition to this, his privilege of sleeping through the night had been unceremoniously revoked by Bird, through a bit of clever trickery meant to make the whole thing appear legitimate. Bird had circulated a note to his staff that all line officers were to be put on *watch and watch* until after the Cape had been crossed. The order hadn't named anyone specifically, but since Piper and Grady were the only other line officers, and both were already subject to this schedule, the change affected only him. He was required to attend to every other watch, allowing him no break throughout the day and night longer than four hours. The well-rested warrant officers like Harvey and Thomas commiserated with him in the wardroom and agreed that the Pelican had overstepped his bounds, but none cared enough to sign a formal complaint on his behalf.

At the end of each watch, Rand would lay in his bunk for nearly an hour, trying to calm himself, trying to sleep because he so desperately needed the rest, but unable to because of his nagging anxiety that he might not sleep at all, that time was passing and every moment he did not sleep was one which he lost forever to uselessness and misery. When he did sleep it was only shallowly, counting the strokes of the ship's bell until it called him back to duty.

He did not understand how they all did it—the seamen who'd maintained this schedule for three years, the sheet-anchor men who'd lived this way for their entire lives. Even Piper and Grady seemed to be full of pep.

To Rand, it felt like all the color was slowly being drained from the world. As they made their way south, the sea itself seemed to change its color, shifting from blue and green to gray and dark, reflecting the overcast skies they sailed beneath. He told himself that he would get used to it over time, but every day that passed he only felt further away. He stood on the deck layered in coats, fighting to keep his eyes open, wondering what was real and what was not. More than once he fell asleep standing up, for only a moment, before being startled back awake as his body began to slacken. He mumbled commands, forgot where he was and what he was doing. Sailors stood before him, awaiting orders. He did not know their names, or how they'd gotten there, or what he'd said to them only a moment before.

He began to lose things. One day, it was his Bible. It was a family heirloom, its pages almost entirely separated from the spine. It had been carried from England, almost one hundred years before, by his great-great-great grandfather. Its leather jacket and the edges of its pages had been worn to smoothness. It was full of passages that both he and his forbears had underlined in pencil, pages marked thoughtfully with lengths of ribbon, and the thought of losing it filled him with a desperate panic. He searched up and down the ship for it for an entire shift, only to find it resting atop a cannon on the gun deck where he must have absentmindedly placed it hours before. On another day, he could not locate his mother's hairbrush. He spent his entire four-hour sleeping shift overturning and replacing everything in the cabin. When he returned to the deck, he confronted Grady as he was coming off duty. "I was curious, Mr. Grady, if you had accidentally taken one of my belongings?"

"What's that?"

"One of my belongings," he mumbled again.

"Yes? What is it?"

"An ivory hairbrush."

Grady stared at him for a while and then removed his cap to show off his hair, recently cropped to a stubble by the ship's barber. He said, "Does it look as if I have any use for a hairbrush?"

He felt as if he was descending, deeper and deeper, into some nightmare realm. On one occasion, he had the sensation, though he hadn't seen it, that the ship had been passed over by a great bird, so large it blotted out the sky. Several other times, he thought he saw the captain's boy Victor, eyeing him from afar and menacingly brandishing a knife.

Ice began to gather on the uppermost yards at night. He kept the crew busy, chipping it away each morning, though even without their effort it would all melt before noon. The sailors began to supplement their uniforms with all manner of makeshift jackets, some painted over with tar to keep the water out, improvised mittens made from woolen socks. John Black, sailing into these regions for the first time, declared the air so cold he could not breathe it, and was punished for abandoning his duties to catch his breath by the warmth of the galley stove.

It became too cold for Rand to find rest even during those few hours he was afforded, and then sleep left him completely. The stove in the wardroom could not chase the chill from his cabin no matter how he stoked it. To pass the time while he was not on the watch, he sat upon his bunk with a blanket wrapped around him like some old Indian chieftain, shivering and compiling a long letter to his father that seemed to have no end. All his previous letters home had prior to this been pleasant, empty affairs, meant to be read aloud to the entire family. He'd never complained of Bird, or of his unhappiness. He did not wish to be seen as a malingerer. But this letter was addressed only to his father, and he withheld nothing. He wrote of Bird as he saw him: drunken, sullen, vengeful, entirely unfit for command. He wrote that the Lieutenant held a personal grudge against him, *due to nothing more than jealousy at our family's prominence in the Service of our country.* He complained of how he was being punished, deprived of sleep and made to work night and day.

Of Alice, he wrote: *She is kept on the ship like a slave, or worse, locked in a room with her own filth like an animal and she is not permitted any liberty. Lieutenant Bird treats her as a private plaything, refuses her the company of others. It is so much Father that I can barely stand to watch and I sorely Hope and Pray that he is one day brought to Justice . . .*

As the days passed his letter continued to grow, page after page with no end in sight. In September, they gammed with a clipper that could take their mail through Panama, but Rand did not mail it. It felt incomplete to him. He knew that there was more he wished to say, but he could not yet find the words.

16.

. . .

Bird had warned her there would be a squall; the word meant nothing to her, though. She'd known storms on the island, sometimes fierce and terrible displays. But even when the wind howled over the sea and the sky opened, she could always retreat into the protection of the forest, where the warm rains would drip down through the canopy and over her body as she lay against the soft, wet earth. Nothing could prepare her for what came: first, the temperature dropped sharply and she lay shivering beneath her blankets, with a feeling like her arms and legs were burning in a cold flame. Then the ship began to toss; gently at first, but as the swells grew the boards beneath her began to rise and fall, each time carrying her higher into the sky only to cast her into a seemingly bottomless chasm. There was a roar of water against the hull, so loud it sounded like thunder in her ears. As cold as she was, she began to sweat until her dress was drenched through and she had a terrible dizzy feeling she could not escape. She felt something stirring within and opened her mouth to retch up the contents of her stomach. Even afterwards, her insides continued to twist and contort themselves as if they sought to wring every last drop from her. This was a *squall*, she thought, and it was terrible.

She pressed herself up onto her elbows to search in the darkness for something she'd hidden beneath the thin mattress of her bunk: it was a stiff picture card, which showed a line of men in coats standing in front of a building. Bird had let her keep it, thinking she admired the picture. But he didn't realize how clever she was—none of them did. She had recognized at once that the picture card could serve as a key, one with the power to free her from her prison. She'd learned to listen from her cabin until the sound of men moving on the decks above and the blowing of whistles subsided and there was only the mournful and occasional ringing of the bell, and at these times she would slip the card between door and jam, slide it upwards until she could feel the bolt lift from its catch, and walk out upon the ship, taking care to avoid the lamplights of the sentries. In the great dark belly of the vessel there were spaces that men rarely came to, black aisles of lumber and crates and folded sailcloth. There, she could move freely, her eyes adjusting to that dim light that filtered from above.

Only once was she discovered; she had come upon a man down there, in the shadows cast by the single lamp near the ladder, crouching behind some barrels as he rubbed his hands together and blew into them. His skin was dusky and covered with black lines and shapes. When he saw her, he stopped what he was doing and fixed his bright white eyes upon her. They did not speak, but something in his manner convinced her that he wouldn't reveal her—she understood that he was hiding from the others, just as she was. She'd approached him slowly, in curiosity, and he'd permitted her to trace her fingers along those dark lines that encircled his body.

Near to her cabin, there was a long room with a table and many doors. She would sometimes listen at the doors for the sounds of men sleeping, and then quietly enter to search through their belongings for things that interested her, a button or a golden ring. Behind one door, she'd even once discovered Mr. Rand, lying beneath his blankets, his mouth agape. For a time, he'd come to pray with her, but then he stopped because she'd done a wicked thing: she'd kissed him, when she was already married to another. On that night, she stood over his sleeping form for some time, trying to determine if she still felt the same desire for him—she could clearly remember the pull of his warm body and soft voice, her fervent wish for him to wrap her in his arms, to comfort and protect her as William had—but found she felt nothing at all. Later, she would remember this night and think this was the last time she saw him.

Whenever she returned to her cabin, she always carefully held the bolt up with the card as she shut the door and allowed it to fall into place behind her.

∼

She stumbled through the narrow corridor, keeping a hand on the wall to steady her as the ship pitched. Her dress was stained with her own filth and as she walked, she lifted it from her shoulders and dropped it behind her onto the boards. In her sickness, she'd forgotten to latch the cabin door after leaving, and it hung open. Her piglet emerged cautiously behind her, and after sniffing at the discarded dress it turned to scurry away into the darkness.

She reached the ladder and found herself climbing upwards. She'd never before dared to move on the upper decks at night, but now she thought the only thing that could cure her terrible sickness would be to witness the squall; to leave behind this stifling darkness and be among the wind and the rain.

The gun deck was silent and empty, all the ports buttoned up against the weather and the cannons waiting quietly in rows like soldiers. Bird's cabin door was shut fast and she could see a small light beneath his door. She continued to climb, clinging to the ladder as the ship swayed and fell, until she reached the hatch that would permit her above. But she could not see anything through the grating. She poked her fingers up through the spaces to feel the rasp of canvas. The rain beat against it and she could read its tumult on her fingertips.

Then there was a light. She dropped to the deck and hid herself between two cannons until the sentry passed below and the darkness was again complete. The ship rolled to one side and the sea hit the hull with a sound like a thunderclap. She could hear the roar of water rushing on the boards above her, and then the splashing sound of it pouring through a hatch somewhere at the fore. She felt her way toward the sound, using the ends of the cannons to guide her, until there was cold water on her feet. Above, more of the frigid sea sluiced through the grating and ran over her as she climbed. She put a hand against the grating and managed to slide it aside; then, she was above.

All around her the storm raged; wind filled her ears and tiny hailstones pelted her as she rose to her feet on the shifting deck. No sails hung on the yards, and only a few lanterns lit the night like dull stars. Above her there was nothing but a dark void. The sea too was black and barely visible, so that it appeared as if the ship was the only thing in the world that remained, tossed upon nothingness.

Standing there naked, she finally felt nothing—not cold nor the wind nor the sting of frozen rain against her body. The storm had consumed her, and there was no part left to feel anything at all.

Then she saw the barely visible form of a man, wrapped in coats and scarves. Her instinct was to run, but something about the way he stood motionless made her pause; the figure was so still that she might have thought it was not a man at all, but some kind of stuffed scarecrow or a snowman, like the ones she'd built with her mother as a child, if it hadn't been for the eyes dimly staring at her from beneath its woolen cap.

They regarded one another for only a moment before a wave crashed over the deck, and a rush of icy water carried her away.

For as long as Alice could remember, things had been disappearing. It had begun in the dim fog of her childhood, a time she could hardly remember and which felt no more real than a dream. She had lived in a beautiful house then, with many rooms and carved wooden bannisters along the stairs. Then she went on a ship with her father and mother and first their beautiful house and then Boston itself had disappeared over the edge of the world. Her father told her that in California they would have a new house. But before they had come to California, father and mother had disappeared as well. She thought of them often, drifting away from the ship in a small boat with the captain and some others, bobbing over the swells as they vanished into the night. Sometimes she even forgot their faces.

After her father and mother were sent away, Alice had fled from the wicked men who remained on the ship. She'd seen them all before: sailors hardly noticed amidst all the excitement of the sea voyage, but on that terrible night they'd been changed into devils, dark-eyed and jeering, carrying with them sharp knives and boat hooks and grinning at her in the moonlight. They taunted her as she ran, snatched at her dress and her hair. There had been no direction for her to go but up, to escape them. She'd climbed into the rigging, up and up, afraid to look back. Even as a small girl she'd been able to climb, clambering upon the furniture and among the boughs of the pear tree in the yard. He father had teased her that she was like an orang-utan. She saw nothing but the ropes and spars around her as she moved into the night sky under a bright moon. At the top of the mast she'd come to a little platform and she'd pulled herself up to hide there, her knees tucked against her chest, afraid that at any moment she would see the hand of a man clasp the ledge or grab her leg to throw her into the sea. But none arrived. Where had they gone, her pursuers? It was as if they'd disappeared, too.

For three days she remained there atop the mast, not daring to look over the edge. It was as if the ship beneath her had ceased to exist and there was nothing left except for her, balanced between sea and sky. During the days she burnt in the sun and at night she shivered under the stars. She felt hunger and thirst as her lips became dry and cracked. She imagined that she was perched in the eye of a great needle that bobbed up and down as it sewed the water to the heavens.

It was on the third day that William had come. The man who would be her husband. She sensed only that someone brought water to her lips. Then slowly she could see his face, framed by his curly ringlets of hair, and she could hear his soothing words. She need not fear, he told her. The men below would not harm her. *They are a rough lot*, he said, *but they have chosen the Lord, and for that I give thanks* . . . He carried her down and laid her upon a wide cool feather bed in the dimness of the captain's cabin. He nursed her and put damp rags on her head until her fever subsided, and spoke to her with great joy of the message he had received from an angel: He had been given a special task by the Lord, to find a new land and begin the world again, in accordance with all of the holy principles; to create a kingdom that would last forever, where nothing would ever die. And there was more, he whispered as he brushed a tangle of hair from her forehead. The angel had also shown him a vision of her. He had known her face and her voice before he'd ever seen her or set foot upon this ship. Because she had been appointed to be his queen.

17.

APOCALYPSE

Rand closed his eyes and opened them. Closed and opened them again, his vision blurred by the ice gathering in his eyelashes. She was still there. He thought at first that she must be some kind of mirage brought on by the storm, or a vision of lust come to tempt him, because she appeared as she did in his imaginings, unclothed, as if the storm didn't touch her. It seemed to him that somehow, in his exhaustion, his dreams had found a way to walk into the world.

He realized with mounting horror that she was no dream only when a wave crashed over the deck and knocked her from her feet. He grabbed onto a shroud as the frothing water came over him and watched helplessly as it carried her across the boards, slammed her into the bulwark, and then sloshed over the side. A dizzying grief: he thought she'd gone over with it. But when the ship pitched and the waters dissipated, she was still there, wet and struggling to rise. She had come for *him*, Rand thought. Because he'd thoughtlessly encouraged her love, and then left her there alone, without any word of explanation. And if she was swept into the sea, that too would be his fault.

He tried to run but he'd been out in the cold for hours; his feet were numb save for a dull pain from the vicinity of his toes. He called her name but his voice was muffled by his scarf and then lost in the storm.

There was pandemonium as every man on the watch joined the chase. They pulled themselves along, holding onto lines and pelted by hailstones, as she dashed across the tilting deck, the only living thing in a world of slow phantoms. She leapt out of their reach as sailors lunged and slid and went sprawling on the boards, until finally several managed to encircle her at the foot of the mainmast. Before any could grab her, she turned to take hold of a shroud and within seconds had climbed beyond the feeble light of their lamps. Mr. Piper screamed at the panicked middies to find sailcloth, so that they might use it as a rescue trampoline.

Rand felt himself being grabbed, shaken. A sailor had hold of his shoulders and was shouting at him. It was John Black, water running over his tattooed face. Icy rain drowned them both.

"I'll fetch 'er down, sir!"

The Maori was big as an ox and one of the most sure-footed men in the rigging, but Rand worried his frightful appearance might startle her and cause her to lose her grip. He surveyed the others. Downturned faces, eyes that would not meet his. None wished to climb the mast in that storm. He felt the Holy Spirit filling his frozen limbs with strength. The Lord had given him this task. She had come because of him, and it would be his responsibility to bring her down. He ordered that none should follow but couldn't know if they heard.

He grabbed a line and pulled himself up into the storm. He'd only climbed a mast once before, at the midshipmen's academy, on a ship resting at anchor in a calm harbor. It was not so difficult, he'd thought at the time. After he'd rung the bell at the top, he'd not descended immediately, but had paused there, to survey all the roofs of the houses along the harbor, the treetops and little streets he could see with their miniscule bustle, feeling a deep sense of peace in that scene, and knowing he was so high above it.

He groped upwards now through sleet and ice, feeling for the yards, his eyes aslant against the wind. He paused on his knees upon the main-top to work his stiff fingers. The ship lurched and he hugged the mast as a wave rushed over the deck. He cast a glance downwards to see the little lights of the sailors scattered by its force, some men struggling to secure a boat that had come loose. He braced himself against the mast and stood to reach for another line. As he continued to ascend with the waters surging beneath, it felt to him almost as if the ship was no longer there. There was only this mast, protruding from the waves. The endless task of pulling himself upwards.

It was then that he experienced a kind of vision, something he could only consider a visitation of grace sent to strengthen him: in it, he saw himself in the future, as the pastor of his own congregation. He was standing in a tidy kitchen, a small stone church house visible through the window. The sun was shining and he was not alone. She was there, too, but with no mark of wildness on her features, only softness and care. She stood at the counter in a plain housedress, preparing a meal for him and the children. And she turned to him and said, *Truly, you are the one who has saved me.*

He finally caught sight of her naked, scrambling legs above him, then her back arching as she reached for a higher line. He was only a few yards beneath her—such a short distance to close. He called her name again but couldn't hear his own voice.

At that height, every yard was coated with ice. He reached up to grab another and as he strained to pull himself up, he felt his foot slip. For a brief moment he hung suspended there, both feet kicking to find purchase, with the terrible knowledge that his grip would not hold. That he would fall to his death. And from a small pulpit within his own heart, he told himself: it did not matter. It did not matter if he died. It did not matter if they were both tossed into the sea, because their souls had been prepared. Sorrow was an illusion, and God had no end.

His fingers lost the yard and he felt himself pass into emptiness. All through his life, when he rehearsed his own death in his mind, he'd imagined that the Heavens would part to accept him, revealing golden light, a chorus of angels. But there was nothing. He fell an impossible distance through an impossible space, waiting for the bell that would wake him, and bring him back to a more familiar world.

18.

Portsmouth, January 1857

Snow was falling as two boats pulled the *Fredonia* out of the deepwater channel of the Elizabeth River, toward the Gosport Shipyard. Thick chunks of ice clogged the Chesapeake Bay and had made their last few days' progress difficult and slow.

The old familiar wharves and buildings rolled by under Bird's gaze, all blanketed with snow. It was a peaceful scene, but he noticed at once that something had changed. Portsmouth displayed none of the usual activity of a busy port, even at this time of year. There were few ships at anchor, fewer still entering or leaving the channel. No carriage wheels or horses' hooves disturbed the snow gathered on the streets that ran up to the waterfront. The massive drydocks of the Gosport Yard were empty and silent. Only one other ship rested at anchor, and the sight of it caused Bird to cringe: it was the *Antioch*. Three years prior, he'd known it to be under the command of Captain Lucas Rand, elder brother to his deceased first lieutenant.

Rand's death had hung like a cloud over the remaining days of the voyage. Christmas, as they'd crossed the Gulf of Mexico, was celebrated only with a plum duff and an extra tot of grog for the crew. At the New Year, sixteen bells were rung and Fledge had proposed a toast on the quarterdeck. *To dear acquaintances, old and new*, he said, raising his glass. *Both those we shall soon see again and those we shall not.* His eyes had flashed at the others with hidden meaning and Bird wondered if this was some form of sly admonishment. They all blamed him for Rand's death, he knew, but they said nothing. At least not within his hearing. And for his part, Bird consoled himself with the knowledge that he did not require their approval. Only their obedience, and even that not for much longer. They had slowly sipped their Champagne in silence as they all stared out into the fog, waiting for some familiar sign of home to heave into view.

For two days after their arrival in Portsmouth, the *Fredonia* was abustle as stores were tallied and unloaded and the ship thoroughly scrubbed and polished for her surrender. The crew were paid off and released, no doubt to squander their years of earnings as quickly as possible in dockside taverns. The officers nearly all fled as well, to be housed in the new officers' quarters at Gosport. Of them all, only Whitlocke elected to remain on the ship to await his orders, not out of any fidelity toward his commander, but only because the old Puritan preferred to avoid any hint of extravagance.

Rand's belongings were ferried over to the *Antioch*, along with a note expressing Bird's condolences. His sentiments were sincere. He well remembered the sting of losing a brother. His older brother, Laird, had always been the old man's favorite. He'd been thrown from a horse right before his sixteenth birthday. A few days after he was put in the ground, right next to their mother, Bird had left the farm for good, hiked all the way to Norfolk with nothing but an apple and a jackknife, ready to give himself over to the sea. He could not bear to remain there alone to suffer the old man's disappointment.

Bird spent the days following the *Fredonia*'s arrival preparing his reports and strolling on the now-silent deck. Those few tranquil days on the empty ship offered a peace he'd not known in a long while. The snowy wharves, the ice-choked harbor, the city near-silent as if time itself had frozen. He was struck by how odd it was to see the ship emptied of its crew, after three years in which it had been impossible to look in any direction and not see men gathered in every conceivable state of work or rest. He might have gone ashore, but he did not feel quite ready for that. These days resting at anchor provided him with an intermediary state to linger in, neither at sea nor truly on land, where he might prepare himself for the inevitable shock of the transition. As challenging as life at sea could be, somehow that which was lived on land had always seemed to him to be denser, more complicated and difficult to navigate.

He retained a small staff to attend to his needs: only Skully the cook to prepare his meals and of course Victor. He sent the boy ashore to post his letters and retrieve all the newspapers he could find, which Bird devoted himself to with zeal. He read every article, every advertisement. He soon learned of the tragedy that had befallen the city: an outbreak of yellow fever, on both sides of the river. Thankfully it had come to an end, but only after leaving the population much diminished. He read of the cold spell the entire Northeast had fallen under, railroad accidents, endless legislative debate; the British, in what was surely an act of hubris, had gone to war with both Persia and China at the same time. Everything was recorded there, side by side, from the most momentous events of the world to local trivialities. Right after reading of a terrible earthquake in California, he read the words: *A great mouse hunt recently came off in this vicinity, consisting of two parties with forty men a side, with a large number of dogs, which succeeded in killing, during a day's sport, 959 rats and 31¼ bushels of mice . . ."*

Often, for as long as his ears could stand the cold, he stood on the deck with Alice and her pig, which had been rescued from the forecastle on the night of her escape by Mr. Hooper, where several sailors were plotting to make a meal of it. The animal was grown so large now—over five feet in length and easily topping two hundred pounds—that it had to be penned in the galley, but Skully had devised a ramp so that it might access the upper deck when Alice wished to take it for a stroll. It followed her around like a faithful dog as she walked, her wrapped in an old coat of Bird's that was so weathered it had faded to gray from its original blue.

He had moved Alice into his own small sleeping chamber, for the warmth. He hardly ever used it anyway—he always wound up sleeping upright in the armchair in his dayroom. While cleaning out her old quarters, Victor discovered a number of surprising objects that she'd hidden around the cabin: a small golden cross, two or three coat buttons, a watch fob, a gold coin. Where or how she had gotten hold of it all he couldn't fathom. He almost smiled to see that she had taken possession of Dr. Mallory's lost set of teeth. The largest item was an ivory hairbrush of very fine workmanship. Probably worth a few dollars, he mused. He knew he should punish her for the thievery, but she'd already suffered so much. If these things brought her some comfort, he thought, let her keep them. He put them all into a pail, which he left for her to discover in her new quarters.

The Elizabeth froze around the *Fredonia*. A few skaters from both shores ventured out onto the ice, eager to shake off the gloomy cloud of the plague with old-fashioned winter cheer. Despite the harsh cold that reddened her cheeks, Alice spent much time on the deck watching them arc and glide in circles in the distance, her breath making warm clouds, the pig sniffing at her empty fists for corn.

"Have you ever skated on the ice?" he asked her.

"Yes," she answered. "When I was a child."

"Perhaps we will be able to get you some skates, so you can join them." He indicated the happy skaters.

"No," she said.

"But why not?"

"I don't like it." He could see her carefully choosing her words, struggling to express herself more clearly. "I like to watch them. But I am afraid the ice will break."

"The ice is thick enough," Bird reassured her. "You can see there, they have been skating all day and the ice has not broken."

"That is because I am praying for them," she replied.

~

Bird was in his cabin when he heard a commotion without. He emerged to find Victor with a bloodied nose, standing opposite an unfamiliar boy of roughly the same age, if a bit larger. Victor instantly stiffened and wiped at his face.

"What is this?"

"Orders from the Commodore," the new boy said, and handed Bird an envelope. He dismissed them both, but made a note to himself that he would mention the incident when he next spoke to the Commodore.

The letter announced the date of a court of inquiry, which would be tasked to investigate the girl's situation, and requested that he forward all relevant materials for their review. This much he'd expected. But he was unpleasantly surprised to find that the court had been given a supplemental purpose: to examine his conduct over the course of the mission, in order to discover if there had been any *actionable offense or breach of duty on the part of the Lieutenant Commander, due to several concerns raised*. Concerns? Raised by whom? His face turned red and he felt a familiar rage turning in his stomach. He immediately suspected some sort of political machination . . . Rand's family might have instigated some sort of play to hold him accountable for the death. Did they intend to court-martial him?

Flustered, Bird immediately penned a businesslike letter of reply informing Commodore Price he would do all in his power to help the court reach its stated goals, though his full report on the girl was not complete and thus could not yet be delivered. He gave the letter to Victor, with the sly admonition, "Put a stone in your pocket this time, and if that boy tries to fight with you again, hit him in the face with it."

~

After she'd been carried down from the mast by John Black, shivering and insensible, Alice had not spoken for weeks. She'd shown no reaction whatsoever when Bird informed her of Mr. Rand's death, though he'd told her in no uncertain terms that it had been directly caused by her disobedience.

Then, when she did begin to speak again, he sensed that something had changed. Some secret willfulness had vanished; she was like a taut line that had gone slack. With enough laudanum in her, she would begin to babble almost incoherently—names, fragments of incidents with no connection or context. By the time they docked in Portsmouth, he was able to establish several important facts, including both the name of her ship and what he assumed was its port of origin, or at least a place where she'd resided. He'd also begun to realize that what she had carried with her from the island was not wildness, as he'd thought, nor was it idiocy, as Mallory had guessed. He had come to suspect that it was madness.

He'd discovered her family name quite by accident. Each day he would scratch a simple lesson for her onto a slate, usually just drawing and naming various letters and numerals. He thought at first the experiment was a failure, because she showed no interest. But one day, in frustration, he rose from the table and stood gazing out the aft windows. He heard scratching behind him and assumed she had taken up the chalk to make marks upon the slate, as she sometimes did. It was never anything revealing, or even comprehensible: jagged lines, sometimes a crooked shape, as if she was only pleased to see the action of the chalk leaving its mark. He turned to scold her and was shocked into silence when he saw the slate. In a childish scrawl, it said *ALICE KELLY*.

"Your name is Alice Kelly . . ." he asked slowly.

She nodded once.

"Was your husband named Kelly?" he asked.

"No," she said. She rubbed two fingers across the name, smudging and making a path through the letters.

He tried to gently ply her for more. "But you have told me that you married. When a woman marries, she takes her husband's name. Tell me your husband's name, and we shall put it here," he said.

Her face darkened. "No," she said. She raised a hand to push the slate away like an emptied plate.

In the weeks leading up to the inquiry, Bird prepared his report. He was able to corroborate and augment what little he had through correspondence with the current harbormaster of Boston, a genial man named Jeremiah Heep, who had been in his post for some years and luckily kept meticulous records. Bird was not much of a wordsmith, but he admired his finished product nonetheless:

In late May of 1850, the ship Lady Fortune *departed Boston for San Francisco via the Cape Horn route. A 500-ton, three-masted clipper, she had completed two previous voyages along that route, in 126 and 133 days respectively, as supported by the advertising cards attached as exhibits a. and b., courtesy of the Culver Dispatch Line. Her Captain was George Kinney, who held a reputation as a stern and reliable man.*

Among the passengers was one Thomas Kelly, occupation listed as a manufacturer of men's handkerchiefs and table linens, along with wife and daughter. Alice Kelly, the daughter, has dictated or confirmed much of what is to follow, and to all available information she may be assumed to be the last person to survive these events.

At an undetermined point in the voyage, it seems that there took place some form of uprising among the crew, though the precise cause of this event is unknown. Those few details of the journey which she can provide are unimportant and do little to clarify these matters.

She can recall their crossing into Pacific waters, as it was celebrated and commented upon by the crew. It was at an unspecified time following this that the passengers were woken in the night by armed crewmembers and made to come out upon the deck. She recalls that her mother was in fear and was not permitted to dress, and her father was roughly handled by the men when he tried to display his tickets.

It is my belief that some faction among the crew had formed under the leadership of a man she has named William. The crew list corroborates that there was indeed a seaman who gave his name as William H. Christensen. He was listed as a greenhand. It was most probably this William Christensen who gave the command to put Captain Kinney, his loyal crewmembers, and all the passengers into two longboats, each secured with an amount of food and fresh water meant to bring them safely to land. He also called for the girl Alice Kelly to be taken from her mother and kept upon the ship in the company of the mutineers. His reason for this act remains obscure, but it was assuredly not honorable.

It is assumed that Captain Kinney, along with all the other passengers and crew who were put off the ship, have perished. Surely if Kinney had been fortunate or skilled enough to arrive on some shore, then by now his story would be known.

As far as it can be determined, the mutineers appear to have had the design of forming a permanent colony on an island, in order to live in accordance with religious principles touted by W. Christensen, who may have been some form of lay preacher.

The Lady Fortune *did land at the isle I have described in my previous report, which for the sake of convenience I have referred to with the nickname of "Bird's Land" bestowed upon it by my boat crew. At some point, under mysterious circumstances, the ship burned at anchor. All seem to have eventually perished, save for Miss Kelly, who persisted alone until I discovered her while on a watering expedition. The ship's log of the* Fredonia *contains further details on the state of the girl when she was discovered, &c.*

Note: *Miss Kelly has often and repeatedly made the claim that she was wed to W. Christensen and considers him to have been her lawful husband. This is certainly not the case. Any mockery of the ceremony of holy matrimony which occurred was obviously enacted without the presence of any authority which custom would require, including the ship's legitimate Captain Kinney, and should thusly be disregarded by this honorable Court.*

Thank you.

A few days after the arrival of the Commodore's letter, Bird discovered another visitor skulking on the docks near to the ship. He was ruddy-cheeked and spectacled, and wore a woolen coat but lacked a hat, despite the weather. His ears were so red that Bird at first assumed him to be some wandering vagabond, and he regarded the man for some time from his high perch on the quarterdeck, wondering how he'd gained access to the shipyard. Noticing Bird's attention, the man straightened himself and called up, "This is the *Fredonia*, is it not?"

"It is."

"I wish to speak with Captain Bird, on an important matter."

"I am Lieutenant Commander Bird. And with whom do I have the pleasure of speaking?"

"Mr. August Kind, on behalf of the *Richmond Dispatch*."

When he'd boarded, Bird noticed that the man's thick spectacles distorted his eyes, giving him a slightly monstrous, fishlike appearance. He presented a folded clipping from his breast pocket and pressed it into Bird's hand. "Is there any truth to this report?" Bird almost scolded him for not saying "sir" and then caught himself—the man was a civilian, of course. He scanned the article, yellowed and possibly many months old:

> THE FEMALE ROBINSON CRUSOE – The following information has been furnished by Captain Amos Snow of New Bedford, Mass., who reports a curious encounter in the South Seas. The whaler *Sea-Witch* departed 1852 with Capt. Snow as master and Edward Brigby as mate, and spent four years abroad. After a profitable voyage and with 600 barrels in her hold, she came to Nukahiva and heard a tale from an American naval officer that could rival Melville and Defoe's popular stories for drama. Captain Bird, of the U.S. *Fredonia*, reported that he had rescued a true "cast-away" who had been living alone on a desert isle,

and that this wretched soul was not even a "he" – this was no hardy seaman but instead a female child born under the *stars and stripes!* What is even more astonishing, Captain Snow reports that this young lady is said to have lived like a wild beast of the forest, without a stitch of clothing and running upon *all fours* . . .

"It's all true," he said as he returned the article. "More or less."

"She is here? On the ship?" Kind peered over Bird's shoulder as if searching for her on the empty deck.

"She is below," Bird answered. "And her name is Alice Kelly. You may write that down."

Kind fumbled open a pocket journal to make the note. "That article was printed across the country," he said as he wrote. "And I have been anxiously waiting to speak with you." He looked up. "Am I the first?"

"The first . . . ?"

"The first to speak with you?"

It took Bird a moment to process what he meant. Then he said, "Oh, the first newspaperman, yes."

"If you would permit it, I would very much like to have an interview with Miss Kelly, for the edification of our readers."

He considered that it would be a boon to have the press in his pocket, if the court of inquiry were to turn against him. But he was in no hurry. He would wait until he knew their strategy, so he could best determine how to counter it.

"We will certainly be able to accomplish that," he said. "In fact, there are a great many things I'd like to set straight in the record, concerning my discovery of the girl, and I can assure you that you will be the first one to hear about it . . ." He could see Kind's anticipation rising, and then added, "but unfortunately, at present I find myself occupied by my duties. Won't you call again in two weeks' time?"

Kind regarded the empty deck, the bare masts, with a look of puzzlement. Bird offered him a polite smile.

∼

Shortly before the inquiry, Bird finally dared to venture into Portsmouth. He walked through a crunching inch of snow that had accumulated in flurries overnight. Many houses and buildings were boarded up, emptied either by death or the flight of those with money enough to relocate themselves when the plague struck. Occasional windows were fogged by the warm stoves within, a few bundled forms trudged in the streets. Ragamuffin children huddled on every corner and in every doorway, begging for pennies.

His destination was a dressmaker's shop, thankfully still where he remembered it. Facing the window display, he felt a sudden fear, a kind of panicked embarrassment particular only to men when faced with the accoutrements of the opposite sex. Bonnets and lengths of lace ribbon were arranged in the front window, flowers made of silk and wire to brighten the display. Inside, he could see two females he took to be clerks and a single customer browsing a rack of ready-made dresses. The idea that he must enter this place and communicate somehow with these creatures seemed so much more frightening to him than anything he had ever faced at sea.

He cringed at the sound of the bell on the door. All three occupants turned to momentarily regard him, and then mercifully went back to their business as he wandered, lost, among their wares. The shop contained an overwhelming number of options: dresses of satin and taffeta, linen and wool, those with floral patterns and those that were plain, in a rainbow of colors from white to deep indigo. There were items whose function he could not even identify: a few looked to him most like harnesses for some exceedingly delicate animal. Did she require a petticoat, or was this unnecessary for a girl of her age? He took a bonnet and nervously turned it in his hands until one of the shop girls asked if he required assistance.

"You are shopping for your wife? Or your daughter?"

"My daughter," he heard himself say. It was simpler that way. It required fewer words.

"How old is she?"

Where to even begin? He offered a hand to indicate her height.

The shopgirl was merciful; she required nothing else of him as she swept around the shop selecting items to lay on the countertop: a choice of linen dresses (*dark colors for winter*, she explained . . . Bird was thankful he'd never had to navigate such complications), a bonnet and shoes with silver buckles, as well as a lengthy chemise and two sets of knickers.

On the morning of the inquiry, he presented Alice with a parcel wrapped in tissue paper and finished with a bow.

"A gift for you," he said.

She unfurled the paper and placed the items onto the floor before her, one at a time. She touched and regarded each piece without emotion. Beneath the coat she'd inherited from Bird, she still wore the blue dress she'd gotten on Mangareva, her only article of clothing, stained and threadbare from the months of wear.

"It is time for you to be a lady," he urged her. "Can you dress yourself? I can have a woman come to assist you."

He had no idea how he might accomplish this in the shipyard, but was relieved when she answered, "I will do it."

He waited without for some time, listening to her shuffling within his sleeping chamber. Finally, she emerged wearing the new dress, blue like the last but a deeper blue, less of the sky and more the color of deep water, with a crisp white collar. She was holding the shoes, one in each hand. He noticed with surprise that her cheeks were red. He quickly realized that she was ashamed. He did not say a word, but took them from her, and bent to slip them on her feet. As he fastened the buckles, he felt a pang of unexpected emotion. His mind drifted to the vague image of the daughter he'd never met. If she had lived, how many countless times would he have repeated this act? As it was, it was an unfamiliar motion; his fingers fumbled with the clasps.

There was a second part to his gift. After visiting the dressmaker's, he'd gone into Clark's Department Store, whose shelves and racks he'd found only sparsely populated, to purchase her a new woolen coat and mittens. She allowed him to replace the weathered gray jacket she'd been wearing, but would not consent to wear the mittens, and so he gave them to Victor, who, in his freezing quarters in the steerage, was somewhat more grateful for the gift.

~

The inquiry was to be held at the Spottswood Hotel, in Portsmouth. A sly maneuver, Bird thought. He would have expected it to take place upon another ship, but with the *Antioch* the only vessel at the shipyard they no doubt wished to avoid any appearance of conflicting interests. He stewed on this as a hired coach carried them across the bridge to Crawford Street. Alice sedately watched the town slide by out the coach's window. If she was excited to return to the land of her birth, she did not show it. As the coach rumbled over the cobbles toward their destination, her breath fogged the glass and she turned her attention instead to the brass buttons sewn into the door's upholstery.

The hotel was sleepy and warm, with only two patrons in the taproom and a great fire roaring in a fireplace wider than the span of a man's arms. The hotelier was a congenial man named Swanson, with a bristling moustache and a gravy-stained apron. He brought Alice a glass of milk and Bird a hot toddy. He'd foregone his usual morning whiskey, thinking it prudent to appear sober before the court, but was thankful to have something strong pushed into his hands.

After some time, the hotelier showed them up to a cozy second-floor chamber, the curtains closed to contain the room's warmth. Two gaslamps gave the room a soft glow. The three officers of the court were already assembled there in full dress: Commodore Price as the president, flanked by Captains Morris and Wood. Their uniforms were all festooned with more medals and epaulets than Bird's. Price was well-advanced in years now—one of the few remaining officers who'd seen service in 1812, the last real war if you discounted the Mexican fiasco—and time seemed to have mellowed him. He acknowledged their arrival by slumping in his chair like a sack of apples.

Bird led Alice to a seat and took the one beside her. The two rows of chairs meant for witnesses and audience were otherwise completely empty. The hotelier seated himself at a smaller table next to the officers of the court. Bird wondered if he was waiting there to take their lunch requests. A clerk sat off to one side at a writing desk. His quill began to move as Price addressed the room:

> Price – As no more suitable candidate was available, Mr. Swanson, the proprietor of this establishment, who has read some law, will be serving as judge advocate. I will remind everyone that this is not a trial, and that the position of judge advocate is, in this court, only a formality.

For nearly an hour after this they engaged in various official rites: the order of Secretary Dobbin establishing the court's authority was read in its entirety, after which the judges were sworn, the hotelier was sworn, the clerk was sworn, Bird was sworn, and they attempted to swear Alice with only moderate success. When he sensed Alice beginning to shift in her chair, Bird placed a hand on her shoulder to still her. He understood her impatience. He could barely sit through this nonsense himself.

> Price – Due to the unprecedented nature of these proceedings, I will suggest that we proceed by the issues. We will deal first with the situation of Miss Alice Kelly, and tomorrow we shall address remarks that have been made concerning irregularities in the command of the ship *Fredonia*. Unless there are any who object to this?
> Bird – I object.
> Price – Upon what grounds?

Bird – Where is the complainant?
Price – There is no specific complainant involved with this inquiry.
Morris – We have been tasked by Secretary Dobbin simply to establish certain facts, and to make recommendations.
Bird – If there is no complainant, then who has made any "remark" concerning my conduct?
Price – What?
Bird – Who has made the suggestion that my conduct was inappropriate?
Wood – There has been no such suggestion.
Bird – You just said there have been remarks.
Price (*to Wood*) – What is he saying?
Wood – There have been remarks, but not suggestions.
Bird – I would like it to be noted that I find all of this to be rather unorthodox.
(*Wood turns to clerk*)
Wood – Let it be noted that the Lieutenant finds things unorthodox.

Bird was invited to read his report into the record. They listened with blank faces. When he was finished, Morris asked to have one other item added to the record: the island at the coordinates Bird described in the ship's log had been identified as "Biscuit Island," three hundred miles northeast of Tahiti.

Bird – Biscuit Island?
Morris – Yes, that is it.
Bird – And who has given it that name?
Morris – I do not believe that is a matter of record. Though we have checked your coordinates on all the charts we have housed at Gosport, and where there is an island shown in that location, it is Biscuit.

Bird – That is not much of a name. Can we be absolutely sure that this Biscuit Island is the same island?
Morris – They are recorded at the same coordinates.
Bird – Yes, but can we be absolutely sure they are the same island?
Wood – It seems that the lieutenant wishes for us to progress into questions of metaphysics . . .
(*Laughter among the officers of the court*)

They questioned her later in the morning. Bird had counseled her on how to address the court, but her attention was directed toward her feet. On the buckles of her shoes, which she was pleased with.

Morris – Please state your name.
Kelly – Alice.
Morris – Please state your full name.
(*Pause*)
Morris – Do you affirm that you are the Alice Kelly referred to in the report we have heard?
Kelly – Yes.
Morris – Miss Kelly. This court presumes that you are the last living person connected with these events we have just heard of. Is that statement agreeable to you?
(*Long pause*)
Morris – Miss Kelly, do you agree with the statement I have made?
(*Kelly looks to Bird; Bird nods*)
Kelly – Yes.
Morris – Can you confirm for the court that you were aboard this ship, *Lady Fortune*?
(*Kelly nods. Morris makes a motion to the clerk, who notates*)

Morris – And can you confirm that there was a mutiny aboard that ship?

(*Pause, private conversation between Bird and Kelly*)

Wood – Lieutenant Bird, we would ask that you do not coach the girl in her responses.

Bird – I am not coaching her.

Wood – What are you doing, then?

Bird – I am encouraging her to answer.

Wood – Well, then we would ask you not to encourage her.

Morris – Miss Kelly, can you confirm that some of the crew of this ship *Lady Fortune* took unlawful control of the vessel, and put the captain and many passengers, including your own family, off the ship?

(*Long pause*)

Kelly – Yes.

Wood – Can you provide us with the names of any of these men?

(*Long pause*)

Morris – You need not fear, young lady. The men who did this cannot harm you here.

(*Long pause*)

Price – I would remind you that if you do not provide a response, you will be held in contempt of this court.

Bird – I would remind the court that Miss Kelly is not a Navy man. You are speaking to a child.

Price – I do not need you to tell me what a child is. I have fathered eighteen of them.

Morris – Miss Kelly, I assure you we only seek a good outcome. This is a chance to inform us of anything you know, so that those who are responsible for this event are brought to justice.

Price (*addressing Bird*) – I am well aware of how to deal with a difficult child.

(*Morris motions to clerk, then continues*)

Morris – In your knowledge, have all the men who did this perished?
Kelly – Yes.
Morris – Did they perish on Biscuit Island?
Kelly – One died on the ship.
Morris – In what manner?
Kelly – Shot with a pistol.
Morris – And who fired this pistol?
Kelly – William.
Morris – And what was the cause of this?
Kelly – He said good day to me.
Morris (*frowning*) – A man named William has shot another man with a pistol for saying good day to you?
(*Kelly nods*)
Morris (*to clerk*) – Please mark that she has nodded in the affirmative.
(*Conference among officers of the court*)
Morris – Can you tell us more about this man you have named William?
(*Long pause*)
Price – If this was not a court room I would take you over my knee.
(*Morris motions to clerk. Further conference among officers of the court*)
Morris – Is it true, Miss Kelly, that you claim to have been wed to this man William? Can you tell us of the manner and circumstance of that?

Bird realized, a few moments before the others, that she had no intention of answering any further questions. Alice squeezed her fists at her sides and let out a whine. Bird heard water dripping and looked down to see a trickle of urine escaping from the hem of her dress and pittering beneath her.

Bird – Please, sirs. I believe she has had enough for one day. If we could excuse her?

Swanson – Shall I take her downstairs and give to her a pie?

Price dismissed them with a small, disgusted gesture. The hotelier took her by the hand and led her out. The court broke for lunch soon after, and Bird found Alice quite a bit happier downstairs, cleaned and dried off by the fire and now being stuffed with tarts by the hotelier's wife. Bird was given a plate of meatloaf and boiled potatoes.

Price, Morris, and Wood took their lunch in the court room. When the court reconvened, they were prepared to record their determination regarding these matters: They advised that the *Lady Fortune* be reported as wrecked with no other survivors. Only the government, Bird thought, could labor for an entire day just to establish things that were already known.

They were uncomfortable labeling it a mutiny, at least in the official record, due to Alice's lack of cooperation. It would not do, Price explained, to go ruining men's reputations over the disordered ramblings of a girl.

Bird asked what would become of her. He'd exhausted the avenues available to him to search out her family and had reported this all to the court: Her father had owned a manufactory, which there was record of as far back as 1837. It had closed its doors in 1849. He'd been unable to locate any living relations, or family friends who might take her on—Boston was overrun with Irish named Kelly, which made the matter difficult.

Morris – I have arranged for Miss Kelly to be lodged here at the Spottswood temporarily, until we have word on her from Secretary Dobbin.

Bird – Will she be sent to an orphanage?

Morris – It is not likely. President Pierce has taken a personal interest. He has a soft spot for the young and unfortunate.

Wood – His boy was killed in a train wreck.
(*Morris motions to clerk*)
Morris – He has established a stipend for her care, until such a time as any family can be located.
Price – On the way out of office and throwing around the public's money.
(*Morris waves a hand again at the clerk*)
Bird – But where will she go?
Morris – We can't say at the moment. Inquiries are being made in the town, if there is perhaps a childless couple.
Wood – A finishing school seems out of the question.
(*Long pause*)
Bird – If it would be acceptable to this court, I have made a promise to the girl that I would see kept.
Morris – And what is that?
Bird – She has a little pet, and I believe it is very dear to her. I've promised her that she might keep it, wherever she goes.
Price – A pet?
Morris – A kitten? Or a dog?
Wood – Or a songbird?
Bird – A swine, sirs.
Morris – We will take this into consideration, Lieutenant. Though unless she is to be housed on a farm, we cannot provide any assurances.

Exhausted and stuffed full of pastries, Alice slept in the carriage all the way back to the shipyard. She'd gotten a jam stain on her new dress; it appeared as a dark splotch on the blue just beneath the clean white collar. Bird licked his finger and tried to rub it out but only ended up making it worse. She stirred and pushed his hand away without fully waking.

On the second day of the inquiry, he was surprised to find the courtroom almost full when he arrived, and most of the faces familiar to him. There was Mr. Fledge, whispering to Mr. Thomas. A stony look from Whitlocke, who had just two days before packed his sea chest and left the ship. He'd given Bird only the necessary salute, and no parting words. Piper and Grady both appeared uncharacteristically taciturn. Grady's hair was plastered to his scalp with an unrealistic amount of pomade. The only one not among them was Mallory.

Bird had arrived alone. Alice would no longer be required, and he'd left her on the ship in the care of Victor. As he took a seat which had been reserved for him at the end of the front row, he received only an uncomfortable nod of greeting from Mr. Fledge.

Commodore Price spent a long time knocking his gavel before beginning:

> Price – We assemble today to investigate if there has been any irregularity in the command of the United States ship *Fredonia* by the Lieutenant Commander Henry Aaron Bird.
>
> Bird (*standing*) – At which I have lodged a complaint. May we have this read out to the court?
>
> Wood – Lieutenant, please, we have only just begun. All of your concerns will be heard.
>
> Bird – Yes, that is why I wish for my complaint to be read. Is this not relevant to your investigation?
>
> Morris – This is not an investigation. It is an inquiry.
>
> Bird – A sham inquiry.
>
> Price – What is this noise? To Hell with you man. I have seen your kind before and mark my words you will never make an officer.
>
> Wood – The Lieutenant is a lieutenant, Commodore.
>
> Price – I'll be damned if he is.

Morris had given up on signaling the clerk to omit the Commodore's remarks, but Bird noticed that the man seemed to know instinctively when to lay his pen down.

It was obvious from the start that they were against him. There was not a single breath of air in the room that did not call for his downfall. Witness after witness was called from his staff and asked questions of an egregiously general nature, all of which served no other purpose than to paint him as a man of low character. They spoke of him as negligent in his duties and enamored with drink; a commander who cared for nothing but sitting shut up in his dayroom to play games with a child. Grady confirmed that Bird had shown no enthusiasm for anything but feeding the girl bonbons and sequestering livestock for her amusement. Whitlocke, with beard freshly squared, claimed that for three years he did not see Bird once consult compass or sextant.

The hotelier had stoked the room's stove to an unbearable heat, Bird thought, and he could feel the air thinning, becoming harder to grasp. Even Mr. Fledge betrayed him in the end. It was revealed that the purser had for some time run an informal betting pool, on the amount of time Bird spent in his cabin each day.

They came again and again to the point of Mr. Rand. The officers unanimously attested that they believed Bird had been *working him up* as punishment for the incident at Mangareva. When they finally came to Bird, they questioned him on little else.

> Morris – How would you describe your relationship with Lieutenant Rand?
> Bird – Professional. Courteous. I do believe he looked up to me, as more than just his superior. I had great hopes for him.
> Morris – Did you ever find yourself displeased with Mr. Rand's conduct on the ship?
> Bird – Only once. I refer to the aforementioned incident of direct insubordination at Mangareva.

Morris – And at that time did you perform any punitive action?

Bird – No, I did not adjudge it necessary. Any error Mr. Rand made at that time, I attributed to his youth and inexperience, and not his character. I think he would have continued to develop into a fine officer one day, and that the service has suffered a terrible loss.

Morris – Is it true that you were working him up?

Bird – I don't understand the question. It is my duty as commander to work my officers.

Morris – We have come to understand from the ship's log and the testimony which has been given here that Mr. Rand was lost while climbing the mast. Is this correct?

Bird – Yes. I gave him no command to do so.

Morris – Do you find it odd that the first lieutenant of your ship has climbed the mast?

Bird – Odd? I think not. When you are at sea, every man must be something of a jack-of-all-trades.

Morris – Had you ever witnessed or heard of a first lieutenant climbing the mast on any other occasion?

Bird – No, I have not.

Morris – So if not "odd," you will admit at least that it was a highly unusual occurrence?

Bird – If you're going to continue suggesting words you wish me to say, we will save a bit of time if you would just fabricate my testimony.

Morris – Allow me to amend my inquiry then, Lieutenant. For what purpose did Mr. Rand climb the mast on the evening of September the 14th?

Bird – It was reported to me by Mr. Piper that he pursued Alice Kelly, who had exited her quarters in defiance of my order.

Price – Was any punitive measure taken against Miss Kelly after this event?

Bird – Miss Kelly remained confined to her quarters for as much time as was practicable without amounting, in my judgment, to a punishment that would be overly cruel.

Morris – Was it your experience that Alice Kelly was disobedient or very unruly whilst a passenger on the *Fredonia*?

Bird – Somewhat. The court must appreciate the girl's condition. She was little able to comprehend the order of the ship. Where is Dr. Mallory? I wonder why he has not been called, for he would attest to the necessity of my acts.

(*Officers of the court confer*)

Wood – Dr. Mallory has not answered the summons to attend this inquiry, and he is believed to have abandoned his commission.

Bird – Oh. I see.

Wood – Might we return to our line of questioning?

Bird – Yes, proceed.

Price – What use are further questions? It is clear to me that this man has allowed a ship of the United States Navy to be the playground of a spoiled child. I would remind you, Lieutenant, that there is little difference between a child and an animal. They both respond to the rod.

There was some further whispering among the officers of the court, a shuffling of papers on their table, something passed between Price and Wood, and finally to Morris, who held it up for all to see.

Morris – Enter into the record, a letter written by First Lieutenant Evan Rand, addressed to his father, Commodore Jonathan Rand, received by this court from his brother, Captain Lucas Rand, currently in command of the ship *Antioch*. Selections from this letter will now be read for the court by Mr. Wood.

By the time the court broke for lunch, their assassination of Bird's character was complete. He did not have the years left to weather such an attack. They had destroyed his reputation, and even if he wasn't drummed out of the service, he would certainly never be permitted to rise above the rank of lieutenant. He would die, he realized, with only a single epaulet on his coat.

He tried to settle himself with this idea as he descended to the taproom. The hotelier's wife, a stout woman of Polish descent, carried out trays of hot meat and onion pies. Price, Morris, and Wood dined together, talking in low tones. All the officers of the *Fredonia* sat together as they had in the wardroom, passing a flagon of cider among them. Bird shuffled among the tables, searching for a place where he would be out of their sight—he couldn't bear the idea of sitting there alone under their gaze while they all quietly mocked him. Then, in disgust, he turned to the door and pushed out into the cold street.

The fallen snow was largely undiminished, save for the occasional track of a horse. It felt cold and dry and like the snow might resume at any moment. And then it did, as a few lazy flakes drifted over the street.

The only other eatery near the Spottswood was a luncheon counter that exclusively served liverwurst on toast. He ordered a whiskey.

The man sitting next to him was impressively drunk. His head hung over the counter, and he seemed to be speaking to his empty plate. Bird downed the whiskey and ordered another. It was commonly said that *a tour in Washington is worth two in the Pacific*. Bird reflected sadly that not even this was true—he'd already sailed the Pacific twice, and had come no closer to earning anyone's respect. To those men, he would always be a poor farmer's son.

Something was coming to an end, he realized. It was the dream he'd had as a boy: that he would go to sea, and through the strength of his character he'd rise to become a renowned explorer. This dream had sustained him, like a deck he could stand upon, a ship that carried him smoothly above the roiling decades of his life. But now it was beginning to feel less like a ship and more like a worn shoe that had seen too many miles.

The drunken man next to him raised his head, muttered something.

"Excuse me?"

"They fail to appreciate my greatness," the man slurred.

"A pity," Bird answered. He left a few coins on the counter and went back out into the street.

The *Fredonia* was still frozen in place beside the wharf, gently rising and falling with the movement of the river beneath the ice. Bird wasn't due back at the hotel for another hour, as the officers of the court deliberated. Enlivened by the whiskey, he'd walked all the way back to the shipyard, and his nose and cheeks were bright red and stung with cold. As he came up the gangplank he was greeted by the pig, who snorted at his arrival and then returned its attention to the empty burlap sack it had been dragging across the deck.

Alice was sitting by the galley stove, turning the pages of an illustrated volume of birds. Skully peeled potatoes. The cook saluted him but Alice did not look up. Bird strode past them with a nod and entered his cabin, where he immediately took up pen and paper to draft the letter he'd been composing in his mind on the long walk back to the ship. He wished to write it quickly, before he sobered up.

He tendered his resignation from his country's service in three concise lines. Then, in a further paragraph, requested that they name him as Alice's guardian. There was nothing else waiting for him back at his small house in Norfolk. There was no one else in the world who needed him but her, and no one else who needed her but him. He was confident they would accept the proposal; with his resignation, the letter would rid them of two problems at once. Aside from the maudlin President Pierce, he doubted that any of them cared what happened to the girl. When he completed the letter, he immediately began to make his first copy. He would need four in total; one to Secretary Dobbins, one for the officers of the court, one for the press, and the last he intended to send directly to President Pierce, for whom he'd included a number of sentimental notes about how, on the long voyage, he'd come to consider Alice as like a daughter to him.

After finishing his letters, he dismissed Skully and Victor. He did not plan on returning to the ship that evening and would no longer require a staff. He could send for his few belongings. He asked Victor to remain behind for a moment on the quarterdeck, so that he might have words with him. The snow was falling again now in earnest, floating over the city, over the river. The boy sensed that something important was happening and stood nervously before the Lieutenant.

"I will be leaving the Navy," he said, unsure of why he was telling this to the boy.

"But what will you do, sir?"

"I am not certain yet what further path my life will take. But it will not be on the sea, I can say that much. You have been a good boy, and I have written you a strong letter of recommendation."

Victor's eyes were wounded. Bird considered him, almost a head taller than when he'd boarded, and now with almost a full scruff of beard. His arms too long for his frame, and only his disheveled haircut to still mark him as a boy. If he shipped again, Bird thought, it would be to a harder life than he'd known before.

"But . . ."

"What is it? Spit it out, boy."

"It's just that, my mam and my pap are gone. I haven't anywhere to go, sir. And it is so cold outside."

"There are public houses. Surely . . ."

The boy blurted, "I wonder if you would consider allowing me to continue with you?"

"For what purpose?"

"I could serve as your valet."

"I will not be in need of a valet," he said. "But I will offer you something even better." Hope flickered in Victor's eyes. The Lieutenant took a golden double-eagle from his coat pocket and held it before the boy. "When I was your age, I left my home with less than this in my pocket. I had not a dollar to my name. I enlisted in the Navy as a cabin boy, just as you have, and worked my way up the ladder to the man I am today."

Victor eyed the coin with a slight confusion, uncertain if he should take it or if it only served as some prop in the Lieutenant's story.

"But the Navy is a pitiless career, and I would advise you not to return to it. Not if you truly desire to make something of yourself in this world. And so that is why I am giving you this." He pressed the coin into the boy's lavender mittens. "Take this and make something of yourself. Do you understand me? You have in your possession the most valuable thing in the world, and that is youth. You have the time and energy left to do anything you wish. And now, you have an advantage. I would like to see you take this money and invest it. You might begin by starting a business, selling cigars or newspapers or something like that. Then you might save your earnings to buy yourself an apprenticeship in a trade. And thus, with this coin and your own hard work, you will build your reputation."

Victor looked at the coin dully in his own palm, as if waiting for it to move.

"What are you waiting for?" Bird asked him. "Gather your things, Victor! The world awaits! Go out and make your mark!"

He clapped the boy on his back and went below to fetch Alice and pack the few things he would be taking with them. Victor did not leave immediately, as Bird had suggested, but instead remained standing at the head of the gangplank to watch them depart, the last remaining soul aboard the *Fredonia*, the coin still clutched in his mittened hand as snow gathered on the deck around him.

The Second Part
Portraits
1857–1860

1.

CORRESPONDENCE

Spring came all at once to Bird's small house on North Cumberland Street. Norfolk lay under a thick blanket of snow for much of February, March, and into April, longer than anyone had expected, impeding progress along the roads and all but halting commerce on the river. Bird had been watching the weather every day through the frosted windowpanes, waiting for it to break, worried it might affect their travel plans. Then suddenly he awoke one morning to find the snow reduced to scattered islands of white, revealing the matted and soggy earth beneath it.

With the newfound optimism that accompanied such a shift in the weather, Bird donned his coat for his daily walk to the post office. He still wore his Navy coat, with its single epaulet. He would not let them have the satisfaction of taking that away from him. He'd made the seven-block walk to the post office every day through the long winter, no matter the temperature or the state of his knee. Aging was a slide that went only in one direction, he thought, and only through constant, vigorous activity could one hope to slow its progress. Even when the wind was howling against the glass he would take a shot of sherry to brace himself and push out, feeling no less intrepid in that moment than Franklin and his men, still lost somewhere in the Arctic.

Today, the air felt wet and somehow open, as if an oppressive covering had been lifted from the world, and for the first time since they'd settled in for the winter he found himself actually enjoying the stroll. He lingered to watch some boys playing in the street. A woman was casting open doors and windows to sweep out the winter's accumulated soot. There was something about the first hint of spring that was perhaps more intoxicating to him now as an old man than it had been when he was young.

The postmaster, his face still concealed behind a woolen scarf, was so used to this exchange that he passed Bird's correspondence through the window without comment and returned to his sorting. Bird ambled toward home as he leafed through the thick stack of mail. There was so much arriving that he'd been forced to dedicate a good portion of each morning just to keep up with it. Much of it was for Alice: from admirers, well-wishers, or the merely curious. It had been this way ever since the first article in the *Richmond Dispatch*. The newspaperman, Mr. Kind, had written up a piece that was very favorable to them, and it had been picked up by the wire service and published across the country. Other writers had followed, including one from *Frank Leslie's Illustrated Weekly*, read in a staggering fifty-thousand homes, which published an article that dubbed Alice "The Wild Girl of the Pacific." The cover of the issue had been decorated with a woodcut which was supposed to represent the mutiny upon the *Lady Fortune*; the central figure of the print was a menacing man Bird assumed to be William Christensen, wild with rage and waving a pistol in the air as frightened crew and passengers were ushered into a longboat. There were two depictions of Alice: on the cover, she was shown as a terrified child in the background, being torn from her mother's arms by rough sailors. There was another small sketch of her within, inserted into a column of the article: in this one, she was depicted dressed in furs for some reason—Bird supposed they could not reveal her naked, after all, and he forgave the artist for taking this license—with a ferocious snarl across her features and her hands raised in the air like bared claws. He'd shown the article to Alice, and she had looked at it for a long while without comment. He'd wondered if she even realized that it was supposed to be her.

The weather was so pleasant, and the pile of mail so oppressive, that he regretted it when he arrived back at the house. His dwelling looked shabby and cheerless among the snowmelt, like a wet rat that had just crawled up a riverbank. It was not a poor house by any means: three rooms with a large attic loft that was inhabited by Alice. It had a stove in the kitchen and another in the sitting room and they had been quite comfortable all winter. The house had so rarely been occupied since his purchase of it—he'd bought it for Margaret to inhabit, following their hasty wedding, but after she discovered she was with child she'd returned to her parents. When he'd arrived with Alice that previous February, he'd not seen the place in nearly four years. There had been a family of raccoons living in the crawlspace beneath the house, who had evidently been using the lower floor of the house, in its entirety, for their toilet. Alice had watched him from the doorway as he crouched in the snow, jabbing a broom into the dark space and hissing gibberish to frighten them out. *Where will they go to live now?* she asked him after they'd been driven off, stark and frightened in the daylight. Exhausted from the struggle of inserting himself into the crawlspace, he'd snapped at her *I don't damn well care as long as they are not beneath our feet.* Later he'd felt remorseful about the incident, and he'd tried to provide her with a more patient explanation, showing her the droppings in the pantry and kitchen and explaining that they were thieves.

There was little greenery around the house. It sat on a square parcel of what was now mud, with a corduroyed walkway of half-buried logs leading up to the front door. He idly thought to himself that he and Alice might beautify it by planting sunflowers around the outside—it would be a fine thing to do together, and might awaken the girl's interest—but he knew full well they would be far too occupied that Spring with the tour for anything of the sort. He entered the front room, stepped around the newly-purchased luggage in the process of being packed, a black steamer trunk and a smaller valise, and after feeding a small scoop of coal into the bottom of the stove, he sat at his writing table to begin sorting the mail into piles.

He split the seal on an envelope addressed to Alice and pulled out a scrap of paper covered in thick pencil markings. It smelled vaguely of manure and the letters were smudged as if by a clumsy hand:

WE HAVE HEARD OF YOUR ADVENTURE AND ARE GREATLY CURIOUS IN YOUR ESTIMATION HOW MANY DAYS WOULD YOU SAY YOU WERE ON THE ISLAND?

He looked at the postmark: Indiana. Too far outside the route of their tour for him to consider sending a promotional card. He placed the note to the side to begin his burn pile.

There was a voluminous correspondence concerning his lecture tour, which they were to embark upon in less than a week. To save the money that would have been wasted on agents and promoters, he'd been organizing the two-month, twelve-city excursion himself, writing dozens of queries to theaters, newspaper offices, local organizations who might wish to host his presentation. He'd engaged in all the negotiations concerning their travel and accommodations, the sale of tickets, advertisement for the events. Money, or the lack thereof, had recently become an item of some concern—his naval service had not been entirely lucrative, and Bird had recently received a letter explaining that the stipend the U.S. Government had pledged to provide Alice would not be continued. After the inauguration, the new president, Buchanan, had gone on a spree, dismantling some of the more flagrant expenditures of his predecessor. The letter announcing the cancellation had been signed by Buchanan himself. *Your country thanks you for your service*, it read, *and wishes you the best of luck in your future endeavors*. Though its contents were disappointing, a personal letter from the president was nothing to sneeze at. He'd stored it in a cubby of his rolltop desk, thinking to frame it someday.

He opened a letter from the theater owner he was working with in Baltimore, and examined the enclosed handbill with some annoyance:

> *Old Market Theatre, Baltimore on Church Street*
> **MUTINY!!! SHIPWRECK!!! MURDER!!!**
> A YOUNG WOMAN REDUCED TO *SAVAGERY*
> **Witness the Celebrated and Extraordinary**
> ALICE KELLY
> described as "The Wild Girl of the Pacific" and Hear Her Recount
> HER TRAVELS AND ADVENTURES
> To be accompanied by the reminisces of
> LIEUTENANT HENRY BIRD and tales of life at sea
> *WEDNESDAY THE 8TH OF MAY*
> *ONE NIGHT ENGAGEMENT*

This was not at all representative of their presentation—he'd been quite clear, in all of his negotiations, that he would be the sole speaker, and the focus of the program would be a sort of memoir of his naval career. He had a number of anecdotes in mind that he thought audiences might find thrilling: the entire first portion of the program would be dedicated to the Wilkes Expedition, with what he felt was a particularly riveting narrative of that terrible incident at Malolo, when the Feegees had turned upon the landing party. He'd not been among them, thankfully—he'd been safely aboard the *Vincennes* at the time—but he'd seen and heard enough to insert himself into the action. He would describe for them what he'd witnessed later that same voyage, those terrible, awe-inspiring southernmost latitudes, the desolate, frozen vistas they had traversed to discover Antarctica. It was no large embellishment to claim that he had been the first to sight the southern continent, no more than a distant ridge of mountains, barely visible in the haze, across a vast and unbroken field of white. In truth, the discovery had been credited to a sailor named William Reynolds, on another ship in the squadron entirely, the *Peacock*. All Bird could remember was staring out into the hazy distance, trying to locate the mountains that had been reported but seeing nothing, trying to warm his frozen hands in his pockets as he and others went about the drudgery of taking the endless soundings of the ocean's depth that would eventually confirm that the sea floor did indeed slope upwards toward land. Hadn't he seen it, though? Right around the same time as Reynolds? Hadn't he looked in that direction, both after and before, and might he not have unknowingly directed his eyes toward some vague thickening or shape or line? It seemed to him that he had. Or at least that he very well might have.

The rescue of Alice Kelly occupied only the last quarter hour of a two-hour-long monologue, the notes for which were still scattered about the house in various states of revision, and which needed to be organized and recopied before their departure. Try as he might, he could not think of much to say about her. There was the wreck of the longboat, of course, a scene in which he omitted his own near-drowning. The mystery of the ruined settlement, and the feral state she was discovered in. Of her time on the ship, he discussed only how, through his patient tutelage, he'd helped her to regain her speech after all the others had dismissed her as a deaf-mute.

At the very end of the program, he would bring Alice out for a brief appearance and a minor exchange of dialogue to provide evidence of her recovery. Theater owners who had requested more of the girl had been flatly refused—he found their curiosity about her a bit ghoulish, to say the least. Some had even suggested that she might appear dressed in furs, as she had been depicted in *Frank Leslie's*. That she might crawl on all fours and gnaw upon bones. He supposed it would do no good to complain about the misleading billet at this juncture—the Baltimore promoter had probably already printed and distributed hundreds of them. He placed it into a second pile of things he meant to save, as souvenirs of the tour.

One letter was battered and creased and bore a postmark from San Francisco. Intrigued, he slit it open with his knife. The last time he'd seen San Francisco it had been a rough mining camp. He'd heard, of course, that the city had grown tremendously since the gold strike, but he couldn't shake the idea that it was a place of dirty, bearded men squatting in mudded creeks and pissing just outside of their tents.

The letter painted a vastly different picture. It was from a man named J. Galloway who claimed to own the finest theater in the city, which he described in an overblown manner as *the most resplendent jewel in the crown of the first true Western Metropolis*. Bird had never heard of him, and as far as he knew had no business with the man. His own lecture tour would not push any farther west than Ohio, due to the high cost and risk of travel. He had no desire to deliver his lecture to a bunch of rowdies in some sawdust-floored saloon. The theater owner requested that they sail for California at once, to partner with him in the creation of a play based upon Alice's life. He even offered to pay for their travel expenses. The man was obviously a crackpot. Expenses or no, to think that they might travel all the way across the country for something as nonsensical as a stage play, with its wooden trees and prancing actors. Galloway had also included, for some obscure reason, a newspaper clipping. It advertised a performer known as Great Ignatius, whose act, as far as Bird could tell, consisted of taking a punch in the stomach from any man in the audience. Both clipping and letter went into the burn pile.

Bird rose and opened a window. He lit his pipe and made a halfhearted attempt to waft the smoke outside. The room was already smoky enough from the leaking stovepipe he hadn't fixed, and the day had warmed. He heard a noise above him that indicated that Alice was moving about in the loft. When he was done with the mail, he thought he might try to entice her to eat. She had grown too thin over the winter, and still she refused meat, which he hoped might strengthen her.

Settling back at his desk, he opened a letter from Boston, addressed to Alice. It contained another crude note written in pencil, this one barely literate. Its contents, however, caused him to bite down hard on his pipestem:

Dearest Alice,

I do not now if you recal me I am your Uncle Frank the brother of your Pa. I have just got back to Boston an herd from the news paper that you are Alive and Well with a Navy man an what troubel you have seen. I am sad to here what has happen to your Pa and Ma I have been out West for many year an I have not layed my eye on you since you was a babe. I do not have a horse I had one name of Sue I will tell You about she was a good girl but I have Lost her so when the weather turns I shall have to come to you on my own 2 feet. It may take me some time God Bless and please say God Bless to Lt Bird for his Charity to you my dearest Niece.

F K

Bird's first thought was that the man must be an imposter—the fact that President Pierce had offered the girl a stipend had been well-publicized; the fact that President Buchanan had withdrawn it had not been mentioned in the press at all. Perhaps this *Uncle Frank* was some unscrupulous rapscallion, looking to have her regular income directed his way . . .

Bird moved to the bottom of the ladder that led up to the loft and listened. His pipesmoke rose in little puffs that disappeared into the dimness of the attic. All winter long, Alice had remained sequestered up there, mostly by her own choice. He'd tried a few times to entice her to come down, to venture out into Norfolk with him so that she might come to know the world again. Even in the dead of winter, there was plenty to do and see in the city. He'd invited her to attend recitals at the church, to view the skaters on the old mill pond, to walk with him as far as the confectioner, where he promised to purchase for her a hot cup of chocolate. She'd refused every invitation and instead remained wrapped in a blanket like an old Indian at the far end of the loft, by the small attic window that showed only gray and white and rattled under the wind. He'd tried to lure her out by building a snowman in the yard. He rolled four large snowballs and stacked them neatly atop one another, gave it arms made from two sticks of kindling, coat button eyes, and one of his old, burnt-out pipes sticking out from its impression of a mouth. As a final decoration, he'd put one of his old blue Navy coats and a lieutenant's hat upon it. When he called her down to see it, she'd only stood in the doorway for a few moments with a look of distress on her face and then turned to go back inside. She had even lost interest in her pig, who resided, full grown and now useless, in a shed Bird had hired his Negro handyman to build behind the house.

"Alice?"

There was no answer. He climbed the ladder just high enough to stick his head into the loft space. He could hear meltwater running off the roof above. Alice was in her place at the window.

"It is a lovely day," he called out. "Do you know that?"

"Yes," she said.

"You spend so much time indoors," he said to her. "You will wilt like a flower in the dark."

She said nothing else—he had long ago given up the hope of ever engaging her in any sort of lively banter. He wondered, privately, if the theater owner in Baltimore would have truly wished for her to be the main attraction if he knew how *dull* she was.

He cleared his throat to gain her attention, in case it had wandered. It was often difficult to tell. "I wished to ask you, do you ever recall having an uncle, by the name of Frank?"

"My father had a brother," she said without interest.

"Did his name happen to be Frank?"

"Yes."

Bird remained there perched on the ladder, feeling a bit woozy and unsure what all of this would mean to them, to his lecture tour, until she added, "My father said that he died."

A flood of relief. "Dead? You are quite sure?"

"Yes."

Despicable, he thought as he descended the ladder. Once your name was in the public eye it seemed like the worst elements of society, crackpots and schemers and criminals, all began to emerge like lice from the woodwork.

As he returned to his writing table, the Lieutenant was momentarily chilled by the image of this unscrupulous sharper, even at that moment on some country road, moving slowly toward them. Well, they would be long gone by the time he arrived in Norfolk, and hopefully he would turn around and return to whatever hole he'd crawled from. If not, then Bird would have some choice words for him upon their return. Bird folded the letter for no reason and then tossed it and its fellows into the bottom of the stove.

2.

THE TOUR

On the morning they were to embark, Bird asked Alice if she wished to say farewell to her pig. He had hoped, with the warm weather, her fondness for the animal might be restored—he could not say why, but her interest in the creature had made her seem more *human* to him, less like a disconnected phantom and more like what a girl should be. He'd arranged for his handyman, Mr. Franklin, to care for the animal in their absence, as well as to keep an eye out for any further varmints that might think to take up residence in the crawlspace while they were gone.

"No. It does not matter," Alice replied.

"What do you mean? You don't wish to say goodbye to Marcy?"

"I think I shall never see her again."

"That is nonsense. We will return in twelve weeks."

Alice did not care to explain herself further. Once they had boarded the waiting cab and the driver had lashed their trunks to the top, Alice asked if she might remove her shoes and Bird said he would allow it—but only until they reached the ferry.

The first leg of their journey was a pleasant ride up the James River to Port Whitehall, where they would catch the train to Richmond. Standing on the deck of the steamer, Bird thought he cut a distinguished figure in his new traveling clothes: a vested suit of dark green wool with a straw boater. Since leaving the service, he'd let his hair grow out, a pleasure he'd not experienced since he was a boy. There wasn't much on top anymore, but the sides grew to the point where he could tuck them behind his ears and wavy gray curls hung to the back of his neck. Still, he could not commit himself to the extravagance of a moustache. As a necessary and small concession to his infirmity, he'd also finally adopted a walking stick, with an intricate carved hound's head for the grip. With the amount they would be traveling over the next weeks, he could no longer fool himself that he could do without it. He was glad to have it now, as all the available benches on the ferry's deck were quickly taken up by women, and he had no desire to go below. The deck was crowded with passengers, watching the mills crawl by on the bank. The millworkers didn't even look up from their labors, so accustomed were they to the steamer's daily passage.

Alice leaned against him to watch the unspooling of the river with empty eyes. He'd given her a strong dose of laudanum before boarding—he suspected it would be as necessary for her on this trip as his walking stick was for him. He'd packed two bottles to last the length of the tour, in case they found themselves in a place with no reputable chemist—he would not buy the concoctions sold on the street, for fear of their uneven quality and his suspicion that they contained more alcohol than anything else, no matter what the vendors claimed. Over the long winter, he'd tried to wean her down to a few drops a day, because he thought it made her sleep too much and stole all her liveliness. But he could not refuse it to her entirely; when he did, she would become willful, sometimes violent, and exhibit the scattered symptoms that Bird feared were the signs of her madness. Her thoughts would become twisted and confused; she thought they were still on the *Fredonia* and mistook him for the deceased Lieutenant Rand. She sometimes claimed that rats gnawed at her legs.

She began to move about sleepily among the crowded travelers, with Bird keeping half an eye on her. There was something boyish about the way she moved, a clumsy confidence without grace or reservation. She was dressed in a yellow spring dress, a darker yellow than her fair hair, clean and combed and hanging down now nearly to her shoulders. She wandered among the legs of the travelers, some of the men nearly twice her height. She stopped to study a group of children playing at fivestones beside one of the secured boats, but did not approach them.

Bird reflected on how odd it felt, to ride on a ship as a passenger rather than an officer. To be undistinguished in a multitude, jostled this way and that by rude people. With no one deferring to him, no one clearing his path or saluting. A man whose face had been marked by smallpox wooed his sweetheart loudly in Bird's ear.

He looked up from his thoughts to find Alice again but did not see her anywhere on the deck. She had only stepped out of his sight a moment ago. Seized with a minor panic, he began to push his way through the crowd, but then found her almost immediately. She was asleep on a bench, her head cradled in the lap of a burly, dirty man smoking a rancid-smelling cigar. The man patted her head when he saw Bird. "There's your papa now," he said to her. Due to her diminished size—a relic of her ordeal Bird supposed would never be corrected—she was often mistaken for a girl much younger than her actual age. To Bird, he smiled a wide brown smile, his teeth stained by tobacco, and said, "Children are God's joy, are they not?"

At Port Whitehall, Bird bought peanuts from a vendor and shelled them for Alice as they waited for the train. When it rolled into the station belching steam and coalsmoke, brakes squealing on the tracks, the shells rumbled and danced at their feet as if they were alive.

Bird felt his vest pocket for the tickets, then searched for a porter to help them with their baggage. The station had a modest crowd in the early afternoon. A well-dressed man boarded the train with a newspaper tucked under his arm, a bonneted schoolmarm pulled along a line of children holding hands—but he saw no one in a uniform. He took the leather handle of one of their trunks and began to drag it toward a train car.

What had he brought that was so heavy? Just clothing, his lecture notes, a spare pair of boots . . . his officer's uniform which he thought to wear on stage . . . Alice had insisted on bringing some of her small treasures, her hairbrush and coins and trinkets, but certainly these could not be what was making the trunk so impossible. He had only dragged it halfway across the platform when a conductor stepped off to blow his whistle and shout *All aboard!*

"All aboard," the man repeated flatly at the Lieutenant, as if he hadn't heard.

"Can you not see that I require assistance?" Bird snapped.

"What can I help you with, sir?"

"My baggage."

A look of irritation crossed the conductor's face. He looked at Bird, then at Alice who stood chewing a mouthful of peanuts, and nodded curtly. "Alrighty, old-timer."

Bird showed him the tickets and he brought them to a cabin where they sat across from a mother and her boy, a foppish little thing in short pants. Bird had splurged on first-class travel the whole way—the idea of crossing overland intimidated him, and he thought that with this luxury he might perhaps insulate himself against its rigors. He imagined sore backs and rumps, muddy roads, unpredictable meals. As they entered the cabin the mother nodded politely and returned to her knitting. The boy picked at a scab on his knee until it bled.

The train lurched into motion. Alice sat with her face pressed against the window, watching the city and outskirts and then the rolling fields of tobacco as they sped past. Seated next to her, Bird watched as well, over her shoulder, both of them mesmerized. They passed through a small town without stopping and the houses and yards and fences, the horses and cows and the occasional farmer ticked through the window as quickly as they could be recognized. Standing on the quarterdeck of a ship, he'd always had the feeling that the world was vast and empty, that all through life one moved slowly and alone through a void. Riding in a train car through a populated landscape, he was faced instead with the vast multiplicity of life, a crowdedness to the world that astonished him. He had not ridden a train in many years, and he found himself awed at the speed of modern travel. To imagine that they could leave Norfolk in the morning and arrive in Richmond that evening to deliver a lecture—when he was a boy, the world had seemed so much slower. He wondered if there was any end to it, to human progress, or if things just got faster and faster until they pulled apart at the seams.

"Have you ever ridden on a train?" he asked Alice. As he spoke the woman sitting across gave him a cool glance, angered that he'd broken their communal silence, and then pretended she was not listening. The boy flicked the first scab away, wiped a red smear onto his leg, and began work on another.

"No," Alice said quietly, her attention still fixed on the landscape passing through the window.

"At the front of the train," he explained, "there is a steam engine. The engineer stokes the fire, which boils the water into steam, and the steam is what moves the wheels of the train."

She looked as if she was considering this, then said, "I have seen a steam engine."

"Yes? Where was this?"

"On the ship. It was all in pieces."

Another memory, floating to the surface. Even after all this time, it never failed to surprise him when some moment, some new impression rose up from her depths. He was silent, to allow her to continue, if she would.

"William told them to bring it up. They brought up all the things from below. There was a piano and wheels and tools and a steam engine all in pieces. And they threw them all into the sea."

A ripple passed through the knitting woman, and she could hold her tongue no longer. She sternly intoned, "Little girls should not fib," then smiled and nodded once at Bird, as if she'd done him some service. Not knowing what else to do, he smiled in return.

∼

In Richmond, the newspaperman Mr. Kind met them at the station, a box of confections in his hand for Alice. He'd been an invaluable ally and had helped to arrange for Bird's presentation in that city.

The lecture hall was modest but adequate. Not the grand amphitheater he'd sometimes imagined himself standing in, but large enough to hold the few hundred souls willing to pay fifteen cents to hear him speak. Bird remained backstage reviewing his notes as the audience began to trickle in. Mr. Kind had taken out a large advertisement in the paper he worked for, and by the time Bird was to deliver his lecture, the hall was full to capacity.

He'd stood to address crews much larger than the crowd that gathered there, but as he walked out onto the boards to witness the dozens of faces looking up at him expectantly, he knew at once that this was somehow different. Though he wore his uniform, he was not protected here by his rank. The audience owed him no deference; any respect they would offer him would have to be won. He looked out over the crowd to see men and women, all types of faces from farmers to spectacled society gentlemen, eager young wives and frowning old dames, all trained upon him, waiting for him to speak. He felt his voice wavering slightly as he began, like a trembling hand that he could not still. Out in the darkness he heard a cough.

He began in his youth, but found the details spilling out so fast that before he knew it, he was battling cannibals at Feegee . . . he was emboldened by the sound of one woman gasping in fright as he described their sharp, filed teeth and ornaments fashioned from the bones of devoured enemies. Pressing on, he tried to whip the audience into a patriotic spirit with an anecdote of the Mexican War, in which he and a boat crew of twelve others had singlehandedly claimed and defended a Mexican fortification for several days before receiving the order to retreat. In truth, the presidio had been mostly abandoned, roamed throughout by mules and chickens.

As he turned his monologue to the events surrounding Alice's discovery, he felt a palpable change in the atmosphere of the room. Before, they had been waiting . . . now, they were *listening*. The rush he felt was like no other—it was like an intoxicant. Every soul in the room hanging upon his every word, leaning toward the stage to get a better view of him. He delayed bringing Alice out for as long as he could, abandoning his notes and spinning every little yarn he could think of: how she could not be coaxed to dress, and how he'd trained her with the bell. He even found himself, against his better judgment, describing her escape during the storm at Cape Horn, and the death of Lieutenant Rand.

Mr. Kind waited with her in the wings, and when she was introduced, he ushered her out onto the stage. She walked forward in her yellow traveling dress to stand beside Bird. He heard another gasp from the audience; perhaps it was the same woman who had gasped at the Feegees, now somehow astonished by the girl's unremarkable appearance.

"May I introduce you all to Miss Alice Kelly."

"Hello Lieutenant Bird," she said.

"You must speak up Alice."

"Hello Lieutenant Bird."

She stood just at the edge of the stage looking out over the crowd. He had worried that she might be afraid, but the look in her eyes was the same he had seen as she gazed out the window of the train. This whole world, he thought, was new to her. Just as it was new to him.

"Lecturing is a fine vocation, I think," he later declared with flushed enthusiasm to Mr. Kind, after a dinner of steak and several celebratory toasts of port. They slept that night on cots in Mr. Kind's bungalow and were off in the morning to meet the next audience.

During these first weeks of the tour, Bird felt as if he had been reborn into the life he'd always been meant to lead. Everything else had been an extended, though necessary, prologue. Thanks to the article in *Frank Leslie's*, Bird's name and reputation preceded him. Packed halls greeted them wherever they arrived, and he was afforded at least a few standing ovations. Everyone in the country, he thought, was eager to hear him speak, and to see the girl. People waited at theater doors to ask questions when he emerged; women asked to touch the single epaulet on his coat.

They ate in all the best hotels. Bird dined now exclusively on rare, fresh beefsteak, a luxury he'd been mostly deprived of since his childhood. More than once, their dining table was approached by the other guests, to ask for his autograph, and to ask for hers, if she could write it out for them.

"She speaks," Bird told them, "but unfortunately she cannot yet read or write."

Alice looked up from her soup.

Seeing their collective disappointment, Bird then offered, "But she is still known, on occasion, to consume a raw fish." He directed his attention to the waiter and asked, "Is there any fish in the house?"

They were invited to meet several aldermen, two mayors, one industrialist whom he was told was a millionaire. In Washington, Bird was informed backstage that following the lecture former president Pierce was keen to meet Alice, and to share a cigar with him, if his schedule permitted.

That evening's lecture had gone particularly well. By this point, Bird had learned how to pace his storytelling, to modulate his tone from grave to light-hearted where appropriate, to adjust his posture and position on the stage and add little hand flourishes for dramatic effect. After the presentation, Pierce was waiting for them in front of the theater. His face retained a boyish plumpness even in middle age. He was accompanied by his wife, Jane, a diminutive woman only a few inches taller than Alice and looking quite frail, dressed all in mourning black. They were attended by several men of distinction who were rapidly introduced and then forgotten. After the introductions, they all stared at Bird, as if waiting for something. Was he expected to say something? Should he offer to kiss Pierce's wife's hand? Then he realized what he'd forgotten . . .

"Miss Alice Kelly," he said, ushering Alice toward Pierce with a hand between her shoulder blades.

Pierce looked down at her and patted her head. "Jane and I were touched when we heard of your misfortune, weren't we, darling?"

She made no comment to this, but instead stepped forwards to clasp Alice to her chest in a long embrace. Then, with some discomfort, the men realized from the soft noises she made that the woman was weeping. They busied themselves with the activity of distributing and lighting cigars until this had passed and Jane Pierce released Alice and retreated into a standing coach.

"My wife has been greatly affected by our own losses," Pierce explained in a low voice.

"I understand completely," Bird said. "Women feel what we do not, so that we may act where they cannot," he mused, garnering a round of nodding and approval from the men at this bit of wisdom.

"Are you married, Lieutenant?" one of the men asked.

"My wife has passed," he said. He drew on his cigar—it was a fine one, wrapped in a tight green leaf—and watched the ember brighten and then dim into ash.

"My condolences," Pierce said, with deep sympathy. The man had a warm way of speaking that made it plain why he'd been chosen as president.

"It was long ago," Bird explained, suddenly feeling embarrassed by his pity.

Pierce congratulated him on the lecture, and added, "And I must say, it is a shame your contributions have not been given due credit, with regards to the Wilkes affair."

"I'm sure you know something about the thanklessness of government work . . ." His comment caused a ripple of laughter among the men; Bird imagined he was becoming something of a wit.

Pierce remained for only a few more minutes of chatter and was not yet halfway done with his cigar when he excused himself to escort his wife home, dispersing the men into the twilit streets of the capital. Bird looked to see that Alice had sat down on the theater steps and seemed content to watch the traffic pass in the street, and so he lingered there on the sidewalk for a long while as the sun set, determined to smoke the cigar that had been given to him by a United States president down to an impractical stub.

∼

Trouble came to them in Baltimore, as he'd expected. Kennedy, the man he'd been working with there, had rented out a large hall on the poor side of town. It had a high stage and threadbare velvet curtains—hanging up in the rafters there was a lighting contraption that Kennedy claimed he did not know how to operate. He held Bird backstage until well after the appointed time, trying to pack more attendees into the space. Finally, Bird emerged into a vast, dim hall before a crowd that was jammed to the walls and seated in balcony boxes above. They were loud and rowdy and he stood and stammered with his hands raised. They never fully quieted.

He began his lecture, having to raise his voice to be heard. He'd hardly reached the end of his "humble beginnings" portion, which climaxed with the death of his brother Laird, a recent inclusion meant to win over the audience's sympathy, when the first heckler called out from the general din, *Where is the girl?*

"Patience, dear sir. I tell you that the extraordinary young woman known as Alice Kelly is with us tonight and will be appearing shortly."

Bird found himself agitated and thrown off his rhythm, omitting details, mumbling through all his stories of the Wilkes Expedition. Just as he'd reached the Mexican War, well ahead of schedule, a bottle flew from the audience. It did not break, but simply clunked against the stage and skidded off beneath the back curtain.

He again held up his hands to quiet them and said, now shouting, "If you will not behave yourselves, I will not be able to continue! Now if you will please be silent!"

Something else flew at him, this time much closer. It looked like a bundle of dirty rags. At the sight of Bird flinching away, a woman in the audience cackled with delight.

He would not subject himself to such poor treatment, and he certainly would not endanger Alice by presenting her before such an unruly crowd. He turned and parted the curtains and walked off. He found Mr. Kennedy sitting in the rear of the theater and counting the cash box. Alice, whom he was supposed to be watching, had wandered over to examine a stack of dusty canvas backdrops; the topmost depicted a verdant, dark forest.

"I cannot continue under these conditions."

"What is the matter?"

"The audience will not quiet. They wish to see the girl, and I suspect that this is largely due to your misleading promotions."

"Well, show her to them."

"I will not."

"If you refuse, you will not see a red cent from me."

Beyond the curtain, he could hear the crowd growing more unruly.

Making a decision, Bird strode over to Alice and took her arm. Without another word, he led her out the back theater door into an alleyway, leaving Kennedy to deal with the angry mob he'd created. They proceeded directly to their hotel to gather their belongings, and left Baltimore that evening on an overnight mail coach.

∽

Manhattan, in Bird's view, was both a wonder and a sort of sieve that collected all the worst parts of humanity. Tenements that looked like houses of cards, laundry draped on lines between the buildings, dark-eyed Italians staring emotionlessly out of their windows at the cab as it passed. It seemed to him more like a warren or an anthill than a proper place for human beings to reside. Immigrants poured into this port from every corner of the world—Bird supposed that all those with honest ambition would push on into the country, to someplace where they might make something out of their own hard work. Those others, who lacked either the will or the know-how or both, remained exactly where they had arrived, like a sediment washed up on the shore.

After two well-received lectures at the Bowery Opera House, a building which Bird doubted had ever seen an actual opera, they spent a few pleasant days taking in the sights. They visited the Crystal Palace and toured the lobbies of the great hotels, dizzy monstrosities of architecture the size of a city block. Together, the old man and the young girl stared up at their immensity, no less amazed than if they viewed the spectacular remains of some ancient kingdom.

They turned west. In Trenton, Bird gave his lecture in a converted barn on the outskirts of the city, where he discovered himself to be on a bill that included several other acts. Alice dozed against him in what used to be a cowstall as they waited through a minstrel show, the clowns barking feeble jokes and strumming plantation songs. After that, there was a prize fight, ropes strung around the corner posts of the low platform they were calling the stage to mark out the ring. A Prussian and an Irishman beat the tar out of one another as the crowd urged them to further violence, the soft thudding sounds of their fists nearly lost in the clamor. When it was finally time for Bird's lecture, he shook Alice awake to wait for his sign and took his place in front of the crowd. On the way, he passed the badly bloodied and swollen Irishman as he was assisted from the stage. The man's face was destroyed, beaten to the point where it looked as malleable as clay, as if Bird might simply reach over and push his nose back into its proper place, smooth over the egg-shaped lump above his swollen eye. Waiting for the crowd to settle, Bird looked down at the crude stage and realized that one of his shoes had come to rest in a smear of drying blood.

Three days later in Harrisburg, he gave his lecture to an indifferent crowd of Germans in a church, who were so silent and puzzled-looking that he wondered if they spoke any English at all. Then a long ride along the Pennsylvania Turnpike, through all the unbroken and somewhat frustrating plainness of that state. Pittsburgh smelled heavily of smoke, and the workmen who filled the small hall regarded Alice with weary disinterest, as if she was merely some colorful and harmless menagerie animal.

Their final lecture was to take place in Columbus, a spread-out farm town under a wide sky that smelled of manure and sawdust. The coach deposited them across the street from the Regency Hotel, where he registered and settled Alice in their room for a nap.

The room contained only a single double bed. The wide feather beds of these fancy hotels were more than adequate for a thin old man and a girl, and even with the money coming in he hated to waste the expense of renting a separate cot. The room was dim; it didn't have a glass window but only a stretch of canvas over a frame that permitted some light and air. The last two days' journey had exhausted Alice, and after giving her a few more drops of laudanum he helped her shed her dress, covered in road dust, and slip into a limp nightdress. Their clothing was in need of a cleaning—perhaps he could drop a few articles off at a laundry before they left, to be fresh for the journey home. The girl too looked as if she could use a bath. All these details one must consider, when caring for a child—he often found himself fretting over her, perhaps unnecessarily. She was almost a woman, it was true, but he couldn't help but to think of her like this, as a helpless thing, incapable of navigating even the most basic of daily activities. He sometimes doubted she would even eat, if he didn't put food in front of her. He could never reconcile himself to the fact that she had survived all on her own on the island. For years. It could have only happened in the Pacific, he thought. Anywhere else, and she would have surely perished. He drew back the sheet to allow her to climb into the bed, then pulled it up to her neck.

"I'll be gone for a few hours," he said. "If you require anything, the hotel man downstairs will bring it to you."

No response. Her eyes were open though. She was curled on her side, turned away from the bright window to study the wallpaper on the other side of the bed. It showed flowers, branches and vines, various perched birds, all connected by their intricate linework, etched in a dark blue on a background of eggshell white.

"Are you feeling well?" he asked.

"Yes."

"Are you hungry?"

"No."

He paused. "You're missing your little pig, aren't you? Well, don't worry, for we shall be going home soon."

In the hotel restaurant he interrupted a few sandy-haired farmers, their hats in their laps, who looked up briefly from their eggs and newspapers as he made a promotional announcement. Then he pressed out into the nearly empty midday street. They were being hosted by that city's chapter of the Women's Temperance Society, as a fund-raiser. He felt it a worthy cause—nothing touched his heart more than the sight of a woman ruined by drink, her wastrel children clinging to her dirty skirts as she begged for charity in the streets.

Their hall was a one-story brick-fronted building, like a schoolhouse. Inside, an empty space set with rows of wooden folding chairs. A lectern for his notes. Just as he'd instructed, two American flags had been hung from the rafters at stage left and right. Mrs. Bloom from the Society met him there, her hat covered in a pile of ribbons and artificial flowers that added a foot to her height. Bird took her offered hand uncomfortably. He knew how to shake a man's hand, but he'd never fully understood how to shake a woman's. He held the limp thing for a moment and then let it drop.

"Miss Kelly is not with you?"

"She is resting at the hotel."

"Of course, the poor thing must be tired, with so much travel and excitement. How many cities have you done?" she asked politely.

"This will be our twelfth stop. And after this, we're for home."

"We are all quite excited to meet this daring young lady." She spoke loudly, projecting her voice as if she was speaking to someone at a much greater distance. They were the only people in the large, empty room.

"I am certain she will be pleased to make your acquaintance."

Mrs. Bloom rippled with pleasure at the comment. Then, as if remembering something urgent, she began to rummage in her handbag.

"Before I forget . . ." she said, "this arrived for you some days ago."

She passed him an envelope neatly folded down the middle. He unfurled it and regarded the slanted handwriting of the address and felt his stomach drop. He opened it at once and read it standing there in the empty lecture hall.

Dear Lt Henry Bird,

I have arive in Virginna to late to see you but I have speek with your Boy who tells me where your gone. I am name of Frank Kelley and Uncle to Alice Kelley I have been West for many a year to find my Fortune but that did not turn out good and now I am come Home to learn my Brothers girl is Alive and well. I did not have a good relation with my Brother Tom but I always had hope we woud make it up some day. Now I am regretful it is to late for that but I wish to make amens by caring for his Girl as it is proper I shoud. Lt Bird I here you are a good man and I know you will not bear a gruge that I have made a bed in your hog shed to await your Return as I do not have Cash for any other accomodation. Your Boy said it would be all rite.

FK

His *boy*, Bird assumed, was the aging Mr. Franklin, who had been provided, in case of emergency, with their itinerary. Bird folded the note and stuffed it into his pocket, suddenly annoyed that Mrs. Bloom was still standing there, staring at him like a pigeon waiting for some crumbs. He excused himself hastily; he could not stand in the shadow of her hideous hat for another moment.

As he walked back to the Regency, Bird considered his options. In truth, he'd been so wrapped up in the whirlwind of the tour that the issue had completely escaped him. It was not cowardice that made him shrink from the idea of a confrontation—he would not mind calling this man the imposter that he was to his face, but he had no wish to expose Alice to such unpleasantness. And what if his claim was true? Perhaps she indeed had a living uncle, and what then? She had no connection to the man; he might as well have been any one of the strangers that she passed in the street. Bird had come to believe that he was the only one with the necessary experience with the girl to best understand how to manage her and provide her with a steady life. But would a judge see it this way, and favor him over the coincidence of a blood relation to some destitute, illiterate fortune-seeker? He understandably had little faith in the justice of the courts.

The more he considered the situation, the more he found that he could think of no compelling reason why they must return to Norfolk at all. His career at sea had made him immune to any sentimental attachment to a particular place. One was as good as another, and they were mostly the same. He did not think the girl favored Norfolk, either. She'd seemed quite a bit happier since their departure. Secured in the hotel safe, he had a valise stuffed with banknotes. The house could be sold through an agent. The pig could be bequeathed to Mr. Franklin, to furnish his breakfast table. What else held them to any past arrangement? Their connection to anything in the world but each other seemed tenuous at best. The tour had been like the start of a new life for the two of them. Why not embrace it, he asked himself, and give them both a fresh start in a new location? Preferably somewhere so distant that this irritating man could not follow them.

He expected to find Alice still sleeping in the hotel room, but he found the door unlocked and the room empty. He checked at the front desk but the clerk had not seen her. Still, he proceeded to the dining room. It was not the dinner hour, and it contained only one man who held his long beard to the side as he slurped his soup.

He found her, finally, out on the hotel gallery. She was standing alone at the railing, barefoot in her nightdress, watching some activity in the street: a handful of men were working to get boards wedged beneath a stuck cart wheel.

"You will catch your death if you do not wear any more than that," he said to her.

She looked at him but didn't answer.

"I have never been to Columbus before, have you?"

"No."

"And have you enjoyed this trip so far?"

"Yes," she said.

He lit his pipe and took a few puffs to stoke it. "I have been considering something at length," he said. "In fact, I would like to ask your opinion on the matter."

She said nothing as he took a few more puffs and felt the bowl warm beneath his fingers. The days were getting longer, and though the sun had dipped they were still a long way from dusk.

"You are aware that tonight is our final presentation, before we return to Norfolk."

"Yes."

"But what if we were to continue our travels? Would that please you?"

"Where will we go?" she asked.

"What would you say to a trip to the West? To California?" Remembering the letter he'd received from the theater owner, California seemed as distant and possibly lucrative a prospect as he possessed.

Alice was silent for a moment, lost in her thoughts, and then she answered, "My father told me that in California there is a dog that can do wonderful tricks."

She was placidly watching as the wagon in the street was finally pushed free, with an enormous effort, by several men. With a wave of thanks, the driver cracked his reins. The vehicle wobbled down the street as the men wandered back to their ordinary business.

"I think I have heard of this dog," Bird mused as a cloud of his pipe-smoke dispersed into the air over the street. "They say he is a marvel to behold."

3.

. . .

"I would like to introduce to you, Miss Alice Kelly, of whom I have spoken a great deal tonight. As I have told you, she is quite shy, and I ask that you refrain from making any noise or commotion that might frighten her . . ."

The theater did not have a hidden place behind the curtains, as some of them did. She'd been waiting in a chair in a back room, a kitchen, where women were frying something made from dough and onions. The smell of the grease hung in the air and coated her skin, and she was glad when Mrs. Bloom gently touched her arm to guide her up and toward the stage. She went through the door and was instantly surrounded by people. She could feel them all looking at her, looking to see if they could tell that she was wild, that she was not like them. She did not look up at them yet. She kept her eyes on her feet until she was at the set of three stairs that led up onto the stage.

The stage was just high enough that she could look out and see them all at once, a sea of heads and astonishing hats. When she was not on a stage, most people towered above her; she felt lost in a dark forest of moving figures. Now it was as if the audience waited patiently behind glass for her to examine them. She imagined that they were beings made of mud, newly fashioned and imperfect. She looked from one man's bald crown, covered in red splotches, to the wildly curly hair of another man with dark, girlish eyes, to the colorful display of flowers atop Mrs. Bloom in the front row, a woman who had cooed and fretted over Alice before the show. She smelled, even at this distance, like an impossible number of roses, and her breast was as wide as an unfurled flag. Next to her, a severe old crone with an expression like a hawk. A man with a long face whose mouth hung wide open. She looked at each of them in turn, and allowed them to breathe and be named.

Bird stood beside her in his blue coat and hat, just as he'd worn on the ship, and looked down at her with no expression to loudly say, "We are all so delighted you could join us." She looked out at the crowd and curtsied as he'd instructed her. She felt their eyes following her, as if even this simple movement was astonishing.

The next day they boarded a train that they would ride for two entire days without disembarking. Bird showed her how their seat turned into a bed, which they would take turns resting upon, though in truth he never requested a turn and dozed upright on the opposite bench the entire time as they sped through flat landscapes. In all their traveling, Alice had come to regard train voyages as her favorite. Only a train, with its smooth motion upon the tracks, its steady rumble, allowed her to feel as if she was a stable and unmoving center around which the world shifted and changed its arrangements. She could stare out the window of a train forever, she thought, and never lose her interest. There was always something new flying through her vision, just long enough for her to think its name.

"Will the train go to California?" she asked Bird, stirring him from his own silent vigil at the window. The sun was low on their second day, and its light winked through the trees that silently glided by.

"No, no," he said. "The train goes east. California is to the west. We will take a ship to California."

A ship. The thought filled her with dread and she brooded during their final hours aboard the train, as it rushed alongside the Hudson River. She had only begun to see and claim this vast new world for her own—she was certain that if she boarded a ship it would all go away, and she would never see it again.

"Are you worried about Marcy?" he asked her.

She looked at him blankly, unable to find any meaning in the name.

"I have told you that when we arrive in California you shall have a new piglet, or even, if you wish, a kitten?"

Oh yes, she remembered. That was the name of the pig.

At the port of New York, men on the docks were drawn to the commotion as Bird tried to drag her onto the ship. Finally, red with embarrassment, he reached into his coat pocket and came out with the bottle of medicine and gave her just enough to soften her fear.

Once she was on the ship, she could no longer even recall why it had frightened her so. The sun glinted on the swells in the harbor, and she could smell the sea. It was comforting to her, as if she was on a stage, and her audience would be all the dolphins and fishes. The clipper was named *Liberty*, Bird told her, a sleek vessel that was smaller than those she'd been on before, with only two masts but with a vast spread of white sail, nonetheless. He spent a good deal of time admiring the neatness of the rigging, and named the sails for her in turn, from the jibs to the spanker.

They sailed for many days. She was allowed to move about on the upper deck when the weather permitted, and the weather for their entire journey was clear and bright. Bird remained sequestered in the steerage, reading the same newspaper he'd bought in New York over and over again, holding it up to catch the light that came through the hatch, as she walked among the other passengers on the deck, or watched the crew as they scampered up and down the masts, adjusting the sails whose names she had forgotten.

There was a young girl who sat on the deck with her legs folded beside her, whispering to a ragdoll, in a quiet place behind one of the boats. The girl wore a pale dress and did not notice as Alice approached. All of her attention was on her doll, whom she spoke to urgently. Alice accidentally startled her when she asked, "What is his name?"

The girl looked up to study Alice. She had small, sharp teeth and wore a colorless dress. "Peter," she said, after judging that Alice was no threat to her or her doll.

"And what do you say to him?"

"I am telling him secrets."

"Let me speak to him."

"He could not understand you," the girl explained with some annoyance. "You do not speak his language."

"He will understand me. Let me tell him something."

The girl shrugged and handed her raggedy man to Alice. Alice took it to her lips and whispered, *You are a pretty boy.* The girl affirmed again that Peter did not and could not ever hear her.

Her name was Sally, and she traveled with her mother to meet her father in a place called Brazil.

The girl was neither curious nor intelligent; she asked Alice nothing, not even her name. Alice was content to sit and watch the girl play, remembering a time—was it so long ago?—when she had felt as if everything was alive, as if she could speak to dolls and objects and they listened and felt the same things within them as she did. Later, when the girl's mother came onto the deck and called for Sally, the girl ran off without saying goodbye. Alice heard her mother ask *Who is that girl?* and the girl said *I don't know.*

Alice searched for her whenever she was on the deck and was disappointed when she wasn't there. When Sally was seated in her customary place, Alice remained at her side, happy for any crumb of attention the girl provided her. She was overjoyed when, finally, the girl claimed that her doll Peter wished to tell Alice something, and held the doll up to Alice's ear as she pretended to listen. "Did you hear him?" she asked. Alice said that she did. Then the girl said, "He says that we must tidy the kitchen," and she began to furiously sweep and organize things on the deck that were not there.

There was a man on the ship who wore a blue suit. He was slightly round, and had a collar that looked too tight, as if his body was being squeezed out of his clothing. Above it, his neck hung in folds. He watched them playing for a long while, as Sally passed Alice pretend dishes that Alice arranged on a pretend table.

"Is this your sister?" he asked Alice, and Sally said that yes, she was.

"Two pretty sisters," he said. "Which one is prettier?"

"I am prettier," Sally said as the man stood over them, shadowed by the sun.

He asked if they would like to hear a funny poem, and they did, but first he made them promise they would not tell it to anyone. It would be their secret.

"We promise," Alice said.

"Tell it to Peter," Sally said, holding up the doll scrunched in her fist. "He likes poems."

He squatted on his hams to whisper to them, both girls stifling their laughter as he recited a naughty rhyme. Sally, her hand over her mouth, turned red. The man grinned from ear to ear as he finished, and then, as a sailor passed by, he quickly stood and strode away, as if he hadn't been speaking to them at all. Afterwards, the girls were rapturous over the rhyme, and repeated the parts of it they could remember for the rest of the voyage. It was a secret they shared that brought them closer, and while under the watchful gaze of Bird or Sally's mother, it was enough to send them both into fits of uncontrollable laughter if one of them so much as whispered the word *Nantucket*.

Alice woke in confusion. She was no longer on the ship, but she could not remember disembarking. She was on another train—she could tell that much by the rumble of the tracks below her, the sound of a chugging engine somewhere ahead. She was arranged on a hard wooden bench, her neck sore, her feet pressing into something soft and yielding that she realized was Bird's leg. She brought herself into a sitting position and looked out the window. All she saw was a deep, dense jungle, the foliage so close that wide fronds dragged across the glass as the train pushed slowly through it.

"Ah. You are awake. You have had a good, long rest," Bird said. "You woke just in time to witness the fourth bridge."

"Where is Sally?" she asked.

Bird's face wrinkled. "Oh. Was that the name of your little friend? I'm afraid she has not come onto the train. She remained on the *Liberty*."

Alice considered this, and realized she would never see the girl again. The thought settled within her, a mild discomfort, a flicker of sadness, and then, nothing.

"Is this California?" she asked.

"No. We are in Panama."

There were so many places in the world, she thought. Panama. Pittsburgh. New York, Norfolk. The world was so much larger than she'd ever suspected, all these places the same but different, separated by vast plains, ranges of mountains, countless trees. He explained to her that they crossed a narrow bridge of land that separated two great oceans. The train would carry them through uncrossable swamps and mountains. "There has never before been a train such as this," he said.

Alice turned to regard the length of the car, lined with humble benches, a few scattered passengers each sitting alone. She did not understand what was so impressive about it. It looked just like the other trains she'd ridden and was perhaps even a bit plainer.

Bird checked his pocket watch and leaned over her toward the window. "Here it comes," he said. "Look . . ."

As she turned back to the window, the foliage disappeared completely, and she could see nothing but the sky. The car filled with sunlight. She stretched herself up on the bench to look downwards and could not even see any ground beneath them. All she saw was an immense drop down to the thin blue line of a river snaking through a valley far, far below. The train seemed to soar through the air. She felt her breath escape her.

Bird sighed with shared admiration. "There is nothing that mankind cannot accomplish," he said, "when we set ourselves to it."

They remained for weeks in a place called Panama City, due to a problem with their tickets. She did not understand it all from Bird's complaints; she knew that they were supposed to board another ship, but the ship had been full and their tickets useless. Bird claimed they had been swindled and moved back and forth between their room at the American Hotel and the lobby, where he engaged in long, fruitless arguments with the manager.

They had been traveling for so many days now that Alice didn't mind lounging in the hotel room as they waited for another ship to arrive. Bird was so sorely distracted by their predicament that he gave her as much medicine as she wished for; she spent her days wrapped in the oppressive heat of the place, drifting in and out of consciousness beneath a layer of mosquito netting that made the world appear hazy and insubstantial. Whenever Bird returned to their room to pace and fume, he brought her strange types of fruit she'd never seen before. She saved their pits in the drawer of the nightstand.

There was no glass in the window and no cloth: it was an open portal with shutters to close when it rained. From the window she watched that city made of white stone. The city slept too in the heat, only alive for a few hours in the morning and the early evening. The people there were slow-moving. Donkeys waited patiently, tethered to trees, their heads hung low, their swishing tails the only motion in the street. Just before dawn, the city would teem with scrawny cats, leaping from one tiled roof to the next, engaging in fierce battles over scraps. She made it her ritual to be awake to see them each day; by the time the sun had fully risen, they seemed to disappear completely, but for a short while she could imagine that they were the city's only inhabitants, and she witnessed some long-abandoned kingdom that now existed only for them.

One morning as the light rose, she saw a hump in the middle of the road, a man lying as if he'd fallen asleep there. She realized from his clothing that it was the same man she'd seen on the ship, the one in the blue suit who'd told her the naughty poem. His face was turned away from her. She looked to see if Bird was awake, but he was still snoring in a hammock. A few of the city's cats sniffed their way cautiously toward his prone form, licked at him and gathered around, and that was when she realized that he was dead. A woman carrying jugs of water skirted around him without taking notice. He remained there until midmorning, when two dark-skinned men in soldiers' uniforms, rifles slung over their shoulders, marched out to take him by his armpits and drag him away.

That was the day their ship finally arrived.

4.

. . .

All the passengers crowded onto the deck when it was announced that the steamer *Elizabeth* was entering the bay of San Francisco. Bird told her that she would never forget her first glimpse of it: the greatest natural harbor in the world. She followed him up onto the deck only to find that a haze had descended, and instead of the grand vista they'd all expected, the passengers pushed against the railing to squint their eyes at nothingness.

Progress through the fogbound bay was slow. The great engine of the steamer lessened to a rumble beneath the deck. Alice looked down at the slowly passing waters and saw that they were littered with debris. Scraps of lumber and driftwood, pages of newspapers gone translucent, tangles of cloth and sacking, bobbing barrels, an entire straw mattress partially submerged like a sinking raft. Then a hulking shape began to form in the fog. An island, she thought. No, she could make out the shape of a tilted mast. It was a wrecked ship, listing to one side, water lapping into a great breach in the hull. She could see right inside the ship as they passed near it: the brass fittings on the doors that stood in a few feet of frothy water, a single floating boot caught in an eddy. Before this sight had even finished disappearing into the haze behind them, she saw another wreck, a ship standing mostly upright but sunken to a point where a foot or more of water washed over the deck. And another, and another. So many abandoned ships. Some of them had nothing wrong with them. They were perfectly sound, floating at anchor, without a soul aboard that she could see. Their masts bare of sail. They floated into and out of view, two and three at a time. The steamer had slowed to a crawl to navigate this misty graveyard.

"What happened to them?" she asked Bird.

"To who?"

"To the ships."

"They appear to have been abandoned."

"But why?"

"I imagine there is no one to sail them." He saw this didn't satisfy her, and explained, "Their crews have probably run off to find gold in the hills."

Later in the afternoon, the sun burnt away the fog in time to reveal the San Francisco waterfront, a chaotic sprawl of piers running at odd angles, a forest of masts attached to every type of craft from the great clippers to little fishing vessels, interspersed with an abundance of rowboats, junks, rafts, and barges. As they descended the steamer's gangplank, she saw a great assortment of men there on the docks as well: bare-chested sailors, dusty cowboys in ten-gallon hats. Chinamen like she had seen on one of the islands, dressed in colorful silk, their ponytails swinging as they hoisted and tossed sacks and barrels. Negroes with fishing poles. Great clouds of ravenous gulls fighting each other for tidbits.

Bird paid a coin to a Chinese porter to carry their luggage as they pressed into the city. Alice was overwhelmed by the sights and sounds—she knew at once that San Francisco was unlike any of the other cities she'd visited. It did not present the tall, imposing stone buildings of New York, but what it lacked in size it made up for in color and variety. It looked as if it had been cobbled together from the discarded fragments of other cities, dream cities: Proud brick storefronts cast their shadows over haphazard wooden shacks. A chaotic sprawl of houses climbed up the sides of the hills. Hotels with broad galleries, streamers and bright flags flying from their fronts, along with every other manner of sign and enticement. One structure even appeared to have been built out of a seagoing ship, nestled between two more conventional buildings, as if it had been sailed there during a flood and became trapped between its neighbors when the waters receded.

Some of the streets were neatly planked and others were washes of mud. She looked down one narrow thoroughfare and saw men pulling and pushing at a horse; the animal kicked its front legs in terror as the men fell away from it. There were bands playing on balconies and in front of the hotels, so many of them that their sounds mingled into a din that only occasionally sounded like music.

Bird mopped his brow with a handkerchief, blinking against the bright sun as he turned down one street after another, constantly checking a piece of paper. Rather than keep turning to look for her, he pulled her along by the forearm. The Chinese porter followed behind them, their steamer trunk hoisted on his back and two valises clutched in one slender hand, unspeaking and seemingly untroubled by his load.

Alice noticed that there were no women in the streets at all. She tried to recall the last woman she'd seen . . . perhaps it had been the Spanish maid in their hotel room in Panama, who had slipped in and out of the room at the edges of Alice's awareness. From there they'd been crammed into the steerage of the steamer, full of men, all of them burning with their own private anticipation. Now, through every open saloon door, she could see more men, roomfuls of them, table after table surrounded by men, counters lined with men. Men in neat suits and others dressed like farmers, side by side, and almost all of them smoking. Pipes, cigars and cigarillos—every man was followed by his own little cloud. Several red Indians, dressed in old coats and feathers, huddled on a streetcorner to pass a single lit cigar between them. As if in answer to some call she could not hear, Bird fished his pipe from his pocket and absentmindedly started stuffing it with his thumb.

Men were lined on a plank sidewalk in single file, all facing the same direction. They extended for an entire block or more, a line of hats and smoke clouds, tall and short, hunched and straight, all peering over each other's shoulders to glimpse the head of the line. She thought they must be moving toward some great reward.

"Where are they going?" she asked.

Bird was mopping his brow again with his handkerchief as he studied his scrap of paper and the street. "What's that?"

"What are they waiting for?"

Bird turned his eyes toward the queue and followed it to the door the men were entering. Above it was a sign. "Fried oysters."

Wherever they went, men stopped in their tracks to regard her as if she was a rare animal, and did not resume their motion until after she'd passed. Some lifted their hats from their heads. Bird didn't notice, so intent was he on finding the hotel the steamer captain had recommended.

"The Oakley House?" he asked a cluster of old men, who stopped staring at her for just long enough to confer. One pointed in the direction they'd come from.

"I suppose any hotel will do," he muttered to himself as they retraced their steps.

"What about this one?" she asked him. "This is one for women."

Alice pointed to a broad, two-story building. The front of the structure was lined with windows: eight of them, four above and four below. In each open window was the figure of a young woman, as if they existed within picture frames. They wore colorful scarves and flimsy, open garments. One of them wore no clothing at all—she held her breasts cupped in her hands, pressing them together and shaking them playfully at the men who stood cheering in the street. Another woman leaned out of her window dangerously, laughing all the while.

"That is not a hotel," Bird grumbled, and he grabbed her arm, as if the sight of these happy women was something he wished for her not to see.

She twisted her neck to view the women for as long as she could. When she finally turned to look ahead, there was a man with a monkey on his shoulder.

This was the place she had been meant to come with her father and mother when she was a child; suddenly, all the intervening years seemed to her like nothing more than a long dream, a period of waiting. She felt as if she belonged here, in this city full of marvels. And she would be one marvel among the rest.

∾

After her arrival in 1857, Alice Kelly would become one of the city's most famous inhabitants. Even after the public's interest faded, she would long be remembered as an anecdote, one more colorful character woven into the tapestry of that place that was known for its host of eccentrics, proof of what the city had once been: a wild place that existed only for a short while as the American frontier reached its terminus at the Pacific. She would watch buildings rise and fall and rise again, as the nineteenth century gave way to the twentieth. And even then, she would persist, mostly forgotten, her feet moving every day along familiar routes as she eked out her existence by scavenging from the city's excess. Stranded there by life, no less shipwrecked than when she had been on the island, with not a soul alive who knew that the old woman they saw wandering the streets was the one who'd once been called The Wild Girl.

∾

"Ah," Bird finally said, regarding a disappointingly plain-looking building. "This is our hotel."

He gave the porter another coin to carry up their luggage. Their room was nearly identical to many of the others she'd known: the same bed, basin, and washstand. A small wardrobe. Only the design on the wallpaper seemed to differ. This room was papered in brown, with a repeated pattern of tall golden columns topped with fleurs-de-lis.

Bird closed the shades to hide the room from the late afternoon sun. She wanted the windows open, so she could look out into the street. There was so much more to see; she thought that the wonders the city could produce would have no end.

"I will be going down to the lobby."

"I want to go," she said.

"You are exhausted. I think you should sleep."

"I don't want to sleep."

"Sit and count sheep," Bird encouraged her. He gave her a full dropper of medicine and as it washed over her, she dimly heard the shutting of the door, the turning of the key in the lock.

5.

The Impresario

Bird leaned on his stick with one hand and gripped Alice's arm with the other as they moved through the crowded streets, searching for another elusive address. The city's organization was haphazard. There were few street signs. Some of the buildings were numbered, but the numbers made no sense. He had just passed seventy and then seventy-five, and yet here was a brick-fronted bank that proclaimed itself as number thirty-five and one-half. The terrain of the city was so uneven that progressing even a short distance required significant effort, and the idea of backtracking filled him with dread.

They had been in California for three days, and he still could not get over his amazement that there was a city there at all, where before there had been only a sleepy mission house, a miners' camp. Where had it all come from? He felt a particular weightlessness when he opened the curtains of the hotel room window each morning, to see it all still there, and to realize that he stood at the very edge of the civilized world. Something in the West had called to him, as it had called to so many others: the prospect of a new life. The idea of leaving all his failures behind him.

Since their arrival, he'd more than once been seized by a momentary panic that he'd made the wrong decision. The city was full of brothels and gambling parlors and was crowded with Chinese and a particularly murderous breed of Australian, who stared at them from shaded alleys with eyes that suggested a great capacity for violence. But then he would view the new faces of stone buildings, the crowded harbor, the bustle of streets full of men all rushing off to their business, and reassured himself that this was the face of progress. It was difficult not to be caught up in the spirit of it. He'd seen enough destitute men in the streets to know the rumors of limitless wealth had been exaggerated, but still there was a pervading sense that all of the men here were somehow collaborating in the same great endeavor. The entire city had burned to the ground no less than six times in the past ten years, and each time it had been built back up within the year, better than the last.

"Where are we going?" Alice asked him again.

"I told you. I have arranged a meeting with a business associate. He wishes to meet you."

He followed Pacific Street up and down its entire length twice before he found the place he was looking for. There was no sign outside the building that would have identified it, save for a small placard in a ground floor window that showed a crude image of a bird sitting in a disembodied hand, broad lines of the same blue paint. This, then, must be the *Bird-in-Hand*, where the dramatist J. Galloway took his lunch at eleven. The man hadn't been hard to track down—his grand theater, it turned out, was still under construction, a project plagued with financial difficulties that had been discussed in the newspapers. And when Bird contacted him, he'd been eager to meet.

It was a small, quiet lunchroom with six or seven round tables and a bar. The floor was swept clean. The barkeep was a tidy man who acknowledged their entrance with a nod. A few men played monte at one table, and at another, a man was fast asleep with his head cradled in his arms.

The only one who could have been Galloway was in the corner. He was a compact man in a tight-fitting olive suit, a derby hat on his head, a flower through one of his buttonholes, and a thick graying moustache drooping over his lips. He was seated beneath a long painting of a fleshy, nude woman reclining on a divan, her breasts hanging like overripe fruit. Alice's eyes immediately found the painting and she would not be distracted from it as Bird tried to usher her toward the table.

"Mr. Galloway?"

"Ah! This is Lieutenant Bird! The great man! Come!" He had an accent Bird guessed to be Russian. Before him, a cloudy glass half-full of something brown, a plate that contained only greasy crumbs, and a newspaper neatly folded down to a small square of print. "And this must be Alice!" he announced, leaning to kiss her on both of her cheeks. She recoiled from the assault of his moustache and wiped her face with her palm.

"But what will you drink?"

"Whiskey will do."

Galloway called to the bartender for whiskey, and the man brought over two glasses and a bottle. He poured one for Bird and one for Alice, which Bird frowned at and slid away from her before she could take hold of it.

"Milk for the girl, please."

"We don't have milk," the bartender said.

"Water?"

He was back in moments with a glass of something only a shade paler than the weak-tea color of their whiskeys. Bird was skeptical of both beverages, and his feeling was validated when he lifted his glass to take a tentative, inquiring sip.

"This is not whiskey," he stated, wrinkling his mouth at the taste.

Galloway shrugged off the comment and asked if they would like anything to eat, offering to put it on his bill.

"No, I think not," Bird said. If this was whiskey, he didn't wish to see what they called food.

Galloway told the barkeep to leave the bottle. Bird had never been good at small talk, and wondered when the man would get down to business; he wiped his mouth and said, "If I may ask . . . your accent? Where is it from?"

"Gdańsk," Galloway replied.

"Is that . . . Danzig?"

"Yes, yes. In German, is Danzig."

"You are German?"

"No, no. Polish." He pointed at his chest, as if there might be some confusion.

"I only ask because your name . . . it sounds Scotch, if I had to guess."

"I have made this name in America," he said. "My name before this was not American. Ignatius Czwojdziński. Who will go to Czwojdziński's theater? I think no one."

Czwojdziński, or Galloway, explained his design to Bird. Much of his talk was artistic, and difficult to follow. He believed that San Francisco would soon be considered one of the major cities of the world, to rival New York or London, and that the men who lived there would require a new kind of theater. The man of the frontier, he explained, had no stomach for the tiresome routines of antiquity. They required a *living theater*.

"That is why it is good, very good you have come. The man of the West does not wish to see history," he said. "He does not wish for *Cleopatra*." He spat the name with something like contempt. "What is history here? No, they wish for *realism*."

"Realism?" Bird repeated.

"Yes!" he declared. He indicated Alice with both of his hands. "This!! This is *realism*."

Alice's attention was not on Galloway. Her eyes were following two women—prostitutes, Bird surmised—who had entered the establishment to circulate among the customers. They were covered with sequins and sparkling jewelry made from nothing more than cut glass.

"I'm not entirely sure what you mean," he said. "You'll have to excuse me, I am not normally involved in the theater."

"They see a play about the girl," he said, shaking his hands at Alice, "and then . . . they see the girl. You see? *Realism*. It is not history. She is here."

"I see," Bird said. He finished his drink and reached to start on the one the bartender had poured for Alice. "What you desire," he slowly reasoned "is a kind of authenticity, and immediacy. You wish for the issues your theater deals with to touch the lives of contemporary men, in a direct way."

Galloway said, "I can see that we will be very good to work together. You are a man who is very wise."

"If authenticity is what you seek, I think I have something to offer you . . ."

Galloway took a moment to drain his own glass in celebration.

"I happen to have put together a lecture, about the girl's discovery. We have performed already in twelve cities. I have brought some notices," he said, fishing in a vest pocket for a few worn and folded newspaper clippings, which Galloway did not look at.

Galloway waved at them dismissively. "The man of the West does not wish for lectures."

"But what could be more authentic than hearing it straight from the horse's mouth? The story of how I discovered her?"

"Please," Galloway said, closing his eyes as if suddenly weary. "Please, no. You have said, you are not involved in the theater, yes?"

"Not until recently."

"I am in the theater all of my life."

"Well, I am sure you know your business."

"Yes. I will do my business." He revealed that he'd already written the work he wished to present, which he'd titled *The Bride of the Sea*.

Bird wrinkled his face. "Isn't that a bit lurid?" he asked.

"No," Galloway replied, nearly offended. "There is nothing *lurid*."

Alice watched as one of the prostitutes led a card player up the back staircase.

"Where are they going?" she asked quietly.

"Do not mind them," Bird said to her. "It is none of your concern."

The whiskey, or whatever it was, was in fact very strong, and Bird's mind felt sluggish. He registered that Galloway was saying something important: he was offering a sixteenth of the profit from the play, in exchange for their participation, though Bird still wasn't entirely sure what this entailed.

"And you mentioned reimbursing the cost of our travel?"

"Yes, yes, of course . . . you will have it all to the penny when we see the receipts."

"I will be in the play?" Alice asked Galloway, surprising them both when she spoke up.

"Yes, yes," Galloway assured her.

"Wait. I did not think that was the arrangement," Bird complained.

Instead of replying, Galloway stood and pulled a handful of coins from his pocket and then threw them on the ground.

"I want to buy for every man in this house," he called to the bartender.

"If you pick that back up and hand it over we'll do it," the bartender said.

Galloway, or Czwojdziński, swayed in place like an old pine. "It is my pleasure to announce on this day that a company has been formed to create the first great work of the Western stage. And it will be only in one theater, and that is *Galloway's Dramatic Museum*."

"What's it about," one of the card players called, without looking up from his hand. Bird noticed that the man who'd gone upstairs with the prostitute was already back at his seat, playing cards again. Both women were gone.

"You have heard of the female Robinson Crusoe?" Galloway swung his arm toward Alice, causing her to wince away.

"Who's that?" one card player asked another. The table-sleeper had now awoken and was regarding the whole conversation with drunken skepticism.

Galloway raised his empty glass, though his money still lay upon the floor.

6.

A Warm Reception

Before the premiere of the play, Galloway worked to put Alice's name in every mouth in the city. Californians were a peculiar and insular tribe; the thrust of his campaign was to paint Alice as *one of them*, a famous citizen the new state could claim as their own. The first article that appeared, in the *Alta California*, was titled "A Very Long Journey." It did not focus on her wildness, but took a more sympathetic tone, calling her *San Francisco's lost daughter*, and highlighting the fact that she'd been waylaid on one of the early clippers headed there during the gold rush. It was as if a prodigal daughter was returning.

They attended a grand "welcoming ceremony" in Portsmouth Square—a treeless plaza that lay across the street from City Hall—complete with the presence of a city councilman meant to make it appear as an official gesture, though Galloway had paid for his attendance. It was held on a sunny Sunday afternoon and drew many passersby with large banners proclaiming there would be a free lunch. Buckets of beer were offered by nearby saloon-keepers. There was a German band and Galloway had invited a speaker from the Society of California Pioneers. Bird made some remarks from the stage as well, the parts of his lecture that focused on Alice (pared down to five minutes at Galloway's request), after which Alice mounted the small and hastily-erected platform to wave at the crowd and receive great cheering and applause from those who'd been lured there by the promise of roast beef sandwiches.

After the presentations, Galloway paraded them among some of the more important men in town. Bankers, manufacturers, newspaper publishers, men in every sort of business. Galloway knew all of them, and steered Bird from one to the next, prodding him again and again to tell the story of how he'd shared a cigar with Pierce.

Bird was introduced to a prominent land agent named Jacob Mirmiran and was fascinated by his story. He'd been stranded in the West as a common soldier when his regiment disbanded at the conclusion of the Mexican War. He hadn't possessed the money or the means to carry himself back to Cincinnati—the army had left him with five dollars and a mule in a rough and uncivilized country. Since those days, he'd pulled himself up by his bootstraps. He claimed that he'd tried his hand, in one fashion or another, at almost every enterprise known in the city: shipping, mining, speculation in coffee and tea, and now land and real estate. Bird was filled with admiration for the man's grit: there he was, rubbing shoulders with the city's best, when only a decade earlier he'd wintered in a cave and been forced to eat his beloved mule.

The city councilman was eager to be seen escorting Alice around the park so that every man could tip his hat to her. Bird overheard her ask him, "Where is the dog?"

"What was that?" he heard the councilman answer.

"My father told me of a wonderful dog," she said.

Bird smiled as he stuffed his pockets with offered cigars.

∼

Galloway invited Bird to attend a performance, a play titled *Mazeppa*, to see a young ingénue who'd been stirring up the city's press for some months prior with her scandalous performance. He suggested she might be the one to play the part of Alice.

The play was being presented in a rough theater, the hard benches occupied by porters and livery men. It took Bird until halfway through the first act to even realize which role he was meant to be watching—the actress was playing the role of a man, a young prince. He'd seen men playing women before, of course, in seamen's theatricals, but nothing like this. Then, at the very end, Bird had sat rigid in his seat, astonished at what occurred on the stage. Seized by soldiers, the young prince was roughly stripped of his (or her?) velvet cape, breeches, and plumed helmet, and stood apparently naked before the hooting crowd. Actually, she was in a flesh-colored body stocking, but the effect was shocking. He did not know if he should blush or hoot or hide his eyes for shame.

"This . . ." Galloway said, speaking loud enough to be heard over the clamor from the crowd, "this is *realism*!"

"It is something," Bird replied. "I'll give you that."

The naked boy-girl was roughly taken and tied facing upright on the back of a "wild horse," a feat of flexibility that made it impossible not to see the curve of her breasts beneath the stocking, the rising mound of hair that covered her sex. The horse, really a tame nag, then trotted right through the audience, who were whipped into a delighted frenzy by their passage. They all stood and followed her out the door. Bird and Galloway followed the rest outside, where night after night the audience watched the spectacle trot off down Pacific Street to excited cheers and catcalls.

"This one knows her business," Galloway assured him, and Bird was forced to agree.

～

As word of Alice's arrival spread, they entertained visitors in their hotel room, made up of more people who wished to meet her. For Mrs. Sutter, a society woman, he made sure Alice was thoroughly medicated—too much so, in fact, because as Sutter and her cronies cooed over her and drank tea on folding chairs brought up by the hotel manager, she only nodded off and would not answer any questions. The famous Lola Montez also visited and did her spider dance for Alice, in which she removed carved whalebone spiders from a hidden pocket in her dress and then stamped them to powder on the floor. When she was finished, Alice followed in her footsteps, making sure they were all dead.

But they could not stay in the hotel forever. Bird was considering putting down roots in the city and had contacted Mr. Mirmiran to show him suitable properties. They arranged to meet at Meiggs' Wharf, which extended nearly two thousand feet into the bay. Something about it disturbed Bird, and Mirmiran caught him scowling.

"Are you suffering from dyspepsia?" he asked. He offered Bird a pinch of cocaine, which he declined.

"Why the devil would they build it here?" Bird asked, studying the shape of the waterfront. "And not past the breakwater to the east? This is a terrible place for a wharf this long."

Mirmiran could offer no explanation. As they walked along the waterfront, he presented Bird with unrolled maps and pointed out into the bay to show him water lots which might be purchased.

"Are you trying to sell me land that is under five feet of seawater?"

"No, no," Mirmiran chuckled. "They are filling it in. Look there," he pointed at two men dumping wheelbarrows of what looked like crumbled stone and broken furniture off the edge of a small pier. Other men were tossing sandbags. Mirmiran explained that local real estate had become inflated to such a premium, they'd resorted to creating entirely new lots in the shallow cove. The deepwater stood far off, anyway, and the long piers required to reach it were being slowly swallowed by the city and turned into bustling streets.

Mirmiran chattered all the while about how there was nothing to do right now but to *buy*. Bird's knee struggled with the hills and the land agent again offered his cocaine, presenting a small mound on a tiny spoon.

"Just give that a strong sniff," he encouraged Bird.

This time, Bird took it, desperate as he was for relief. His first reaction was only to sneeze and then sneeze again, with a peculiar tingling, burning feeling in his sinuses.

"I don't feel any effect at all!" Bird shouted.

They walked across the city all day, up and down the hills, sniffing cocaine as Mirmiran pointed out various properties. They viewed an abandoned flour mill, a petite cottage, a weedy patch of ground that was home to several discarded wagon wheels. Each one seemed to contain a different kind of promise, a different life that could be led in that magnificent city. All of the possibilities flew through his mind . . . it was hours before he realized he was carrying his walking stick and no longer needed to lean on it. He felt like a young man again, climbing the side of a mountain in Patagonia to survey a new land.

He bought the most expensive property that Mirmiran had to show him. It was a two-story building, made entirely of brick (good insurance against fire, Mirmiran commented), which sat between two less impressive structures: a private house and a small dental parlor advertised with an enormous model tooth that hung above the door. It was on Montgomery Street, not far from Rincon Hill and South Park, where the wealthy made their homes, and was also close enough to the bay that he could smell the brine and hear the cries of the gulls if he stood at one of the upstairs windows. The entire second story was a French-style apartment with kitchen, sitting room, and two small bedchambers that could easily be their living space. The bottom floor was wide open. It had formerly been a saloon, though you could not tell save for the short bar counter. Mirmiran suggested it could be rented out to a business, to create a permanent stream of revenue.

Bird walked slowly through the emptiness where there'd once been tables and chairs. He opened the shutters so that light could come in and splash on the walls. He breathed the dry odors of wood and plaster and imagined paper on the walls, a good cleaning and a coat of polish on the floor. Something was taking shape in his mind, an idea he hadn't possessed until he'd walked into the building, but which already felt familiar to him, as if it had been his design all along.

"No," he said to Mirmiran. "I have other plans for this."

7.

. . .

The new house was better than the hotel room, because she at least had the freedom of moving between several rooms—kitchen, sitting room, her small bedchamber where she kept her belongings—and there was a bay window that overlooked the street. It had a bench she could sit on to watch the life pass below her, allowing her to feel safe and enclosed, high above it all. Montgomery Street offered a changing landscape: in the mornings, the vendors put out their wares, bushels of fruit in front of the grocer's and shovels lined neatly near the doorway of the hardware store. They swept their front walks, moving the dust into the street where it would be trampled down by the first passing horses and carts. By the middle of the day, the street was full of men rushing about. In the evening the traffic thinned, and she could see a few women among them. They moved like the cats she'd seen in Panama, emerging from nowhere all at the same time, alone or in pairs.

When she tired of the street, she retreated into her bedchamber to be among the things she'd collected: her hairbrush; the ragdoll she'd stolen from the girl on the ship, the names of both girl and doll lost to her now; her feathers and coins and smooth stones; her line of teeth on a string. Each thing made her think of something, sometimes no more than a feeling she wished to preserve. She longed to be like them: unchanging. No matter where she was, her things remained what they were. There was a small shell that made a sound. She couldn't remember where she'd gotten it. But each time she took it in her hand, it retained the same ridges she could feel with her fingers, the same caramel swirls in its coloring. When she put it to her lips and blew, it always produced the same note.

There was a golden cross that most often made her think of William. Christ had been hung on the cross, and William had told her that Christ was only one messenger in the world and that every man could be a prophet like Christ if he would only stop and listen to hear the voices of the angels.

"And what is each woman?" she'd asked him.

"Women are God's grace," he'd answered, and gently kissed her head.

Mr. Galloway wished for her to be seen about the city, so Bird took her with him as he strolled along the wide thoroughfares. They stopped to place orders at all the shops for the furniture and other things they would require. Bird ordered pots and pans for the kitchen, a bed for her with a feather mattress; for the downstairs parlor, he made more extravagant purchases: plush upholstered chairs, elegant mirrors, bookshelves and books to put on them. In one store full of fancy things—candelabras and polished pewter and delicately carved statuettes—he purchased a massive orb on a wooden housing that allowed one to spin it in any direction. A globe, she realized as she deciphered a coastline, the blue of the water and the brown of the land. Different countries, large and small, with little markings of mountains and waves. While Bird was occupied in his haggling with the shopkeep, she placed her finger on the globe, on the places where she had been, and she believed now that she had been to them all. It was another one of the things for Bird's parlor. He'd explained to her that she would not be permitted there—it was to be a room for men.

In another shop, Bird invited her to select the printed pictures that would hang upstairs in the sitting room. Alice approached the task with great seriousness. She had never been given authority over such an important decision; they must be pictures, she thought, that could be looked at again and again, day after day, without ever growing tiresome.

The shop that sold them was narrow as a hallway, with small, colorful images hanging on both sides above bins filled with more of the same: scenes of ships and horses, court justices, poets, and other notable men whom Bird named for her. A snow-capped mountain. A pasture, attended by a herd of smudged sheep. She studied each one, trying to determine if she wished to see it forever.

Alice wandered back and forth in the narrow shop for some time and finally she selected an image of a red Indian smoking his long pipe, wrapped in skins, a cluster of feathers in his hair. She reached up to remove it from its peg on the wall. Bird was waiting impatiently behind her and took it from her hands.

"Very well, let's get this one . . . come along."

He made his way up to the counter at the front of the narrow store.

"But you said I can choose four . . ."

"We've spent enough time here." Bird turned to the counter man, who had waited silently as she made her choice. "Give us three more," he said. "Anything will do."

Alice stood on her toes to watch the counter man's busy process. Behind him were more rows of bins, from which he selected rolled sheets of paper. Then he produced wooden box frames from somewhere beneath him, out of sight, applied paste to them with a thick brush, and then fixed each image onto one of the box frames with a tool like a rolling pin that flattened them. His movements were sharp and swift as he ran the tool over each picture exactly five times, with the same rhythm of *up-down-up-down-up!* Then he passed the four completed, framed prints over the counter as Bird's hands burrowed for his money purse. Alice saw her red Indian there, or one just like it, and three others that were not as good: a wagon being pulled by a donkey, the stern face of a man who was not known to her, and one that showed only words, arranged in an elegant script. She tried to read it but the words were as unfamiliar and impenetrable as the face of the man. Before they had even made their way to the door, the counter man waddled out from behind the counter to return the original red Indian to his place on the wall.

Farther down the street, they passed a display window full of dazzling garments like those worn by saloon women, draped over headless wooden mannequins. Flashing brassieres and feathered scarves, delicate webs of lace.

"I want to go in this one," Alice insisted, half to test him.

Bird's eyes followed hers to the window and he quickly said, "No, absolutely not."

"I will," she announced. Still angry with him for not allowing her to select all the pictures, she abruptly strode through the shop's door, setting off a bell that tinkled daintily.

Inside, she saw all the colorful lace and cloth, now hanging shapelessly and uninvitingly on racks. When not arranged on the mannequins, they appeared no more interesting than rags. There was a man inside the shop. He smelled like flowers even at a distance and smiled at her in a way that made her want to leave.

Bird opened the door behind her and leaned in. "Come here," he hissed. He could not enter this place, she thought. Some power held him back. "Please," he said. "I will give you a dollar and you can buy whatever you like, if you will only come outside." He looked up and tipped his hat to the man behind the counter, who was still smiling grotesquely.

"Something for the young lady?" the counter man asked.

Bird said, "No, thank you," as she took his offered hand and left the shop.

True to his promise, once they were safely outside, he gave her a coin and said that she could spend it in any other store. He suggested the candy shop. "Or," he suggested, "you can put it in the bank to gain interest. It is your decision. Though I recommend the bank."

She held the coin in her hand as they moved down the street. For once, Bird was following her, rather than pulling her along. She took pleasure in it, and strolled slowly, carefully perusing every window display. She moved all the way along to the cross street and stopped and looked at him. He had a searching look on his face. She turned and wandered around the corner.

"Where are we going?" he asked her.

"I know a place," she said. "You said I could spend it on whatever I wished."

"What do you wish to purchase?"

"Follow me." She turned and hurried away.

"Wait! Alice, you're getting ahead of me!" he shouted after her. She heard the panic edge into his voice. "Alice!" There were men and horses and a wagon with slowly turning wheels. She wove among them, moving on the plank sidewalk and the mud of the street. She didn't know where she was going. It was like a game. She turned and saw Bird struggling along, and then he was out of sight. She turned another corner. She hurried along, now looking at each storefront until she saw one that gave her pause. Its display window showed several carved wooden heads—the only reason she knew them to be such was that they wore hats. Each head was egg-shaped and featureless, with only a smooth raised swell where the nose would be. They looked to her like a faceless tribunal, men and ladies all sitting to consider some grave matter. The hats they wore seemed to give them different personalities; one was a stern man who said *no, no, no*; another, a woman who laughed at everything. She heard the chorus of their voices all at once.

Bird, breathless, grabbed her arm roughly.

"This one!" she said. She pointed at the window.

"A hat?" he said. "You wish for a hat?"

She studied the hats in the window. Her eyes were drawn to a particular one; it had a brim that curled up slightly on either side. Not as tall or posturing as the elegant top hats, nor as short and stubby as the straw boaters. It was made of a rich black material that could almost reflect the light. A band of ribbon wrapped around its base.

"This is the one," she said. She moved to the window and touched the glass.

Bird's face wrinkled. "That is fifteen dollars."

"I want it," she insisted. She took a step away from him.

He relented, and finally said, "Well, come on then," with a sigh. He moved to the door of the store and held it open for her. Inside, she was allowed to try it on. She turned and regarded herself in a small mirror positioned at the center of the shop, which had to be tilted down for her to see. The hat was too large for her head and came to rest on her ears. Still, it made her look taller, she thought, as tall as a man.

"We have lovely hats for young ladies," the salesman offered.

With a mischievous smile and a wink to her, Bird said, "We'll take this one. No need to wrap it, the girl will wear it out."

~

From that day, the hat would become inseparable from her, both in fact and myth. She would stuff its crown with Bird's old newspapers, stolen from the crate beside the stove, until it hung just right on her head. She'd wear it both in and out of the house, often falling asleep with it on as she napped at her customary place on the bench before the bay window.

She wore it during the second and final photographic portrait that would ever be taken of her, at the small shop of daguerreotypist George Robinson Fardon, at Galloway's expense. It was the only clear photograph of her that was ever taken, the only evidence of what she looked like.

Fardon captured her against a dark cloth backdrop, from the waist up, the small stool beneath her not visible. She wore a dark dress that, in the portrait, is of an indeterminate color, similar to that of the backdrop; the only bright spot in the image is her face, framed by the pale hair that hung to her shoulders and the white lace collar of her dress. Her expression was firm and blank, staring at something behind the camera without interest. The hat was darker than her dress, darker than the backdrop; it provided a sharp contrast to her face and seemed to consume the light.

Hundreds of copies of the image would be printed and sold for a nickel to theatergoers and tourists who wished to bring a remembrance with them back to London, to Paris, to New York, as some tangible proof that they'd visited a wild place at the edge of the world. And they would settle for this portrait, of a taut girl wearing an ill-fitting man's hat that gave her, along with the black and undefined smudges around her eyes, the impression of madness.

∽

"Alice, someone is here to see you . . ."

She looked up from the carpet, which was littered with postage stamps. Bird had left them on the writing table in his bedchamber, and she had taken it upon herself to separate them—they had been all together in a sheet and she had folded and torn them carefully along the perforations. She thought they looked like tiny windows. Out of each window stared the same square-jawed, white-haired man. Who was he? She thought he looked like an old king. And why was the king looking out so many windows? He must have been waiting for someone to arrive.

Bird was standing in the doorway and frowned when he saw what she'd done to his stamps. There was no one with him.

"There is a woman who wishes to meet with you. She is waiting downstairs."

She was so rarely allowed to descend into that world Bird had built. The downstairs parlor was full of books on shelves, armchairs covered in leather that had been worked to a bright cherry shine. Men had arrived with crates full of bottles that were lined up behind the bar. On a sideboard, an array of cut crystal glasses. There was striped paper on the walls, above a wood-grained wainscoting nearly as tall as her. Carpets on the floor woven with intricate patterns. The parlor had taken on the air, for her, of a secret temple. While Bird slept at night, she would always check two doors: the one that led down there, into the dark mystery of Bird's parlor, and the one to the cabinet in his bedchamber where he kept her medicine. Neither ever yielded.

A woman was waiting in one of the armchairs. She was thin, almost delicate-looking, with dark eyebrows and a youthful face. Her hair was raven black and kinked, hanging in loose curls. It was almost as disheveled as Alice's own hair, never combed or brushed, hidden under her hat.

"There's our gal," the woman announced. She took a hand and swished one of the two wrinkled scarves that hung from her neck.

Bird had placed a bowl of boiled eggs on a low table near her. Alice settled in a chair and then picked up her legs and tucked them beneath her. The woman studied her movements with pretty eyes the color of dull emeralds.

"Alice, I would like you to meet Miss Ada Stanley. She is an actress who will be in the play. She would like to meet with you and speak for a while. Miss Stanley, this is Alice Kelly."

"Alice, that's your name? I think it's a lovely name. My mother's name was Alice. Pleased to meet you."

She leaned forwards to offer Alice her hand. A wrinkle of displeasure passed through Alice as she considered the idea of another woman possessing her name.

"Would you like some coffee?" Bird asked the woman.

"Thank you kindly."

"Cream and sugar?"

Stanley craned her neck to study the bottles behind the short but well-apportioned bar. "Yes, and a bit of whiskey if you don't mind," she said.

"Do you go on a stage?" Alice asked.

"I do."

Bird poured coffee from a pot into porcelain cups and then fetched the whiskey and gave a generous shot into each. "A woman after my own heart," he said, but Stanley was too intently focused on Alice to notice.

"I've played many different roles," she said. "I have been Cleopatra . . . can you imagine that? Me, as an Egyptian queen?"

Alice entertained a dull hope that this woman would take her away from Bird and carry her off to a stage where she would stand night after night. She would live with a family of actors and acrobats, she imagined, all sorts of characters who could flip and juggle, and perhaps the dog she had been thinking of. Ever since their arrival in San Francisco, she'd been entertaining small fantasies like this, of what would happen to her when Bird himself disappeared, as everything did in time. But she kept waking each morning to find him still there, and the door of the apartment still locked.

"I will be an actress, too," she replied.

Stanley considered her and said, "I would be happy to teach you what I know. There are so few great women in the craft. Would you like that?"

"Yes."

"Can you show me your skill? What role can you play for me?" Stanley asked her.

She was embarrassed; she could think of no answer. She saw herself on a stage singing, but she could not hear the song. They were all watching her, the men and women in the audience, hypnotized by her beauty.

"No," Alice answered. "I don't like to do that."

"But an actress must play parts." Stanley sipped her coffee and gave Alice the space to answer.

Bird thought to help her: "We have come off a lecture tour? You haven't heard? It was very successful in the Northeast. But I suppose the news is slow to make it all the way out here . . ."

"Well, congratulations. I am about to begin a new production myself," she winked at Bird. To Alice, more gently, she said, "I will be playing *you*, did you know that? My next role is to be Alice Kelly, in a play about all your grand adventures."

Alice went silent. She felt a kind of heat in her face and hands as she came to understand that this woman would play the part she thought was meant for *her*. Then she was on her feet. "I will be in the play. Mr. Galloway said I will be . . ."

"Please, Alice," Bird said. He picked up his walking stick, leaning against the side of his chair, and stamped it firmly on the ground, twice.

She could see the actress was already pretending to be her: Stanley had drawn her legs up on the chair, just as Alice had.

Alice took two steps over to the actress and grabbed at her necklace of pearls. The white globes seemed to contain her pride in little milky bubbles. Alice wished to see the necklace break, and for them to scatter on the floor. But it did not, and her effort only yanked Stanley forwards roughly in her chair. Stanley swiped an arm at her involuntarily and said, "Oh! Oh!" then froze with her arm still held in the air, to fend off the next attack.

"I will not have it!" Bird spat. He rose and grabbed Alice and held her arm as he fished the medicine bottle from his pocket. "Open," he said to her. He shook her and repeated the word until she complied and then he put some drops on her tongue. "I apologize. Alice is having one of her spells," he said to the woman.

Was she having a spell? Within moments she felt her anger wash off her, as if it had been insubstantial to begin with. A film of sand. Somehow, she'd been returned to her chair, but she couldn't remember getting there.

She looked at the actress, still holding a frightened hand at chest height. When she saw Alice once again regarding her, she dropped it and made an effort to return to her more casual posture.

"It's alright," the actress cooed. "Do you think them pretty? Here . . ." She reached up and removed the pearls from her neck and slipped them over Alice's head. "What's in the bottle?"

"It's laudanum. It's from a doctor," Bird said.

"Can I see it?"

He hesitated and then passed her the dark brown bottle. It had no label. She pulled off the cap and smelled it. "Do you mind?" she asked.

"You require it?"

"It is good for my nerves," she said. Without waiting for permission, dabbed the bottle onto the balled-up edge of her scarf and held that to her lips. She breathed in deeply, as if smelling the loveliest of flowers. "Will you have some?" she said, offering him the scarf, as if they were guests that she entertained in her own parlor.

Bird looked up from his tin, which contained a powder he'd told Alice was for a toothache. He inhaled sharply and then said loudly, "No thank you! I am perfectly healthy!" Then he reached around, looking for his walking stick as if he wished to stamp it on the ground again, this time to display his vigor, but it had fallen to the ground and was out of easy reach. Instead, he began to pop boiled eggs into his mouth.

"I must say," Stanley said to Alice after a brief silent moment. "My nerves are calm. Are your nerves calm as well?"

"My nerves are calm," Alice mumbled, but it felt as if she was not saying the words, only repeating them like a parrot. She looked over and saw that her hat had fallen from her head. It sat top down on the carpet, as if waiting for someone to fill it up.

8.

THE SHIP

Bird found California's lack of seasons disorienting, and time seemed to be moving too quickly. The day of the play's premiere was set for April 1st, in the spring of 1858. They had been in San Francisco for nearly six months already, and in that time, Galloway had completed the construction of his theater. In the printed announcements and handbills, the title of the play had been changed from *The Bride of the Sea* to *The Wild Girl of San Francisco*, an alteration Galloway had failed to mention or explain.

His design was such that Bird had never truly understood it. Galloway seemed to think it vitally important that Alice appear on the stage at the end of every performance, to provide the audience with a link, however small, with the real events that had inspired the play. In addition to this, their participation gave the play a kind of sanction that the inevitable copycats and imitators would lack. Theirs would be the one "true" account of Alice's life, disregarding the fact that Bird had not been consulted and Galloway had, as far as he could tell, made the whole thing up. Still, it seemed to be only a modest amount of work on Bird's part for such a reward—Galloway assured him that the production, if a hit, would make them rich men may times over.

He invited Bird and Alice to visit the new theater before the opening. Galloway's Dramatic Museum was an impressive edifice of stone on a prominent corner, with tall double doors opening into a richly decorated lobby. It was every bit as large as the Jenny Lind Theater that had been converted into the new city hall, and which had loomed large over the welcoming ceremony in Portsmouth Square.

Inside, gold leaf covered everything possible: the balustrades, the ticket windows, the arms and backs of the lobby chairs. Green velvet curtains hung over the windows; the entire scene was illuminated by gas lighting fixtures on the walls and an ornate chandelier that seemed to float in the space above. A wide velvet staircase allowed patrons to reach the balconies and private boxes. Just seeing the impressiveness of the theater put Bird's mind at ease. There was a sense, when entering, that one was climbing into a dream of opulence. He wondered how the man had ever raised the capital for such an undertaking.

Galloway strode through the lobby, pointing at this and that like a proud father. Alice had been excited to see the theater where her play would be performed, and asked Galloway again and again when it would open, and how long it was until then.

He said, "Two weeks, my chickadee," without looking at her, intent as he was to point out flourishes in the architecture.

They followed him through another set of doors into the theater itself. He bragged that it could seat two thousand, in the rows of plush upholstered seating. Bird could not imagine how many seamstresses it must have taken; he imagined an army of old women on their knees, sewing up seat cushions with the slight, sure movements of their fingers. He was a part of this, he thought. All this elegance, this majesty. Somehow, his name had become attached to it, and every guest who sat in the theater would see his story, how he'd rescued the girl, and would know his name. He was almost overwhelmed by it, and felt momentarily ill.

There was no one else out among the seats save for an old man sweeping the floor. The sound of hammers and sawing pulled them down the wide center aisle, toward the back of the building. Alice walked before them, slapping her hand against the backs of the seats. Next to the stage, men were hoisting something into the rafters with ropes and pulleys.

Galloway jogged ahead, waving his cigar in the air. He shouted, "They are supposed to be *green*, you imbecile!" Partially hidden in the wing, a workman was slathering blue paint upon something half as high as a man. Galloway hoisted himself up onto the stage, like a seal mounting a rock, and hurried behind the curtains to chastise the man. Alice followed, sliding up onto the stage and back onto her feet with a quick movement, and then she was gone as well. Bird found the stairs at stage left and limped after them. He passed the workman Galloway had reprimanded and saw that the man was painting wooden cutouts of overlarge seahorses.

When Bird found them backstage, Galloway was showing Alice a number of painted backdrops that had been created. Tranquil island scenes, a jungle that was a riot of swirling greens and browns. A vast oceanic horizon. He pulled this wheeled display aside to reveal a San Francisco street, full of recognizable storefronts and landmarks. The painting contained little fragments from all different parts of the city: One half looked like Telegraph Hill, though without any obvious indication of the nasty business that went on there, while at the other side of the panorama were the stately mansions of Rincon Hill. Galloway pulled up props as well, spears and headdresses. "We have hired greasers to play the Feegees," he explained. "For *realism!*" He used the word so freely that Bird was beginning to wonder if it truly meant anything at all.

Galloway no longer even seemed to be speaking to him; he'd become lost in his own line of thought, defending a thesis he'd obviously long been developing. "The work should be mundane!" he declared. "Any melodrama will do. It is the *setting* which is important. The eye must be tricked into seeing a different world . . ."

Thoroughly lost now, Bird searched for something that would not offend Galloway and decided to use the man's own words. "Wait . . . you are saying you wish for our play . . . to be *mundane*?"

"Please," Galloway intoned. "When you see it . . . here . . ." He swept his arm to move a curtain aside as he strolled back toward the front of the stage. "Then, you will see!"

Across the width of the stage, hidden from the auditorium behind another set of curtains, he showed them two painted rows of wooden waves. At his behest a few burly men yanked them back and forth from the recesses of stage left and right to imitate the movement of the ocean. It was uncanny, the way they almost made Bird feel the motion of water beneath his feet. Alice tugged at a rope that had been hooked onto a peg in the wall. Galloway shouted, "Don't touch that!" The rope fled upwards, and only a moment later a bag of sand thudded against the stage a few feet from her, spilling its contents. She did not jump, but only stared at it like it was a dead bird dropped from the sky.

Bird took her arm. "Don't touch things in this place." He looked up into the darkness above the stage and saw dim shapes: catwalks, a web of lines like those on a ship but whose purposes he could not guess.

They followed Galloway through the second set of curtains and back into the emptiness of the auditorium. Untroubled by her near-accident, Alice wandered to the edge of the stage and looked out at the rows of seats. "There will be people in all of these seats," she said. Then, more a question, she looked to Galloway and said, "They will come to see me?"

"Of course!" Galloway went over and guided her back away from the edge of the stage. He was excited to show them his *pièce de résistance*, which he summoned by shouting, "Benny, let me see my ship!"

A young man in a cap and spectacles poked his head out from behind one curtain to give Galloway a hand signal, then retreated back from whence he'd come. Bird heard a squeal of a crank or winch somewhere unseen. It was so loud that Alice took a few steps away. Then the drapery parted to reveal the prow of an enormous ship, almost half the size of the real item, sailing impossibly toward them with a sound like thunder—the entire thing was carried along on wheels affixed to metal rails. It lurched to a stop a few feet from them as both Bird and Alice stood in awe of it. Galloway, unmindful of their astonishment, or perhaps relishing it, laughed and climbed a rope ladder up the side of the ship. When he reached the deck, he stood upon the prow with his foot proudly up on the figurehead, a bare-breasted ivory-colored woman without nipples or eyes or a face.

"Have you ever seen such a thing?" he shouted incredulously down to them, as if he was just witnessing it for the first time himself. "Now this . . . this is *realism!*"

On the deck there was a wheel, a capstan, and a stub of a mast that only extended above where it could be seen by the audience.

"Benny, pull this curtain," Galloway instructed the man scurrying in the wings. "And give me my waves!" The back curtains parted to reveal the painted waves they'd seen before. They began to slide back and forth again like the teeth of a saw. The open air of the huge auditorium could almost seem like sky. "Can you smell the salt air?" he asked them.

"I can indeed," Bird said. He inhaled deeply and looked out across all the empty theater seats. It was not entirely a lie.

9.

THE WILD GIRL OF SAN FRANCISCO

Bird read the brief newspaper item several times without looking up, a look of stern disapproval resting heavily on his face. He and Galloway were seated in the downstairs parlor, across from one another. Bird's cigar burned steadily in the ashtray like a distant signal fire.

> *MESSAGE FOR,*
> *The One and Only*
> *Wild Girl of San Francisco*
> **ALICE KELLY**

My Dearest One,
Ever since I have first laid my eyes upon you, I must confess that my very SOUL has been in TORMENT. *THUS* . . . I, Phinneas T. Goldwater, being of sound mind and recently established in this FAIR CITY which you call HOME, do hereby request your HAND in MARRIAGE to alleviate such pains as my HEART has ENDURED. . .

If you accept to my PROPOSAL, I pledge that I will build you the finest GRASS HUT on the SHORE where we can eat COCOANUTS in the GENTLE BREEZES. HOW ABOUT IT???

Please reveal your dispensation at:
GALLOWAY'S DRAMATIC MUSEUM
on the eve of the WORLD PREMIERE
OF THE NEW PLAY BY EUROPE'S FOREMOST SCRIBE
J. GALLOWAY & *Company*
THE FIRST OF APRIL, 1858
LIMITED ENGAGEMENT TO FOLLOW
(reserved seats avail. private boxes, galleries)

"Well?" Galloway asked. "What do you think of that?"

"Is this man cracked?"

"Do you find it surprising?"

Bird frowned without looking up at him. "Surprising? I would say so, yes."

"And you might be so curious, in fact, that you will buy a ticket to this play, to witness her reply?"

"I have no idea what you're talking about. You know we'll be at the premiere. And if I meet this fellow, I might have some choice words for him . . ."

Galloway wished for them to arrive at the theater in a spectacular style, and had rented a coach which was pulled through the streets by a team of trained African zebras. On the back of the coach was hung a placard announcing the fact that it carried the celebrated Lieutenant Henry Bird and Alice Kelly, The Wild Girl of San Francisco. Alice was excited by the animals, which she'd never seen outside of a picture book, and was allowed to examine and poke at them as they swished their tails uncomfortably. The coachman had no experience with them—they'd been rented from a traveling menagerie—and held the reins tightly as they careened through the streets, sometimes starting and stopping without apparent reason.

The coachman had been instructed to take a circuitous route back and forth across the city, as a form of last-minute advertisement. When Bird and Alice were finally able to stagger down dizzily in front of the theater, he saw that all of Galloway's promotional work had paid off—it seemed the entire city had gathered for the premiere. Bird saw pale, soft-cheeked and spectacled clerks next to grizzly, bearded men who hunkered like mountains. There were hayseeds, foreigners, dapper swells, society ladies in fine dresses and hats. Witnessing this motley assortment, Bird realized that one of Galloway's odd, rambling ideas had been entirely correct: he'd always insisted that Alice was the perfect heroine for their particular city. Her story, he'd predicted, would unite young and old, rich and poor, because at the end of the day, they were all Californians. And she was a Californian most of all. A beauty without a past. That is what these people had come to see. Though perhaps this was too optimistic, Bird thought, eyeing a disheveled drunk in filthy clothes craning his neck to get a glimpse of her—perhaps some had only come to see a young woman lope around like an animal.

As their arrival was announced by the coachman, the crowd greeted them with exuberant applause. Bird smiled and held up his hand. Alice drifted toward the grand entrance alongside him, where a man in a comically oversized suit was greeting everyone at the door. In one hand, he carried an equally oversized ring of metal, large enough to fit around a man's arm, painted gold with a polished glass stone meant to look like a diamond. He was lifting his hat and handing out small, printed cards to all who entered, which littered the carpeted walkway where patrons had dropped them. They read:

YOU'VE BEEN HAD!
Courtesy of "Phineas T. Goldwater"
WELCOME
TO
GALLOWAYS

As they passed him, this comical figure dropped to his knees and silently wrung his hands, miming that he was begging for her to accept his proposal. The crowd laughed. Alice hid behind Bird.

The lobby, full of people, seemed smaller than Bird remembered. Galloway was nowhere to be found—he was no doubt behind the scenes somewhere, preparing for the curtain's rise. An usher led them up to their box, which provided them with a clear view of the stage and the cheap seating in front of the orchestra pit. Bird and Alice stood at the railing of their box and Alice waved as she was instructed. Another round of applause, more scattered, from this rabble. The general din of hundreds of conversations, the occasional piercing shriek from some low woman.

At the appointed time, the house lights went down and the audience began to settle, though they would not fully quiet until the appearance of the massive prop ship, which was wheeled slowly out onto the stage among sound effects of thunder and lightning emanating from backstage, covering the telltale sound of the ship moving on its runners. Bird looked to Alice and saw she was watching the scene intently. He did not know if she'd ever seen a play before, and certainly he'd never seen a production so lavish.

Standing on the deck of the ship was the actress, Ada Stanley, quickly introduced as a young woman traveling with her mother and father. Her age at the time of the incident had obviously been fudged in Galloway's script. She wore a blond wig; there was no visible trace of her kinked black hair. The expression on her face was one of awestruck innocence; whether she had been thus stricken by the fury of the storm, or something else, was not indicated.

"Do you see?" he now asked Alice, leaning toward her. "This is supposed to be you."

"It is not," she said, too loudly. A few necks turned below them.

"It is Miss Stanley, do you remember her? The actress? She has been done up in your likeness."

"When will I go on the stage?" she asked.

Bird shushed her. "Patience," he said. "We must watch the play first, and then your time will come."

He gave her a drop of laudanum to ease her into the seat, and they returned their attention to Galloway's creation, which, Bird quickly realized, was entirely ridiculous. Galloway had explained that his intent was to capture all the forms of drama—tragedy, comedy, history—in one play, so the audience member did not need to look elsewhere for any type or variety of entertainment. It had sounded like a bad idea to him at the time, and now, seeing it in front of him, it was a train wreck, soaked in melodrama and cheap thrills, without the slightest seriousness. Galloway had taken several liberties with the facts as well, the most notable of which was that William Christensen, in this version of events, was no villain. The mutiny on the *Lady Fortune*, early in the first act, was led by a swarthy, dark-skinned sailor with a shaven head and a dangling earring. He was not meant to represent Christensen but instead was given the made-up and slightly sinister-sounding name of Ernesto. Christensen, played by a broad-chested blond man of striking good features, was presented as a sailor loyal to the captain, who had fallen in love with Alice Kelly from afar. He only pledged himself to the mutiny, faking a change of heart, when he realized that they intended to kidnap her. Galloway had made the alteration because the play needed a hero. "There can be no play with only a damsel," he told Bird. "What kind of a play would that be?"

"I thought I was the hero?" Bird had asked him.

"Yes, yes," Galloway had replied. "But only in act three."

Throughout the first act, this more heroic version of Christensen bided his time in the background and occasionally performed lonely songs and soliloquies on the ship's deck when no others were on the stage. At the climax of the act, he scuffled with Ernesto when the villain began to menacingly approach "Alice," and Christensen wound up casting the man overboard. The actor playing Ernesto did an acrobatic flip, head over heels, off the back rail of the ship and out of sight, letting out a yodel-like cry of defeat. At that moment, several other mutineers, not important enough to be bestowed with names and characteristics save for their ragged clothing and raucous behavior, appeared on the ship from stage right. A terrific swordfight ensued, with Christensen leaping among the men to parry their blades. The whole spectacle was ended with another terrible storm (Bird wondered if there was any rule as to how many storms one play might contain), effected in a most realistic manner, once again highlighting Galloway's skill, at least, with those effects of *realism*: water was thrown on the stage, dousing the actors, and thunder rang out from sheets of tin shaken behind the curtains. And then, the ship shook and retreated from the stage and there was a terrible noise that sounded like nothing in the world Bird had ever heard.

He looked to Alice and saw that she was gripping the arms of her chair. The stage was dark. She looked to Bird with worried eyes and said, "Tell them to stop it."

"Stop what? The play?"

"Tell them it was not like that," she urged Bird. "They must stop."

He had come to know her well enough to sense when she might fall into one of her spells, and now he saw the signs of one approaching. She fidgeted and would not sit properly in her chair. Hoping to head it off, he applied a few more drops of laudanum. This seemed to settle her a bit, though as the stage lights went up again, she said loudly, "That is not William." Her words, cast out into the pregnant pause before the second act began, were heard by all.

The second act began with both Christensen and Alice washing up onto the shore of a deserted island (the wreck of the ship was something beyond even Galloway's capabilities, and thus was implied to have occurred offstage). Here, the tense conspiracy of the first act was replaced with a light, romantic farce as he began to court her (Galloway's deliberate refusal to acknowledge her age now worked to his advantage; between acts, numerous small flourishes had been added to Stanley's appearance to make her look older). Bird yawned through several clever amorous advances and their comical rejections, until finally she relented when Christensen cooked her a dinner of turtle soup on the beach, a scent she could not resist, which drew her from her hiding place in the forest. After this, they built a house of palm fronds and set up housekeeping, being married in a native ceremony after they were visited by canoes, also mounted on runners, containing scantily-clad Mexicans who were meant to represent the inhabitants of nearby islands. To mark the occasion, Christensen made some high-minded remarks about the marriage customs of all cultures being equal before God.

Alice had begun, over the course of the second act, to find the events of the play humorous, and she bubbled with laughter, even when the natives inexplicably turned on the couple and another swordfight ensued. This time, Christensen was stabbed through by a native spear, which prompted another round of cackling from Alice's chair. It was loud enough that Bird saw one of the Mexican actors look up at their private box as he was departing the stage. They paddled off in their canoes, their motives still as obscure and incomprehensible as their fortuitous arrival, just in time to allow Christensen a tear-stained farewell to his bride as he lay dying on the shore.

If there was anything at all that could be praised about the play, it was the performance of Stanley, who managed at turns to encompass all the various forms of womanhood: innocent child, helpless damsel, coy mistress, and then finally faithful wife. Following Christensen's death, when she had been left alone on the island to fend for herself, she sang a beautiful song to the gathered beasts of the forest, represented by wooden parrots and a small and shifting group of docile goats. The painted sea horses, now the correct color, rose from the waves in the background so that they might hear it as well. At the end of the song, live turtles and clipped, flightless seagulls were coaxed out onto the stage by handlers behind the curtains, and one poor, misguided turtle tipped off the stage and into the orchestra pit. It was the end of the second act.

There was then a brief intermission before the third act, and the house lights rose. Few left their seats. When the play resumed, a remarkable and completely unexplained transformation had been wrought in Stanley. The act opened on the now-familiar island backdrop, devoid of life until Stanley came loping onto the stage like a wild dog, eliciting little gasps from the front rows, so abrupt and disturbing was her entrance. Galloway, ingeniously, had clad her in the same sort of flesh-colored body stocking she'd worn for *Mazeppa,* only now, he'd added on top of it some scanty, crude clothing of animal hide, much like that which Alice was pictured wearing in *Frank Leslie's.* Every time she turned on the stage, it seemed the inadequate garments were just about to reveal something unmentionable: a breast, or the pale, fleshy moon of her rear end. The audience on the ground was delighted; those wealthier theater-goers in the upper boxes, Bird would later find out, were scandalized (though this would not wind up hurting ticket sales). But of course, the body stocking made it all acceptable. Never for a moment was Stanley actually unclothed. Galloway had topped *Mazeppa*—rather than just make his lead actress falsely appear nude, he hid the false nudity beneath clothing and allowed only tantalizing glimpses of it, discouraging any scrutiny that might reveal the seams of her costume, adding layer upon layer to her mysteries.

Stanley snarled and bared her teeth, twisted into strange lupine postures. In one feat, which would have been impressive even for a man, she carried herself all the way across the stage by swinging from one fake tree branch to another.

The discovery of this wild creature by Bird's landing party, and the long and complicated pursuit that followed, was a slapstick comedy of errors that saw the blundering, blue-coated officers falling and tumbling over one another as Stanley barreled across the stage on all fours. The actor who played the part of Lieutenant Bird had a full head of steel-gray hair and cut a distinguished figure, he was happy to see. The rest of the navy men, middies and lieutenants and sailors alike, remained nameless.

Finally, this overlong farce came to its close, and Alice was captured and carried directly to San Francisco, where Stanley adopted a top hat and, in one of the play's more ludicrous turns, was instantly cured of her wildness by the pleasant California weather. Here she performed another song and dance about how happy she was to have finally arrived in the greatest city in the world, and she was joined by actors done up to represent all the various types of citizens who could be found there—the rough miner, the old dusty cowboy, the merchant, the rich investor counting his bills, a Chinaman played by a white actor in heavy makeup—who all jumped and leaped and sang with her, in front of the lavish city backdrop Bird had seen which displayed all the landmarks of San Francisco beneath a radiant painted sun.

After the curtain had closed, the entirety of the cast gathered on stage for a long and raucous ovation. The same usher who had greeted Bird and Alice in the lobby now arrived to guide them down a narrow stairwell and through a door to the backstage area, so they might emerge and allow the audience to view the real and the fictional Alice Kelly, side by side. Beyond the curtain he could feel the rush and roar of their approval. In his attempts to quell her outbursts, he'd given her a few drops too many of the laudanum, and now she leaned heavily against him, unaware of where they were or, he thought, what was occurring.

He walked out onto the stage with her tottering beside him. Just as Galloway had requested, he deposited Alice next to Stanley and took a place in the rear, next to the silver-haired gentleman who'd played him. Alice at first made to continue following him but Stanley, seeing her confusion, took her hand and held it up. The audience rose to a new height of ecstatic applause. Alice looked out at the crowd, as if surprised to notice them. She took a few shuffling steps toward the edge of the stage. With a deft motion, Stanley snatched Alice's hat from her head and switched it for her own identical hat. Alice turned sharply to grab it back but lost her balance. Bird watched in horror as she disappeared into the orchestra pit with a crash of music stands and a sickening thump. The audience fell silent, all at once.

10.

・・・

On the night William disappeared, they'd fled from the colony to hide in a gully as those wicked men searched for them, roving over the island with torches. He'd told her to stay silent, and to remain hidden, that he had business to finish. Then he'd kissed her and left her there, and she never saw him alive again. That was the night that the ship had burned.

    The flames rose from the ship so high that the night carried an orange glow, though she could not see the ship and didn't yet understand what William had done—it seemed to her that perhaps Hell had opened itself up. She crouched there in the darkness, paralyzed by fear and waiting for him to return. She didn't think the sun would ever rise, but it did. The next day, she crept through the forest, back to the colony. Peering from the dense vegetation, she saw the men moving among their shanties on the rocky shore, the smoldering hulk of the ship still visible above the waves, but William was not among them. Later, two men dragged a body up from the shore and she knew that it was him. They dug a hole in the sandy soil and tilted him into it, and all those who remained gathered around in the raucous mockery of a funeral, firing the single pistol he'd possessed and singing sailors' songs. With tears drying on her cheeks, she quietly retreated back into the forest, and none of them would ever see her again. But sometimes, in the dead of night when the men were snoring away in their dilapidated shelters, she would visit his grave and dig her fingers into the soil, thinking that in this way she was closer to him.

And then, one by one, the men disappeared into their own graves as well. They fell by disease, by blade or pistol ball as they squabbled amongst themselves or over the meager spoils that had been saved from the ship. One survived much longer than the rest. He lay in a fever in a little tent of sailcloth in the forest, calling out to her. She sat where he could not see her and listened. After he stopped calling, she ventured closer, and was fascinated by the process she saw unfold. He blackened and swelled and then later became a putrid mass and then just a set of bones coated with shreds of meat and ants crawling in lines, carrying him off one piece at a time. His jaw hung crookedly from his skull, as if frozen in a joyous greeting, until it fell off altogether. How long did it take for him to vanish completely, to be overgrown, until she could hardly even locate where his little lean-to had stood to shelter him? A long time. She did not count the days.

In time, everything was lost. She hardly noticed when her dress fell from her body. Even her own name left her, became a sound that no longer had meaning. And the island was silent once more.

11.

HIGH SOCIETY

The Wild Girl of San Francisco *would prove to be one of the most popular entertainments in San Francisco for the remainder of the year 1858 and into 1859, after the inaugural performance made the front page of the* Alta *under the headline "WILD GIRL TRIES TO FLY – BREAKS WING." It was the only production that ran in Galloway's Dramatic Museum for its first, and only, year of existence, after which Galloway would take a scaled-down version of the production on a tour of the East.*

This period would be the pinnacle of Alice's fame: Galloway's play had enshrined her as San Francisco's most celebrated resident. A table was always reserved for her at a nearby restaurant on Montgomery Street, with a placard set above it to inform diners that this was where The Wild Girl took her breakfast. A column appeared in one of the city's satirical publications, entitled "NOTES FROM A SAVAGE KNOW-NOTHING," which purported (in jest) to be written by Alice, and to contain all of her views on local and national politics. The sheet music for a song was published as well—"Sweetheart of the Cannibal Isles"—which found its way onto most of the city's multitude of saloon pianos.

Several copycat plays sprung up which presented variations on her story, usually involving at least one shipwreck and several bestial acts. On the waterfront, crude peep-shows were available that claimed to have her on display, and though the patrons of these establishments knew that the girls they saw, some eight or ten years old, were not the famous Alice Kelly—her photograph had become so ubiquitous that none might mistake her for anyone else—they paid their pennies anyway to view whatever was on offer.

~

She was seen the same night by a physician named Burrows, who declared her arm to be broken. The physician was a friend, a member of Bird's budding social group that met in the downstairs parlor on most evenings. He gave her a shot of morphine before setting it; it took several drops of laudanum just to get her to accept the steel syringe. As she slept it off, he wrapped her arm tightly against a wooden frame.

He asked if he could perform a full examination of her, to check for any *abnormalities* that may have been caused by her time on the island.

"For what reason?" Bird said.

"To record them."

He did not speak for nearly an hour as he performed the examination, which was far more thorough than the one she'd undergone on the *Fredonia*. She remained completely insensible as he measured every part of her limp form with a tape, from the lengths of her limbs to the circumference of her skull. He examined her with the cool detachment of an assayer, prodding and poking with a steel wand. Then he asked Bird to leave the room so that he might remove her clothing.

"Is that necessary?"

"Without a doubt," he said. "She must have an inspection of her feminine parts. There are a number of diseases associated with them, which a trained eye must look for."

"Such as what?"

"Labial cancer, for one. Inflammation of the ovaries. Syphilis. Should I go on?"

"I can remain present," Bird said. "I've seen it all before. She was naked when I found her."

"Please. It is not appropriate. She is not a girl. This is a mature woman."

"Why, then, is it appropriate for you?"

"I am a scientist," Burrows answered.

Bird waited outside of her bedchamber as the doctor completed his tasks. In ten minutes, he opened the door with a disappointed look upon his face. He declared to Bird, "There is nothing of interest here."

"Nothing?"

"No, she is a typical female," he said. "There are no anomalies."

"What of her health?"

The doctor was packing his implements into his handbag with soft precision. "I found a fungal overgrowth and administered a suppository of a solution of boric acid. That should knock it out." On his way out the door, he asked, "How long have you been administering the opium?"

"Since the beginning," Bird said. "She has had a distemper, it is like madness. It is not always present but when it turns up, she is . . . difficult. Is there any other treatment you would recommend?"

He shook his head. "Continue the opium," he counseled Bird. "But not too much. I had a patient who drank down a bottle to commit suicide. Too much will stop the heart. Good day and thank you for your time, Lieutenant."

∼

A young woman in the public eye could not avoid offers of marriage, and it was no different for Alice, despite the fact that she still resembled a girl. She would not in her life ever grow above four and a half feet tall, and she ate so little that there was barely any flesh on her small frame and her chest remained flat.

Most of her suitors were instantly dismissible, from San Francisco's seemingly inexhaustible phalanx of crackpots and perverts. But some seemed legitimate, men with prospects who'd fallen in love with Alice somehow by seeing Stanley portray her upon the stage. There was one, a twenty-five-year-old man who owned a profitable fruit stand, whom Bird could find nothing at all wrong with. He was handsome, and seemingly sincere in his intentions. Still, Bird thought of some excuse to send him away.

Some part of him realized that he shouldn't be so opposed to the idea of her taking a husband; he wouldn't be there to take care of her forever, after all. He had begun to feel his age lately, his body slowing and sending ominous signals: sharp pains in his arms, a shortness of breath he could not account for. He thought it a particularly gruesome torture, to be aware of the unmistakable traces of senility entering his mind. He noticed little lapses in his memory, missing details in the past: For instance, what was the name of her little pig? He just didn't have hold of it. That fact had cut itself loose from his mind and drifted away. What else had he lost? What was Lieutenant Grady's first name? Each time he delved into his memory, he found more missing, until he stopped testing himself altogether for fear of what he would discover. He felt sour more often, and quick to anger. When he woke from a nap in a foul mood, it would sometimes seem as if everything was out of its proper order and could not ever be put right.

A cruel irony, to experience this just as he entered the period of his life when he felt he should be celebrating. He had money in the bank, a name that was known and respected. He'd hired a servant girl named Nettie to visit their home twice a week to clean and cook for them, an extravagance which now felt both necessary and appropriate.

He'd appointed the downstairs parlor to be a kind of gentleman's club, with armchairs of stiff leather, maps on the walls, and souvenirs from far-off places. It was easy enough in San Francisco to purchase bric-a-brac from the South Pacific: a native's carved mask, a shrunken head like one he'd once been shown in Jakarta. He envisioned the parlor as the future home of a society dedicated to the spirit of the old explorers. Of whom, he was most certainly the last. A place where the memory of these great men could reside in perpetuity, now that the business of exploring and conquering the globe had been completed.

Mr. Mirmiran was one of his first regular guests. He'd done much to help introduce Bird across the city. Through him, Bird had met doctors and politicians, lawyers, even a famous jockey. Soon, he was inviting them all to the house on Montgomery Street, and they were happy to sit around drinking his sherry and congratulating one another on their accomplishments. Each night the room filled with a cloud of cigar smoke so thick that it fully replaced the air, and produced in Bird a humming buzz which, when balanced with a precise amount of whiskey and cocaine, put him in a kind of happy trance. Whenever he wished to speak, he stamped his cane on the floor and they would pause in their deliberations to hear him opine.

He thought to call their little society *The Neptune Club*, but dithered on proposing this until after his regular guests began referring to themselves only as "The Group," a moniker which unfortunately stuck, and made its way into the society columns.

Friends invited friends. Some nights Bird was introduced to so many new faces that it seemed they might be wandering in off the street. He told his stories again and again: of the landing party on Biscuit Island, of how he'd shared a cigar with Pierce. They cheered his tale of the Mexican War, as Bird described how he raised the stars and stripes over the old presidio. He wished that his father could crawl out of his grave to see this: his good-for-nothing son Henry being celebrated on stage and in the newspapers, rubbing shoulders with the best men of the city. Then, he could crawl back into Hell.

It was even suggested that Bird should run for office.

"He is a man of the people," Mirmiran declared one night, sloshed on apple brandy. He clapped Bird on the back with a lit cigar in his hand that would scorch a hole in his vest, unseen and unfelt.

∽

At first, Burrows had predicted that the splint might be removed in eight weeks, but Alice would wear it for almost six months; she pulled out of the bandages and managed to renew her injury several times, causing her arm to heal with a permanent crook between elbow and wrist. Bird increased her dose of laudanum to manage the pain.

Much to Galloway's consternation, Bird was adamant that she make no more personal appearances at the theater. He focused now on helping her to heal, both in body and spirit. He shut her off from all visitors except for Stanley, whom he thought was a good and comforting friend to the girl. There were perhaps things that another woman could give to her that he could not, and he would not deprive her of that. Stanley herself was on a kind of whirlwind celebration of her success—she was, at that point, the highest-paid actress in California, and her name was being spoken in New York and London.

When asked about The Wild Girl, she'd said to one reporter, *I don't see her as wild at all . . . I see a young woman in need of a friend.*

Alice was happy to sit upstairs with her and listen to Stanley chat about the roles she'd played and the famous people she'd met. She would read to Alice from books or articles, sometimes overly romantic novels—stories of depraved criminals and kidnapped women—which seemed in Bird's mind to have little instructional purpose.

It was clear, though, that Alice felt an intimacy with Stanley which Bird could not achieve.

"How many men have you kissed?" Alice asked the actress one day. Bird coughed in surprise and took a sip of his whiskey. Stanley waved him off when he began to stammer apologies.

"No, it's fine," she said. "A young woman is curious about these things." To Alice, she said playfully, "I have kissed more men than I can count. And what about yourself?"

Two, Alice whispered.

"Were they very handsome men?"

"My pipe is downstairs," Bird said, red-faced. He excused himself to allow the women some privacy. "Are you sure you'll be all right with her?" he asked the actress.

"We'll be fine, I think."

"We are very fine to-day," Alice half-said, half-sung after him.

～

On another occasion, the actress brought over a kit containing stage makeup, and applied it to both Alice and herself, adding rouge to their lips and cheeks and ashy shadows around their eyes encircled by a thin golden line.

"Is there a mirror?" Stanley asked.

"Downstairs, in the parlor," Bird affirmed. The three of them made the trek so that Alice could see her face, all done up, in the gilt-edged mirror behind the bar. At first, Bird thought she was frightened of what she saw there. But then he realized she was enthralled. She raised a finger up to touch her cheek as if testing its solidity. Her mouth hung open, and she smeared the rouge on her lips with the finger.

"Now," Stanley said, "look how beautiful you are."

Stanley left the makeup kit behind, a slim leather case lined with blotches of color, a selection of thin and fat brushes and small-edged tools which Bird immediately confiscated. Without the benefit of a mirror or Stanley's trained hand, Alice could not apply the makeup in any semblance of order, and Bird would find her with a riot of colors swirled on her face, smears of red on her forehead, one eye blackened, flesh-colored powder sprinkled on her clothes and the furniture. The effect was hideous, and made her appear like some deranged moppet come to life in the candlelight.

"I am a great beauty," she sleepily intoned to him one night, as he rubbed it from her face, watching the colors spread and then transfer themselves from her flesh to the damp rag in his hand.

12.

. . .

It was an overcast day, and Bird had been repeating for hours that a car was being *sent for them,* walking back and forth between the windows to witness its approach. It was a great honor, Bird explained to her, to be invited to a fancy *ball* at the home of Mr. and Mrs. Charles Sutter.

She wore a dress of rich, deep green that had been made for her by an Italian dressmaker, a small, dusky man with a pencil-thin moustache who'd come to the house to measure every part of her and show them samples of different fabrics and patterns. She had been allowed to choose the fabric and even the design of the dress herself, from a book of pictures, but now she found that she hated it, even though both Bird and Nettie assured her that it was very beautiful. It had taken their combined efforts to maneuver the dress over her splinted arm, because it possessed a framework of wire hoops that caused it to open at the bottom like a bell, a moveable cage that followed her wherever she went. It became caught on the furniture and she could not sit without assistance. As it was, she was standing stranded in the center of the room, watching Bird move his pipe between the different pockets of his coat, as if trying to find one that satisfied him.

When she tried to take a step forward she nearly tripped, and she began to clutch and bunch the folds of the dress up in her hands, to lift it from the floor.

"What are you doing? Don't do that. Leave that."

He came over to her and swatted gently at her hands.

"Put the fabric down," he said.

Before being introduced to the hated dress, she'd been awaiting the evening of the ball with great anticipation. After Bird had shown her the invitation, an elegant card covered with a lace cutout, she'd carried it around with her for days. She'd studied the mysterious dark letters within to find those that spelled her name, and others that she thought said *ball*. Though she could not read anything else, she recognized that the invitation carried a special significance; it was like a ticket, the thing that would finally free her from her imprisonment. She'd been locked in the apartment day and night since the play, with only a few visits from Miss Stanley and her window overlooking the street to entertain her—the only thing that made her life tolerable was the medicine, which, for a brief period, made her feel as if she was not contained in anything at all.

"Will Ada be at the ball?" she asked.

Bird made a face like he hadn't heard her, and then answered, "No, no. She moves in different circles."

"Why can I not wear my hat?"

"I have told you, it is not appropriate for this event."

He was wearing a three-piece suit of black wool, with a new hat to match it. He looked small in the new clothes, which seemed to hang off him like those of a scarecrow.

The buggy that arrived had an open top, and the driver was a proper Englishman, who hopped from his seat to open its door for them as they exited the house. "Car for you, milord."

Bird helped her up and onto the seat, where she was forced to hold the wire hoops up above her waist. Then he said to the coachman, "Don't you know you are in the United States? We have no royalty here."

"Sorry, sir."

"That's more like it," Bird said, and clapped the man on the shoulder.

They did not have far to go. The Sutters lived on Rincon Hill, in a house that was large enough to be a palace, two stories tall and with a candle burning in every window. As they drove along the wrought-iron fence that surrounded the property, Alice saw a splendid garden within, complete with fruit trees casting long shadows and flowering bushes and benches, and even a little pond.

A riot of coaches and buggies deposited their occupants at the broad front doors, framed by long columns. When it was their turn, they were greeted by a man with a thick middle, practically popping the buttons on his vest, who approached as Bird was struggling to help her down from the buggy.

"Lieutenant Bird!" he called out. "We meet at long last."

"Mr. Sutter . . ." Bird said.

"Please, just call me Charlie." He extended a hand to shake Bird's vigorously, and then he was looking down at her, pulling the cigar from his mouth. He smiled at her. "Miss Kelly! I'm so pleased to meet you. My wife has told me so much, and I have seen the play. You must tell me, is it all true?"

"No," she said.

"There were minor embellishments," Bird added quickly. "A necessity in the theater trade, I am told."

He was not listening to them. "I bet you would like to have a look at the fishpond before we go inside?" he said. She looked to Bird, who gave no sign, and then she gently nodded to indicate that she did.

Sutter waved to some other guests with the cigar in his hand and then led Bird and Alice away from the brightness of the house. The trees were spaced evenly and each was identified by a small card close to the ground. Bird expressed approval of the labeling system and examined every one. He squinted in the falling light to read out: *Pyrus Calleryana*.

"Chinese pear," Sutter called back.

The pond was small, encircled by a shoreline of bricks and a neat, isolated clump of reeds. A kind of bird walked near it, like a blue turkey with a long tail of colorful feathers. At their approach it strutted away, and then suddenly turned to spread its tailfeathers into a marvelous fan. For a moment Alice could no longer recognize the animal's body, it was only a vast arc of shimmering green eyes. The bird hissed and shook its feathers angrily at them.

Sutter kicked some gravel at it, which caused it to turn from them and bob away. "A peacock. Nasty animals, these, but pretty. It was a gift to my wife, on the occasion of our thirtieth wedding anniversary."

The bird strutted into some nearby bushes as Sutter bent over the water and began to name the fish in the pond for them—they had names like racehorses, *Cossack* and *Sir John Percy*.

"What kind of fish are they?" she heard Bird ask.

"Oh, damned if I know. I would have thought a Navy man would know them."

"I have little experience with freshwater varieties."

As the men were engaged, Alice edged toward the bird, which was still visible among the shrubbery and keeping a wary eye on them. It shifted nervously from one leg to the other as she approached, but did not retreat any farther. She pulled the front of her dress close to allow her to wade into the bushes after it. It took a cautious step toward her, perhaps looking to see if she had come to offer it some crumbs of bread. When it was within her reach, she quickly grabbed at one of its tail feathers and yanked as hard as she could. It let out a sound like an angry trumpet and then ran at her, hissing and flapping its wings. Within two steps of her hasty retreat, she became caught in her dress and tumbled to the ground, taking most of the fall on her fractured arm, which lit up with pain. Then the bird was over her, pecking madly as she swung her free arm to ward it off.

"God damn this bird!" Sutter exclaimed and was there in an instant. With a hearty kick, he sent the peacock skittering back into the shrubbery, where it flapped and hopped away.

Bird had turned his walking stick upside down to hold it like a baton. Sutter helped her to her feet. Her dress was soiled. "My God, I'm so sorry . . . it has never done anything like this . . ."

As he turned to Bird with his apologies, she quickly ducked to snatch the feather from where it had fallen, and tucked it up under her dress, weaving it beneath one of the wire hoops.

"Well, it's getting dark," Sutter said, and it was.

The hall inside shone with the light from hundreds of candles up in the chandeliers. There was heat radiating from them, and from the bodies in the room and a great fire in a hearth. The kitchens, too, emanated a warmth that smelled of roasting meat. Women fanned themselves with white cards. Alice looked among the men and ladies for the small forms of orphan children that she had expected to be there. Bird had told her that the ball was meant to honor the opening of a new orphanage, which Mr. Sutter had paid for, but in the bright hall there were no children at all. At the far end of the room a band was tuning their instruments.

Mr. Sutter led them toward a woman. Alice had a loose memory of her, like a tooth about to fall free: of her cloud of perfume and the way her face powder gathered in the folds of her flesh. As soon as she saw Alice, she raised one of the white cards in the air and waved it, calling her name as if they were old friends.

"My wife," Sutter said to her, "whom I believe you're already acquainted with."

Mrs. Sutter stood with four other ladies, their names quickly announced and then forgotten. Alice had trouble telling them apart, save for the fact that their dresses, the cuts and styles nearly identical, were different colors: lavender, sky blue, yellow, and pink. They huddled around Mrs. Sutter like four fleshy angels meant to carry her to Heaven.

"But you must have other guests to greet, dear," she said to her husband. "Take the Lieutenant. We will entertain Miss Kelly."

"I would prefer to remain on hand, in case Alice requires my attention . . ." Bird said politely.

"Oh, I won't have it. Go and be sociable. Miss Kelly can remain with the ladies tonight. There is so much we wish to ask her."

Mr. Sutter spoke up. "Henry and I are just getting to know one another. Henry, come along and I will introduce you to the boys."

"The girl . . . Miss Kelly, you see, she is sometimes moody, and I wouldn't want her to impose upon you in any way . . ."

"Oh, don't worry yourself, Lieutenant. I swear," she said, now more to her husband, in a playful tone, "you men think nothing can happen without your oversight. Miss Kelly, I'm sure, will be fine company."

Mr. Sutter took Bird by the shoulder and whisked him away as he continued to stammer his protests.

"Tonight," Mrs. Sutter informed her with a twinkle, "you will be one of the ladies."

Alice watched Bird disappear into the crowd, then turned back to Mrs. Sutter and ventured to ask, "Where are the orphans?"

The old woman became ecstatic. "Oh, my dear thing! My sweet thing! Why, they are all sleeping, safe and sound in their new home. Did you hear that?" she asked her companions. "She wishes to know where the orphans are! The dear thing . . ."

The ladies crowded around her. She was fenced in by their billowing dresses, cut off from the ball by a shifting ring of color and the sound of swishing crinolines and silk. Their voices seemed almost disembodied, coming from somewhere above and not from their mouths. Their questions came to her so quickly that she couldn't keep up with them:

"Were you very lonely when you were on the island?"

"Did you often think of home?"

"But you must let us know how you kept house—this is something I long to hear about, how even in such adverse circumstances, we women can always find a way to keep house." This comment amused the ladies, and they all made sounds that were not quite laughter.

"I must ask you, when you were trapped on the island, whatever did you eat?"

Alice reached into her memories, as if trying to call back a faded dream. When everything was gone—after she'd stolen what she could from the ruined camp, the dry hardtack, the flour that she made into a loose dough with rainwater—she'd smashed cocoanuts by throwing them from a high place, then scraping the insides of their scattered fragments with her nails and teeth. She could vividly recall the disappointment of the turtles. One night, she had witnessed a hatching of them on the shore, little tiny things like beetles pulling themselves up out of the sand and stumbling down toward the surf, clambering over one another, knocked back by even the gentlest waves. It had seemed like a miracle to her then, to see all the little animals climbing up out of the ground and moving toward the sea. The moon had been high over the waters and it called to them. And then out of the night sky they had come: sea birds with cruel beaks to swoop down and pluck them from the sand. For days, they had been circling the island and now she realized they had come only for this feast. She had been so hungry then herself, her stomach filled with a feeling of scratching emptiness that sometimes welled into a dull ache. She felt hot and weak and her hands trembled as she walked out onto the sand, scattering the squabbling gulls around her, to collect up as many of the turtles as she could into the front of her dress. They crawled up the cloth, trying to tumble out, but she held it shut with a fist as she retreated into the forest. There, still clutching her dress so the turtles could not escape, she got down on her knees and with her free hand dug a pit into the loamy soil, into which she deposited the turtles like stones. Then she watched them kicking and writhing on their backs, a squirming motion in the pit like it was a nest of vipers or worms. She reached in to pick one up. It wheeled its little legs in the air. She held it up to her lips but could not bring herself to bite it. Instead, she put the little thing on a stone and hit it with another stone, to still its motion. Once crushed, it resembled little more than a smear of grease and the filaments of bones. She dipped her fingers into it and brought them to her mouth but the taste had been like salt and metal and mud—she had spit it out and could not bring herself to continue. She wiped it from her mouth, then wiped her fingers on her dress. The rest of the little turtles, she'd abandoned in the pit to starve. Later she would return there to see them, all shriveled and desiccated, as if they had never been alive at all.

"I ate fruit and some things that I found," she finally answered, and the ladies tittered approvingly.

"You must tell me, for I have been very curious of one thing. Did you pray, when you were alone on the island?"

"No," Alice said. In truth, she had only prayed with William. She could recall kneeling in the sand with him when they finally reached the shore, to thank God for bringing them to their new home where they could live forever in harmony.

"But my dear, why not? Didn't you know that the Lord would never abandon you? He was watching over you the whole time, I am certain. The fact that you are here today among us is testament to that," the woman said.

Alice felt that they wanted something more from her, though she did not know what, and so she said, "Sometimes I pray for souls, to save them." This was met with a murmur of approval.

"I shudder to think how frightening it must have been," the lady in blue said, "to face that wicked Ernesto."

Alice struggled to fit the name to one of the faces in her memory, but she found there were no faces other than William's. Then it seemed to her that there was one, a man with a shaven head and a golden hoop in his ear, the one who had argued with William, perhaps the one who had killed him. She thought this might be the man they spoke of.

The ladies' attention shifted as Mrs. Sutter called out to a young woman, summoning her into their circle. She was fully a head taller than Alice, with a thin, bloodless face and large hands that she clasped before her.

"My daughter, Fanny," Mrs. Sutter said to Alice. "I am so glad you two have the opportunity to meet. Fanny is entertaining a good number of offers," she added, now speaking to her multicolored angels.

Fanny rolled her eyes. "If you are a marriageable woman in this city with all of your teeth, I promise you will have suitors crawling through your windows by the light of the moon."

The comment caused another gentle eruption among the ladies. Alice hated Fanny at once—the way she held herself so proudly and her words came tumbling out with ease. Fanny spared Alice only a quick, disinterested glance before begging her mother's permission to return to the dance floor.

"This is youth," Mrs. Sutter sighed aloud after she'd left. "To have someone as fascinating as young Alice here to converse with, and to care about nothing but filling your dance card."

Mrs. Sutter took Alice's hand and followed her daughter, all of the colorful ladies now tracking across the room like a cloud. The pain in her arm had dulled to a throb that would not leave her. It was maddening, and made her wish to be out of her body. She stumbled on the edge of her dress and Mrs. Sutter reached over to steady her. As they were paused there, Alice quietly twisted her feet from her shoes and left them behind unnoticed, to be lost beneath the forest of moving ballgowns.

They took a position at the edge of a wide-open area, from which she could more clearly see the musicians, including one who sat at a wide piano. There had been a piano in her home, when she was very small, which no one had played. The keys had always been covered and her mother had scolded her if she touched it. Once, someone had played it. She tried to remember the melody but found she could not—all that she could remember was the feeling it had given her. A sweet dream, a lullaby of tinkling notes, cascading over one another like the water in a stream.

Across the hall, the band began to play.

The first dance involved only eight participants, four men and four women. Fanny was among them. The men wore identical suits and hats.

At first, they did not even seem to dance. They stood in couples, across the emptied dance floor, and then began to walk and greet one another, moving in such precise concert that they seemed to be like train cars moving on their tracks. Sometimes the men exchanged women, twirled, and continued, following the same routes with new partners. Alice watched them, Fanny especially, with an emotion somewhere between envy and burning hatred.

With a sudden burst of speed, they began to twirl. They formed into two wheels and spun round and round. *Man woman man woman man* they flashed, moving with lively sidesteps. It seemed that their feet barely touched the floor. The band swept them in circles, their movements perfectly timed to the music. She thought with a mounting, giddy terror, that they could not stop; they were prisoners of the music, forced to twirl for as long as it continued. Their faces were blank, and they moved like puppets on strings.

When the music ended and they were finally released, there was polite applause. The dancers bowed and made way as others began to drift onto the floor to participate in a waltz. Mrs. Sutter's colorful ladies moved off to find partners or to distance themselves from the sudden confusion of bodies. Alice looked around to realize that Mrs. Sutter was several paces away, engaged in conversation with someone new.

Unobserved, Alice walked out onto the dance floor. Twirling dancers carefully arced around her. Some smiled down at her, at least one woman glared in annoyance. She could feel the breeze of their dresses twirling and smell a bouquet of floral scents all covering the ripeness of countless bodies in motion beneath the warm chandeliers.

She came before the band and stood to watch them for a long while. Their eyes were fixed on their sheet music and she became lost in their activity as they huffed and puffed, their fingers and mouths on their instruments, the violinists sawing away with their bows. The piano player's hands hovered over the keys: they barely seemed to move at all, but somehow, he created an unending string of notes that tickled her ears and sounded almost like laughter.

When they ceased playing again, they laid down their instruments and one man stood to announce that they would return in one quarter of an hour. The dancers all fled to the edges of the ballroom, leaving Alice there alone on a vast, bare plain, its polish scuffed dull by a multitude of feet.

Someone appeared at her side—the woman in the lavender dress. "Do you wish a partner for the next dance?"

"No."

"Oh. Do you require assistance, in finding the Lieutenant?" she asked.

"I wish to play the piano."

"You play! I am sure we would all love to hear one of your pieces." She looked around, as if disappointed that they were not observed, and said loudly, "Is this some surprise Heloise has dreamed up?"

Alice walked away from her, crossing to where the instruments lay on their chairs as she made her way to the piano. She looked back to see that the woman in lavender was calling for others to come, to hear what she would play.

The piano stood taller than her and seemed to be waiting. Cautiously, she pressed one of the keys. A low note growled at her and then stopped as she quickly removed her finger. She played another, higher, and held the key down so it could ring out across the room. Still, it was the wrong note. She looked to see the woman in lavender still watching with her hands clasped in anticipation. She pressed her hand across many keys at once and the piano made a murky sound. Frustrated, she then lifted her broken arm and brought the wooden frame of the splint down on the keys as hard as she could. The piano made a strangled cry; it was the first sound that had pleased her. She brought her arm up and down again and again on different parts of the keyboard. A haphazard collision of notes. It was her music, she thought. A new and better kind of music.

Each time she brought her arm down she was met with a sharp pain in her arm, but she did not stop because it made such a glorious, angry sound, and the pain enlivened her. She could *feel* something, through the dull haze of her medicine. Her splint became loose and the bandages that held it to her hung down in tatters. The throbbing pain that remained darkened the edges of her vision.

Alice clutched her arm to her chest and turned to survey those gathered around her—a half-circle of now-silent men and women in their finery, with horrified looks upon their faces. Then, she shrieked as loud as she could at the woman in lavender, her voice echoing in the quiet hall: "*Why are they not dancing??*"

Bird had been too tired, too used up by the commotion of the ball to scold her, but he'd spent the ride home in a stubborn silence. When they arrived, he'd given her a strong dose of medicine to quiet her illness and then fell asleep almost instantly. His bedroom door was half-open and he was lying face down, gently snoring, his boots still on and both his feet hanging off the bedside. Her splint had been retied, and the pain in her arm was now distant, and soft. There were no lights in the house, but a moon in the window cast shadows across the floor. Bird had left her in the dress but she'd managed to wriggle out of it on her own, and now it lay in a pile on the carpet, diminished into itself like the shed skin of a snake.

She bent to search in the folds of the dress for the peacock's feather; once found, she fetched her hat where she'd left it on the bedside table. When she put it on, she felt a lightness in her chest, as if her holy soul was lifting itself from her body. She thought of the ladies at the ball: elegant women wrapped in cloth and wire who moved softly, as if they were made of clouds or cotton batting. Women who spent their lives appended to husbands and suitors, who performed their proper dance steps, never deviating. She thought of the girl, Fanny, and felt a twinge of hatred. She wished dearly that someone would shoot Fanny with a pistol, and she found herself imagining it and imagining how she would cry out and bleed and then die. Then she thought of Ada, how the actress had leapt wildly across the stage, and Bird's comment that Ada *moves in different circles* . . . it seemed to her that Ada was a different kind of woman. She thought of the saloon women she'd seen in the streets and in the windows of the hotels, laughing gaily, their faces brightly painted. There was something that these saloon women shared with Ada, a quality Alice could not name but which she desired for herself. This was the kind of woman that she wished to be.

She searched in her bedroom for the makeup kit that Ada had left for her and brought it over to her seat by the window, where she began to daub at the makeup with a wadded-up cotton ball, reduced from many such usages, to apply it to her face. She did not need to see herself; in her mind she could clearly see the beauty she was becoming.

The street below her was at its quietest, in the hours before dawn. The windows of the other buildings were all uniformly dark, the only figure a lone man with a haversack slung over his shoulder, making his way down the center of the street without any urgency, a silhouette in the moonlight. As he approached, she rose to her knees on the bench. Silently, she commanded him to look up at her body and he did. At first he squinted, and even raised a hand above his eyes to block the light of the moon. She pressed her naked body against the window so that he could see it better. In her hand, she held the peacock feather, and brushed it along her neck, over her breasts, as she'd seen a saloon woman do. He stood rooted to his spot on the street, unable to move or look away.

She began to do a slow dance, undulating back and forth in the window as the feather traced the glass. This finally broke the man from his frozen position. He shouted something up at her, but the words were muted by the window. Then he walked urgently toward the house and out of her view.

A few moments later, she heard an insistent knocking coming from downstairs. She moved to the locked door at the top of the stairs to better hear it. She could imagine him standing at the front door that opened onto the street, waiting to be permitted. Her beauty had pulled him there; he was in her power, just as the dancers had been slaves to their music. His efforts paused for a while and then resumed, more urgently.

In his bedchamber, Bird stirred but did not rise. Then his snoring abruptly ceased. She crouched against the door at the head of the stairs as below the man began to rattle the doorknob, the sound of it as pleasing to her as the drilling of a far-off woodpecker.

13.

SKETCHES

There is nothing in the world that appeals more to an old officer than the sturdy bulwark of an unbroken routine, to help ease the passage of the days. Thanksgiving and Christmas of 1858 passed with small feasts prepared by Nettie, who was permitted to bring home the leftovers as a show of Bird's graciousness.

For the first time in his life, Bird began to sleep late. When he rose, sometimes even as late as nine, he always tried to encourage Alice to eat something, though she ate less and less. Her splint had been removed, but her illness, he thought, had grown worse. She was increasingly willful and scattered her belongings across the house, tore his pile of newspapers into strips, so at times the upstairs apartment came to resemble an animal's den more than a proper living space, with fragments and debris strewn across the floor. A rat had somehow become trapped in the flour bin and died, and she'd hidden its carcass for weeks. Their rooms were mysteriously filled with flies and the smell of decay until Nettie happened upon the limp, rotten thing hidden under Alice's bedcovers. The girl's antics terrified the poor housekeeper, who had found her several times walking around the apartment unclothed. Bird was at a loss as to how to control her and applied her with more and more of the medicine to quiet her nerves.

In this way, her madness became his compass, her routines becoming his own and giving shape to his days. Her meals and dosings, her periods of calm. Alice in the morning light with her belongings spread on the floor, always being arranged and rearranged according to some complex calculus that only she understood. Alice drooping in the twilight, Alice curled asleep in the window like a cat. He kept watch over her as an old salt studies the sky and the clouds, without thinking, waiting to see what each day would bring.

In the few hours of peace that followed a dose of her medicine, he would go out to stroll upon the promenade, hoping to be recognized, engaging in long conversations with shopkeeps, stable hands, old men on their porches, and anyone else who would consent to stand with him in the street to bemoan the chaotic and declining state of the world.

He would return home for dinner, cooked fresh on Tuesdays and Thursdays by Nettie and reheated in the pot every other day, and then apply himself to the task of reading the newspapers and engaging in any necessary correspondence. This would normally carry him through to the evening, his favorite part of the day, when Alice drifted toward sleep and he would retreat into the cocoon of the downstairs parlor to mingle with those members of "The Group" who arrived to guzzle his Scotch whiskey and hear his opinions on everything from the transatlantic telegraph to the slavery question, upon which he was a vocal moderate (though disturbed by the sight of human beings in bondage, like many old men he also hated the very idea of things changing too much, or too quickly, and carried with him the persistent impression that the world had been in its best arrangement in the days when he was young). Mr. Fairbanks, the owner of one of the last few gold mines still turning a profit, had dropped by a few times to dominate the conversation with fascinating talk of the relative values and properties of metals; Gus the dentist had become a regular fixture, and he'd offered a discounted rate to all the members of their club who might need teeth pulled. More often than not, after the departure of the last of his guests, sometime after midnight, he would continue to sit down there in his armchair, emptying and refilling his whiskey glass alone in a cloud of staling smoke, to rehearse what he had said, what he should have said, what he would say tomorrow. At some point nearing dawn, he would fall asleep for a few short hours, finally run down from the manic fits of wit and loquaciousness bestowed upon him by the cocaine he'd sniffed that evening.

In the early part of 1859, he was surprised to receive a card in the mail from Ada Stanley. Her visits with Alice had become much less frequent as of late, and Bird was inclined to think this was for the best. The papers had been reporting for some time on her extravagant and wild behavior about the city in the wake of her success: cavorting drunkenly in saloons, gambling, spending lavish sums of money. One report even made note that she'd been seen behaving somewhat amorously in public with a mulatto. Though the diversion she'd provided seemed to please Alice, he now wasn't altogether sure the actress was the sort of influence the girl needed in her present condition.

The Wild Girl of San Francisco was still playing, but only once a week, with audiences mostly comprised of tourists from the East, and the actress obviously had enough time on her hands to mount another production: the card he'd received announced the premiere of a new piece for the theater she would appear in, something called *The Seven Ages of Woman*. It credited her as writer, director, and sole performer (playing thirty-seven different roles, something Bird thought was surely a misprint). A brief personal note was included, inviting them to attend, along with two tickets. Of course, Alice would not be well enough to attend, and rather than disappoint her, he kept this news to himself and offered the second ticket to Mr. Mirmiran.

The theater it was playing in was disreputable and small. There were a few dozen people in the room, all men, on hard benches munching peanuts by the handful and scattering the shells on the dirt floor. He insisted that they sit far in the back, so the actress would not see them and possibly try to sequester Bird afterwards to inquire about the girl.

The claim upon the card had not been a misprint: Stanley was the only performer, and she indeed played thirty-seven different roles, each with a full costume and makeup change, representing famous women in history who all either sang or played musical instruments or delivered moving soliloquies. Bird found it to be interminably boring. There was no action whatsoever, only speaking, singing, and occasional stretches where the lone actress sat at a mirror and sighed as she brushed her hair and bemoaned the fate of women, unjustly dismissed and imprisoned by a society of individuals they had birthed. Drunken hecklers interrupted her from the audience. These men had come to see the woman who'd run on all fours snarling, who'd been strapped naked to the back of a horse. They had not asked for Greek soliloquies. Bird fell asleep for an indeterminate amount of time during her silent pantomime of "Diana on the Hunt" and woke abruptly with a little gasp to see her stomping her feet in a French military uniform, playing obnoxiously upon a bugle.

"I did not see the point of any of that," was Mirmiran's only comment as they shuffled out.

The press was no kinder to it. The newspapers said that it was dull, overly self-aggrandizing, and that her argument was inherently flawed. Bird hadn't even been aware there was an argument. One writer was unkind enough to suggest that the performance was beneath her, and that the poor judgment necessary to produce such trash was the result of *an alcoholist's customary delirium.*

He would see the actress only once more. It was a chilly night in early spring. All his guests had left and Bird was alone in the parlor, dozing in his chair and occasionally waking to take sips of bourbon and feed the stove. He was roused from his half-sleep at some point by a sound at the door. His first thought was that it must be a thief. He had no pistol on hand—he'd left his old Navy pistol in Norfolk and had Mr. Franklin sell it off with the furniture—so he went upstairs to retrieve a cleaver from the few implements in the kitchen. Returning to the parlor, he stood behind the door and called out, "Who is that?"

He was startled to hear a slurred female voice. He turned the key to find Stanley leaning in the door jamb, reeking of gin. The makeup on her face was smeared and ran down her cheeks. She was quite scandalously wearing a pair of men's pants, which had mud on the knees as if she'd been kneeling in the street.

"Miss Stanley," he said with surprise. Then, "Ada . . . are you alright?"

"I will be fine once I have my feet on this horse." She laughed. She saw the cleaver and said, "Are you going to cut me to pieces? It is too late, my dear Lieutenant, for that has already been *thoroughly* accomplished."

She did not wait for an invitation to step in and tumble down into a sitting position on the carpet. Bird placed the cleaver on a table but continued to stand, unsure of how to greet this intrusion. The next thing she said was, "It smells like smoked sausages in here."

"Pardon me?"

"Don't mind me," Stanley answered. "I was raised in a barn."

"You are drunk," he said.

"I am drunk? *You* are drunk."

Bird was, but it didn't seem to matter. "I think the difference is that I can hold my liquor."

"I can hold more than you can hold," she said.

"I am not the one on someone else's floor in the middle of the night."

She propped herself up straighter and said, "Maybe so, maybe so . . ." Then she reached over to take an ashtray from the nearest end table and spit into it, a long trail of her saliva hanging until she wiped her mouth with the back of a hand.

"Why are you here like this?"

"I have come to say goodbye to Alice. I am leaving for Europe. Where people want me."

"Godspeed."

"Can I have a drink?"

"I think not."

"May I see Alice?"

Bird considered it. "I think not. You may call on us at a regular hour, when you've sobered up."

Bird fixed himself a fresh bourbon and water and then, in a moment of compassion, he fixed Stanley one as well.

She took a deep sip and slumped to the ground and closed her eyes. "I just need to lie down right now. I just need to lie down."

"I can fix up a bed for you."

"No, just right here. This is all I need."

He watched her sleep as he finished his drink. At length she began to snore and for a while he was content to watch her bosoms rise and fall with her labored breath. Then he finished her drink as well, which she'd barely touched, put out the lamps, and went upstairs, leaving her there in the darkness.

As he was locking the upstairs door behind him, he was startled to find Alice standing in the kitchen in her nightdress.

"Is Ada here?"

"Go back to bed," Bird said, quietly but firmly.

"I want to see her."

"It is out of the question."

"I *will* see her," Alice said. She took a few steps toward the door and Bird caught her by the shoulders.

"Let me be . . ."

She pulled herself from him and backed against the door. Then she turned and began to frantically try the knob and pound at the door.

"Stop this at once."

He grabbed her again, by her good arm, and pulled her through the kitchen. She wrestled with him every step of the way, until he smacked her once, sharply, across the face. The shock of it stopped her immediately. She stood regarding him in the darkened sitting room, her lip quivering, but said nothing else.

"I am going to bed now, but this is not over. We will revisit this issue in the morning, when I expect that you will apologize for these antics."

With that, he turned and strode into his bedchamber and shut the door behind him. As he lay in bed trying to calm his agitated breathing, he listened for some time to see if she would resume her efforts with the door but heard nothing.

In the morning, he found her asleep on the kitchen floor, curled with her back against the door. She was confused when he woke her, and accepted a strong dose of her medicine, after which he walked her to her bed. Downstairs, he found the actress gone and the front door hanging open to admit the morning light and noise of the street.

Over the following weeks and months, he would receive several letters from the actress, all addressed to Alice, and would burn them unread.

※

Alice never mentioned the events of that night, nor did she ask about the actress again. Bird could never be sure how much she understood, or if she blamed him, but it was clear that she was affected by the loss. She became morose. Day and night she sat in her window, studying the street with empty eyes.

In an attempt to cheer her, one morning he invited her to accompany him on an errand. Having a walk in the city, in her better days, was something that had never failed to brighten her spirits. When she emerged from her bedroom, her hair was clumped and matted down beneath her hat and she wore a sullen expression. He did not think she'd changed out of her nightdress in weeks.

The street was packed with foot traffic, mostly men who were dressed in various shades of brown and blue. Men who still recognized her lifted their hats to Alice. She stared through them as if they were not there.

"Do they repeat?" she asked.

"What's that?"

"The faces?"

"I don't understand you, Alice."

"Men have all the same faces," she said.

He watched a few men pass by as they walked: slim and weak-chinned men, broad and hardened men, men with spectacles and doggish jowls. He had to grant her that they all seemed to be variations on a few basic types.

"Maybe there are only so many faces to go around," he admitted.

The address he'd been given was in the Chinese district. Here the streets were more crowded, full of vendors and crowds of young toughs. The air was full of their strange, piercing cries. An old woman was crossing the street with a strangled duck hanging from her fist.

They arrived at a square-fronted structure of two stories that at once looked rickety and newly-built. The sign out front said WASH'NG AND IRON'NG. A broad-chested Celestial with a long ponytail greeted them as they entered. Behind him, twenty or so of his fellows bent over steaming tubs, their arms and faces scalded red by the water. They splashed and scrubbed.

"I am here to see Mr. Swain."

"Billy upstairs." The man smiled and bowed without much effort.

Bird tugged Alice behind him as he moved between two rows of vigorously scrubbing men, using his stick to tap the back of a man who wouldn't move out of the way. The man gave Bird a harsh look. Past him, a narrow and turning stairwell ascended to the building's upper reaches.

Bird had gotten the name of the building's upstairs occupant from Mr. Blakely, a member of "The Group" who owned a small gaming saloon—Swain was a painter who'd done a series of nudes to amuse Mr. Blakely's clientele. For some time, Bird had been troubled by the sense that the decoration of his own parlor was not quite complete. His vision for it, he had to admit, had been slowly evolving . . . a piece here, a piece there, all guided by a design he could only dimly perceive, but which seemed to him to be ever on the precipice of reaching some kind of conclusion. His most recent notion was that several paintings were required, to adorn the walls.

The painter lived in the house's garret. Bird knocked and cautiously opened the door when he heard a vague sound from within. The room was long and had a sloping roof on both sides, cutting off its area, so that only in the center could a tall man stand unobstructed. Sunlight came in through two large dormers on each side. Arranged near one of these windows was an easel, under which was a man, sitting with his legs crossed on the floor and his head in his hands as if he was lost in deep grief.

"Hello?"

He looked up sharply. "Well, who are you?" He studied Bird and then Alice with an owlish look.

"Lieutenant Henry Bird. We discussed the possibility of you performing some work on commission for me. I thought we had arranged to meet at this hour."

"Ah. And now you are here," he said without feeling, pushing himself to a standing position. The first thing Bird noticed was that he was exceptionally short, for a man. Perhaps only a bit above five feet tall. Then, as if just putting it together, he asked, "And this is Alice? The wild girl that people speak of?"

Alice looked at him darkly.

Bird nodded. "Say hello to Mr. Swain, Alice."

Alice wandered a few steps into the room, studying the easel and paints, the Spartan furnishings. Swain ignored her silence and smoothed his cowlick down with his hand. As he donned a wrinkled jacket he said, "Tell me more about this work you require." Despite his short stature, he had a broad, muscular chest. He possessed the build of a dock worker, but with soft and youthful features. Bird could not even begin to guess his age. He had a boyish face and strands of gray in his hair.

Alice turned her attention to a stack of paintings leaning by the door. She dropped to her knees to study the outward-facing portrait closely. A woman with wide hips and pendulous breasts, lying on her side with her hand suggestively resting in between her legs. Alice took her nail and dug into a ridge of almost-dried enamel and it fell free like a tiny crumbling of stone.

"Don't do that," he said sharply. Then, softer, "Please, miss. Do not touch those." He walked over and pulled a sheet over them as Alice retreated to Bird's side.

"I will not waste your time, Mr. Swain, for I find that is one of the worst offenses a man can commit. Time is money, after all. I wish to commission four portraits."

The painter followed Alice with his eyes as she floated across the room. He spoke to Bird with a distracted air. "Describe them for me."

"They are to represent scenes from my life. Momentous occasions that I would like to commemorate. The first would be a scene of battle. In the Pacific. The crew of a longboat facing off a horde of cannibals rushing from the shore. Rifles firing and so on. An active scene."

Swain nodded for him to continue.

"The second would be called *The Land of Ice*. I would like a scene of the Antarctic Continent, which I was the first to witness. A distant line of white mountains, across a vast and unbroken field of ice. Ominous gray skies." He felt in his pockets, came out with a few crumpled and folded pieces of notepaper. "I have written it all down for you."

"That will be helpful," the painter said, but made no move to take the offered notes.

"In the foreground, the viewer will see me surveying this landscape, from high in the rigging of the ship *Vincennes* that I sailed upon."

"The third?"

"The stars and stripes, being hoisted over a liberated garrison during the Mexican War."

"Is your name William?" Alice asked him abruptly.

"Do not be rude," Bird scolded her.

Swain smiled at the sound of her voice, and then said with mock-surprise, "Ah! The wild girl can speak! I have always been called Billy. Even my mother called me by that name."

Bird ignored this exchange and continued, "The final painting would depict me with Alice."

"Ah. And we will call this one *The Discovery of The Wild Girl*," Swain suggested. "Something like this?"

"No," Bird coughed. "I was thinking something more dignified. Portray us as you would father and child. Perhaps seated?" Bird looked around, as if expecting to find furniture, and found none. "It is a fair bit of work but I am told you are the man who can do something like this cheaply."

"Not cheaply. My work is not cheap."

"I did not mean cheap."

"I should hope not."

Alice walked behind the easel and the painter followed her, trying to angle himself between her and his uncovered work-in-progress. He picked up a small, stretched canvas on a frame. "Four canvasses, perhaps of this size?"

"No, I should think much larger. The viewer must be impressed, with the majesty of nature you see, that sort of thing."

"It will not be cheap."

He began to discuss figures, a down payment needed for the canvas and supplies. The numbers sounded high to Bird, much higher than he'd expected. How much effort did it take to swab some paint onto canvas? He had no idea. In truth, Bird had begun to fret over money. His profits from Mr. Galloway's play had, thus far, been a pittance—the impresario had put him off, claiming that more was forthcoming when the previous year's accounts were settled, but recently the man had been difficult to get ahold of. Bird had spent too much already, he thought, on the house, on the parlor, on the crates of liquor necessary to keep it well stocked for "The Group." He'd considered charging some sort of membership fee, once he'd formally announced it as *The Neptune Club*, making it an official society with bylaws and rules, but Mr. Mirmiran had discouraged him.

"Perhaps we can work out some sort of arrangement . . ." Bird began, but in fact he could think of nothing to offer the painter. Then he thought of Gus the dentist, and the discounted dentistry afforded to "The Group." "I do have little gatherings at my house, I could introduce you around to some of the better men in the city, to help you attract more business?"

Swain did not answer for some time. "I will also need sketches," he mumbled, oblivious to Bird's offer as he moved toward Alice, who was gazing out one of the windows at the blue sky. He placed a gentle hand on her shoulder. She stopped, turned to regard him. He stooped before her, bringing his head level to hers. With one hand still on her shoulder, he moved his other to brush some hair from her face. When he tried to nudge up the brim of her hat with a finger, she pulled away.

"Wait," he said quietly. "Stay here." He reached over to the easel and took up a slim brush, which he held vertically, a foot away from her face. "Can you see it?" he asked. Alice nodded once that she could. "Keep your eyes on it, keep looking at it," he said. Slowly, he moved the brush up, then down. Her eyes followed it. He moved it left to right across her field of vision, seeming to study the track of her eyes, the shape of her chin.

"I have another project . . ." he began, distracted by her face. Then he turned to Bird. "I have been searching for a model, for a piece I have in mind. She would be perfect."

"Oh, we wouldn't be interested in anything like that," Bird said, thinking of the nude woman waiting by the door.

Swain caught his meaning, and said, "If you're worried that I'll require her to take her clothes off, I assure you I mean nothing of the sort. It is a historical piece, *The Revenge of Medea*. I would only need her to sit for me a few times, in addition to the sittings for your portraits. If you could consent to that, I would offer you a reduced rate."

"You will paint me?" Alice asked him.

"That is my meaning, yes," Swain said to her.

"I would like that."

"You would?" Bird asked.

"She would be perfect," Swain repeated.

As Swain rose and stood in front of Alice, she looked up and said, "I am not wild, you know."

Swain looked down with a bemused expression.

"That was just an actress in a play," she said. "It was not real."

"Of course," he soothed her. "You don't look very wild to me."

14.

• • •

The smells of laundry soap and turpentine hung thickly in the painter's garret. All the steam from the washtubs below rose through the boards, filling the space with warmth and a fog of moisture that seemed to slow the afternoon's light. The painter was seated on a side-turned fruit crate, moving a lump of coal furiously over the pages of a book that was balanced on his crossed leg, occasionally looking up with dark eyes, as if what he saw angered him. An easel near the windows had a canvas upon it, an open paintbox at its side, but he had not touched them. He had been drawing her with his coal for hours, but she did not mind. She enjoyed standing motionless in the painter's warm garret, feeling his attention focused only on her. Challenging herself not to move a single muscle, not wanting to displease him, fighting to still the trembling in her hands.

Bird was seated near the doorway on a hardbacked chair, looking bored, his hands folded in his lap. The only sound had been the scratching of the coal on the paper. Bird cleared his throat and broke the silence. "You must tell me something that I have always wondered: Is great art something within you, or is it the product of schooling?"

"Both," Swain said, without interrupting his drawing. "If you do not have it within you, you will not create, it is as simple as that. But schooling gives the work form. I was schooled in Paris." He raised his eyes briefly and it was clear he was speaking only to her when he asked, "Have you ever been to Paris?"

"I have been to many places upon this globe, but France is not one of them," Bird said. "And I say that I have not missed it. I did have the occasion though once, while sailing in the South Pacific, to dine with a dozen sober Frenchmen . . . there is nothing worse in the world, I say, than a sober Frenchman."

Swain let Bird's words hang in the air unanswered. He placed his book and coal on the floor and crossed over to her, to reposition her arms. His touch was gentle; his hands were thick and muscular like a seaman's; they did not seem like they should be able to make such delicate suggestions upon her body. She took a small step as he gently pressed her hip to reposition her. These small motions, when his hands hovered outside of her clothes, when his fingers touched her neck, were like words to her; it was as if they held a private conversation that no one else could hear.

"I will take San Francisco over any city in the world," Bird said, undiscouraged in his attempts to start a conversation.

The painter returned to his seat and took up his implements. Finally he replied, without interest. "Paris was already there when the Romans came. How long has all of this stood?" He nodded toward the recessed windows that gave a view of variegated rooftops climbing a hill, plumes of smoke, one angling gull. "It has been here for ten years and will be gone in just as many." He returned to his scratching at the paper.

"I would ask, why are you here, if you detest it so much?"

"It is easier for me to sell work here. Paris is full of artists. San Francisco is not."

"Is your work not to the French taste? That is no mark against you."

The painter closed his eyes. "Please," he said. "I cannot work with this level of interruption."

Motes of dust turned in the sunlight. She wished that she were small and made of air, so that she could step from one to another, use them as a ladder to cross over to him. Instead, she slid her left foot a few inches and shifted her weight onto it.

The next time Billy looked up from his book, he exhaled sharply through his teeth, threw his stone to the ground, and ran his fingers through his curled hair. Then he stood and returned to her. He was small enough that she could look up directly into his face. He took her shoulders firmly and moved them back to the original position. Her foot, he tapped with his own until he was satisfied with its place.

"You must remain still," he said.

"Yes, Alice. Stand still for Mr. Swain, or we will be here all afternoon. We have already been here long enough."

They fell into silence as the painter resumed his work. Every so often, he would look up from the book and she would try to catch his eye with her gaze. Finally, he noticed her staring at him, and their eyes remained locked for a long while, as if it were a contest. Then, defiantly, she shifted her position again, in his full sight.

This time, he did not throw his coal to the ground in anger but put it quietly into his pocket. He stood without a word and went over to her.

"Has she moved?"

"Please. Silence."

He placed a hand on each of her hips. She pressed herself into them, so he was the only thing keeping her from falling forwards. Only a slight movement, hardly noticeable from where Bird sat. For the briefest moment her weight was in his hands. There was a silent agreement between them, communicated with the smallest of gestures: the way he allowed her to settle into his palms, curled his fingers around her as if to keep her there. He took her hand into his own for a moment and lifted it up, lifted up her crooked arm as if he wished to do something with it, but then let it drop back to her side.

∽

For weeks they continued like this. Every Tuesday, in the afternoon when the light was most appropriate, Bird and Alice climbed up to the painter's garret so that he could make his sketches. He made a few of Bird in different positions, reaching his arms above his head, which Bird did stiffly like a pelican, or holding a broom handle as if it was a rifle, but these took up only the first portion of one day. For the rest of the time they remained in the garret, Billy made sketch after sketch of Alice, never satisfied with what he'd created.

On the days between her sittings, she would sit at the window and wait to see him again. It had always been a dull frustration for her, to see all the life in the streets she could not partake of. Separated from the world by glass. It waxed and waned as she received her medicine: a gnawing sense of her confinement, of the possibility and adventure in the world she could not experience, which would subside only when she had a full dropperful and could retreat into her own colorful fantasies where she lacked nothing. But now there was a new edge to her frustration; it had become longing, a more powerful thing that was not as easily diminished. She studied the faces in the street below, waiting for his to appear among them. When her vision was distorted by the haze of her medicine, she thought she saw him again and again among the bustling commotion of Montgomery Street, each time wearing a different hat. Each time, it was only some man who looked nothing like him. She trained her eyes on the corner, watching every figure that came around it, telling herself that he would be the next.

She heard Bird hovering behind her, uncomfortable in his silence.

"You are wasting away. I have brought you a cup of broth."

She did not turn to receive it, fearful that she might miss him when he appeared. "Is it Tuesday?" she asked.

He clicked his tongue at her. "You asked me that question yesterday, and I told you that it was Thursday. Tuesday does not come after Thursday. Stop pretending that you do not know the days."

Bird's patience waned. He began to bring his morning newspapers with him to the painter's garret to angrily riffle through them, searching for any tidbit of news that had escaped his attention the first time he'd read them. While his attention was thus occupied, the painter allowed his hand to caress her neck, to cross over her breast. When he moved her leg, he slid his hand up, until it was under her dress, resting briefly on the hidden pale flesh above her knee. It was a place she had never been touched.

Eventually Swain left his sketchbook behind and began to work on a canvas. He spread and mixed colors on a piece of board, selected and abandoned brushes. At the close of their sittings he turned his easel toward the wall, unwilling to allow them to see it.

Until one day, he did. He took the canvas down from the easel without a word and leaned it against the wall facing outwards. Alice looked at it and saw only swirls of color, the most basic shape of her body. Swain set about stretching a new canvas over a wooden frame, fastening it with little tacks that he tapped in with a mallet.

"What is this? You're not starting all over again, are you?" Bird's voice carried his annoyance.

"I am doing what the work demands," Swain answered as he placed the fresh canvas upon the easel. He stood and came to reposition her, careful now that Bird was watching. He moved her into a new position, slightly bent over, her crooked arm curled against her chest. He eyed her a final time and said, "Wait. Wait just like that." He quickly crossed the room to rummage among a stack of items, and returned with a small sack of flour, half-full. "Can you hold this? In your arms? Yes, like this . . ." He showed her how to cradle the sack in one arm. "This will help . . . imagine that this is your babe."

"How much longer is this going to take?" Bird consulted with his pocket watch.

"Mr. Bird. You can see that this process is taking time. And it will take more time than necessary if I am constantly called upon to stop and explain my every act to your satisfaction."

Bird rattled his newspapers and coughed but said nothing else. Swain took and raised her arm, the one that remained perfect and straight, until it was poised high above the sack. He brought his face close to hers and whispered, "You love your babe, but with this hand . . . you hold a knife, which you will use to kill your very own child."

"What are you saying to her?"

"Can you do this?" he asked her softly. She nodded once. As he returned to his easel she stared down at the slumping sack and tried to feel for it a burning hatred. She thought of it as Fanny, Mrs. Sutter's daughter, whose fading memory filled her with an anger she could not explain.

"What is this?" Bird demanded.

Swain stood behind his easel and stared at her with a distant intensity. Then he spoke, more to himself than to Bird. "Medea . . . she is most often depicted as a proud, ample figure. She must have been, they reason, to possess the strength to do what she did. But there is a lie in that. This is where my work will differ. My work will be honest. It will show her as what she was . . . selfish, immature, unable to contain her own rage. No more than a child herself, in spirit as well as body. A child killing a child . . ." He trailed off. Then without another word he took up a brush and dabbed it against the palette and began to make long, rasping strokes on the canvas.

Bird only made a sound of acknowledgment like *humph*, to indicate that he either disapproved or did not understand. For a while he looked to the painter as if he might speak again, but then he only slumped in his chair, his newspapers so thoroughly picked through that they could offer him nothing else. In the warm and quiet atmosphere of the garret he began to slowly nod. His head drooped, then raised. It drooped again and remained there, his mouth hanging slightly open, his chin on his vest. Eventually he began to snore. Swain stopped his work and looked for a moment as if he might scold the lieutenant for this further interruption, but then he seemed to reconsider and quietly put down his brush. Alice still held the sack of flour, both of her arms now burning from the effort. She would not drop it though. She would show him how loyal she could be.

He stood and came over to her. He took another look at Bird to make sure he was still asleep, and then brought his head down to touch his lips against her forehead, her nose, her lips. Each touch was brief and carried with it the smallest bit of moisture that she could feel cooling, fading on her skin after his lips were gone. He flashed her a mischievous smile as he pulled away, and then he cleared his throat loudly, startling Bird awake and putting an abrupt end to his snoring.

Before taking their leave one afternoon, Bird declared that there would be no more sketches, no more sittings. "I am quite sure you have more than you need," he said. "And I simply do not have the time to accommodate you any further. If I had been at work digging ditches, I might have made enough money already to buy the paintings at full price, for all the hours I've sat here."

Alice felt something within her drop—a weight had been suspended by a thread and the thread had been cut. She felt dizzy as it plummeted. She looked to the painter, waiting for him to object, to say that she must come again. That his work was not done. He did not look up from his painting, which he'd been working at with intensity for some hours, hardly noticing either of them. All that he said was, "Very well."

"When will my paintings be finished?" Bird asked.

"Very soon."

He did not look up at her as they left.

In the street, she found that she could not walk, and Bird was forced to hire a Chinaman to carry her home. As she lay on the sofa, he complained that he was being forced to waste money on her foolishness. She felt a hatred for him then unlike any she'd felt before, even when he'd struck her.

Nettie was cutting up onions and throwing them into the stewpot. Alice slept. Later she woke to find the woman had gone for the day and Bird asleep in his chair. She rose and moved into the kitchen. As carefully as she could, she took two linens from the sideboard and used them to grip the handle of the stewpot without scalding herself. She lifted it from where it simmered and placed it on the floor. Then she pulled up her dress to squat and release a trickle of urine into it, all that she could muster, before replacing it on the stove. When Bird awoke for his supper hour, he complained that it was salty and said that he would scold Nettie for the error.

∼

Days and then weeks passed without any order. Her thoughts moved slowly under the weight of her illness. Still, a thought was forming in her, like a tangled line. Why did he not come? To save her? She thought that perhaps he required something more, some better display of her faithfulness. She could recall the night when she huddled in the little house William had built for them, the first of their colony. The sound of William arguing with the men. They had grumbled and complained continuously on the island, but on that night, she heard a man threaten to kill William and take the ship. William's voice was patient and calm as he tried to explain their error. She felt calm then as well, as if his strength, or perhaps the grace of the Lord, had entered her, and told her what must be done. She'd found the captain's pistol where William had hidden it in their little domicile and put the bullets in as he'd taught her. She'd carried it down to the rocks, where they stood around a fire that whipped and flared in the wind. And when she went to his side and placed the pistol into his hands, he'd said to them all, *Do you see? This girl has more faith in her heart than the lot of you.*

∼

Alice waited and watched for an opportunity. Then, one morning as Nettie was gathering the laundry, it came. Bird was growing more forgetful; the housekeeper discovered his key still in the pocket of his vest, and placed it on his bedside table, where she often put the pipes and dried scraps of tobacco that she salvaged for him before taking the washing away. As soon as she'd left with the basket, Alice slipped into the room where Bird still lay sleeping, the tangle of white hair around his head like a crown, and placed the key in her mouth for safekeeping.

All day it remained there, like a word she could not speak. Bird didn't notice its absence until after his supper. He'd started his drinking early and was already quite drunk; he shambled around the apartments like a sleepwalker for some time, checking his pockets, before he asked her, "Have you seen my key?"

"No," Alice answered him. The sharp taste of the metal filled her mouth.

He searched the living room, and then rifled through her belongings, in her bedroom. He scattered her shells from the windowsill and tore the blankets from her bed.

"Alice. Did you take my key?" he demanded.

"No, I swear it." She pulled away, as if afraid he might strike her.

"I'm only asking you questions," he said sheepishly, suddenly embarrassed by his own outburst, and then seemed to let the matter drop.

He seemed to believe her story. That night he locked the door with his spare key, the one he would sometimes loan out to the housekeeper and which she suspected resided in his medicine cabinet. As soon as she heard the click of the lock, Alice rose from the window bench, where she'd been pretending to sleep, and pressed herself against the door, listening to the arrival of Bird's guests. Before long, there were a dozen voices or more. Tobacco smoke drifted up the stairs and under the door so that it smelled as if the house was burning in the night. She clearly heard one man shouting about a cargo of walnuts he'd acquired. He called for a toast to celebrate. *To all of our ventures,* he said. *May we arrive at fruitful pastures.* She waited. She heard their voices grow louder as they guzzled their drinks and Bird told again the story of how he'd discovered Antarctica. It was met, as it was every night, with a rousing cheer. Their evenings were as predictable as clockwork, and eventually the front door began to open and close once more, ejecting the men into the street like seeds spit into the night.

She waited for a long time, listening to the silence, and then slowly inserted the key in the lock. She paused after the tumbler clicked and listened again before quietly opening the door. There was still a lamp lit down in the parlor, its light set so low that it flickered through the bannisters. Her bare feet made no sound on the stairs. Bird was asleep in a chair with his head tilted to the side. She smelled stale whiskey, and staler smoke. Empty glasses and overflowing ashtrays were everywhere. She heard Bird's deep and uneven breathing, as if his lungs were struggling to draw each breath. She crossed the room, trying not to look at him, lest her gaze somehow wake him. She held her breath as she tried the knob on the front door and found it open.

No one noticed her as she hurried along the route she knew so well; she had rehearsed each step in her mind countless times. Dawn was hours away, and only a few lights shone over the doorways of the saloons. She remained in the shadows of buildings and shop awnings; the only ones in the streets were women and drunkards who did not even notice her small figure moving from one shadow to another.

With each step, she felt her life with Bird loosening its tendrils, fading behind her. She did not even spare a thought for all her things, her feathers and coins, shells and stones, her hairbrush that still after all this time smelled of Mr. Rand. She could leave it all behind as easily as she left behind her bedchamber, her window over the street, even Bird. None of it had any hold on her. She had taken only her hat.

The Chinese laundry was silent and dark. The front door was not locked. The washtubs all sat emptied and turned over, leaned against the walls. As she approached the back stairwell, she could hear the Chinamen sleeping all in the same back room, curled on mats on the floor.

She climbed the twisted staircase up to the garret and found yet another unlocked door—it was a sign, she thought, that angels were surely watching over her, as William had promised her they would. The moon hung low enough over the city that its silver light spilled through the windows and across the floor. The garret was unoccupied. The wide canvas he was working on remained upon the easel, covered with a sheet. She wished to see it but she knew it would displease him, and so she sat on his bed, a straw-stuffed mattress atop a pallet in the corner, and regarded the covered canvas from across the room.

The sun had begun to rise when she heard footsteps tromping heavily up the stairs. The Chinese had already begun their day's work and she'd been listening to the sound of them clanging their washtubs below. He opened the door and she saw him, humming an indecipherable tune, swaying, his shirt unbuttoned down to his navel. He took a few steps into the room before he noticed her, and then he stopped, studying her, his eyes narrowed as if trying to decide if what he saw was some apparition.

"You've come . . ." was all he said. He wrinkled his face, searching for more words. But then his features softened into a warm smile. He said nothing else, only collapsed onto the bed next to her, rested his tangle of hair in her lap, and immediately fell asleep.

15.

AN UNINVITED GUEST

Bird awoke to a terrific headache and the pudgy jowls of someone shaking a newspaper in front of his face. He could determine from the light in the windows that it was day, but knew nothing else.

"Have you heard?"

"Which one are you?"

"The Dramatic Museum. It's burned to the ground." Mirmiran had obviously taken the liberty of letting himself in, or else perhaps he had never left from the night before.

Bird's eyes found their focus and he read the headline.

"And I hear there's going to be an insurance claim. This Galloway is either very prudent or very crafty, I can't tell which."

Bird tried to process it all but couldn't find the thread. Thanks to his nightly carousing, his mornings had become more fragile, and he found he could do little but sit and sip a cup of coffee and try to remember things for the first few hours of each day, unable to read or to venture out into the bright sun. He had a painful feeling in his bladder, but he was not yet up to the task of urinating—he sometimes imagined that tiny beavers had built some sort of dam within him, and he could only get a little to dribble over the top with a great effort.

"What about my money?"

"That is another matter."

Mirmiran took the time to pour them drinks and light a cheroot before sitting down. "I've looked through the papers you gave to me. And I must scold you, Henry. Why did you not have me look through them before you signed?"

"I was not aware at that time that you practiced law." He looked at the whiskey in his glass. He would have preferred some coffee, but the pot was upstairs, cold and impossibly distant.

"You realize you were in breach of your obligations."

"That bastard made his money. And I have obliged him. He must owe me something."

The Wild Girl of San Francisco had packed the Dramatic Museum for nearly an entire year, yet Bird had hardly seen a penny from it. He and Galloway had disagreed vehemently on what fair compensation might be once it was clear that Alice would not be appearing at any more performances. Still, hadn't they engaged in all his ridiculous promotional stunts? Hadn't Bird given his blessing to the whole enterprise, allowing it an authenticity Galloway's competitors lacked? For months, he'd been pressing Galloway on the issue, both through a persistent letter-writing campaign and by skulking around the alley behind the theater, hoping to catch the man as he left his office. It pained Bird to skulk, but Galloway was slippery as an eel. When he did manage to corner the man, he'd been put off by a host of excuses: the latest receipts had not yet been tallied, the actors were pressing for greater salaries . . . On one occasion, he'd simply told Bird that he refused to discuss business at suppertime. Bird had recently received a parcel, delivered by a stagehand, stuffed with ledger books that he'd not been able to decipher. Mirmiran now explained that these documents indicated that no further money was owed to him, as *The Wild Girl of San Francisco* had somehow, incredibly, not made any profit.

"You saw it yourself," Bird said. "How many people fit in that theater of his? Night after night? I can't understand it."

"I can answer you in one word, Henry. Overhead. It's as simple as that. There are costumes to purchase, coal for the stoves and gas for the lamps. Face paint and such. There was a very sizable cost for the rental of the theater."

"But he owns the damned theater. How can a man rent something from himself?"

"I've seen it happen," Mirmiran assured him. "And then there are the salaries."

"Whose salaries?"

"Everyone. Salary is a *cost*, Henry. To put on a play, there are actors to be paid, set decorators. The boy who sits in the ticket window."

"What was *his* salary?"

"The ticket boy?"

"No. Galloway. I hate calling him that. It's not even the man's damned name."

"What is his name?"

Bird sought it out but his mind grasped only air. "Hell if I can remember. Some Polish nonsense."

Mirmiran consulted the pages for a few moments. "There are four, that he was receiving. He is listed as director, lighting manager, set designer, and writer."

"And where is my salary?"

"You did some work on the play which you weren't compensated for?" Mirmiran asked, Bird thought dismissively.

"I discovered her. That's some work, isn't it?"

Mirmiran shook his head. "You know that won't do."

Bird swallowed a mouthful of whiskey and put his head in his hands. "Well, you are the legal man. Tell me, what do we do?"

"Do you wish to take the matter before a court? We could try. Your reputation is solid, and a judge might see it your way. There are additional costs associated with that, however, and no guarantee we would win."

"What costs?"

"Legal fees, for one. Though I'm more than willing to take a note of credit, due to our personal relationship."

Bird considered the prospect of standing again before some tribunal and admitted to himself that he would rather not. "So, we're stuffed and roasted . . ."

"I'm surprised to hear you giving up so quickly. Is this the same Lieutenant Henry Aaron Bird who nearly turned the tide of the Mexican War?"

"You are buzzing me. I have told you, I cannot abide with buzzing."

Mirmiran squared himself and took off his spectacles. "The way forward, I think is for us to concentrate not on what Galloway has taken from us, but what he's given to us."

"The man has given me nothing. Isn't that the point?"

"Not true," Mirmiran said coyly. He regarded the growing cherry on his cheroot before tipping it into the crystal bowl on the end table. "He gave us something that is worth more than gold. *Exposure*." He paused to let his words sink in. "Think of it—every man in the state knows the name Alice Kelly. She is famous, Henry. That is something."

"What do you propose? That we sell her to the highest bidder?"

"No, that we sell her *story*."

"What do you mean?"

"I am proposing that you write a book."

Bird tested the idea before responding. "A book . . . there's not enough to say about the girl to fill an entire book. Do I catalog every time she says something mad? I don't think I could fill four pages with her."

Mirmiran shrugged. "This is no obstacle. We can embellish the tale. There is no law against that. Everyone does it. You don't know how awful some of these books are, nowadays. Most of them have perhaps one or two good scenes, and the rest of the pages are filled up with fiddle-faddle. We need only have one or two chapters on the girl, and the rest can be furnished with other anecdotes. The one about the Feegees is stirring."

"I do have a number of good stories under my belt, don't I?" Bird mused. "More than other men . . ."

"Yes, exactly. We can present it as your memoir. I've heard you speak, eloquently, grandly, I might add, about your past accomplishments. All that remains is to put it to paper, exactly as you tell it."

"I see," Bird said. His fleeting moment of enthusiasm had already passed, and the daunting prospect of writing an entire book hung over him like a thunderhead.

At that moment there was a loud knock at the door.

"Hell's bells. It's a busy morning." Bird felt around for his stick and struggled to his feet. Mirmiran had not offered to get up and open the door for him, but sat puffing on his cheroot, happy as a clam.

He opened the front door to find a giant on the step, nearly seven feet tall, wrapped in a coat stitched together crudely from the skins of dozens of beavers. He had a bush of beard and wild hair that sprouted from beneath a coonskin hat, the tail still hanging from it. The entire effect of his appearance, Bird thought, made the man look like nothing so much as a mountainous pile of dead animals.

"I'M LOOKIN FOR THE LIEUTENANT!" he announced. The voice was as big as the man, carrying the faint trace of an Irish accent, filtered through perhaps decades of rough living on the American frontier.

"You've found him . . . Who did you say you were?"

"FRANK KELLY!" the giant bellowed. It seemed he could find no way to communicate other than shouting at the top of his lungs. He then leaned over and crushed Bird against his chest. Bird was hit with a nauseating wave of the man's scent. "I APOL'GIZE FER THAT," he said as Bird tried to squirm free and was finally released. "I ALWAYS LIKE TO GIVE A MAN A STRONG EMBRACE."

"Frank?" Bird mumbled as the giant yanked on his arm. "You said your name was Frank?"

He looked down quizzically at Bird. "DIDN' YOU GET NONE A MY LETTERS?"

"Letters?" Bird pretended to search his memory.

"AH WELL. THAT'S THOSE DAMN POST MEN FOR YA." A dark cloud crossed his face as he considered the failings of the postal service. As he pushed past Bird into the parlor, he called over his shoulder, "ME AND THAT NIGGER ET YER PIG."

He settled himself heavily in a chair and placed his feet up on a table, shaking clods of earth onto the polished wooden surface. Mirmiran sat to one side, quietly taking in the proceedings as the line of ash at the end of his cheroot grew longer.

"I'm sorry," Bird stammered. "Who did you say you were?"

"FRANK KELLY. I'M UNCLE TO THE GIRL YOU GOT HERE." He looked around, as if expecting to find her. "WELL, WHERE THE HELL IS SHE?"

"You . . . how did you find us?"

Kelly wiped his mouth. "OLD-TIMER, I TRACKED INJUNS IN A LOW DESERT. IT WARN'T NOTHIN TO FIND YOU. I JUST HAD A TIME COMING."

"You say you've come a long way?" Mirmiran asked politely.

"DON' YOU KNOW IT. I RECKON I CROSSED THIS WHOLE COUNTRY THREE TIMES. FIRST TIME I WENT OUT TO ARIZONNY TO GET AT SOME GOLD AND DIDN' FIND NONE. THEN I COME BACK EAST AND HEARED MY BROTHER WAS GONE AND HIS OFFSHOOT WAS IN VIRGINNY. I WENT DOWN THERE BUT YOU WAS ALREADY GONE OUT TO CALIFORNIA SO I HAD TO WALK ALL THAT DAMN WAY AGAIN ON ACCOUNT OF MY HORSE DIED. AND I SEEN PLENTY A TROUBLE." He held up a hand that had been partially concealed by his furs to reveal two missing fingers.

"That's an astounding story," Mirmiran offered, finally tipping his column of ash into the ashtray.

Kelly looked at the bar and then at Bird and said, "WELL, AIN'T YOU GONNA OFFER A MAN A DRINK?"

Bird fetched a bottle and glasses and poured for them, several times pursing his lips as if he was about to speak. Kelly took his whiskey in one swallow as soon as it was handed to him. Bird sat down and took a sip of his own, and then another.

"Really, an astounding story," Mirmiran said. "Have you ever considered writing a book about it?"

Kelly's mood darkened again in an instant. He regarded Mirmiran with a hardness in his eyes and said coldly, "NO WAY, MISTER."

"Well, why not? If you don't write well," Mirmiran offered, "it is no shame. None of the great writers could write very well, that's the truth of it. Did you know that? Charles Dickens, one of the undeniable greats, did you know for instance that he couldn't spell? Not a single word. His publisher did it all. Give it some thought," Mirmiran said.

Kelly turned icy cold, leveled a murderous stare at Mirmiran, and said, "KEEP PUSHING AND SEE WHERE IT GETS YOU."

Bird forced down another swallow of whiskey, hoping it would start to work on his nerves. He smoothed down his sleep-wrinkled trousers. "I have to admit, Mr. Kelly, I was not prepared for your visit. If you'd like, we can make arrangements for you to meet Alice at some future date?"

"WHAT KIND A DAMN ARRANGEMENTS DO YA WANT? I'M RIGHT HERE, SO LET ME HAVE A LOOK AT HER."

Bird listened and heard nothing from upstairs. "That will be impossible today. You see, Alice is very ill at the moment."

"SHE'S SICK? IS SHE GONNA DIE?" he said, panic creeping into his voice. Unable to contain his emotions any longer, he stood up from the chair and howled, "AIN'T THAT JUST MY LUCK! EVERY PLACE I GET TO, IT'S JUST TOO DAMN LATE!"

"Mr. Kelly . . . Mr. Kelly . . . no, I didn't mean . . ."

Tears flooded his eyes. "I NEVER HAD NOTHING EXCEPT FOR BLAMED BAD LUCK IN MY LIFE AND ALL I SEEN IS ONE TROUBLE AFTER ANOTHER. MY MOMMA ALWAYS SAID I WAS THE BAD ONE AND MY BROTHER WAS THE

BETTER AND YOU KNOW WHAT? SHE MUST'A BEEN RIGHT . . ."

"Please. Miss Kelly is not going to die. She is not fatally ill. Her malady is a disorder of the mind. I'm sorry to say it. She is mad."

Kelly looked up from his lamentations and wiped across his face with the sleeve of his coat—on it, the small, distorted face of one of its beavers was clearly visible. He sniffled and composed himself. "OH, IS THAT ALL?? THAT DON' BOTHER ME NONE. I THINK HER MOMMA HAD A TOUCH OF THAT."

"As I have said, if you would like to make arrangements, for a different time . . ."

Kelly's eyes narrowed and he was silent for a long while. Then he said, "YOU KNOW WHAT, MISTER? I AM STARTIN TO THINK YOU'RE TRYIN' TO PLAY ME."

He followed Bird's eyes to the stairs, and without another word he stood and crossed the room, shouting "ALICE? YOU UP THERE? IT'S YER OLD UNC'! UNCLE FRANK!"

"Please! Mr. Kelly! Excuse me! If you don't stop this at once, I'm going to be forced to summon a policeman." Bird regretted the words as soon as he spoke them.

The giant froze halfway up the stairs. "WHAT IN HELL DID YOU SAY?"

Bird desperately tried to reason with him as he clomped back down to the parlor. "I'll have you know this city is not the lawless place it used to be. We have order now. You cannot just go into a man's house and start banging around. I'm sure we can settle this somehow . . ."

"YER GOD DAMN RIGHT WE WILL."

Kelly's hands were empty one moment and then there was a knife in them. Long and wicked-looking, two sides of a homemade grip tied on with strips of rawhide, produced almost magically from somewhere within his trousers.

"Now, look here," Mirmiran said, adopting a remarkably unaffected tone. "I do not know where you are from, but here in San Francisco this is not how we do it. If you've been insulted, you can at least settle it like gentlemen."

"I DON'T GIVE A HORSE'S SHIT WHERE WE'RE AT," he said as Bird maneuvered to keep furniture between them.

"I understand that you're upset. You feel that your honor has been besmirched, and as is any man's right, you demand satisfaction. But Lieutenant Bird has rights in this situation as well. If he is to meet you on the field of battle, where he may fall, he has a right to put his affairs in order first."

Kelly stopped circling to regard him warily. "WELL, HOW LONG DOES THAT TAKE?"

Mirmiran looked to Bird. "Could you do it on Sunday?"

"Do what?" Bird asked. He felt entirely disconnected from anything that was happening in the room, as if he was merely an observer.

"Meet Mr. Kelly." Mirmiran said. He looked to Kelly, "I understand that you are issuing a challenge to the Lieutenant, is that correct?"

Kelly's face wrinkled with doubt. "YER SAYIN I GOTTA WAIT TIL SUNDAY TO KILL THIS FANCY COCKSUCKER?"

"That would be ideal," Mirmiran said. He had begun to take notes on a little pad he removed from his vest pocket. "And think of the advantage for yourself. In San Francisco, they hang men for cold-blooded murder. But I've never heard of a man being convicted for an honorable duel, no matter the outcome."

Kelly lowered the knife and it seemed like a great machinery was slowly turning in his head. "WELL," he said, "WHAT DAY IS TODAY?"

"Tuesday. So that would be five days hence. Do you have a location in mind, or should we suggest one?"

"WHAT'S WRONG WITH RIGHT OUTSIDE THAT DOOR?"

"It's a busy thoroughfare. There are women and children. I would propose the dunes to the west, out past the mission house. It will give you some privacy, to settle your disagreement."

"FINE THEN. IT DON' MAKE NO DIFFERENCE TO ME."

"And another thing. I believe the Lieutenant would prefer pistols to blades, isn't that right Henry?"

"Pistols," Bird mumbled, as if trying to recall what the word meant.

"To even things out, make a real contest of it," Mirmiran explained to Kelly.

"I AIN'T GOT A PISTOL."

"That is no obstacle. I can provide my own personal brace of pistols, and I'm sure the Lieutenant would not mind letting you have your pick at the time of the duel, to ensure fair play."

Kelly scratched vigorously at his head. "ALRIGHT. I'M AMEENABLE TA THAT." He looked to Bird. "I'LL KILL YOU ON SUNDAY HOWEVER YOU WANT, AND THEN I AIM TO TAKE MY BROTHER'S GIRL."

"So, it's settled." Mirmiran wrote everything down. "Sunday, we'll meet at the mission house at dawn, yes, and proceed into the dunes. I will serve as the Lieutenant's second. Have you any ideas in that regards? As to whom your second will be?"

"I DON' NEED NO HELP TO SHOOT THIS FOOL."

"Well," Mirmiran made another note on his paper. "If you lack connections in this city, I can make arrangements for your second, just to keep everything legitimate. And there we have it." He looked up with a satisfied smile, to see everything so roundly taken care of. "We will see you on Sunday then, Mr. . . . Kelly, was it?"

Kelly tucked the knife back in his trousers and pointed his three remaining fingers at Bird menacingly. It said more than any words he might have spoken. And with that, he strode out the front door into the street.

Bird felt as if he'd left the room at some point, and had only just returned to find everything in hopeless disorder. "You've just signed my death warrant," he sputtered.

Mirmiran was uncommonly cheerful. "No, I've just saved you from being stabbed and bleeding out on your carpet, is how I see it."

Neither he nor Mirmiran moved or spoke for several minutes. Bird's first thought was to run. To start again. Maybe in Mexico. Or farther than that. They'd done it before. But he couldn't. He would rather die than be remembered as a coward.

Mirmiran fished in his pocket for his cocaine tin. Bird searched for his own and found that he'd unfortunately emptied it the night before.

"Would you mind giving me a pinch?" he asked.

Mirmiran took a pinch to his nose and passed it over to Bird. "Good show, Henry. You didn't back down for a second. Fortitude, that's what you possess . . ."

"Is it allowed?" he asked. "To arrange a duel, with such little provocation?"

Mirmiran shrugged. "I admit he was hot-tempered. But a man will have his satisfaction, there is no power in the world that will stop that." He thought about it and said, "We could probably head this off, if you just give him the girl."

"What? No, it is out of the question." Bird tapped out a little hillock of the powder onto his palm and sniffed it. He felt something resembling order returning to his mind, his thoughts sharpening. "You can't truly think I would surrender her to that awful man. Even if he kills me, I won't have it."

"Oh, I'm sure it won't come to that. If you're as good a shot as you've said, we should have no difficulty winning the day."

His thoughts went to Alice, upstairs. He couldn't imagine what she had made of all the commotion. Mirmiran faded into the background as Bird made his way to the stairs and mounted them one at a time. He took the key from his pocket but found the door unlocked. He entered the silent apartment and walked from kitchen to sitting room to bedroom and back again, wondering if she was hiding from him. Playing some game. From one room to another. Studying the wrinkled blankets and her belongings scattered on the floor. Opening the closet. Looking out the windows. Wandering in a growing confusion, unable to add it all up.

She was gone.

"Alice?" he said.

16.

PISTOLS

Mirmiran suggested they hire a Pinkerton to track her. He said that these matters, *matters of the home* he called them, should always be privately handled.

At the company office, their case was assigned to an Italian named Scarlata, his face already darkened with stubble at one in the afternoon. He asked them a precious few questions—his English seemed poor.

"Is there nothing else that you can remember?" Mirmiran prodded him. "Did she say anything else?"

Bird tried to remember if there was any other detail he'd missed. Then something returned to him—he did not know if it was important. Something so small that he'd not attributed it to anything more than her customary delusions: The day before she'd disappeared, he'd found her sitting on the floor of her bedroom with all her belongings arranged before her. She'd been holding something up to her lips, a hairbrush he couldn't remember buying for her, and he'd clearly heard her whisper the word *goodbye*.

The Italian only shook his head, as if this was grave news indeed.

∼

Bird moved through the following week like a condemned man. It felt to him as if a curtain had been drawn over the future, a blackness he was barreling toward. He wished to keep her disappearance from the press, and even from "The Group." What could not escape their attention, however, was the fact that he'd been challenged. Kelly had been visiting saloons in the Australian part of town, bragging loudly to any who would listen that he was uncle to The Wild Girl and that Bird was a dead man.

They offered him empty words of encouragement. Mr. Charles, who speculated on the cargoes of abandoned ships in the harbor, said that he'd been challenged once himself, as a younger man, and over less. He'd asked a girl to dance, that was all, and a suitor had taken offense.

"What was the outcome?" Bird asked weakly.

"Both missed. Agreed to go about amicably after that."

"I hear it happens quite often," Mr. Lutz suggested helpfully.

They all assumed that a duel would be no great affair to one such as the Lieutenant. In fact, he had only once before fired a weapon at a human being. A lone Mexican, watching the approach of their war party from a distant hill. Bird had been so far away, the man hadn't even flinched at the shot.

Within the hour, his guests had moved on to discuss the looming threat of a constitutional conflict. Mr. Anselm declared that there would be a war, and that the South would be victorious due to an army they would form, whose rank-and-file soldiers would be slaves under the command of white generals. *The African is a keen fighter, and the European a keen strategist*, he explained. *And so they cannot lose.*

As much as it had irritated Bird to hear them discuss the duel so lightly, their dismissal of it galled him even further. He felt bile rising in his chest that he attempted to wash back down with whiskey as he maintained an uncustomary silence. How could they sit there and talk of such things at a time like this? What would it matter if the whole country went to war with itself, if he would not be there to witness it? Mirmiran had sequestered himself behind the bar to conspire with Mr. Murphy, who had an eye on the purchase of some water lots. Mr. Haymaker, the grocer, sat in the corner as he always did, only half-listening to the conversation as he chewed and ate his cigars. It disgusted Bird to think of them all next week, prattling on about the same things whether he was alive or dead.

Bird realized that even here, he still felt the pang of his old loneliness. No, this was even worse: this was loneliness coupled with the fear that loneliness was eternal, that he would never have a true friend in his life, that such a thing was not even possible.

He took up his walking stick and rapped it against the leg of his chair.

"Out!" he announced.

"What?" Mirmiran asked. The others just stared at him blankly, like fish in a pond.

"I must ask you all to leave. I need room to think . . ." he began to struggle for air.

"Henry, are you alright?"

He could hardly speak. He pointed his stick at the door.

They filtered out into the night in silence, some lingering just long enough to toss back the remainder of their drink, to tap their pipes into the ashtrays and gently stub out their cigars so they might finish them later.

In the remaining days leading up to the duel, few would return, and those who did—some of the newer initiates like Mr. Dane-Smith, who'd been out of town during Bird's outburst—would wither and retreat immediately at the harrowed sight of him clutching at the arms of his chair, his eyes sunken into his skull and swimming with fear.

∽

The only one who remained at his side was Mirmiran, whose optimism never flagged. "Do you know what this is?" he asked Bird, referring to his situation in general.

"Calamity," Bird muttered.

"Not at all, not at all. This," he said, "is nothing more than another chapter for our book. We can call it *The Duel*. A fitting final act of bravery to round out your adventures."

The lawyer had brought over his brace of pistols with the suggestion that Bird might want to have some practice shooting. "To feel the weight and the action," he explained.

The pistols were long, black Navy revolvers that carried six shots apiece. Bird took them from the cherrywood case into his hands and considered that one of these implements might be the cause of his death. Mirmiran emptied handfuls of firing cartridges out of his jacket pockets and onto a table.

"We need to discuss your last will and testament, before Sunday. It won't take long, I'm sure. And it will be a pure formality, as I'm confident you'll be victorious. We just need to draw up the papers."

He didn't notice Mirmiran leaving. At some point later in the day, he came to his senses and realized time had passed. The pistols were still both resting in his lap. He found the idea of remaining there, helpless in his worry, to be excruciating, and so he took a sniff of cocaine to enliven him and stuffed a handful of cartridges into his pocket.

With the pistols secured beneath his belt, he ventured out into the city. He passed his usual haunts without responding to the nods of greeting. He followed Montgomery to California Street and turned west. The city was growing, spreading and changing so rapidly that he was soon in a section he did not recognize. Whether he was alive or not, it would continue to grow, like some mold that would eventually devour the peninsula, the state, the entire country. Even death did not stop progress.

The buildings thinned and there was more sand between them, more weeds growing up through the sidewalk planks. He took another sniff of cocaine for his knee. He passed numerous saloons and gaming rooms, some open and sparsely populated, some closed, and one that had recently lost its roof and upper story to a fire.

The mission house was not quite white; large swathes of paint had weathered to reveal the muted color of the stone beneath. Here was the place where the city had begun, the first place where men had planted themselves in this country. The roof had lost tiles, like a mouth missing occasional teeth. Many of the fallen tiles lay broken and half-submerged in the mud. Couples and tourists strolled around the grounds—it was a popular spot for walking. It was not near the harbor, but there was a tidal inlet somewhere nearby that Bird could smell. He pressed on, out into the sandy wilds beyond the city's edge.

The dunes around the city were full of abandoned encampments, the garbage of tens of thousands of men who came for their fortunes, found them, lost them, and moved on. A crowd of men in dirty clothes and caps were standing around in a circle and shouting. As he passed, he realized they were betting on bear fights. Two small grizzlies were chained to posts in a shallow depression, breathing heavily, their coats thick and matted with blood.

He found a place beyond them, just out of sight. A few sandy dunes covered with sparse grass, a leaning fence that separated nothing but weeds. He sifted through the detritus to find a number of discarded tins and glass bottles, and then arranged them as well as he could on the lonely piece of fencing.

He moved himself twenty paces from it and fumbled with one of the pistols as he tried to load it. The bullets seemed too large for the holes, too small for his fingers. Those that fell on the ground, he left there.

He raised the pistol and fired once, twice, three times. The shots rang out in the open air but hit nothing. On the third shot, his eye caught a little spit of dust five feet to the right of the bottle he'd been aiming at.

"Hells," he said. He tucked the pistol in his armpit to tap another mound of cocaine onto his palm, which he sniffed to steady his shaking hand. He held up the pistol and took aim again.

He emptied the cylinder, reloaded, and emptied it again, firing like a madman. All he hit was sand and the weathered planks of the fence.

As the last shot rang out over the dunes, he stood panting. His heart was roaring and sweat pooled in his eyebrows, soaked his shirt collar. "Damn this thing," he said, and threw it to the ground. He drew the second pistol, loaded, and fired with similar success.

In the silence that followed, he heard footsteps crunching in the sand and gravel behind him. He turned to find a round-bellied man in suspenders. The man wiped his hands on his trousers, removed a cigar from his mouth, and said, "How about you take a walk, buddy?"

"What? Who are you?"

"An interested party." The man thumbed over his shoulder. "You're spoiling our fun."

Bird briefly wondered if the most reasonable thing to do would be to shoot the man. And for a moment the prospect made perfect, frightening sense.

"What are you talking about?"

"You are making the bear shit," he explained. "I do believe that your noise has demoralized him."

Bird gathered the fallen pistol from the ground and followed him. From the top of the dune, he looked down to see the men attempting to wrangle one of the bears back into the circle. The animal pulled on its chain and grunted with displeasure. It seemed that the man in suspenders had spoken truly—the bear's hindquarters hung close to the ground, and as it was being pulled along it let out a mournful cry and then ejected a stream of loose, watery stool that spattered on the sand beneath it.

∼

Later that night, he was disturbed by a knock at the door. "Go away," he said without rising, hopefully loud enough for the caller to hear.

He'd been steadily drinking since his return, trying to organize his thoughts. The buzz of the cocaine had worn off and left him feeling hollowed-out, unable to sleep no matter how much he drank. All the alcohol did for him was to provide his thoughts with a kind of blessed dullness, to allow him to see it all as inevitable.

The caller knocked again and he rose to open the door. He expected to find one of "The Group," or perhaps Mirmiran, coming again to check on him, but instead he found the painter, Billy Swain, dressed loosely like a Bohemian and carrying a large cloth-wrapped parcel under one arm.

"I have finished the paintings," he stated.

"You have fine timing," Bird said bitterly.

The painter entered and unwrapped the parcel, leaning the four works up against different pieces of furniture. Bird examined them. The battle at Malolo. *The Land of Ice*. They were exactly what he'd asked for, nothing more and nothing less. He turned to the portrait of him and Alice. His own likeness was striking. The man had copied him down to the whisker. But there was something wrong with his depiction of Alice. Though her features matched, she looked like a different person.

"Fine, fine," he said. "That will do."

He moved to show the painter the door. The short man stood rooted in the center of the room, like a pin stuck in the ground.

"There is the matter of payment," the painter said, for some reason staring down at Bird's hand. Bird then realized he was still loosely holding one of Mirmiran's Navy pistols. He laid it down heavily on the bar as he went upstairs for his cashbox. He counted out the two double eagles they'd agreed upon. Swain pocketed the coins and was gone before Bird thought to see him out.

Left alone once more, he walked from one of the leaning paintings to another, looking at each in turn, searching in them for his courage.

17.

. . .

All that Alice could ever remember of her dreams were fleeting impressions, and the terror of being pursued through dark locations by faceless men. When she woke in the painter's garret, she remembered where she was and pressed herself against his sleeping form until these images retreated. The room was full of sunlight.

When Billy woke, he regarded her with sleepy puzzlement, then wrapped her in his arms. Later he kissed her, a new kind of kiss, a kind without restraint. He bit at her lips, her neck, and she surrendered to this feeling of being slowly devoured.

He removed her dress. He removed his shirt, slid his trousers down to his ankles. Their nudity was a kind of honesty she'd longed for. She rubbed her cheek on his chest and felt the small dark hairs there like grasses brushing against her. Then a sharp intrusion, a pressure from within like she was being split in two. She hollered and tried to wriggle free, but his bulk pinned her against the bed. There was nothing she could do but whimper at the pain.

Then it was over, almost as soon as it had begun.

He sat up and leaned against the plaster. She felt a lingering soreness, a heat between her legs. She touched herself there and her fingers came up stained with blood. She'd bled before, but only a small amount—she'd thought it nothing more than a sign of her illness, a reminder there was something wrong inside of her. Billy was staring at the window, his eyes half-closed. Furtively, she clenched her discarded dress and wiped the blood from her leg, hoping he wouldn't see it.

"I should draw this," he said. She did not know what he meant to draw—if it was her, or the sunlight in the room, or something else. Ultimately, he drew nothing, and they lay back down together, warmed by the steam from the laundry below.

For the rest of the day, she could feel her illness gathering. Her skin felt tight and hot, as if it was shrinking. She could not remain still. She hid her head beneath the sheets to shut out the sunlight that seemed like a very loud noise. The sickness spread from her stomach to her chest. It crept through her limbs—there were tiny pricks along her arms and legs like she was being stung by bees—and even seeped into the floorboards of the garret itself, which seemed to slowly pitch one way and then the other like the deck of a ship.

Billy had begun his day's work. He'd been scraping a canvas with a knife for hours, trying to remove all the paint so he could use it again. Eventually, he noticed her suffering and asked if she felt unwell.

"I am sick," she said.

"Should I summon a doctor?"

"I need medicine," she said.

He studied her for some time and passed his hand through her hair. Then, without another word, he left the garret. He was gone for a long, long time. Years, she thought. Longer than the time she was on the island. She felt as if she'd died and her flesh had crawled away, but her ghost was stuck to her bones and her ghost was on fire.

When Billy returned, he had something in his hand, a small sachet tied with string. He rummaged among his belongings for a wooden case and opened it on the bed. It contained a long, carved pipe with a brass bowl, and a small candle in a pewter dish.

He lit the stub of candle with a matchstick and filled the pipe with something from the sachet that stuck to his fingers like mud. He reclined on his side and held the pipe above the candle, just beyond the flame. He puffed a few times but got nothing from it. Then the smoke began to come. He blew it from his nostrils and it had a thick smell, sweet and heavily fragrant like wildflowers.

"This is Chinese medicine," he said. "It helps me some. I believe it will cure almost anything."

"Are you sick?" she asked weakly.

"No. It cures my sadness."

He handed her the pipe. A whisper of smoke was curling into the air. "Like this," he said, bringing it to her lips.

Her first sip of the smoke filled her with fire. She coughed until tears welled in her eyes.

"Here, I'll show you how to do it." He pressed the pipe into her hands and then guided it toward the candle. "Not too close," he said. "You don't want to burn it up."

The second breath was rich and spiced, and she began to feel like she was rising from her body. Her ghost was no longer trapped in her bones; as she rose toward the ceiling, her sickness remained on the ground, already forgotten. "I am dying," she said. She found the words to be funny, and laughed as she repeated, "I'm dying, I'm dying."

"No, you're not," he said. Then he laughed as well. "But I suppose we are?"

Bird's medicine had only dulled the edges of things, as if the world was a painting and someone had wiped a hand over it, giving everything a softer and more pleasing shape. Now there was no shape that she could see. All things bled into each other. Nothing had any edge to it at all.

Time passed and she found he was speaking to her again softly, as if his thoughts were coming to him from afar. "You would love Paris, I think."

"What is there?" she asked.

"The whole city, it's full of trees, and flowers. It's the opposite of San Francisco. Have you ever seen a tree here? A proper tree? Not those little shrubs they have in Portsmouth Square. Little things, barely clinging to life . . . a perfect metaphor, I think, for life in this city. Ha, don't you think?"

"Can we go?" she asked him.

"A fine idea," he said. "We shall raise up the money for the trip. A first-class steamer. We'll eat lobster and drink champagne." She lost herself at the rail of a ship. She was older and wore a flowing white dress and held a lantern over the waters. He said, "We could go to the Louvre. It's a place filled with art. Have you ever been to a museum before?"

"No," she replied. She had only a murky image of what the word meant—she imagined it was something like a church, with paintings on the walls that showed the sufferings of Jesus Christ, the movements of the angels.

∼

Billy accepted her into his life without comment or discussion, as if it was always meant to be. Each day they lay together in bed until almost midday, when a man from downstairs, Mr. Ah Hee, would bring up their dinner. Fish and rice that they picked at with their hands. She adored him as he ate. After their meal, he would go to his paintings. She sat against the wall, watching him move his brushes, his easel angled so that she couldn't see what he was working on. She asked him if she should pose again but he said that he had enough sketches.

He said to her, "You are free now. I am free. And freely, we come together. That is why our love is beautiful."

Now that she'd found him, there was no reason to ever leave. It was a closed, warm little world, up beneath the roof beams. She wanted only to watch Billy paint and listen to the swallows roosting outside. It felt like the painter's garret was a place where time had ceased its motion, a place like the island where she was not troubled by any thoughts of before or after.

He taught her how to prepare the pipe. To separate out some of the sticky substance with the head of an old nail, to warm the opium until it began to smoke. Bird had always carefully rationed her medicine, and she thought that perhaps this was why she hadn't gotten better. The Chinese medicine was better, and as she took more and more of it, she could feel her illness shrinking from her, like a shadow.

She often woke to find him above her. It was no longer painful—in fact, she could barely feel him inside of her at all.

After many days, he completed the paintings for Bird and revealed them to her. The first showed a man raising a flag above an impressive brown house. The figure was small and indistinct, but she supposed it could be Bird. Another showed this same figure, firing a pistol into a horde of angry men rushing through the surf. Then, Billy uncovered the portrait in which she sat with Bird, his hands resting on her shoulders. This was the Bird that she knew. Tall and stooped and old, with a stern, sour expression on his face. But she was more interested in the depiction of her. She studied her own face. It did not resemble her at all.

"After I have delivered these," he said, "we will be free of that awful lieutenant forever."

She felt afraid when he left to deliver the paintings. As fearful as she'd been when she hid in the gully and William went off to his death—afraid Billy would never return, or worse, that Bird would follow him back and that would be the end of her newfound freedom. If he took her away from Billy, she decided, she would take no food or water until she died, and then her ghost could fly free and return to him. She smoked the pipe and thought that this had already happened, and she was sailing through the clouds with Billy riding her like a horse.

Then he did return, with a pocket full of money and a feast in a small sack: fresh bread, wine, cheese, olives, tarts topped with jam, canned peaches. He'd bought a dozen new candles and lit them all to make the garret glow in soft orange light as they enjoyed their picnic.

He told her of his life in Paris; how he'd only dined once per week on stale bread, but that even the stale bread there was like manna from Heaven. She liked to hear his stories, because he required nothing from her. The wine made her dizzy, and later she would recall only fragments of them.

∽

On many evenings he would leave the studio for a few hours, to walk by the wharves. She wished to go with him, but he said that she could not. He said the night was his time to be free, like an alley cat. He told her he had been born with the soul of an alley cat.

"What is my soul?" she asked him.

He considered for a long while, and then said, "You are a little sparrow. High up on your branch. Looking down at all of us without a care in your head."

William had told her that marriage did not require a church or a priest, but only true intentions before God. When Billy returned from these excursions, smelling of drink, she would lie next to him on his thin mattress and search for God's presence, to silently ask if this, too, was marriage.

One night, she heard William's voice reply: *It is not.*

She thought it was a dream. She thought she was asleep.

∽

Alice lit one match after another. She let each burn for a time, then dropped them into the pewter dish where they smoldered. Billy was sitting across the room from her, his elbow on his knee, his chin on his hand, his eyes closed, allowing the sunlight to warm his face. It was not clear if he was dozing or thinking.

She scraped another match against the floorboards and it sprang to life. She watched the flame move toward her thumb, darkening the matchstick. She allowed it to get closer. By the time she felt a warmth, it had singed a black mark on her nail. She dropped it to the floor and put her finger in her mouth.

Billy came over and stamped upon it. "Are you trying to roast us?" Then, more softly, "Alice, this is turpentine . . ." He bent over to pick up a stoppered jug. "If this catches fire, the whole house will burn."

He moved the jug to the other side of the room, away from her and her remaining matches. Then he went over to his cashbox and took out a coin.

"Do you want to see a show?" he asked her. He pressed the coin into her hand. "If you go out and go toward the water. On the left you will see a yellow house. In the building right after that, there is a music show."

"Will you come?"

"I must do my work," he said to her.

"I want to stay."

"But why? There is an entire city out there, full of wonders. You must not fixate yourself on one thing. Go walk about."

She took her hat and shuffled to the door. Downstairs, Mr. Ah Hee found her lost among the workers and escorted her through the washroom.

The street was lined with flags and signs covered with the Chinese writing that looked to her more like animals than words. Snakes and centipedes. Chinese men and women moved past her, taking no notice of the girl with a coin clutched in her hand. She moseyed over to sit on the edge of the boardwalk across the street, facing the front of the laundry, wondering how long it would be before she could return.

A man with a knobby nose caught her attention. He clinked and clacked—there were glass bottles hung all over his body like ornaments, held there by twists of wire, loops of twine. He stopped in front of Alice and looked down at her to say, "Do you want a bottle little girl? A pretty bottle?"

"Yes," she said.

"How much money do you have?"

She opened her hand so he could see the coin.

"I have green bottles and blue bottles, do you see them?" He smiled as if he knew the beauty of his bottles well; like they were a meal he'd once enjoyed. "For that coin, I will give you whichever you choose."

She dearly wished to have one of the pretty bottles, but said, "No, I will not have one." She thought that Billy would be so proud when she returned with the dollar and put it back in the cashbox, so it could be saved for their tickets to Paris.

The bottle man moved on and she pulled down her hat so that it cut off the top of her vision, leaving only a moving sea of legs. For a while she continued to watch the bottom half of things like this.

Then she heard a soft wailing coming from nearby. It was like the sound of a baby, she thought. She had never seen a baby except from afar. She picked herself up and followed the sound into a wide alley between two houses. Behind the house was a yard, framed by other buildings, and in the yard there was a rose bush. At its base, in a slight depression, she found a clutch of kittens.

There were seven of them, a large litter, and no mother in sight. They were batting at the air with their paws, squirming and mewling for milk. One was trying to leave the nest, but kept falling over his brothers. All four of his paws and his front shoulders were white, the top of his head and his rump were black. He scratched at her hand as she picked him up, but his little claws were not sharp and felt only like a rasp on her skin. For the rest of the afternoon, she sat with the kitten in her lap. It fought against its captivity, but each time it wriggled from one hand she would snatch it with the other. Eventually it surrendered and slept, after she tried to feed it sand from her fingertips.

When she returned to the garret with the kitten at dusk, Billy was sitting at his easel with a thin brush held loosely in his hand, as if he might drop it. His canvas remained blank. When she released the kitten from her hands, it darted behind a stack of canvasses and huddled there, watching them from its shadowed space.

∼

Most of Billy's paintings were temporary things. They were begun and completed in as little as a few days. She would only have just seen one—women with grapes, women on couches, one that he showed her with a mischievous glee which depicted two women kissing, their bare breasts pressed against each other—when it would disappear, carried out the door; sometimes he would return with money for the cashbox, sometimes he returned with nothing at all.

There was only one painting he never carried away: the painting of her, *The Revenge of Medea*. He scraped the canvas and started again many times. One day, he took all the sketches he'd made of her and burned them in the small wood stove. He said he no longer needed them, for the work was now clear in his mind.

It pleased her to think he would paint it forever. Each day he would add a line to her, a color. But then he declared that it, too, was complete. He warned her not to touch it because the fixing wash was not dry.

It was smaller than Bird's paintings—only like a tiny windowpane—and less brightly colored. It had a purpled blackness around its edges so deep that the eye was drawn in, to the form of Alice at the center. She was visible from head to toe, clothed in a robe so dark it was barely distinguishable from the background. The only bright objects were her face, sealed in bitterness, the knife she held aloft, and the babe cradled in her arms. An older child, clinging to the robe at her feet, was also lost in the shadows.

"What do you think of it?" Billy asked her. "It's a reversal, in many ways, of how the scene is classically portrayed. Medea is always ample-bosomed. But here, we see her body as frail, almost consumed by her sorrow . . ."

"When you sell it, will we have enough money?" She meant for their voyage to Paris. He knew this, because she asked him the same question every time he sold a painting.

"No, this one is not for sale. We'll bring it to Paris with us, and I'll put it in the Louvre. Then, for centuries to come, they will look upon you. Would you like that? To be immortal, like the *Mona Lisa*? Or Ophelia?" The kitten pawed at the hem of Billy's trousers and he shooed it away with a sweep of his foot.

Alice imagined the painting in the museum. Her own image, frozen in place, the knife still poised in the air, the babe still wailing. A scene that would never resolve, a kind of everlasting life. And he was the one who had given it to her.

~

Billy had told Alice they were having a guest, but the words slipped from her mind until she saw the woman standing in the doorway, peering into the garret. She was thin and fair-skinned, with a few red sores on her face. She wore a round, brown hat with a narrow brim, a ribbon of darker brown tied around it.

Alice studied the woman from her position on the mattress. The woman met her eyes briefly, then ignored her.

Billy prepared a chair for the woman to sit in, and then began to position her, squaring her shoulders, taking a step away to observe and then moving back to rearrange the way her hands fell in her lap. The woman had a tired look, and before Billy had even taken up his sketch pad she'd allowed her shoulders to slump.

Alice was thirsty. She leaned to take up the jug in two hands and tipped it so the wine spilled into the cloudy glass by the bedside.

Now the woman spoke. She asked, "Can I have a glass of wine as well?"

Billy made a noise.

"I am a bit dry."

"We are not here to drink."

Billy made lines on his sketch pad. The woman pouted.

"Please . . ." Billy said. "Can you stop that?"

"What?"

"Your face . . . please."

"What's wrong with my face?" she asked.

Alice drained her glass with feigned relish and stared at the woman, daring her to speak again.

"What is she doing?" the woman asked.

Billy looked to Alice. "She isn't doing anything. Please. Your husband has paid for a portrait. Don't you wish for it to be accurate?"

"But who is she?" the woman asked.

"Alice," Billy said.

"Alice who?"

"What do you mean, Alice who?"

"Is she your sister?"

"I don't see how it is any of your business who she is."

"Is she . . . ?" The woman paused before continuing.

"She is not," Billy snapped. "Many people make this mistake."

Billy stared down at his sketchpad for a long while before he resumed his work. The woman did not look at her again. Alice turned the emptied glass and laid it on its side, then began to slowly roll it back and forth across floorboards with her foot.

Billy said, "Alice . . . please."

The kitten was crouching nearby, watching the glass intently, waiting for it to resume its movement. She paused and then rolled it again, only a little, to tease the kitten. He pounced and swatted at the glass as if it was a mouse, sending it spinning across the floor.

"What is this behavior?" Billy demanded.

"It was the cat," she said. She picked up the kitten and began to stroke its fur.

When she returned it to the floor it began to silently stalk Billy. The woman noticed the cat's approach; Alice saw her eyes following it. The cat crept closer, its head held low, forepaws stretched before it. Billy was hardly moving, making some small circles with his charcoal, lost in deep concentration. The woman looked as if she was about to speak when the kitten pounced, batting furiously at Billy's moccasin and sinking its teeth into his ankle. He did not cry out or look surprised; he only bent to scoop the kitten up into one of his broad hands and said, "We are done."

"That's all?"

"I have everything I need."

After the woman's huffing departure, he held his face in his hands.

"Why must you paint her?" Alice asked.

His hands muffled his voice. "I told you. Her husband is paying for a portrait."

"Paint me," she said.

"I have painted you. I have shown you the painting."

"Paint me again," Alice said.

"Is that what you would like? For me to paint you again and again, to paint nothing but you?"

"Yes. Because I am your wife," Alice said. She thought it fitting, if their souls were joined for all eternity, that he should wish for nothing else to describe with his colors.

He said, "That is a ridiculous notion."

She had a brief, worried thought: If she should die, which of her husbands would she be with in Heaven? Would it be William, or Billy? She imagined that in Heaven miracles would occur, and perhaps there could be two of her, one to stand beside each man. Ada had told her that a woman could marry many times. A woman could marry one hundred men, one thousand, if she pleased. And for each of them in Heaven, perhaps there would be waiting a perfect bride, fashioned for him alone.

Billy rose to find the case that contained the opium pipe, and she knew he would do no more work that day. He didn't look at her as he prepared the pipe. He spoke quietly and in the wrong direction, like he was speaking to someone else. He said, "Sometimes I think you don't hear a word I say."

∼

His foul mood lasted for weeks. He did not paint and the cashbox became empty. He spent more time out in the city and when he came back to the garret, he sat rolling and smoking cigarettes on the bed, unmindful of her beside him. She said nothing, consumed with guilt for having caused his sorrow.

Her stomach became swollen and tight. Her breasts had plumped as well, until they felt heavy and ached, and she was forced to smoke more opium to alleviate the pains and her terrible hunger. She slept all day and hardly wished to move from the bed. She only realized that she was with child when he said that he hoped it would be a little girl, like herself, and not a hopeless miscreant, such as he was.

Then he was gone. She woke one morning to find almost everything had disappeared from the studio: his paints and brushes and his easel. All that remained was a clouded jar of turpentine, and a single canvas leaning against the wall, *The Revenge of Medea*. The kitten skulked behind it, unhappy with the room's changes.

Next to the mattress, he'd left a large chunk of opium and a letter she could not read save for her name at the top.

A day passed, and then a week. Mr. Ah Hee continued to bring up a meal for her each day, though these grew smaller and more meager. One day, he only brought her a pitcher of water and a tiny crumb of opium. As he opened the door to return downstairs, the kitten darted for the door and vanished into the stairwell.

18.

ANOTHER DUEL

Bird stood at Alice's window seat, to see what she had seen as she'd kept vigil over Montgomery Street. Even in the hours before dawn there was always some form of movement below. Dark clusters of men in the predawn glow, still drunk from the night before. The only sound the draw of his pipe.

It was not yet light when a buggy clattered down the newly-planked street. It stopped in front of the house and the driver hopped down to open the cab for Mr. Mirmiran, in a dark frock for the occasion.

Mirmiran took stock of Bird when he came out, dressed in his old Navy coat. It was threadbare, but gave him some comfort. He had shined his single, small medal, won for valor in the Mexican conflict, and straightened his epaulet.

"You are sober and prepared?"

Bird gave a nod and shifted the cherrywood pistol case under his arm. In the carriage he carried the case on his lap and watched the street.

"I have heard from Scarlata," Mirmiran said off-handedly, as if this was not the only news he'd been waiting for.

"They've found her?"

"Not yet. But we have a lead." Here Mirmiran paused, and then said, "The news is both good and bad, I'm afraid. Are you sure you want to hear it before the duel?"

"Yes, yes, what is it?"

"My concern is that it might aggravate you."

"You have already succeeded."

Mirmiran gave a considered pause and continued, "The Pinkerton has received word, a reliable word, that Alice has come under the influence of an unsavory character known as 'Rough Dan.' A . . . procurer of women, Henry. Scarlata believes he has sequestered her within the city, and you can rest assured that we'll find her. And this 'Rough Dan,' whoever he is, will pay dearly."

Bird made no reply.

"Are you now willing to discuss the terms of your last will and testament?" Mirmiran asked. He sniffed a lump of cocaine from a small spoon and Bird took the same.

"If I leave this world today, I trust you to take care of it. Just find Alice. And make sure she is well cared for, that is all I ask."

"Oh hush," Mirmiran said. "I'm sure it won't come to that." He patted Bird on the shoulder. "It is something admirable in your character, that you care so much for her. As if she were your own child."

"I had a daughter," Bird said. Oddly, he could not remember ever having uttered those words before, to anyone.

"Oh?"

"Died in the birthing."

"What was her name?"

Bird searched his memory. From deep within him, he pulled a sound. "Charlotte?" He tried to remember her face, in the photo he'd burned, and saw only a vague swaddled babe with dim eyes, indifferent to the world.

Mirmiran's meaty hand still rested on Bird's shoulder. He gave another gentle pat and said, "Well, I don't think you'll be seeing her today."

Kelly did not arrive at dawn, though they were met punctually by Mr. Knowles, a thin and idiotic man in a jacket much too large for him, whom

Mirmiran had hired to serve as Kelly's second. Something necessary, he'd counseled Kelly, in the event of any legal case being brought against him. Knowles was a hayseed who'd lost everything at the gambling tables. Mirmiran had found him sleeping beneath a saloon's porch. After a terse introduction, he stood chewing a wad of tobacco, waiting to receive his pay and be released.

The three of them watched the sun climb over the tiled roof of the mission. A flock of ducks was raised from a nearby puddle and disappeared in the distance. Mirmiran once again shared his tin and Bird spooned a big load into his nostril. He smoked the end of his pipe, tapped it out, and stuffed it again with shaggy strands of tobacco. He puffed until his tongue and lips were singed.

"Perhaps he will prove a coward," Bird commented.

"Sleeping off his drink, I should hope," Mirmiran answered. "In the event of non-attendance, he will forfeit all right to any further challenge."

"Well, then. That will be that."

"That will be that," Mirmiran agreed.

A few early strollers circled the mission house in their Sunday clothes, the women with parasols tilting at their shoulders. The morning was bright and breezy, so that Bird felt like a man being forced to endure a picnic while awaiting the gallows.

At seven in the morning, Kelly trundled over a nearby dune, holding an enormous hand over his eyes to block the sun. His face was already screwed up in anger as he sauntered over.

"WHERE'S THE GIRL?"

"Sir, I'm surprised you think this occasion appropriate for a woman," Mirmiran explained. He took a deep lungful of dusty air. "No, this is an occasion for men, so we might sort out these matters of honor . . ." he motioned vaguely between Kelly and the Lieutenant.

"I DON' KNOW WHAT KIND OF GAME YER PLAYIN, BUT IT DON' MAKE NO DIFFERENCE. I'LL PUT BOTH YOU IN THE GROUND."

"I can pledge to you, sir, that I offer you no duplicity in this matter. As I've explained, my professional code does not permit it. May I introduce you to Mr. Knowles, the party that has agreed to be your second?"

Kelly did not even spare Knowles a glance. He said, "LET'S GET TO IT."

The dueling grounds Mirmiran had selected were a quarter of a mile away, for privacy's sake. Kelly was insistent upon walking at the rear of their party. The location was flat and sandy and obscured by nearby dunes. A single, struggling juniper grew there, beneath which Mirmiran stopped and dropped to one knee in order to open the cherrywood pistol case. Kelly wiped his hands anxiously on his beaver coat.

Mirmiran spent some time preparing the pistols and then handed one to Bird and offered the second to Kelly.

Kelly reached over and swiped the pistol from Bird's hand. "I'LL TAKE THIS ONE," he announced. He opened the cylinder and checked to see the single shot loaded into it. Bird thought to do the same, but didn't.

The men readied themselves. Kelly drew a flask from his pocket and took a good long swallow. He offered it to Mirmiran and Bird, who both declined, and finally to Knowles, who accepted a swig.

"This is all 'bout a girl?" he asked.

No one answered him. Mirmiran offered his tin and Bird took another lump.

"If you would both stand back to back, I will call your steps. When you take the twentieth step, you may turn and fire."

"I AIN'T TURNIN MY BACK ON EITHER OF YOU WORMY SUCKERS."

"I must remind you, you've agreed to these terms."

Kelly backed away with the pistol. "YOU AND YOUR TERMS CAN GO TO HELL."

"If you are in violation of the terms . . ." Mirmiran began.

"How would you have us do it?" Bird said abruptly. He was impatient to begin, before his courage abandoned him again.

"HOW ABOUT I STAND OVER HERE, AND YOU STAND OVER YONDER, AND THEN I SHOOT YOU DEAD."

"Fine, agreed."

Bird trudged over to the place Kelly had indicated. He worried for a moment that he'd lost the pistol, but no, it was in his hand.

"NOW YOU TURN AROUND AND PICK UP THAT GUN."

He turned to see Kelly, his own pistol held at his side, his elbow slightly crooked. Mirmiran and Knowles stood by the juniper with blank expressions. Neither looked at all concerned.

Bird wondered what death would be like. At one time, all that had mattered was making a name for himself before it happened. This was the only way, he'd thought, to live forever. But he'd made his name, hadn't he? And now he found all he wished for was to be alive, for even a little while longer. To be alive, and to have Alice home again.

He raised the pistol.

Kelly's shot rang out and then Bird's. Kelly made a guttural noise as he jerked backwards and fell to the ground. Bird remained standing, seemingly unharmed. The pistol hung in his hand like a dead animal.

He was overcome with dizziness. Was this relief? Then he felt a slow, sharp pain entering his chest, like something was boring through him. The path of a bullet slowed down as it crawled through flesh. His arms stiffened. He looked down, expecting to see blood where he felt the pain, but there was only his unblemished shirtfront. His vision blurred and he felt the world retreating. The pistol dropped from his hand.

Kelly remained at the edge of his awareness, writhing and groaning where he lay. He managed to spit, "I AIN'T DEAD YET, YOU COCKSUCKER."

Bird didn't realize he was falling until he felt the ground rise up to meet him and heard the distant noise of his own collapse. He clutched at the sand, trying to find something to hold and finding nothing. The blue above him seemed to take on an incredible weight, pushing him farther and farther down. He felt as if he was being pierced by arcs of fire or light. And then it happened. He died.

19.

Awakening

He woke in his own bed, with Mirmiran sitting beside him. Time had passed—he had a sense of it, a stiffness in his limbs, and incredible dryness in his mouth. All the room's edges were dull and clouded.

As he stirred, Mirmiran dropped his newspaper to his lap.

"What happened?"

"Heart attack. The doctors said it should have killed you. But I told them they were not speaking about an ordinary man." Mirmiran beamed. "They were talking about one of our nation's heroes!"

"I'm a hero?" Bird asked, dazzled by the light that came through the room's single, thick-paned window.

Mirmiran shrugged. "Well, you're alive. That's a foot in the right direction."

"Is Kelly dead?"

"Hit in the lung. Expired shortly thereafter. Never forgave you."

"He missed." Bird meant it as a question.

"His shot never left the barrel, because I gave him a bad pistol. And Mr. Knowles, an appropriately disinterested party, has attested to the duel's fairness. The whole city is waiting for your account of it."

Bird rested with this information. When he had the strength, he asked, "Why didn't you tell me?"

"Oh, I know you, Henry. Man of honor and such. I knew you would never agree to it. So, I took the liberty of arranging things in our favor."

"But if he hadn't taken my pistol . . ."

"A calculated risk," Mirmiran interrupted him. "Let's not dwell on it. Mr. Kelly did not seem a complicated man. It wasn't like playing chess. More like checkers. As a magnanimous gesture, I assumed you would pay his funeral costs. It looks good to the public, makes you seem the bigger man."

Bird lifted his hand slightly in assent. He didn't care about money.

"Alice?" he asked.

Mirmiran adopted a more serious tone and leaned toward the bed, as if they might be overheard. "Scarlata has followed her trail east. He believes this 'Rough Dan' character has taken her to Illinois. But don't worry. Our man has promised to turn every brothel in the state upside down until he finds her." He offered Bird a false smile, probably meant to reassure him.

Bird didn't respond. There was nothing to respond to.

"I'm sure he'll find her, Henry."

The room smelled like onions. The smell filled his nostrils, making his eyes water. He wondered if it was real or some effect of the heart attack.

"Are you hungry?" Mirmiran asked him. "Would you like water?"

"Can we open a damned window?"

Mirmiran grunted as he forced up the sash. Bird could smell the harbor on the breeze. The pungent but comforting odor of the tide going out. He thought that as soon as he was able, he would like to see the seals. With Alice. He would like to stand behind her and watch her wonder at things.

"I imagine you would like a day or two to regain your strength, but when shall I tell the man from the *Alta* to come by?"

"I will not be seeing any newspapermen." Bird closed his eyes.

"I understand you're not feeling up to it at the moment. But give it thought . . . it will be an excellent opportunity to begin promoting your book."

"No," Bird said. "There will be no newspapermen and there will be no book. Now leave me alone."

Mirmiran gathered his coat in a huff. Before he left the room he asked, "Were you planning to thank me? For saving your life?"

"Thank you," Bird said. "Now let me sleep."

20.

. . .

Alice stood in the middle of the street as men and horses went around her. She saw nothing familiar and didn't know how she'd gotten there. Across the street, the upper part of a stable door was open. A man leaned upon the lower half, looking out and smiling without any teeth. Horses' tails swished in the shadows behind him.

She walked until she finally saw something she recognized, a sign with Chinese writing in red paint. She sat down on the planks of the road to rest. When she could rise, she found her way back to the laundry and pushed open the door. The men scrubbing, the women folding; they did not look up from their work as she moved between them, so that she briefly wondered if she had died and become a ghost.

She climbed up to the garret and opened the door to find it had changed completely. It was full of new furniture and the smell was different—wood pulp and hair oil. At a round table sat three identical men. Each wore the same faded shirt, the same brown trousers, the same black suspenders. Each had a moustache. One read a newspaper. The other two were speaking in a language she did not know and tossing coins upon the table.

All three looked up at her, standing in the open doorway.

One of them said, with a thick accent, "Yes! Can we help you, missus?"

"Where is my painting?"

The three men regarded one another and conversed in their own language quietly. Finally, the speaker looked back to her and said, "Thank you, we do not know."

She felt a slim hand on her arm. She turned to see Mr. Ah Hee, tugging her gently toward the stairs.

"I tell you. Billy no come here. You no come here."

Mr. Ah Hee took her to the back of the house and pushed her through a door into an alley full of refuse. There was a ladder there with broken rungs. A bucket full of rusted nails and rainwater. Farther down the alley, she found her painting beneath a pile of rags. She pulled it free to find that the paint had greatly worn and come off it in chunks. There was a tear in it, a limp strip of faded color hanging down. The figure of the woman was hardly visible. Only the babe remained clear and bright.

She wandered the streets. The sun rose and fell and each time it rose the city was different. She did not know what city she was in. It was not San Francisco. There was nothing in it she had seen before.

Then there was one thing she knew. The narrow front of a restaurant. She had been there many times, with Bird. There they had a plaque on the wall with her name on it. She stared at the diners behind the glass in confusion, wondering if the restaurant had been moved to this new city. Or if it was a new restaurant that looked just like the old one.

But she was hungry. There was a baby inside of her—she could feel its little pulse of life rattling in her swollen belly—and the baby was hungry.

She entered the dining room and found another man sitting at her table. She stood nearby and watched as he continued to shovel beefsteak into his mouth, and then he looked up from his plate to ask if she would move away.

"This is for me," she explained. She reached into his plate and took a hot potato and bit into it.

"Damn your eyes!" he shouted, and wrestled her for the potato. She dug her fingers into it and screamed.

A man hurried over, saying, "Ah, Miss Kelly. Yes? Miss Kelly?" He said something to silence the complaints of the man at the table. "Your table is this way," he said to her. "For you I have a new table." She thought he looked a bit like the man she remembered owning the restaurant, but he was also different. Like the fat older brother of the man. She heard William say: *It is not the same.* She had a thought that everything was being changed behind her. When she turned, things were being replaced by things that were not quite right.

At a small table in the kitchen, the restaurant owner, or his brother, gave her tomato soup and cornbread. She ate some but found that her appetite had left her. The cornbread was dry and stony, so that she couldn't swallow it. It felt like her mouth was full of sand.

∼

She found a place to sleep beneath a house built on sloping ground, with one side propped up on posts. She could hear people moving and speaking in the house above her. William said they were hunting for her, that they wished to kill her. She remained hidden in the darkness beneath them, where they would never find her.

She cast up the food she had eaten and then continued to be racked with coughing that shook her entire body. She coughed and coughed. She felt a long, deep pain, a sickness, her sickness. The world was hot and cold. She remembered the night of the squall, as the ship had rounded Cape Horn. This was a *squall*, she thought, and it was terrible.

She tried not to make a sound, because the people above were still searching for her. Shuffling and moving chairs. Scraping hungry blades on the floor and whispering *Alice, Alice.* Then something came loose inside of her. There was a warmth on her leg and on the ground she found blood, and among it her child. It did not even resemble a child—it looked to her like nothing more than a little piglet. She left it there beneath the house.

∼

She stood in front of the house on Montgomery Street. She did not know how she'd found it. Her feet had taken her there. The house was the same as she'd left it. A curl of smoke escaped from the chimney.

She tried the knob and the front door opened inwards. The downstairs parlor was clean and empty and dark. No glasses lined the tables; there were no ashes in the ashtrays. She was greeted by the paintings which Billy had made, hanging on the four walls. The battle with the savages, the man raising the flag. The portrait of her and Bird. The vast land of ice, so blue and featureless.

She moved upstairs and found the door hanging open. The apartment was quiet and tidy and seemed unoccupied, but then she heard a slight cough from the direction of Bird's room. Bird was within, lying in his nightclothes although it was the middle of the day.

He was not the same. The man in the bed was sallow and thin, his cheeks collapsed as if they could no longer hold themselves in position. His eyes were rimmed with blue and less alive, as if some measure of his spirit was gone from them.

He regarded her with puzzlement, his mouth slightly open. "Oh," he said. "You've come?"

"Yes." She moved to the cabinet on the wall and tried the handle. "Where is the key?"

It took Bird effort to free one of his hands from the sheets. He pointed to his vest, draped over a stool. "In the pocket," he said.

The key was a thin thing with only a single tooth. It slid into the cabinet's small lock and turned with almost no effort at all. Inside, she found the bottle of laudanum, right where it had always been. Bird watched wordlessly as she filled the dropper and emptied it into her mouth, one time, then again. She felt relief wash over her and sunk onto the stool.

"Will you stay?" he asked in a weak voice.

"I will," she said. "But it will not be the same."

He nodded.

"Of course," he said. "Yes, yes, anything you wish."

She sat with him for a while. She could not tell if he slept but his eyes were closed and his breathing shallow. Then she rose and went into her bedchamber, and there she took up and examined all her old familiar things.

The Last Part
Ghosts
April 1906

. . .

The old woman woke before dawn. Something had disturbed her, a sound she couldn't name. There was a gray light in the window. She listened for the wind—when it blew, the house would whisper and groan—but heard nothing. Then it came again. A sound like a tiny laughter. A tinkling of water over stones. Then the room was quiet again. It continued like this: the sound would come and then it would cease. Soft waves of sound and periods of silence. She listened to it as the light rose and her sight cleared. It was becoming stronger, she decided. When it sounded again, her eyes were drawn to a bell clock on the shelf, covered in dust. It was the Lieutenant's clock. She had never wound it, and its hands were always still; its hammer now gently fluttered between the two bells. She studied the clock through a haze of clouds and decided it wasn't laughing. It was weeping.

One corner of the wooden frame slid toward the edge of the shelf, as if it was taking a tentative step forward. Then it paused, uncertain of whether to continue. The world was full of wonders. She had never before seen a clock come to life.

Everything in the room remained as the Lieutenant had left it: the cabinet, the washbasin, the pipe on the nightstand. She thought that his ghost took comfort in these things always being in their right places.

He'd died on the mattress she now slept on, a flattened thing almost unstuffed and smelling of mildew. It had taken the Lieutenant a long time to die. Each year there had been less of him, until he'd descended into a state like a babe, unable to feed himself or rise for his toilet. She'd cared for him as she could. She'd fed him bits of bread or boiled carrot from her fingers, and washed every part of his body with a soft cloth. When he was feeling well, she brought him a splash of whiskey in a glass which he would hold and never sip. She even came to love him, in the way one could love a helpless thing, like a pet or a child. Eventually, so little remained that death seemed like no great change. Just a tiny step over a threshold, a slight movement from one room to another.

The bell clock resumed its weak cry and shifted its other foot forward. Its wailing continued even after the clock was still. It grew louder, like it was shouting and angry with her. As if she had sinned.

She thought that she was dying now, much as Lieutenant Bird had. Things were falling from her. Her eyes were obscured by wispy gray clouds. It took her much of the morning to regain her sight, and at night it left her completely. Few of her memories remained. She knew she'd lived most of her life in San Francisco. She thought that at one time she'd been a famous actress, and great crowds of people had gathered to admire her. Little scenes of a play she was once in returned to her—a shipwreck, and an evil villain, and her husband William. She would become tangled in these memories, uncertain if she was remembering the play or the events of her own life. She could remember being on a ship, but sometimes the ship was on a stage, the waves beneath made of painted wood.

She had once lived alone on an island, and her memory of this time was the only thing which remained clear to her. She could sharply recall the shore and the sound of the waves. The wind moving against her skin. She thought sometimes that she had been born there, perfectly formed from the sand, without any mother or father.

The bell clock took a final, urgent step and clattered to the floor with a strangled noise. Now there was another sound, a rumble from without.

The house began to growl and creak. As if it, too, wished to stand up and walk.

The Lieutenant came into the room; she knew it was him, because his ghost smelled of tobacco and newsprint. He said *I must ask you all to leave.*

The Lieutenant rarely spoke unless the matter was important, and she'd never known his spirit to be dishonest, as some were. She placed her feet on the boards and shuffled into the sitting room, teaching her legs how to walk again. The room was stuffed with an accumulation of decades—all the things she'd stolen or found in the streets of the city. And all of it was quivering in expectation. As if they were a crowd of people all whispering and tittering, a secret conversation she had stumbled onto. Soiled hats and worn shoes, alone and in pairs, seemed to clamor for her attention. Dulled copper tiling and glass bottles, a golden ring: all rattling. A ragdoll bear that had lost the buttons of its eyes trembled with fear. A pile of matching books toppled. A bird's feather spun slowly on a table. Each of these things had spoken to her in some way, and she had rescued them so they would not become lost. In one corner of the room, a copper brazier she'd taken from the church of St. Mary. A small corner of the roof had fallen in and a bird had stuffed the hole with its nest, and the brazier was placed to catch the water that came in. She could see the little pool of rainwater rippling as if someone had thrown a pebble into it; she was careful not to tread near it because the floor had gone soft.

The entire room began to shake. The red Indian, more familiar to her than her own face, jumped from the wall, leaving a pale square on the yellowed wallpaper. A bouquet of dried roses shimmied from the window bench and onto the floor. She stopped only to take up Bird's old Navy coat to place over her apron. The sleeves were frayed and all the buttons missing, but it still retained its single, dulled medal.

She went down the stairs into the parlor as quickly as she could. All the furniture and the crystal had been sold off after the war. The globe and the fixtures, the elegant curtains. The polished furniture. Nothing had been left in the room after that but some bottles of liquor and the four paintings of the Lieutenant on the walls, the only things he would not part with. Sometime after he died, men came inside to drink the liquor. She didn't know who they were. She heard them downstairs one night, and for several nights after, laughing and shouting, and she had sat against the door listening, wondering if they would come up the stairs to take anything from her. But after a time they were gone, and the paintings were all that remained.

As she crossed the parlor, she cast her eyes at the bare floor so she would not see the faces of these false Lieutenants. If she met their eyes, they would speak evil words to her, but when she didn't look, they were silent.

She stumbled into the street as the ground began to shift and buck. She fell to her hands and knees. It seemed as if the city was a great beast trying to shake her from its back. She looked up to see that all along Montgomery Street the tall new buildings trembled in the sky, and then they began to fall. Huge chunks of masonry broke free, the entire cornice of a proud stone bank crumbled into sand. Up and down the street the cobblestones rose and fell like waves, as if the street was made of water.

∽

How had she survived through all those years? Is it so hard to imagine? How had she ever? It is not such a difficult thing, for a woman to survive.

The city had provided for her. Each day she'd gone out to see what treasures it would give up. She was welcome in the saloons, where there was sometimes a free lunch. For a time, a baker who called her Mad Old Alice had given her stale rolls if she called each evening at his back door.

She could sometimes gain a few nickels by selling copies of her book. It was no more than a pamphlet really, put together by Bird's solicitor, Jacob Mirmiran. After viewing the final product, Bird had refused to allow it to be sold with his name upon it—it was full of fabrications and pictures of unclothed women, with their parts labeled in scientific detail. Mirmiran had left them with hundreds of copies when the two men finally parted company over this disagreement in the sixties. Bird would not even touch the things to remove them from the house, but she had liked to take one up when he wasn't watching, to look through it at all the words she could not read. She would sometimes see her name, and the name of William, and she would tell herself stories that she imagined the other words said, the story of her life as she understood it. When she wandered in the city, she always carried a copy in her apron, hoping to entice lonesome men to purchase one.

Mirmiran's book had been barely noticed upon its publication, and she entered the city news only once more after that. It was in the eighties, when she was discovered by a tax official who'd come to condemn the house. He had been born in San Francisco, one of the first generation, and could recall her name from his youth. He'd halted the building's removal, and came later with another man, from the Society of California Pioneers, who interviewed her for the newspaper. He published an article about the disgraceful state of her affairs, which led the city to waive her unpaid taxes and deed the house to her in perpetuity. There was also talk at this time of establishing a stipend for her care, but nothing came of it.

The world was still again. Clusters of men and women who had been driven outdoors in their nightclothes all gathered in the street in a dazed uncertainty. She could hear a woman wailing and the soft hiss of dust in the air settling around her like snow. Then, in the distance, the urgent ringing of a bell.

As the sun rose, teams of men began carrying bodies out from the wrecked buildings and laying them out in rows. Some were horribly bloodied and crushed, while others looked like they had only gone to sleep. A family—a man, a woman, and two small girls—pulled a table and chairs from their house and then sat in the middle of the street to eat their breakfast as if nothing had happened at all. The two small girls were dressed identically. Seeing them, the old woman felt a stab of worry for her own child. Hadn't there been a child? She could see the image of a brown-eyed boy, calling her *mother*. Had she left him in the house? She returned to the place where her house had been. It had collapsed into a mountain of brick and splintered timbers. The roof tiles covered everything like a blanket. She sifted through the edges of the debris, trying to find things that would tell her what had become of her child. The work was difficult, because she had only one good hand; the other, lost always in her coat sleeve, she rarely thought about. She pulled feebly at large chunks of masonry, afraid that her boy was crushed beneath, but found she could not move them. She found the Lieutenant's armchair, overturned and covered with fine white dust. She heard him say *Now look at this mess. Everything is scattered.* The iron kitchen stove had fallen to the level of the street and still stood on its four feet, proud as a ship's cannon. Then she found something, a small toy coated as well with dust. It was a baby's rattle. She shook it but all of the beads had come out.

~

She walked along streets lined with piles of splintered timbers and the skeletal remains of steel-framed buildings still pushing up into the sky. Others among the buildings remained intact, as if the Lord had chosen some to stand and some to fall.

She saw a line of children holding hands, being pulled quickly along by a stout nun. She searched for her child among them but found that she couldn't remember his face. A group of men stood proudly in a line atop a pile of debris as another man bent beneath the shroud of a photograph machine.

She followed the tracks of the electric train, twisted out of the ground in some places as if they had been bent by a monstrous hand. As her eyesight had failed, they'd always served as her guide. She walked the city staring down at her feet, following the silver lines and counting the intersections. She'd never ridden the electric train because it was crowded and noisy, with a bell that never ceased and men jumping on and off like dogs. It was nothing like the trains of her youth—long and elegant with clouds of smoke trailing from their engines. She could remember a train voyage through a dark forest, with the trees brushing up against the windows, though she didn't know where she'd come from or where she'd been going.

She came upon a train carriage that had been pushed onto its side and lay in the street like a whale. Glass from its windows was scattered over the ground and she picked her way carefully among it with her bare feet.

The church of Saint Mary's tall brick front still towered over the ruins around it. One of the doors of the cathedral hung on a single hinge. A young man who wore a priest's collar met her at the door as she climbed the stairs. There was dust in his sandy hair. "You cannot go in. The roof is down," he said. "You must go to the ferry."

". . ."

"What is your name, grandmother?"

She searched for it, but did not find anything where her name had been. She could not remember the last time she'd uttered it. She did not often speak with the living; it was as if a silence had accumulated between herself and the world, one which she was hesitant to disturb. At one time, she had liked to sit in the church because it was even more silent there behind thick stone walls that muffled the noise of the city, which had become full of streetcars and engines and automobiles buzzing down the avenues. Hammers and saws at all hours of the day and night, always building the city up nearer to the sky. In the church, there were only hushed whispers, the heavy smell of incense, the voice of the father saying holy words in a language no one understood. It was a peaceful place, a place that never changed. The people of the church had helped her, she remembered—their men had come to take away Bird when he died. There had not been money for a funeral or a stone, and she didn't know where they'd taken him. Women from the church had brought her pies and baskets of food.

"Are you hurt? Where are your people?"

"Where is the father?" she asked.

"I am the father, but there is no help here. The roof is down."

This was not the father. The father was an old man with snowy white hair. Long ago she had told him of William and the angel, and the father had told her not to return until she stopped speaking such blasphemy.

She said, "You are not the father."

"Have you found your people? Is there anyone who can care for you?"

She tried to find more words. "I have a son."

"Where is he?"

". . ."

"Go to the ferry," he said. He retrieved something from just inside the door of the church. It was a sealed tin can. He pressed it into her good hand. There was a picture on it of a bowl of corn. She put it in her apron pocket. She could hear William whispering to her, urgently and from a great distance: *Corn is the Devil's crop. Corn shall never be eaten among men. Those who partake of it shall perish in fire.*

Steamships were visible gliding across the harbor, moving under some power she had never understood. She could remember ships with tall, proud masts that needed wind in their sails; at one time, the harbor was full of them. Now the last of their masts had vanished beneath the waves. One long white steamer with a fat chimney sat motionless in the distance, with its passengers crowded at the rails to watch the city burn. And bells were ringing, ringing from all directions.

Men on the piers hurried to load crates and barrels onto the ships. She studied their faces, hoping to find her son among them. Feeling the same dull urgency that drove her through most of her days, no more and no less, yearning for something she could not recall. A hunger in all her limbs that felt as if it could never be satisfied. Her son . . . her son would know what it was that she required.

There was a ferryboat being loaded with people. Already it was full, with men clinging to the rails and falling into the harbor. Still, the crowd on the pier jostled to get closer. She pressed among them, standing no higher than their belts; she felt that she'd been shrinking as she got older, or else the world was growing larger. The air began to fill with smoke. She was lost in a forest of trousered legs, unable to tell what direction the ferryboat was in, now only dimly able to see the men's faces above her. A man stumbled into her and nearly knocked her over; she clung to the pants of another man for support.

"My son has gone to the ferry," she said, in a small voice.

The owner of the trousers looked down in surprise, then waved his arms and shouted, "There are women! We have women!"

Hands grabbed at her, pulled her. Angry hands: she thought they would rip her to pieces and throw the pieces into the bay.

She tore free of them and fled from the crowd and away from the approaching fire, moving along the waterfront. Billowing clouds of smoke rolled over the tops of the buildings so that she could no longer see the water or the piers. Figures passed before her, appearing and disappearing in the smoke. A man whose skin had been blackened carried a crate full of cans away from a burning building. A young woman sat on the edge of the sidewalk with a sleepy look, unsuccessfully trying to wipe soot from her hands onto a bonnet.

∼

After the war, she was displayed for a time in a dockside oddities show. The proprietor, Mr. A. J. Freeley, discovered her as she was trying to solicit men on the wharves, and thought only to place a stray whore he might dress as a child into the burlesque portion of his program. She proved intractable for singing or dance routines, but by the time he discovered this he had also learned, through a pornographic booklet he'd confiscated from her belongings, of her storied past. After that, he displayed her in her own booth, unclothed, a red stripe painted on the floor to prevent the patrons from approaching her. He told them, quite convincingly, that this was for their own protection.

There is little record of this period; the only reason it is known of at all is because Freeley went on to write a memoir of his life as a showman. He mentions that he paid her, like many of his performers, in opium, though he failed to generate enough interest to cause a resurgence in her career. In a reproduced handbill from his long-lasting waterfront show, The Wild Girl is listed only as a minor attraction, well beneath such billings as Speedo the Lizard Boy and some form of acrobatic demonstration known as Two and a Half Women.

Great swathes of flame crossed the city. During the day, the sky was gray with smoke and the fires lit the night. She watched the Palace Hotel burn. When it had been built, they had said it was the greatest hotel in the world. The regal stone face of it stretched the length of an entire block. Now flames had broken the windows and escaped into the sky.

She traveled for a time with a procession of refugees trying to escape the reach of the fires. On every corner, there were men with long rifles and bayonets who would direct them, first down one street and then another. She walked among old and young, rich and poor, families and lone men, women and children. Mules and carts loaded with furniture. They were made to march through thick banks of smoke; she wrapped a rag around her face, but still her mouth and throat were burned dry. She tried to sleep in a doorway but a soldier pulled her to her feet and made her move on.

At some point during the night, soldiers herded the refugees to the side of the road and told them to wait. A caravan of brightly painted wagons was being moved down the street. A menagerie. The horses were skittish from the commotion and the drivers cracked their whips. Their teams pulled great wheeled cages that contained animals: peacocks and zebras and even an orang-utan, all huddled nervously in their confinement. In one cage, she saw a tiger with mottled and dirty fur, pacing from one side of the cage to the other without cease.

They were given water from a barrel, little more than a sip each. She brought her can of corn to one of the soldiers there, hoping that he could open it for her with his bayonet, but he took it and pushed her back into the line. As they marched, she saw a tower on fire and men at its base throwing buckets of dirt uselessly into the flames.

There was gunfire in the night, and for a time, a noise like the firing of cannons. As they marched past, she saw that a team of men were using dynamite to topple a row of houses. She could not understand the activity, except to think that the men had been driven mad and sought to help the fires in their work, and they would not rest until every building in the city was razed to the ground. The sound was so loud that she tried to pull her hat down over her ears, but she found that she had no hat. Where had it gone? It seemed that it had always been there upon her head, and now it was not.

They marched on. The sound of the explosions rang in her ears even after they had ceased. The voices of the soldiers and refugees were muffled, as if they were wrapped in cloth. Then she heard one voice in the din that was clear, and knew that it must be a spirit. It was a man who had drowned in the sea. His face and his name were lost, but she could recall that once he had given to her a toy bird and she worried now that she could not remember what had become of it. She asked the spirit, "Where is the bird?" but he could not tell her—instead, he only said again and again that his feet were cold.

"How can you be cold?" she scolded him. The air was warm and black flecks of burnt paint were carried on the heat. "There is a great fire."

He said: *It is very cold in this place.*

～

She wandered alone among blackened ruins. She came upon the smoking wreck of a jailhouse with metal cages still standing, perfectly intact but emptied of their prisoners. There, she met a man shuffling among the opened cages and asked if he had any water. He was short, hardly taller than her, and waddled when he walked. He asked her if she had rope, because he wished to hang himself. Neither had what the other sought, so he gave her a coin, which she hid in her apron pocket. He said *It is all that I can spare.*

That day she arrived at a vast plain of fine, smoking gray ash. There was no feature to mark the landscape and a haze obscured the distance. She could not tell that there had ever been a city there at all. She continued to walk, hoping to find what lay on the other side of this wide desert. She felt a need like a flame that was burning her away with no water to extinguish it. The tips of her fingers turned to ash that fell away and mingled with the plain. She was surprised to find, when she stopped to examine them, that her fingers were still there. She'd thought that they would be gone by now. She thought that she must find her house. That somewhere beyond this place it still stood, and that her son was waiting there for her. That was where she would find peace at last.

In the silence of this landscape William plagued her with his babble of the commandments of God and the sinfulness of the world. He spoke of Sodom and Gomorrah. He said that all vanity would be cast low and that only in the kingdom of Heaven could there be any greatness. She wished that there was a way to silence him, but when she spoke he never heard her at all.

She slept for a time on the ground. The ashes were comfortable and warm. When she woke in the night, all was dark around her save for an orange glow in the distance. Then she heard another voice that was not William.

Alice, it called to her.

This was her name. She tried not to let go of it again. She rose and shuffled through the dark, seeking this helpful spirit who had returned it to her. Her feet stirred through piles of ash.

Alice.

She felt leaves brushing up against her and she reached out her good hand to grasp them. She was in a forest and a canopy of trees blocked her view of the night. Somewhere in the distance, the soft crush of the sea on the shore.

Alice.

She found him in a small clearing, lying in a little tent he had made for himself of leaves and sticks. His head lay outside the tent. His face was red and his lips dried white. He struggled for breath. She watched him from a distance for some time until she decided that he was unable to rise. Though he was much changed, she knew the face of the man. She had seen him before in a play upon a stage. She thought that his name was Ernesto. He'd been a wicked man, but now he was sick and helpless and she thought there was nothing to fear from him. He heard her as she approached and opened his eyes to look up at her.

Are you there?

"Where is my son?"

Is it you?

"Tell me of my son."

His skin had pulled tight around his bones, his eyes were deep in their sockets so that when he looked up at her his face resembled a skull. He said *Please, bring me water. I am sick. Water.*

"What is his name?"

We are the last. We will build a ship. I will take us from here.

"I would not go with you. And you will not go, either."

His face grew pale with fear.

Are you a spirit? he asked her. *Have you come to take me?*

"No," she said. "You are the spirit. Now fly away."

∽

Her only child to survive infancy was named Henry, though from early in his life he called himself Hank. In his boy's way, he had decided that that was the name of the father he had never known. He could remember little of his mother. There were a few instances he could recall of her tending to him. But as he grew, she seemed to forget him and they lived for most of his childhood more like two animals in a den; both coming and going as they pleased, hardly speaking to one another. He thought that perhaps at one time there had been a grandfather who lived with them, but he could recall nothing more than a silent form under blankets, absent of speech or knowledge.

By the time he was able to look out for himself, he had become just another of the filthy gamins who plagued the city, sleeping wherever he found himself at the end of the day. He had little reason to return to the house on Montgomery Street as he grew. He performed small tasks for men along the wharves to earn the money he would gamble away at dice. When he thought he was man enough, he went on a ship to work but found he did not like the life. He made his way to Oregon where he worked in a logging camp, first as a cook and then as a woodcutter. He did not ever think of his mother or his past.

It was after he'd felt the rush of youth leave him that he became restless and found his way back down into California, staying on for a few years in Eureka before returning to San Francisco. Sorrows had begun piling up on him: there had been no work in the camps and he'd married a girl who had run off after only four months. He wished to see again the places he'd known as a boy, and hoped they would cure him of the sadness and bad luck he'd been gathering.

When he arrived, he found he didn't recognize the city anymore. He knew that the great quake had done terrible damage, but he hadn't expected to find an entirely new city that bore no resemblance to the one in which he'd been a child. He could not find the streets that he knew, or any of the buildings. Even the wharves had been changed. He did not know any of the people. This was not San Francisco, only another city built on top of its ruins. The thought made him melancholy. He found Montgomery Street but could not even determine where the house had been. He roamed the city for a few days, spending off the last of the money he'd made in Eureka. He wouldn't stay, but didn't know where else to go.

One day, hoping to wait out a rainstorm as he continued to delay his leaving, he went into a storefront that housed the offices of the San Francisco Historical Society. The clouded glass door opened upon a parlor full of things that had been salvaged from the past. Colorful advertisement posters, framed *photographs of men whose stiff and unbroken postures somehow suggested the kind of success in life that had eluded him. A harbor full of sailing ships. He browsed among the items collected within. A rusted ship's anchor was propped in a corner. A single pistol that had been used in Senator Broderick's famous duel, though it was not known by which party. This was the city he remembered. He saw clippings and photos concerning all of the city's lost characters: mad Emperor Norton and the two famed street dogs, Bummer and Lazarus. One of them had even been stuffed and stood proudly displayed atop a trunk, his posture noble as he was said to have been. There were writings by the famous Mark Twain and photographs of buildings he could actually remember. Never before had photography seemed so miraculous to him, because he had never before seen a photograph of something that he had known and which was lost.*

He found the picture of her on a rolltop desk. It was Galloway's promotional picture of her, in a top hat. She was younger, but he couldn't mistake her. It was his mother. There were other things gathered on the desk: a faded playbill, an album of brittle newspaper clippings. A placard near this display read Alice Kelly, also known as The Wild Girl. *He could not comprehend it. He knew that it was her—his mother's name had been Alice Kelly—but he had never known of any of this. He could not imagine her living any other life than the one he remembered. He read each clipping slowly, mouthing the words because his reading was not good. He opened a red-covered pamphlet that contained a drawing of a half-naked girl in furs that was not her.*

Just then he heard a sound behind him. A man had entered the room. He was slim and mostly bald, wearing a vest but no jacket.

"Can I help you to find something?" he asked.

"These things," he said. "Are they for sale?"

"No. They are a part of the collection. But we do rely on donations to continue our work here. There is so much of the past that is worth preserving."

He only grunted at this and turned back to the desk.

Sensing his refusal, the man added, "But a donation is not necessary. We are open to the public, and you may browse for as long as you wish."

∽

West of the city, there was a place that had at one time been only dunes stretching all the way to the coast. Later, the dunes had been flattened and a great strolling park had been made, with curving lanes that wound gently around fruit trees and lawns, benches to sit upon and horse carriages for lovers. Now the park was full of white tents in orderly rows and men with saws were cutting down the trees for firewood. She passed one man furiously sawing at the trunk of a twisted old juniper. He sawed for a while and then shouldered the tree, trying to push it over, then began sawing again.

A man wearing spectacles gave her a blanket and told her to wait. For some time, she sat on it and watched another crew of men digging a wide pit in the ground. When the pit was complete, the bodies of people like children asleep were brought over on wheelbarrows and dumped into it. The pit was filled with soil and then the men began their work on another pit, the endless work of folding people back into the earth.

After a while, she forgot why she was sitting there and rose to leave, but an old soldier in a mismatched uniform said, "Hold on there, sister."

He brought her to a table and opened a ledger book. He asked her where she had lived.

" . . ."

"You have come from the city?"

" . . ."

"Bad time where you were at?"

She nodded.

"Do you have someplace to go?"

" . . ."

"Has your husband passed?"

She nodded again.

He wrote some things down in his ledger book. He looked to see if she had a blanket and saw that she had. "What else do you have with you?" he asked.

". . ."

"Do you have children?"

"I have a boy," she said.

"Is he with you?"

"He is somewheres," the old woman said. She looked back to the men who were digging graves, trying to determine if her son was among them. "He is off somewheres," she said again.

"What is your son's name?" he asked her.

She considered this and then said, "William," because she knew that William had been her husband and thought that the boy would be named after his father.

He wrote the name in his ledger book. "You can go over there for bread," the man said, nodding toward a tent.

You may eat of bread, for it is written that the Son of the Lord fed multitudes of loaves and fishes. Bread is to be permitted upon the Earth. Oysters shall not be eaten.

"I will eat what I please."

The old soldier frowned and said, "You can have four ounces now but the president says that soon there will be more for everybody."

The sky had clouded over. The camp was full of women and children who sat outside their tents organizing their few belongings or frying bread in pans. The smell made her again feel the pang of hunger. She found the place to get bread, but the soldier there told her to come back in two hours.

She moved through the camp with the blanket wrapped around her. There was an open white tent full of cots, mostly occupied by men who were sleeping. One man sat at the edge of his cot smoking a cigarette. One of his arms had been taken off and was wrapped in bloody bandages at the stump. A doctor with clean skin and trimmed hair passed among the beds. She saw him administer a syringe to another man, concealed by blankets, and she remembered all at once what she needed to stop the burning, to quiet the whispering voices scratching in her ears. She was ill and she required medicine. She had always been ill.

She followed him until he turned and asked, "What can I do for you, mother?"

"I require a shot of morphine," she said.

"What's that you said?"

"I require morphine."

He looked down at her unsmiling.

"You have pain?"

"I got a bad arm." She raised her arm from the blanket and pushed up the sleeve of her coat. From elbow to wrist, it had wilted on her like a cut flower. The skin wrapped tight around the bones so that she could see the depression between them, the hand curled into a near-useless claw.

He took her withered arm into his hand and examined it. "This is an old wound. It has healed."

"It pains me something."

He released her arm. "I'm sorry, but I need the medicines we have for those who are truly injured."

She reached into her apron pocket to offer him the coin, but her apron pocket was empty. There was no coin in any of its corners.

"You took it," she said as he turned back to his work.

"What?"

"Give it here."

"Please, I must ask you to leave now."

She tugged at the doctor's shirt with her good hand. "Give it to me."

"I haven't taken anything from you."

The doctor looked to the man with one arm, for help or confirmation. The man with one arm calmly watched the exchange as he smoked.

"You stole it," she said, clinging to him.

"Please . . . ma'am. Alright."

He rummaged in his black handbag to take out vial and syringe. She watched the clear liquid rush up into the syringe, and then he took her arm again from beneath the blanket, gray and marked by scars. "I can only give you this one," he said, "because our medicines are in short supply. After this I don't want to see you again."

She felt relief come over her as he withdrew the syringe and wiped it with a cloth. A great warmth covered her like a blanket, and all the ghosts were finally silent.

～

She could smell the sea long before she came to the edge of the cliffs. Both sky and sea were gray and heavy and the wind cut through her blanket. Below her, the Pacific roared and hammered into the cliff face. For as long as she could remember, she'd only known the tame and familiar waters of the harbor.

She turned and followed the cliffs until she could pick her way down to the shore. There were tents and shanties there, but nothing so orderly as the relief camp; men had thrown up lean-tos and structures made of tin and thin wooden boards, with newspapers nailed over the windows. A few fires burned and dogs circled around them.

She could smell coffee brewing in a camp of Mexicans and a few fat raindrops fell. One vaquero in the camp was making his horse perform tricks for an assembled audience. From the saddle, he made the horse rear up on its back legs and then kneel down on the front pair. Each time he did, the other vaqueros would cheer as if it was the first time and the rider would make his horse perform these tricks again. She watched the horse rear and kneel, rear and kneel, and wondered if the spirits of horse and rider both would be forced to perform these tricks for all of eternity.

Farther down the shore, she found a quiet place to get out of the coming storm. A lone tent perched on a dune, nothing more than a thick expanse of sailcloth propped on poles to make a ridge. In front of the tent there was a little cookfire with a skillet of beans warming over it. She saw a man sitting inside, leaning back against a sack in the dim rear of the tent. He had a feeble moustache and he was gazing out at the sea with the kind of blankness she sought, the kind she'd learned to look for in the eyes of drunken men along the waterfront. It looked as if he was an empty vessel, waiting to have his desire written by her. It began to rain more steadily and the rainwater filled his skillet.

He looked up but offered no greeting. She knew the proper words to say. She'd learned them long ago from a woman whose face or name she could not remember but she remembered the words still.

"I'll butter your bread."

"Well, I don't know about that," he replied.

She entered the tent and knelt before him. His shirt was so dirty it had browned to the color of his trousers. He didn't say anything else so she began to rub the front of his trousers with her good hand. He made no complaint. She felt him growing and worked her hand inside to tug at him.

"I find this to be tolerable," he finally said.

She did her work until his body tensed and he let out a single breath. She wiped her hand on his trouser front.

"That was not too bad," he said.

"I can do you again in a bit."

"I did not say I liked it that much. But help yourself to some supper." He made a motion toward the overflowing skillet. "I am full up anyhow."

She knew that she should eat but her hunger had again left her. It seemed to her as she grew older that she could survive on almost nothing: just a few sips of water and a few breaths of air, as if she was almost a ghost herself. She would eat later, she thought, if the beans had not all washed away.

She pulled the blanket around her and listened to the swells beating against the shore. She looked out over the sea to the horizon, as if waiting for something to appear there. Perhaps a ship that would come and take her away to another place. Her son would be on the ship and he would row a boat to the shore to receive her. He would say *I have been searching for you, mother. Where have you been?*

"You can set there a while, grandmother," the man said, "but I can't be taking care of you. Once that rain lets up, you got to move on."

The rain thundered against the canvas but it was dry in the tent and she felt herself drifting toward sleep. Little streams of water poured from the tent's edge to run themselves out in the sand.

"Don't you worry," she said. "I aim to."